Deadly Odds
The Stairway Press Edition

Allen Wyler

Deadly Odds—The Stairway Press Edition

Other books by Allen Wyler (fiction)

Changes
Deadly Odds 2.0
Deadly Odds 3.0
Dead Ringer
Dead Ringer 2.0
Dead End Deal
Dead Wrong
Deadly Errors
Dead Head
Cutter's Trial

Also by Allen Wyler: *The Surgical Management of Epilepsy*

Deadly Odds—The Stairway Press edition ©2020 Allen Wyler
All Rights Reserved

Print ISBN 978-1-949267-62-4
ebook ISBN 978-1-949267-63-1

Visit Allen online at www.allenwyler.com

Cover design by Guy D. Corp
www.grafixCORP.com

STAIRWAY≜PRESS

STAIRWAY PRESS—APACHE JUNCTION

www.stairwaypress.com
1000 West Apache Trail, Suite 126
Apache Junction, AZ 85120 USA

Special thanks to Simone
for her initial read of this manuscript and
feedback.
You rock, Simone!

1

"WHAT, NO TIP?" the cook asked while sliding the medium-size pizza across the chipped Formica counter to Arnold.

See, that's the problem. Do a person one favor and they expect another. Never ends.

But Arnold didn't mind. In fact, he liked the guy. Besides, what's not to like? Always good natured, smiling, always put a few extra anchovies on the pizzas even though he didn't have to.

Arnold glanced over his shoulder to check out who might be nearby. The overheated humid room air was spiced with yeast, grease, and tomato sauce. The only other customers tonight were a couple, eyes glued to the high-def big-screen on the far wall, watching the Mariners, a large pepperoni and pitcher of beer in front of them, half-eaten slices in route to their mouths. Last thing they'd be looking at was Arnold doing business with the cook.

Arnold slipped a folded paper from his billfold, passed it to the guy, pressing it firmly into his palm with the words, "Danny Boy to win in the third. Thunderbolt to place in the fifth. Saratoga."

The cook nodded acknowledgment, casually stuffing the note into his breast pocket.

"Thanks. You the man!"

Arnold began to pull a twenty from his billfold but the guy waved it off.

"Naw, naw, no way. This one's on me, dude. After all," patting his breast pocket, "this more than takes care of it."

Arnold smiled, stuffed his wallet back in his jeans.

"So, we're good?"

The cook laughed with a quick nod.

"Yeah, we good, that is, of course, unless you want to tell me your system."

Arnold cringed. He'd messed up having ever mentioned it. In retrospect, he probably shouldn't have given the guy the first tip and just let it be. But he hadn't been able to keep his big mouth shut—hadn't been able to muzzle his jubilant pride at being able to match Nate Silver's uncanny predictive accuracy—so now here they were.

"Then it wouldn't be my system anymore, would it," making it a statement instead of a question.

Wiping his fingers on the greasy apron, the cook nodded.

"Point made," and shot a glance at the oven where a large meat-lovers pizza was beginning to bubble. "Anything else? Something to drink? Otherwise..."

Arnold thought about that a moment, a whisper in the back of his mind warned of forgetting something.

It came to him.

"Tell you what. Throw in a couple packs of those hot peppers, will you?"

Arnold was hurrying to get home before the pizza cooled, the smell of melted cheese and greasy pepperoni whetting his appetite. He cut down an alley, crossed a side street, then hung a left into another alley. Greenlake, a Seattle residential neighborhood, had been established before World War II in a bygone era of narrow roads, when alleys were unpaved afterthoughts for accessing impossibly small single-car garages.

Years ago, this alley had morphed into a contiguous series of opposing garage doors and privacy fences so high he could see nothing of the enclosed properties other than peaked roofs and brick chimneys. The light on the utility pole halfway down the alley had burned out weeks ago, leaving the chuck-holed asphalt in India ink shadows. But from having spent his life in the house he knew each crack and puddle well enough to navigate the narrow alley blindfolded.

His garage—set back from the alley by two feet—anchored the northeast corner of his property. A 7-foot-high cedar fence enclosed a back yard long gone to seed since his parents' death. A blue recycle and a green garbage bin abutted the fence, providing barely enough room for the garbage truck to navigate its weekly route. He carefully set the box of pizza on the green dumpster to type the six-digit code into the security pad, and the lock emitted a metallic slap. Propping the gate open with one foot, he picked up the pizza and entered the back yard, stopping to make sure the gate had locked securely behind him.

Satisfied, he hurried along the short cement path to the back steps, on up to the porch, through the kitchen door, yelling, "Yo, dude, I'm back."

Heard Howie yell, "Run! Get out!"

Arnold stopped in the middle of the kitchen.

"What?"

This some sort of joke?

BAM. The unmistakable sound of a handgun made him jump. Then Karim was filling the doorway from kitchen to dining room, gun in hand.

Dropping the pizza, Arnold spun 180 degrees and bolted through the back door, arms out, palms hitting the porch rail, his momentum carrying him into a Western roll out into space, into an arching fall ending with both feet hitting the ground. Hard. Jolting, searing pain shot from ankle to knee, almost buckling his right leg.

Then Karim was up on the back porch, yelling, "Stop!"

But now Arnold was limping as fast as possible straight for the gate, hand out to open the latch. Halfway through the gate he recognized Karim's heavy shoes clamoring down the stairs, coming after him unexpectedly quickly for such a big man.

Damn ankle! Sprained. Badly, too.

Arnold only had time to round the recycle bin and wedge into a crouch between it and the garbage bin, back against the fence, knees tucked against his chest before he heard the gate click open and the hinges squeak. He went dead still one second before sensing Karim slip silently into the blackened alley, breathing hard, like a guy out of shape. Arnold hugged his knees, scrunching into an impossibly tight ball, shoulders wedged between bins, his back flat against the chilly cedar fencing. He strained to listen, heard one heavy step hit alley asphalt, then nothing as the big man waited, listening for footsteps or movement, for any sign of him.

A car engine grew more distant, blocks away. A dog barked somewhere on the next block. Graveyard stillness settled over the alley.

Silently Arnold began massaging his ankle, at first pressing gingerly over the spot hurting worse, the pressure producing excruciating pain, tolerable only because he needed to know if it were fractured or not—not that it made much difference if he had to bolt. He covered his mouth with his free hand to muffle his breathing.

Could Karim hear him? Sense him?

He caught a whiff of Karim's nauseating body odor and decided he had to be off to the left, probably just inside the alley at the gate. He gingerly probed the ankle further, deciding the bone wasn't broken, but shit, the damn thing hurt. He continued the massage, hoping it might alleviate some pain, because first chance he got, he'd make a break for it and run. But unless that opportunity was damn obvious, he'd stay still.

"See him?"

He recognized Firouz's voice, quiet and urgent, and figured Karim's brother must be on the porch leaning over the rail.

"No."

"Find him."

A direct order. Shit!

Arnold tensed, ready to spring. If Karim discovered him, he'd bolt before the bastard could react, hoping for the element of surprise…

Yeah, then what? Guy has a gun.

Sheer stupidity to try to overpower him. Certainly, couldn't deck him. Didn't have the moves. Or the fist, for that matter. Running would be his only option. He certainly had the advantage of knowing every path and shortcut around here. Yeah, maybe…

A shadow denser than others slipped silently past from left to right, the tangy stench of BO stronger, overpowering the rank, rotting garbage. Karim silently radiating a presence of mass. Arnold sensed him stop, probably no more than five feet away, almost close enough to feel his body heat. He held his breath, praying Karim wouldn't look between the bins, or if he did, couldn't see him in the inky shadow. Did the bastard carry a flashlight?

A light suddenly flashed on, casting high-contrast trapezoids across the alley. A door clicked, followed by the rapid scraping of claws on wood. Arnold pictured the neighbor's big male German shepherd shooting out across their back porch and down the steps into the enclosed grass yard. Then, a deep guttural growl from behind the fence.

Silence.

The dog began rapidly sniffing as his nose scraped the fence corner where the properties met, about where he sensed Karim standing. The shepherd barked again, deep, threatening barks.

The alley remained deathly still. No movement, no sounds. More barks.

Arnold breathed and probed his ankle once more, this time applying more pressure, palpating the bone. No, not broken. Good enough to run on.

Get ready. Any second now…

"Fritz, no bark."

He recognized the neighbor's voice. The shepherd obediently ceased barking but continued to pant and sniff, his nose glued to the fence corner where Karim's scent had to be strongest.

"Anybody there?" his neighbor called.

Yell to him?

Yeah, and say what? Call 911?

Fat chance. Not with Karim five feet away with a gun. His heart was beating so hard he was certain Fritz could hear it. Surely the pooch recognized his scent. But Karim's strong, foreign smell would be threatening, causing more threatening barks.

Silence.

A moment later the neighbor said, "Come!"

Fritz's tags jangled, followed by the scrape of paws on the wood steps. Seconds later the door latch clicked and the floodlight went dark, once again filling the alley in heavy black shadows. Arnold stopped breathing.

Silence.

The mass moved again, stopped, moved a bit further. Probing, searching, intent.

Water splashed, followed by a muttered curse in a foreign tongue.

Arnold smiled.

Bastard stepped in a puddle.

Wet footsteps squished in his direction as the mass slowly and silently passed, now moving in the opposite direction, to Arnold's left.

Suddenly, the alley lit up, shadows streaking from left to right with the crunch of tires on loose dirt. A car was turned in from the far end, headlight straight into Karim's eyes.

Instinctively, Arnold realized his chance. He bolted, took two steps, cut sharp right, away from Karim, thinking, distance is good, every inch of is one less degree of accuracy.

The odds of survival increasing in his brain with each step he ran, legs pumping harder and faster than ever before in his young life, an adrenaline surge igniting afterburners he never knew were there, fear overriding the searing pain from his ankle.

He was flying through Mahoney's yard, onto the side street, cut another right, shot down a short block as one final surge sent him bursting through the pizza shop front door, breathlessly yelling, "Call 911!"

2

"WHAT EXACTLY WAS your relationship with the deceased?" Detective Wendy Elliott asked. She was sitting on an aluminum chair opposite him, a small metal desk separating them. She seemed to be studying him with a freaky detached curiosity he found unnerving.

The deceased.

The words reverberated through his mind and decayed like the ring of a bell as they vanished into heavy silence.

Howard's dead. Howard is the deceased.

Then the words finally began to sink in, his muscles going lax. He slumped against the hard cinder- block wall. Blowing through pursed lips, he scrambled to grasp the full reality of those words. Until this very moment he'd desperately held onto a thread of irrational hope that the detonation he assumed to be a gunshot had been something entirely different—although he had no idea what that might be. Or if it was a gunshot, it had served as only a warning, a threat, anything but a senseless murder.

His best friend shot dead. Guilt engulfed him.

Had he not gone for pizza, this awful senseless act of violence would never have happened. Meaning, in a perverse way, he was directly responsible for his friend's death.

He blew another deep breath and rocked forward, elbows on his knees, fingers knitted together as an anxious storm of butterflies fought to escape his stomach. The metal chair suddenly became too hard to bear, but fear of moving was paralyzing and he was too afraid to say a damn word. The acoustical-tile walls began squeezing his shoulders together, and this room's air—smelling of sweat and fear permanently embedded in the cinderblock walls—had become too warm and stuffy to catch one satisfying breath.

Glancing away from her, he massaged the back of his neck, suddenly aware this was an interrogation room. He stopped to look again.

Oh, Jesus, am I a suspect? They couldn't possibly think...

The gut butterflies morphed into a gnawing ache.

"Mr. Gold?"

"Huh?"

His attention snapped back to the detective's penetrating green eyes boring into him, but his mind couldn't track her words.

Those contacts she's wearing? Eyes like emeralds.

Jesus, did I actually think that? How ridiculous.

Dude, get your shit together, focus. What does she want?

She asked again, "What was your relationship with Mr. Weinstein?"

And he knew then she must be reading his thoughts.

"Mr. Weinstein? Funny, but he's always been Howie..."

"Please just answer the question."

Sucking another breath, he palm-wiped his face, blinked.

"We're best friends. Have been since grade school."

More than friends...brothers. Having grown up together. Bar mitzvahs only a month apart. Shared their fantasies, dreams, fears...he flashed on the countless hours spent together linked by a love of all things digital, sharing copies of WIRED when other kids passed around comics, building outrageous computers from junked equipment, reading operating manuals and books on languages like C++ just for fun.

She seemed to weigh his answer, deciding something, which, in itself, was off-putting and uncomfortable, as if she was accusing him of something diffuse and intangible. Which did nothing but amp up his restlessness even more—if that were possible.

"That all?" she asked.

He mentally replayed the question yet still didn't see the point.
"Sorry. What is it you want to know?"
"You and Mr. Weinstein. You *just* friends?"
Ah. Now it was clear. Why was he so dense?
"You asking if we're gay?"
He considered a biting answer, finding it unbelievable that she'd ask the question so obliquely.

Should I be offended?

Give her the benefit of the doubt. She needs facts, is all. Don't take it personally.

She raised her eyebrows. "Well?"
He gave a sarcastic laugh.
"No, we're not gay."

And immediately regretted his irritable, sarcastic tone because it sounded so...adolescent. She was, after all, just doing her job. It was just that she was so far off base it actually struck him as humorous. Howie, Mr. Cool Dude, dated about three girls at any one time, his favorite du jour being Nicole, a French exchange student at the UW.

Again, he glanced at the round-face wall-clock and realized it was approaching midnight. They'd been at this for an hour now, revisiting the same ground over and over, just asking the question slightly differently. Seemed like they've been here all day. With a weird detachment he noticed his right hand was splayed across his abdomen, in a weak attempt to staunch the gnawing pain that hovered just below unbearable. The pain came in continuous rolling waves, diminishing temporarily when distracted by a question, intensifying as he considered their answers, back and forth in an endless loop.

Howie is dead.

He'd never forgive himself. Never. Howie didn't deserve to die. Especially not like that. Murdered.

She tapped her ballpoint against the pad of paper on the small table in an attempt to capture his attention.

"See, that's what I don't understand," she said. "Why would someone kill your best friend for a computer? Can you explain that?"

Damned ankle, aching like a sonofabitch. The terror of the alley zapping through him again, sending fresh searing bolts of pain deep into his gut, freezing his mind in mid-thought.

Oh, Christ, she's waiting for another answer.

He scrambled to remember the question, replayed it in his mind.

"I don't know."

But he *did* know.

It's just too complicated to go into at the moment. Maybe never.

Frowning, she shook her head.

"See, this is where your story begins to fall apart."

"Fall apart?"

"Explain something to me. How do you know they were after your computer if you haven't been inside the house?"

Uh -oh. Good point. Messed up on that.

He saw her eyes—laser emeralds—boring straight through his pupils into his brain. Tell her?

"You got a Tums, something like that?"

The weightlessness ratcheting several notches again.

She scoffed. Her tone was demanding, leaving no room for discussion.

"You going to answer the question or are we going to spend another hour playing hide and seek?"

Obviously, she knew he wasn't telling the whole story. His entire life he'd been transparent as a contact lens. Probably always would. Lying just wasn't in his DNA, and truth be told, that was a definite personality liability. Some friends claimed he was too blunt, whereas he considered it simply being truthful. But yeah, had to admit, there was probably something to be said for diplomacy. Exactly what that might be, he wasn't quite sure. He decided to give her something reasonable.

"No, you're wrong. I said I came in the back door. Besides, it's the only thing in the house worth anything."

She shook her head again, not buying that part of his story.

"And you just assume it's gone? Why would you assume that?"

Shit, was it on the table when I came in?

Only thing he could remember were Howie's words. And the gunshot.

"Which reminds me."

She straightened the pad of yellow legal paper, aligning it precisely parallel to the edge of the table. So far, she hadn't written a single word, but he'd seen enough television crime shows to assume the entire interview was being recorded anyway, so why bother, just use the pad as a prop.

"Tell me about the room in your basement."

Yeah, sure, after an hour of questioning this just happens to pop into your head?

He started to say, "What room?" but realized how ridiculous that would sound. Instead he shrugged.

"I like computers."

At least that's the truth.

This time, instead of a scoff, she flat out laughed, the sound ripe with a definite sarcastic ring.

Silence.

More seconds ticked away, each seeming like a minute.

She waited five more silence-filled seconds before saying, "Hey, Arnold, look, I was down there. I saw the whole enchilada. You've got what, a rack of equipment? Special A/C system? Power supplies? Looks more like Google's research lab than the hobby room of a twenty-three-year old. Understand why I might be curious?"

He locked eyes with her in an attempt to settle the issue.

"No, seriously, I'm really into computers."

And he was serious. He'd started figuring out digital circuits in the fifth grade when he was given a castoff PC. Had that puppy dismantled and put back together running better than ever in a few days.

She leaned back in her chair and flashed him a serious dose of cop-eye.

Compelling him to elaborate.

"Ever hear of Nate Silver?" Without waiting for an answer, he started in, finally seizing an opportunity to jabber about something he did want to discuss, hoping maybe to short-circuit some anxiety. "He's, like, the guru of predictions. The last Presidential election? He called every electoral district, every Senate and House seat. I mean he was amazing. He—"

"Can it." She sliced a hand through the air, cutting him off. "Answer the question, Mr. Gold. Who was in your house and why are you so sure a computer's missing? Wait," holding up a finger, "Let me be very specific. What computer is missing? You went into the basement?"

Palm-wiping his face again, he leaned back to stare at the acoustical tile ceiling and try to remember. He was about to contradict himself, he realized. How good was that? Well, he was going to have to start digging himself out of the hole. He straightened back up.

"I just assumed they took my laptop. It was sitting right there on the kitchen table where it always is when I went out for pizza. Howie and I were using it. Like I said, it's the only thing of value someone might take. I don't have jewelry or artwork."

He bent over, started massaging his sprained ankle again, the skin feeling boggy now, and he knew it was swelling.

She tapped her ballpoint against the pad.

"Did you see that it was missing, or do you just assume it is gone?"

Was it?

Thought about that a moment but knew that's what those bastards were after, so yeah, had to be.

"I can't even remember looking. I mean, if I did, I didn't notice. Didn't have time. Like I said, I came in, yelled to Howie, and he yelled for me to run. Then bang, I heard the gunshot…then everything happened so fast…I ran. That's it."

The gunshot echoed through his mind again and he knew it would be embedded there for the rest of his life.

She waited a couple seconds for him to continue.

When he said nothing, she said, "I'm being truthful with you, Mr. Gold, so listen up. The less you say, the more you implicate yourself in this murder. What am I supposed to believe, that two armed burglars forced their way into an occupied home to steal a laptop? Get real. That isn't the way burglaries work. Burglars—real burglars—case a place out so they can break into it when it's unoccupied. They're trying not to get caught, much less identified. Armed robbers, on the other hand, are a different breed. They use ski masks to stick up 7-11s and gas stations."

Arnold figured this wasn't a question, so didn't answer.

Detective Elliott continued, "So then—if I have your story straight—this unidentified armed laptop robber shoots your friend and chases you down the alley. This sound about right to you?"

He resented the sarcasm.

"I'm upset."

The words sounded so lame as to be embarrassing, but what could he say?

She leaned into this answer.

"Upset?"

Even more sarcasm was dripping from the word.

What the hell does she want from me?

He'd told her the truth.

Well, sort of.

"Yeah, upset. Wouldn't you be if your best friend had just been murdered?"

"You're off in the weeds again. These two men—the ones you claim stole your computer and murdered your best friend—what were they doing in your house? You can't get me to believe two armed men just show up out of the blue to steal a laptop. Nuh-uh!"

His stomach killing him now.

"I don't know."

She stabbed an accusing finger at him.

"You're lying. I know you're lying, and you know I know you're lying. What I'm trying to figure out is why."

Her question bounced right off him, his mind too consumed with an endless loop replaying what Howie must have experienced during his final desperate seconds of life. He imagined Howie staring unbelievingly at the gun, defenselessly focusing on Karim's finger as it pulled the trigger, the shock, surprise, and moment of horror at realizing a bullet had just ripped through his body, finally the helplessness of lying on the floor knowing life was rapidly ebbing from his body and that in another few seconds he'd discover the answer to a life-long question. Did he experience pain, or did the shock mercifully shield him from that?

Arnold shut his eyes, pressed the heels of both hands tightly over both

13

ears, and shook his head.

Stop! Thinking! Of! It!

Arnold didn't practice his parents' Judaism. Nor had he adopted any other religion. Yet every night he prayed to whatever God might be out there to not allow him death as a result of a violent or brutal act, to make sure his last living thought—the one he would carry into eternity—would not be one of horror. Exactly what had happened to Howie. He died knowing…

He leaned forward, hands on his forehead, and began to sob. Big, heaving sobs that he couldn't stop, for the loss of his brother. Elliott put a gentle hand on his shoulder.

"C'mon, Arnold, let it out. Tell me. Tell me the truth. You'll feel better if you do."

He blurted, "The truth is if I hadn't gone for pizza Howie would still be alive. That's the fucking truth!"

She continued massaging his shoulders.

"Why's that, Arnold?"

He shook his head, mumbled, "They would've killed me instead."

Her voice stayed soft and soothing, working on extracting the story from behind whatever wall Arnold had built.

"Why's that?"

Arnold simply shook his head and remained mute.

He was thinking back to Howie's warning: "Don't tell anyone about your system."

How prophetic. He had told. And that is the reason Howie was now dead.

Elliott switched back into hard interrogation mode.

"Who murdered your best friend, Arnold? I *know* you saw them."

Suddenly he knew this hammering on him wasn't going to let up because she'd continuing this harangue until he broke down and told her everything. He was totally fucked. He had to end this.

But how?

"Arnold, you're not leaving until we settle this," now sounding like a grade school teacher instead of a detective.

It dawned on him. He slowly raised his head and met those

startling vibrant eyes.

"I want a lawyer."

He thought he heard a sharp inhale, as if she'd just been gut-punched.

"No you don't, Arnold. You want to settle this now."

But now he detected a hint of desperation in her words and knew he'd done the right thing. His confidence grew.

"You heard me. I want to talk to a lawyer."

3

FIROUZ LET KARIM drive, giving him more time to think, regroup, strategize, always his responsibility because that was the way things needed to be with Karim. If it weren't for being brothers, he would never bother using him. On the other hand, he was a devoted believer, a good Sunni, which, in the end stood for something. But the need- less killing now drew attention to them they could ill afford. Not with what was at stake. But there was no sense saying anything more. They now had to deal with what they had, and, God willing, would still succeed.

"The Jew saw you?"

Karim said, "Yes."

Firouz silently shook his head and bit his tongue because the mission was not a total failure. They did, after all, have the computer and were on their way Gjayoor's small apartment in the area called Capitol Hill. Gjayoor was a true believer as well as a brilliant computer expert. He would be the one to examine and extract information from the Jew's computer, determine how he was able to see into the future and predict events as Naseem had explained. The Jew, he knew was smart, perhaps brilliant when it came to foreseeing events, so it was a shame he wasn't sympathetic. Now that he had seen Karim kill his friend, he certainly would give this information to the police. Too bad because this now meant they would have to kill Gold, an outcome that would only implicate them more. Unless of course they could kill him and disappear before the authorities had identified them. He was glad they had the sense to wear gloves when they went to the Jew's front door.

Yes, Arnold Gold would not be allowed to live.

After what seemed like hours sitting on the butt-numbing metal chair, breathing warm stale air in the cramped cinder-block room, steeping in an emotional stew of guilt, anger, and helplessness, the one metal door clicked open. Elliott stepped in, followed by an older, well-dressed man Arnold had never seen before. With three bodies packed in, the rectangular space felt even more cramped. How long had Elliott been gone? Could've been three minutes, could've been three hours, his mind had been so chockablock distracted with worry and self-loathing, that time had simply vanished into unmeasured consciousness. The man a police officer? Looked serious enough to be one, though maybe a bit too dapper. Arnold bet not.

"Arnold Gold?" the man asked, hand extended.

Without a word, Arnold stood and stared from the proffered hand to the man's face. Older, maybe in his 50s, slick dresser, what with the well-tailored suit and polished Farragamos, a gold Movado, precisely barbered salt-and-pepper hair. He'd never paid attention to how well or poorly men dressed until the trip to Vegas. Not that he considered himself any sort of fashion connoisseur.

Arnold answered, "Yes?" not intentionally ignoring the handshake.

Having never been in this kind of situation, insecurity blinded him to his already thin social graces.

The man hesitated before dropping his hand back to his side.

"Palmer Davidson. Murray called me. I came straight over."

Aw, yes, Murray Fein, the only attorney Arnold knew. He'd always harbored an edgy distrust of lawyers for various reasons, but primarily because regardless of what type of law they practice, the majority of their effort was devoted to preying on other's misfortunes. On top of that, they loved to argue, maybe even thrived on persevering with no regard to being right or wrong or what might be just.

Arnold hated to argue. He hated confrontation even more. But preying on people's problems.... the only reason he knew Murray was he had managed his parents' legal affairs while they were alive.

Ah, now he got it. This had to be the lawyer Murray arranged for him. He remembered Murray saying something about needing a different attorney than himself, one who did criminal defense work, and would track one down, send him over to help out. This had to be him.

Arnold nodded, distracted by another wave of guilt.

"Yeah, okay." He paused, glanced around the room again at the walls, ceiling and floor. Even the stains in the acoustical tiles seemed way too familiar, as if this interrogation room had been an integral part of his life for years now. "What do we do now?"

Davidson turned to Elliott.

"Excuse me, Detective, but I haven't been informed of any particulars. Perhaps you might help me by explaining exactly why my client is being held for questioning?"

Elliott squeezed against the small table in order to make room to close the door, trapping the three of them in warm sour air, making the room feel even smaller and more cramped, as impossible as that seemed. She motioned Davidson to the one remaining chair. "Please," and dropped into the chair Arnold just vacated—leaving Arnold standing awkwardly in the center of the floor.

She folded her arms across her chest.

"Since Mr. Gold seems unable to give me any details of tonight's events, here's the story I got from the initial patrol report. He and his friend, Howard Weinstein, were at Gold's residence earlier this evening. Apparently, he exited the residence through the back to go to a neighborhood pizzeria where he subsequently purchased a pizza before returning home. There he reentered the premises through the back door. Once inside the kitchen, he called out to Mr. Weinstein who, in return, shouted for him to run. Mr. Gold heard what sounded like a gunshot and immediately fled from the rear of his residence back to the pizza shop where the owner placed a 911 call. He remained in that shop until a squad car picked him up."

She gave Arnold an expectant look, giving him a perfect opportunity to flesh out more detail.

When Arnold said nothing, Elliott shook her head disgustedly and glanced at Davidson as if to say, "see?"

"He claims two people—whoever they are—entered his home to steal a laptop computer. From his earlier statement it's clear he believes these two people are the assailants but he'll neither confirm nor deny that assumption. In addition, his statement leads us to believe he saw," miming quotation marks, "*them*. But he refuses to cooperate further with the investigation by providing any sort of description of Mr. Weinstein's alleged assailants. And before you ask, a GSR administered to Mr. Gold was negative."

Davidson adjusted himself on the metal chair and crossed his legs, ankle on knee, and smoothed his pants.

"Am I correct in assuming Mr. Weinstein is now deceased?"

She nodded.

"Mind filling me in with more details what was found at the scene?" Arnold thought he caught a glimpse of blush flash across Elliott's cheeks. "Sorry. Assumed you'd been briefed more than this. Howard Weinstein was found dead of a single through and through GSW to the head. He was on the living room floor. Nothing else in the house seems disturbed. There were no signs of a struggle and no signs of forced entry, suggesting Mr. Weinstein allowed them access to the house."

Arnold realized his assumption they stole his computer hadn't been confirmed.

"What about my laptop?"

They both turned to him, Elliott saying, "What about it?"

"My laptop is always on the kitchen table. It wasn't there when I came through the back door."

For the first time this memory actually surfaced into consciousness. His earlier claim that it was stolen had been based solely on assumption, now it seemed to be fact.

They both waited for him to add more, but when he didn't, Elliott told Davidson, "Now you can see how it's been all evening. Nothing. You might want to explain to your client that he's not doing himself or us any favors by withholding information."

Davidson nodded vague agreement, perhaps processing the information.

After a moment, "Mind if I speak with my client alone?"

Elliott was already pushing up off the chair, probably in anticipation of this request. She gave the vaguest hint of relief, perhaps assuming Davidson would be able to convince Arnold to provide needed information.

"Knock yourself out. I have paperwork to complete before I finish my shift."

Davidson bowed slightly.

"Thanks," and waited until she was out of the room and the door securely shut before removing his suit coat, folding it lengthwise, then draping it over his thighs once he was sitting again.

He motioned for Arnold to take the chair across the narrow desk from him. Davidson leaned forward, hands clasped, forearms on the desk, a gentle disarming expression on his face.

"Will you talk to me?" the words sounding more inquisitive than judgmental.

Slowly, for the first time since being brought here, as if surfacing from anesthesia, Arnold scanned the four bare walls of floor to ceiling acoustical tiles searching for any evidence of hidden cameras or microphones. Surely, this room was monitored. He'd watched too many episodes of The First 48 to believe differently. But he saw nothing to confirm this suspicion. Didn't mean anything, though, because wide-angle camera lenses could be tiny enough to easily embed in a hole of an acoustical tile, making it impossible to spot during cursory inspection. Every zit on his cheeks was probably being recorded in stunning high definition.

"No problem. Just not in here."

Davidson seemed surprised at this.

"Oh? Why's that?"

Arnold swept a palm around the room. He let out a sarcastic grunt.

"Really?" And shook his head, "You're kidding." Pause. "Aren't you? Think they're going to let us to talk in private?"

Davidson slowly nodded.

"Tell you what. I'll see what I can do, but you know, don't you, with this being a homicide investigation they have every right to hold you for several more hours if they so choose, especially if they believe you're willfully withholding critical information."

News to him.

"Why? I didn't do anything."

The hell you didn't. Howard's dead because of you.

"That may be, but here's the thing: at the very least you're a material witness. Meaning they have legal right hold you for questioning." Davidson dropped his voice a notch. "But, realistically, face it: they're human. Refusal to cooperate accomplishes nothing but piss them off. Not only that, it makes you look guilty of something. Especially if they have no idea of the degree of your involvement in your friend's death. Following me?"

Made sense.

He liked the way Davidson said it; open minded, non-judgmental, as if they were in this mess together.

"Yeah, I get it. It's just…I don't, I can't, talk about it here."

And circled a finger around the room to indicate this entire conversation was probably being recorded.

Davidson stood.

"Let me see what I can do," and opened the door.

4

"GIVE ME ONE good reason to cut him loose?" Elliott asked. She was leaning against the cinderblock wall outside the interrogation room in the West Precinct, her intense green eyes boring deep, straight through Davidson's retinas, arms crossed in a challenging posture. "Your client has refused to cooperate. Which, I gotta tell you, does nothing but convince me he's withholding information vital to an active investigation. I mean, let's get real here; this is a cold-blooded homicide we're talking about, not some petty-ass auto theft or DUI. There's obviously something going on that I fully intend to get to the bottom of."

Davidson stood next to the open door to the interrogation room, wanting to keep the conversation out in the hall rather than in the room with its thick stale air and body odor so strong you could probably peel it off the wall with a spackle knife. His suit coat remained draped over the back of the metal chair he'd vacated minutes earlier. Damn room was hot, too, as evidenced by little crescents of moisture darkening the armpits of his crisp white shirt. Most of all, he wanted his client to hear this conversation so the gravity of his predicament just might sink in.

Davidson scratched the angle of his jaw.

"Look at it this way: hold him for several more hours and I can pretty much guarantee he's not going say another word. You want that? What good's that going to do anyone? Why not let me have a chance to talk with him, find out what's going on? Improves the odds of you getting what you want."

Elliott shifted weight, pushing off the wall, dropping both arms and straightening her broad shoulders.

"Let me tell you something, counselor, that attitude of his is, at best, not helping him or his cause. What's to guarantee he won't disappear if I cut him loose?"

"Come on, Detective, kid's scared to death." Davidson inhaled audibly, maybe a bit too dramatically, but drama had always served him well when working the legal system. Sometimes it generated quicker and better responses than cold logic. "Let's be realistic. Look at him," jerking a thumb in Arnold's direction, this being the first time during the entire negotiation they had acknowledged his obvious presence. "We're not talking professional criminal in there. He look like the kind of seasoned slime ball who's likely to flee?"

The incredulous emphasis in each word drove home his point.

Elliott gave her signature sarcastic laugh. "Didn't realize they had tattoos on their forehead spelling out 'Flight Risk.'"

Davidson sucked a tooth and considered how to better plead his case. Was Elliott serious or was she simply play-acting to increase her odds of prying loose Arnold's cooperation? Whatever the motive, he didn't believe it was going to make Gold cough up the information she wanted any faster than her present tactic. Not yet at least. She'd have a much better shot at obtaining it if he were permitted to talk with Gold someplace away from this intimidating environment. How to convince her of that?

"What I mean is this; you have a, what, a twenty-three-year-old kid with no priors whose best friend was allegedly murdered in cold blood during what is presumed to be a home invasion. A robbery, maybe. Maybe not. But a robbery of what? A laptop? Get real!"

Davidson gave a dismissive grunt.

"What's the big collusion here? Explain that to me, because I just don't see it. And, by the way, the reason he doesn't want to tell me his story in there is because it looks like it's right out of Guantanamo. To be absolutely blunt about it, he doesn't trust you guys. What's to keep you from recording every word we say?" He quickly raised both hands in a don't-shoot-the-messenger surrender. "Not that I'm suggesting you would actually stoop to such low tactics, but put yourself in his shoes. Think about it a moment. What would you do if you were him?"

Without even blinking, she countered with, "First of all, I'm not him. And I damn well guarantee you he knows whose finger pulled that trigger. So, if you want to play what-if games, put yourself in my shoes. I got a witness who can identify the shooter and he's not saying word one."

Touché. Tough negotiator.

Wish I knew more about the kid.

Davidson scrambled for more ammunition to buttress his logic but came up blank, so he reverted to the time-honored tactic of simply rewording his previous argument.

"Hey, look, the kid doesn't even have one outstanding parking ticket."

Now that was a stretch, a total shot in the dark, having never laid eyes on the kid before. For all he knew, Arnold Gold might owe a small fortune in delinquent fines or speeding tickets or have a felony warrant pending in Duluth. But that didn't fit the picture he was seeing of the emotionally demoralized innocent wringing his hands inside the room.

Elliott sighed and shot Arnold another look, seemingly weighing Davidson's argument. She glanced at the lawyer, then back to Arnold once more.

"You'll take full responsibility for him until we get this sorted out?"

He thought about that a moment before answering. All he knew about this young man was the first impression that had formed after a few minutes of discussion under stressful circumstances. He decided to carve out some wiggle room for himself. He didn't want her coming down on him some time in the future with a ginned-up infraction of their understanding.

"That all depends on what you mean by full responsibility. Define that."

She finger-combed her short blond hair.

"Most importantly, I expect you to know his whereabouts when we need to interview him again, which I guarantee you will be within the next twenty-four hours. In other words, I call, you have him on such a short leash you can have him here," pointing at the floor for emphasis, "in fifteen minutes. You clear on this?"

Davidson struggled keep the corners of his mouth from curling up. "Thanks, Lieutenant."

Elliott flashed a double take.

"How'd you know about that?" referring to her recent promotion.

Davidson just smiled and turned toward the vulnerable young man slumped in the metal chair, a thousand-yard stare glazing his eyes.

"Got everything? If so, let's get out of here."

Arnold trailed Davidson past the heavy aluminum-framed glass door, into the early morning chill, out over the small patterned-concrete plaza with Virginia Street straight ahead. Even though it was now early morning, he registered traces of car exhaust from yesterday's rush hour, a lingering urban smell that never fully dissipated once a temperature inversion trapped air pockets between the Olympic and Cascades mountain ranges.

Davidson said, "I'm parked up a block. Where would you prefer to talk?"

Not usually out and about in the city at this time of morning, he had no idea what might be open. Regardless, he doubted there was any public spot in which he could feel totally at ease discussing the story. Certainly not back at his house. Besides, that was probably still an active crime scene, and now, thinking about it, he had no idea when he'd be allowed to return. Assuming he would even want to go there again.

"How about your office?" Before Davidson had a chance to answer, he added, "Where is it?"

"Yeah, that'll work." Davidson pushed up his coat sleeve to check his watch. "Tell you what. Let's pick up a couple cups of coffee. Looks more and more like this is going to take a while. But, in answer to your question, the Smith Tower."

Davidson turned right off of James Street into an almost empty multistory parking garage in the heart of Seattle's historic Pioneer

Square district. The building façade—stone with arched windows, brick, and concrete—seemed a mosaic of additions and renovations spanning more than a century of service. Davidson nosed his car into a space with the word 'reserved' stenciled in black military-style letters on the bare concrete wall at the back of the narrow stall. Arnold opened his door carefully to keep from banging its edge on a thick concrete pillar of flaking pale yellow paint. He squeezed out and stepped onto well-seasoned concrete. From the ease with which Davidson navigated the tight garage, he assumed he'd been renting this parking spot for some years. He stepped away to admire the car: a metallic gray Mercedes e350 Coupe. Beautiful. Definitely a car Arnold could easily get used to.

Without a word, Davidson headed toward a glowing green exit sign, Arnold hurrying to keep up. He followed Davidson down an open flight of concrete steps—the slap of the lawyer's leather soles echoing against the sharp angles and hard surfaces—out of the garage, on up James toward First Avenue, Arnold's Nikes making no sound.

"Over there," Davidson said, with a nod toward the Smith Tower, a venerable Seattle landmark, one of the nation's first skyscrapers to very briefly hold the distinction of the country's tallest building outside of Manhattan.

Arnold trotted along, trying to match Davidson's long stride without having to actually run, thinking he probably thought everyone walked this fast. He estimated him at 6'1" and in pretty good shape for a guy in his early to mid-fifties. Husky but not overweight.

Did he work out regularly?

Davidson's office seemed to Arnold something straight out of a 1940s movie set—heavy, darkly stained mahogany furniture—and now that he thought about it, seemed to fit perfectly with the building's time-warp interior. Davidson had carried the theme even further, decorating the walls with Seattle photographic reprints from the early 1900s. There was even a brass banker's lamp on the desk and a Persian carpet heavy in maroons and blues on the polished hardwood. Yep, right out of central casting. Took a lot of thought, but Arnold wasn't sure it was his taste. They continued through the small reception area into Davidson's office.

Davidson slipped off his suit coat and carefully hung it from a hook on the back of the office door before settling into a classic wood desk chair, its spring emitting a protesting creak. Arnold had several seating options to choose from: two chairs and a small couch in brown leather, all very masculine and cozy. But his antsy, nerve-jangling anticipation of finally having to explain his story made it impossible to sit or remain still and not fidget, leaving him to pace, his mind unable rid itself of the awful sound of that gun in Karim's meaty grip, the gun that murdered his best friend.

Hands clasped behind his head, Davidson pushed back in the chair, propped one foot on a half-open lower drawer, waited for Arnold to start.

When Arnold ignored him, he said, "Okay, out with it."

Arnold opened his mouth to ask, "Out with what?" but realized what a cheesy way that would be to delay the inevitable, that he risked Davidson losing patience with him and dumping him as a client. Sooner or later he would have to tell his entire story, difficult as that might be. Where to begin?

"How much detail you looking for? I mean, where do you want me to start?"

"How about at the beginning?"

The beginning.

A flush of embarrassment rippled through him. He paced a tight circle, searching for the words, and cleared his throat, knowing he was simply stalling.

The beginning...

"Come on, son, we don't have all night."

Son. One word. Enough to weld a link between lawyer and client. Felt good, that word. It suddenly connected him to another person, one he believed to be sympathetic. Arnold nodded and stopped, eyes closed, reliving the events.

"Just wanted to get laid, was all...."

5

Six Weeks Earlier

ARNOLD STUDIES THE image staring back at him from the mirror; acne scars, black curly hair, the "Jewish nose" people make jokes about and that Nazi propaganda cartoonists exaggerated. He hates his face. Hates this damn sports coat, hates the slacks and polo shirt draped over his gangly frame. He can even discern outright loathing in the dark brown eyes as they stare back. He sees a 23-year old virgin who lacks the social skills to rectify the problem and who will never have a girlfriend. In other words, he's totally hosed. Put another way, he stands a 0.001 percent chance of getting one. He is the quintessential cliché of the computer nerd, the social outcast, the toe-dragging hem-hawing geek, the guy who will eventually enter a retirement home having never scored.

"Fuck it. I'm not going to do it."

He rips off his sports coat and throws it on the floor. With an exasperated sigh, he turns from the mirror so Howie can scope a head to shoulders frontal view.

His stomach aches with dread and anxiety.

"What do you see?"

Howie picks up the sports coat, makes a point of brushing it off, and shakes it open for Arnold to slip back on.

"I see a great guy with a big heart who has a lot to offer any girl he wants. Seriously, dude. There's someone out there who would love to meet you. Believe me. And you're the smartest man I know. Smart goes a long way."

Lip service, nothing but goddamn lip service.

Then again, what do you expect from your best friend? He knows Howie not only means well, but his friend also loves this role of coach to the socially downtrodden. This confuses his emotions even more, as if he's a damn charity case or something.

"Bullshit. I'm ugly. You know it, I know it. Everyone in the goddamned nebula knows it. So why don't we both save ourselves a shit-load of grief and go out for a beer instead of persisting with this charade?"

Howie bobs the coat like a matador goading a bull, encouraging him to slip it back on.

"Come on, Arnold, we've discussed this, like, how many times now? Too many."

Arnold shakes his head. He hates the sound of his petulant whining voice but seems unable to open his mouth on this particular subject without it spilling out like Niagara fucking Falls. Just another reason to cancel the evening. It'd be way simpler if they just went out for beers and talked computers.

"Easy for you to say. I'm not going."

Howard steps closer, now holding the coat in his left hand and making a come-here wave with his right.

"Oh, yes you are. You'll do fine. Just take this first step. You're never going to get yourself out of this..."

"Out of what!" he says too loudly.

Arnold snatches the dangling coat from Howie's grasp and throws it on the bed in a huff.

Immediately regrets his tone and action and wants to say, "I'm sorry," but fears it'll come out whining again. Goddamn it! He'd punch the wall like he's seen real men do in the movies, but knows that would hurt like hell and will accomplish absolutely zip to diffuse his mounting frustration.

Why do people do that, punch walls, it seems so...stupid.

29

Howie sighs. A parental sounding sigh, one that makes Arnold feel even more infantile than a moment ago. Now he's as furious at Howie as much his is at himself. Jesus! There's no way to win.

Backing up a step, Howie raises a palm at him.

"Whoa. Take a deep breath, calm down."

His friend is right. He knows this. So, he pauses to do exactly as instructed, but it doesn't help because he still wants to scream and stomp his feet, just do something—he's not sure what—to short-circuit his self-loathing. How juvenile is that? Pretty damn juvenile.

Howie says, "Listen to me. We need to find a way to get you out of this...this isolation. You're trapped. You're mired down in the damn quicksand. Okay, so I get *it*: you feel awkward around women," he says in a sing-song voice of having heard it so many times he wants to puke, "like you don't know what to do. That's the way every guy feels at the beginning. That's why it called the beginning. The only way you're going to fix that is to take the first step and start dating. Might be a little, ah, uncomfortable the first time out, but come on, dude, you got to do it. I know you can and you know you can."

He pauses before dropping the bomb.

"You don't, people are going to start thinking you're gay and you don't want that, do you?"

Arnold scoffs. The Gay Threat. Can't believe Howie actually stooped to such a snake-low level. But why be surprised? He's done it before. On multiple occasions. Didn't work then either. But he does have a point: his social isolation is beginning to make him feel, well, weird. And the weirder he gets, the harder it's going to be to rectify the situation. He knows all this intellectually. But actually, taking action and doing something about it, well, that's a whole different ballgame.

Arnold shakes his head side to side and blows a long breath through pursed lips. Still doesn't help. He glares back at Howie.

"Start dating. Just like that, huh. Easy for you to say. Look at you!" Arnold gives him a head to toe appraisal. "You're the guy who's got it all: good looks, you know how to talk to people—especially women—and you're dating at least three girls I know of. God knows about the ones I don't know about. You got it made."

Only thing I have over him is smarts, he thinks. And even that's close. But he would never tell Howie that. He envies Howard. Dude is everything he wants to be. The other thing he'll never admit to him is the huge crush he has on Rachael, his sister. He's secretly been in love with her since puberty when he started to notice girls.

Howie offers up the sports coat again with a little nod to say, come on, put it on. Grudgingly Arnold does just that. Then Howie runs his palm over the shoulders smoothing out a wrinkle or two.

One of these days I should splurge and get a sports coat, one actually tailored for me, Arnold thinks.

Then again, why? I never have to dress up.

Howard says, "Come on, I'll drop you off. We'll go out for a beer afterward and you can tell me about all the great girls you met."

The bell rings.

Relieved to have this agonizing period finally come to an end, Arnold pushes away from this table and silently shuffles to his right, to the chair just vacated. He drops in, sighs, lets his eyes drift up from his knees to the woman directly across from him, a distant look on her face, as if to say, "Okay, here's the next clown."

Aw, Jesus, drop-dead gorgeous too.

Arnold's mind blanks. The buzzer sounds.

"Hi, I'm Debbie." She's beaming now—stunningly, with perfectly aligned white orthodontics and flawless complexion—as she extends a slim hand across the table, suddenly transformed into Ms. Personality now that they're on the clock.

Arnold stares at her delicate fingers, the perfectly painted and manicured nails, as heavy silence settles over his head like a blank cartoon speech-bubble.

Shake it, you idiot.

He reaches out, gently grasps the warm soft skin, gives one brisk pump before dropping it like a lump of toxic uranium. She'll probably wash it in the ladies' room as soon as this particular encounter finishes.

"Arnold…. ah, Arnold Gold."

He starts massaging the knuckles of his left hand, eyes drifting down to the surface of the table, his mind racing for something, anything, to contribute.

Aw, shit, say something. Do not repeat the last disaster.

Remembering Howard's advice, that it's going to be uncomfortable initially but then gets easier, he opens his mouth, but no words come.

Come on...

The ambient noise level increases with chatter as couples— perhaps ten of them—are now well into their three-minute conversations. She studies him, waiting for an initiation of conversation. His gut cinches into a rock-hard square knot and he feels warmth ascend his face like a rapidly spreading brush fire, and, for a moment, hates Howie for forcing him to attend.

Hears her ask, "So, Arnold—oh, may I call you Arnold?—what do you do?"

"I..."

He'd love to tell her, to describe the artificial intelligence he's been developing since age twelve, to ask if she's ever worked in the Linux environment and if so, how does she solve certain problems. But he knows this wasn't greeted with shrieks of joy during the last feeble attempt at conversation, so why repeat the mistake?

"Ah...nothing," he mutters, watching his right-hand squeeze into little white pearls of knuckles.

"Okay," she says.

Did he hear a twinge of disappointment in that single word? Or is he simply projecting? Would she be impressed if he told her about his work? Of winning his grade school science fair in sixth grade? Of being advanced into the special mathematics program in high school, a junior level college course? Would she even believe him? She's beautiful, which only amps up the cloud of cotton candy fluffing around his stomach.

I'm dying here. Do something.

"Want to hear a joke?" he asks, face now radiating like a megawatt space heater.

"I'd love to."

He swallows, inhales, rallies his nerve.

"How do you recognize an extroverted engineer?"

"Don't know. How?"

"They stare at your shoes instead of their own."

She laughs, but he can tell it's forced, which makes him even more anxious than a moment ago—if that's possible. He shifts position on the chair and starts to massage the back of his neck, forcing himself to look at her face. He wants to tell her she's beautiful but suspects she knows that only too well. That kind of person always knows.

Howie advised him to act interested in women he talks to, so asks, "What do *you* do?"

But his heart really isn't in this anymore. Guys like him don't have a snowball's chance of ever dating a woman this fine. If he stood even the most miniscule chance of getting close to her, he'd exert a bit more effort, but she's so damned gorgeous she wouldn't be caught dead talking on the phone with a nerdy, pimply, gangly geek like him, much less agree to a date. And she knows he knows this.

Life is so damn unjust. So unfair. Beautiful women, for example.

They have such a huge advantage over the average guy. Well, maybe not over the Tom Bradys of the world, but the middle-of-the-road guys. Engineers, accountants, mid-level managers; your basic average salaried schlemiel. Beautiful women can pretty much write their own ticket in life. They only marry good-looking guys with money and power. And, in contrast to men like him, they can get laid whenever they want, by whomever they want. They have life so damn easy. And now, instead of being simply envious of her drop-dead beauty, he's jealous as hell of her. Why does she get all the breaks while he only gets the short end of the stick? Life is so damn unjust.

Shaking his head, he scans the chatting couples around them just as the beauty across the table asks, "This your first speed dating experience?"

Aw, Christ!

"That obvious, huh?"

Now she pities him. This only twists the knife into his gut further. His right hand, he realizes, is splayed against his belly as if counterpressure will somehow ease the pain.

"Yes," he lies, desperately hoping to save face.

Actually, this is his second try at pounding square pegs into a round holes, this experience just as disastrous as the last. He'll be damned if he'll fess up to that, because that'll simply evoke more pity.

"It gets easier," she reassures him. "Believe me."

Bullshit.

What would a girl like her know?

"Hey, look, I'm sorry," he says, pushing out of the chair. "I just can't..."

Without another word to anyone, he almost runs for the door, wanting nothing more but to end this torture. Never again.

He sits at the small kitchen table—a comforting space for him—with a frosty longneck Anchor Steam beer in hand, Howard slouched in the chair across from him. Arnold shakes his head, face burning with embarrassment even though it's only Howie. Step by agonizing step he recounts the disastrous experience, leaving nothing out, making no attempt to salvage any self-respect. As if confession is now penance for his sins. Howard stares back with a pained expression, listening, not interrupting, not asking questions, and in no way being judgmental. Thank God. Howard could be a great psychiatrist, Arnold believes. It's a damn shame he's chosen to be a computer engineer.

"Awful is the only word to describe it, but that's like saying the universe is bigger than an electron," Arnold tells him. "You can't relate, but it's terrifying, not knowing what to talk about, what to say. There got to be some way, some sort of finishing school...some place where someone can teach me how to act with a woman. I guarantee you, until some miracle happens, I'll never willingly submit to that type of humiliation again. Never. Not unless I have some..." searching for the right word, "training, some coaching."

Training? Really?

Yeah, well, it's the first word came to mind, so it must be right. He shakes his head, overwhelmed by yet another pang of self-pity.

"Can't change the way I look," although he had considered consulting a plastic surgeon last year. "So, there's nothing I can do about that. There's got to be some way to learn to be more comfortable..." he says, letting the thought trail off into nowhere land because Howie's heard it so many times there's no reason to drag him through it yet again.

He wants to cry or smash the beer bottle or scream, just do something to release the frustration eating him alive like a goddamn rat scurrying around his gut, its little claws and teeth chomping at him. Any minute it'll pop out of his chest like the Alien.

Howie picks up his bottle, uses his shirt cuff to wipe away a ring of water condensation on the red Formica tabletop.

"Know what I think? I think you need to get laid."

"Well, duh." Arnold coughs out a sarcastic sound. "What do you think I've been talking about? Can't get laid without a female. Well, yeah, I can fantasize…"

"No," and up pops a just-a-second finger. "Hear me out. I think we need to take you to Vegas, get you laid."

A moment of silence deafens him until his hearing slowly returns.

He knows it's returned because now he again hears the soft hum of the refrigerator and, in the distance—through the open French doors— the wail of a siren off toward the University District. The air carries spring warmth and the scent of freshly mown grass and pollens. Allergy pollens. Suddenly, he's acutely aware of these myriad sensory stimuli while Howie's suggestion echoes though his mind, turning a distant possibility into an actual reality.

Did Howie actually suggest what he thinks he did?

"I'm serious," Howie adds, apparently reading his doubts.

Arnold watches his thumb swipe condensation off the bottle, embarrassed by having to respond to the suggestion.

"I know you are," he mumbles, embarrassed even more by the stew of emotions suddenly bubbling up inside: lust, yearning, fantasies, more embarrassment followed by another loss for words. The story of his pathetic life is now floating below the surface of consciousness, making him feel naked and exposed.

He forces his eyes to look at his best friend, sees him sitting there, silently waiting for an answer. Arnold drops his gaze to the bottle again, too embarrassed to admit the very same thought has crossed his mind numerous times in the past months. It is, however, the first time Howie has put the topic on the table for open discussion. Now, hearing his fantasy actually suggested by his best friend—a person whose judgment, especially when it comes to women, he admires and trusts—it becomes...what, more realistic? Not so fantastic, not unreasonable? Doable?

Seeing a pro would certainly solve the biggest problem. Isn't this the way some guys lose their virginity? There was this movie a couple months back on late night TV, an old film, a comedy/drama about sailors—*Cinderella Liberty*, he thinks is the title—where that's precisely how one sailor was indoctrinated into the mysteries of consensual sex.

It's just...actually...implementing the idea.

Boy!

He sucks a deep breath and shakes his head at nothing, the idea now niggling away at him like a loose tooth, painful, yet curiously demanding to be played with.

"Well?" Howie presses.

Aw, Jesus, dude's not going to let this one go by.

Arnold drops his hand from the bottle to the table, the insurmountable problem of a few moments ago now distilled into an exceedingly simple solution. To say no would strip him of any justification to ever complain about this again. Yet to accept would mean actually having to follow through and go to Vegas, because he sure as hell isn't going to see a call girl anywhere within miles of Seattle. A ball of cotton candy now spins in his chest, fueled by an accelerating heartbeat. Thoughts fly past at warp-speed. No, there's no way of dodging an answer, and he realizes this has just become a pivotal point in his young life. For a moment he hates Howard for forcing a solution upon him.

"What do you want me to say?"

"How about, thank you, Howard for providing me a solution to my misery?" Howie nudges the laptop toward him without a hint of goading in his tone. "Google Las Vegas escorts."

Arnold's face is doing the space heater thing again.

"I...can't."

Howie gives him that sideways squint he mastered in grade school, an effective non-verbal message the meanings of which are always appropriate to the situation.

"Why not?"

The two friends stare at each other, Howard's face dead-ass poker-serious now. And that's when Arnold knows the proposition isn't a joke, that Howard isn't simply jerking his chain to see what kind of a reaction he'll get. Has to admit this is just another example of why he loves Howard, looking out for him like a big brother. Although there are times...

Jesus, how can emotions flip-flop so quickly?

Howard taps the computer again.

"Ever looked before?"

That a trace of a smirk?

His face amps up ten more degrees.

"No."

"Well, just for laughs, let's sneak a look, see what kind of woman appeals to you." Howie scrapes his chair around the table next to him. "Just because you look doesn't mean you have to actually do anything about it. Right?"

Warm tingling begins to stir his groin as his mind slips into fantasies never shared, even with Howie. What does it feel like to touch a breast? To feel a nipple at your fingertips? To slide a hand down...he swallows and inhales into air-starved lungs and realizes he's actually inching the laptop toward himself.

What the hell harm would it do to look? After all, Howie's his best friend, the one he's shared everything with. Well, almost everything. There are things...

Howie says, "Type, Las Vegas escorts, into Google, see what comes up."

Other than my dick?

Arnold types in those words and watches the screen fill with pictures of women, some shots blatantly provocative, others coy, catering to just about any imaginable preference. Tall, short, plump, skeletal, Caucasian, Asian, African American, she man, leather dominatrix all decked-out with riding whips and Stormtrooper caps, you name it, it's there for the choosing.

Allen Wyler

Howie's beside him now, reading the screen, pointing to the one shot.

"How about her? She's really hot."

Arnold swallows again. The top half of the webpage contains two rows of thumbnail shots, the women's names bannered below each one. He double-clicks one at random, watches the page change to her nude body in profile, wavy auburn hair tumbling over a bare ivory shoulder, eyes lowered in false modesty. Heather is her name. Which he's sure isn't the one on her birth certificate. The rest of the page contains a description of activities you might enjoy during an encounter with her. Also included are blank fields to complete should you wish to contact her for a "date." Arnold reads her sketch word by flaming word, his groin now tumescent with explosive pressure as seminal fluid inches into his cotton briefs. Suddenly, his embarrassment over Howie leading him into a forbidden website is trumped by raw curiosity. So, after backing out of Heather's page he clicks on Judy, a statuesque blonde who claims to love threesomes and taking it up the tailpipe.

"Well?" Howie asks, sitting back in the chair, shooting him a funny telepathic expression of knowing Arnold is intrigued.

But by now, all Arnold wants is to relieve his pressurized groin, to go upstairs and privately fantasize about Judy or Heather or, best of all: Rachael.

Instead, he side-steps to the subzero for another beer in an obvious attempt to hide his bulging crotch, which Howard undoubtedly notices.

"I don't know...want one?"

Howard has the good grace to not joke about the obvious.

"You don't know what?"

That stops him. Good question. What exactly doesn't he know? Whether or not to finally experience sex with more than a curled palm? But it is somehow extremely difficult to admit he's actually considering...

Why not fly to Vegas for a day or two?

Seriously.

What's preventing him? He's not formally employed. He does have the time. He can afford the flight. The only question is: does he have the nerve?

The ungreased skids of being able to negotiate sexual intercourse with a living, breathing female—a prospect he'd never before considered to be anything but a distant fantasy—comes crashing down on him. Yes, it could happen. So damn forehead-slapping simple, too. Just book a flight, fill out one of the forms for the girl of his preference, and the entire transaction could be a done deal in the matter of a couple minutes.

"Think it'll do you some good," Howie offers supportively.

Arnold responds with a vacant nod, his mind working through the logistics.

But the moment his mind visualizes the reality of stepping from an air-conditioned 737 cabin into the hot desert air at McCarran airport, sobriety sets in. Making him flat-out reject the idea.

Just can't do it.

Then again, if I don't, I'll end up in this chair 40 years from now wondering what happened to my life, asking how come I turned out to be a virgin curmudgeon, why didn't I take the chance?

He nods.

"Why not?"

Howard waits. But Arnold just sits there, doing nothing.

"Well?" Howie goads.

Why not? What's to prevent me from doing it?

Embarrassment?

Maybe.

Howie's right, this would help guide him over the hump of social awkwardness, instill in him a bit of the confidence so desperately needed. Sure, he can spew out an endless litany of reasons not to—everything from contracting a flaming case of STD to getting ripped off in a scam, to say nothing of the morality of prostitution—but why not give it a try? At least, he will have done *something* to rectify his pathetic situation.

Howie sits back.

"Know what you're thinking. You really don't want to use your real name. But computers and maintaining online anonymity are your thing, dude. You can probably get two to three false identities before I get home. Which, by the way, is where I'm headed."

He scrapes his chair back from the table.

Can't wait for Howie to be out of here.

So much to think about. . .

6

TWO WEEKS LATER, Howie is back in the kitchen sitting across the table from Arnold, drinking another long-neck Anchor Steam brew, asking, "Taylor? Why the hell Taylor?"

Arnold thinks, *what the hell difference does it make?* It's only a name. He hesitates, trying to decipher any underlying tone in Howie's question.

"Well, I wanted something that doesn't sound Jewish but is sort of common, but not something as common as Smith. I mean, that's way too obvious, right?"

Howie takes a pull of the beer and belches.

"Yeah, but probably ninety-percent of the johns book those girls under phony names. Ask any of them, they'd probably be shocked to hear someone actually used their real name. And if we stay with that logic, use Gold and they'll figure it for an alias anyway. But hey, Taylor's as good as anything, I guess. What'd you come up with for a first name?"

That one was a tad tougher, taking longer to decide. He figured as long as he was going through the hassle of creating a false identity, he wanted something that, well, resonated with him.

"I narrowed it down to two names, actually. Trevor Taylor and Toby Taylor."

"Toby?" Howie wrinkles up his face like a bad smell. "You're kidding. Sounds like a name you hear on a grade school playground. Don't you want something more adult, something more macho?"

Why bother defending the choice? Howie isn't the one who might follow through on the deal.

Yet, for some ill-defined reason, he feels compelled to justify the choice.

"There's a country western singer named Toby. That macho enough for you?"

Howie laughs. "Shit-kicker, huh?"

Neither one of them listens regularly to that music genre, although when Arnold is really feeling down in the dumps, he admits that some of the lowdown tears-in-my-beer country-western lyrics provides a touch of solace in knowing others out there on the planet have felt just as shitty. Otherwise they'd never be able to come up with those words and situations. Makes him feel less emotionally isolated. Maybe in a group therapy sort of way.

"You got trains, trucks, honky-tonk girls, prison, and hard drinking. Can't get more macho that that. Right?"

"You forgot Mama. Lots of country songs have Mama in there."

"Whatever."

Howie arches his back, stretching both arms high overhead, and yawns, not bothering to cover his mouth because they're the type of close friends who don't have to even worry about muffling farts, and in fact, often laugh at them, sometimes seeing who can gross out the other. Howie slips him a sly grin.

"Okay, so you've taken care of the name. What about the woman?"

"Not yet, still working on developing my," he mimes quotation marks, "persona. You know, credit cards, driver's license, everything."

Howie laughs.

"Figured you'd stall. Why not just go ahead and do it?"

Arnold jumps on the opportunity to explain.

"No, no, listen, it's not what you think. I'm really getting into this. Pretty interesting actually, developing a fictitious persona."

He remembers the high when he opened the envelopes and saw the actual physical pieces of Toby Taylor's identity materialize: California driver's license, VISA card, Social Security number.

Howie reaches for the beer again.

"What's the big deal, I mean, why go through the hassle if all you want is to get laid? Not like anyone really gives a rat's ass who you are when you're there. Certainly not the girl. All she wants is your money."

Typical Howard. So literal.

Hands clasped between his thighs, shoulders hunched, Arnold rocks forward in the chair, eyes downcast, staring at the table, mind searching for the words to describe the voyeuristic thrill of creating the guy he wishes he could be.

In the end, he answers with a simple, "You wouldn't understand."

No way can he explain to a guy slick as Howard Weinstein how it feels to stand in front of the mirror and see Toby Taylor transformed into a young man with a clean slate, one that can become just about any person his fantasies dictate. How it feels to create an entire backstory along with a real career. Perhaps make Toby a law student, or Wall Street options trader, or movie star.

Toby can do things Arnold Gold would never in a million years hope to even try. More importantly, in developing Toby's character down to the granular level, he's gaining the confidence to be with the woman who will strip him of sexual naiveté. These are feelings and emotions Howard would never comprehend for the obvious reason that he's always had life by the balls.

Sure, an element of luck modulates everyone's life, but it's also true that to a large extent you create your own luck and opportunities. They are very different people, he and Howard, meaning there's no way in hell to explain this feeling in a way he'd grasp. In spite of being best friends their entire lives, Howard can't begin to fathom a life shackled by insecurities.

"Yo, Arnold," Howie says, miming knuckling a hard surface: knock-knock.

"Sorry. Got off on a tangent. What?"

"You picked one," fingers making air quotation marks again, "yet?"

Arnold feels his face burning once more.

Damn it!

This time Howard, reading him correctly, grins broadly.

"I take that to mean yes. Show me."

Arnold has her page bookmarked on the Tor browser, right up there on the toolbar for easy access. He clicks it, pulls up the picture and text, rotates the laptop for Howard to see.

"Here."

Howard elbows him.

"Using Tor, huh? Man, you are paranoid."

What's to say? Wish to stay anonymous when web cruising, don't use Internet Explorer or Firefox, go Darknet via Tor. He can see no upside, and a definite downside, to leaving digital signatures for anyone—including the NSA—to follow.

Howard studies the picture, absentmindedly pulling his right earlobe.

"Huh. Didn't think you'd go for a darker one for some reason. What you think, Pakistani, Indian, Tajikistani?"

"Christ, Howie, how the hell would I know? Or care."

But the thing was, he didn't want to pick a girl who resembled Rachael. He wanted his fantasy about Rachael to remain, what, unsoiled? Yeah, perhaps.

Jesus, how crazy is that?

"Well, she certainly isn't a two bagger."

"Huh? What's a two bagger?"

Howie grins.

"That's a girl who's so ugly you put a bag over her head and then one over your own, just in case hers falls off while you're screwing."

Arnold laughs.

Howie studies the screen a moment longer before starting to read aloud in a bad imitation of a female voice.

"Hi, I'm Breeze, the exotic treat you've been craving. With my petite five-foot three-inch frame, toned physique, and flawless skin, our meeting is guaranteed to be unforgettable. I'm not just a pretty face though; my naturally sweet and sensual personality will be just as enjoyable for you during our time together. Call me now and we can enjoy an erotic, sensual encounter today." Howie pauses a moment before returning to his normal voice. "I'm getting hard just reading this. What you waiting for? Call her."

Deadly Odds

He rotates the computer, sliding it back to Arnold.
With him listening? No fucking way!
"C'mon, dude, stop farting around, do it."
What the hell. After all, I'm Toby Taylor now.
Arnold picks up the phone, his stomach churning with butterflies.

7

ARNOLD STANDS AT the floor-to-ceiling window, gazing down at the impressive circular pool with ever-changing streams jetting twenty feet skyward as colored lights refract and shimmer off droplets, creating the impression of the hotel's jeweled crown. His left hand holds a tumbler of ice and scotch. His right hand presses to his ear the technological umbilical cord that links him to familiarity and security as he listens to a hollow echo of microwave energy travel through air and wire at the speed of light to form a magical connection from his ear drum to Howard's lips, the entire trip measured in milliseconds compared to the hours spent flying the same distance in a jet.

One ring, then another until Howie answers with, "Yo, Dude, the hell you wasting time calling for? You're supposed to be down there getting laid."

Arnold rocks the heavy crystal tumbler back and forth, sloshing amber fluid around the sides and over the rounded cubes, diluting the alcohol he hopes will bring him—trite as it sounds—courage. He wants a dose of his friend's reassurance as an antidote for the straight-up, flat-out frightened ghost niggling away in the back of his mind. But he sure as hell won't admit that to Howie. Howie would only laugh at him and tell him to loosen up.

Yeah, easy for Howie to say.

He wondered how many times his friend has had sex with girls and just where he learned how to do it, both subjects the two friends have never discussed in detail. Was Howard as nervous losing his virginity as he is now?

Highly doubtful.

The actuality of meeting the escort isn't the biggest nerve-grating issue. And hey, the scotch will help him slide past that part. No, his nervousness stems from the knowledge that prostitution is a business surrounded by myriad wide-ranging criminal activities. Not only is he sexually inexperienced, he's criminally naïve: the wide-eyed kid in a chocolate store. Which makes him a ridiculously easy mark for a hustle. What's to say that when he opens the door—even after looking through the wide-angle security lens—some thug isn't going to Bogart his way into his room and rob him? Well, he tells himself, this is exactly the reason for having booked an "independent" escort. From all he's read, most of these girls are exactly that: independent. They don't rely on pimps and are not necessarily supporting drug habits. Especially the really attractive ones. Some of those women—if the pictures are truthful—must spend hours sweating in gyms while dieting 375 days a year. They're not the meth-mouth, burnt-out, beat-up, 50-miles-of-bad-road specimens the vice squad busts at truck stops and street corners.

Besides, he asks himself, what about gambling? Isn't that activity equally permeated with criminal activities?

I gamble and I'm no criminal.

True, but online gambling isolates him from any street element.

Besides, he's never done anything even remotely encroaching on the line of criminality. People, he believes, gamble out of greed and the lust for fast bucks and zero work. He, in contrast, gambles because he knows from objective hard cold data that, over time, his computerized analysis will be right more frequently than wrong. That's why he keeps refining his system. The more frequently and more accurately it can predict outcomes, the less "gamble" it entails. He is now at the point of being able to earn a respectable living from his winnings. Simple enough. He views the small improvements he occasionally achieves as similar to what any well managed business would do under the guise of research and development. "Improving, always in all ways," is his motto. Besides, what about our federal and municipal governments and the tons of revenue they generate peddling lotto tickets? So, they have, in essence, legalized gambling regardless of whether or not they admit that seemingly minor fact.

Perhaps that's a rationalization but it's one that works.

Now, standing in this beautiful Bellagio suite, in a city developed by and devoted to organized crime, he intends to add a few bucks to their sustaining fund. But that still bothers him somewhat because, regardless of Breeze's gentrified job title of "Escort" she is—and let's not beat around the bush—a prostitute, a whore. The intended act is to exchange money for sex and, therefore, is likely to be associated, directly or indirectly, with criminal elements.

This thought ripples another chill of fear through his gut.

"Just calling to check in, Mom," he jokingly tells Howie in a lame attempt to mask his nervousness in spite of knowing his friend can probably sense it in his tone of voice.

They're that close, and good friends are canny that way.

Howard laughs.

"Okay, son, but why aren't you getting your brains blown out?"

Arnold nervously checks his titanium Movado, a new watch purchased in anticipation of this trip. The big bulky timepiece is so Toby Taylor and so not Arnold Gold. Big, black with orange in the dial. Very cool. One he saw in a full-page WIRED advertisement. Not close to anything he's ever owned. Living this fictitious life is definitely turning out to be a rush.

"I'm waiting. She's supposed to call from the lobby so I can give her the room number."

"Ah-ha, so you haven't even seen her yet?"

Why did I even bother calling?

"What does it sound like?"

The multiline phone on the desk trills in muted European notes he finds pleasing, not the usual jarring ring so characteristic of American phones. Time comes to a screeching halt. Another cycle of trills echo through the room before Arnold can get his act together.

"Oh shit, that must be her on the house phone. Hold on."

After transferring the cellular to his left hand, Arnold picks up the

48

handset.

"Hello."

Her voice is pleasant, the tone soothingly warm and breathy.

Sexy.

"Toby?"

His mouth immediately dries, making "Yes," come out as a croak.

"What room shall I come to?"

He tells her the room number, hangs up, and says goodbye to Howie without mentioning being scared shitless. He sets his drink on the table and walks to the door to peer through the fisheye peephole as he waits.

Will she look anything like her picture?

A soft knock on the front door of the suite releases an adrenaline rush in spite of his having mentally prepared for this moment. His eyes zero in on the stylish chrome door handle and the two-tone plastic "Do Not Disturb" sign obscuring the solid steel dead bolt. In a strange detachment, he watches Toby Taylor's hand reach for and then touch the cool metal handle. He knows he is about to unlock a fresh chapter of his young innocent life.

He pauses, swallows, closes his eyes and thinks of all the reasons to consummate this encounter. Will she sense his nervousness?

Has to be a complete fool not to.

But isn't the idea to get him over the hump? So to speak...

He laughs at the double entendre. A bit of humor, he thinks, might be just the thing to get him moving again. He opens the door.

"Breeze?"

She flashes unnaturally white teeth.

"Uh-huh, and you must be Toby Taylor?"

Once again, he thanks himself for using the alias. It's so incredibly liberating that he can't imagine going through with this under his real identity.

"I am."

They stand at the threshold, Arnold with the door in one hand and the jamb in the other, thinking she looks a bit different in the flesh than the website picture. Can't explain exactly what, perhaps the same reason people look different on television than in person. Same woman, just different. Attractive, maybe mid-twenties, gorgeous lustrous black shoulder length hair, her slim body outlined by a clingy sleeveless black dress, one strand of black pearls around an unwrinkled neck. Iranian or Pakistani, or of a nationality from that area, just like Howie guessed. Now that he thinks about it, he realizes what makes her different from his expectation is that, for whatever reason, he assumed an "escort" would be trashy. Breeze strikes him—in voice, posture, makeup—as just the opposite: very classy.

She looks past him, into the room.

"Nice room. May I come in?"

"Oh, yeah, sure."

Still holding the doorknob, he backs away, allowing her to enter, then quickly shuts the door behind her, his mind scrambling for something to say. He is NOT going to repeat all of his bumbling dumbass mistakes of the past. This time it's different. He's prepared a series of conversational topics to run through, should they spend time chatting. Now that she's here, how the hell does this work? What is he supposed to do?

She stops in the center of the suite's living room and does a 360, repeating, "Nice."

Perhaps sensing his nervousness, she points to the cut crystal tumbler of scotch on the table by the window.

"I'll have whatever you're drinking."

Relieved to be tasked with something other than gawking like the putz he is, he goes to the wet bar and begins dropping ice cubes in a glass, listening to the deep resonant impact of frozen water on real crystal. You can always hear real crystal, he thinks. He senses her watch him, which seems to make his herky-jerky movements even more robotic, if that's possible given his present state. He imagines actually dancing the robot and laughs at the absurdity.

"Which would you prefer I call you, Toby or Mr. Taylor?"

He sloshes scotch over the ice without any attempt to measure what a reasonable pour might be.

"Toby."

There, that wasn't so difficult.

He sets down the bottle, turns to see her sitting casually at one end the small love seat flashing a coy, seductive smile. She pats the cushion next to her.

"Why don't you sit here, and we can get to know each other?"

He retrieves his own drink, carries both of them to the couch, hands off hers, and settles in at enough of an angle so they can see each other without craning necks. And tries to smile.

"This your first outcall?" she asks, swirling the ice with a perfectly manicured index finger while maintaining eye contact.

"My what?"

She samples the scotch, nods appreciatively, then, setting the glass on the table, "Don't be nervous, I won't bite. Unless of course you're into that kind of thing." She giggles and raises her perfectly shaped eyebrows. "Well, are you?"

He scrambles for some witty repartee, something smart and clever, but comes up empty, so instead, opts to sip his scotch, knowing full-well how transparent the ploy is.

With an empathetic smile she reaches out to gently stroke his cheek with her fingertips.

"You're cute. Know that?"

The C word? No one's ever called him cute before. Of all the adjectives he can think of, cute isn't one. Oh, that's right, she's being paid to please him.

Still, he relishes her flattering words.

He wants to say something, but his heart is hammering away, lodged in the base of this arid throat.

Open your mouth and you'll probably croak again.

He takes another sip to wet his mouth.

Her face becomes more serious.

"How about we take care of business before getting lost in pleasure?"

Not knowing what this means, he nods, relieved with allowing her to take the lead.

She opens the thin silky purse in her lap, slips out a piece of paper. "Your email requested five days, is this correct?"

"Yes."

"Such a lengthy time is a bit unusual. What exactly do you have in mind?" She touches his hand. "But before you answer, I want to make sure of a few things. First of all, do we understand that you are asking only for my companionship and that my presence tonight is neither a solicitation for, nor an offer for, sex?"

No, not at all. What's going on?

"Toby?"

"I thought—"

She repeats the statement/question more emphatically.

"Answer yes, please."

"Yes."

"Fine, it is understood, then." She nods. "However, if our relationship should develop into a sexual one, well hey, that can happen with consenting adult men and women. Don't you agree?"

Ah, now I get it.

"Absolutely."

"The second thing you need to be clear about is that I do not charge money to be with you. Now, having made this absolutely clear, also want you to understand that I do accept gifts and it's quite common for men to demonstrate their affection for me in the form of money that is placed in a plain white envelope and left on, say, this table here," motioning to the one on which their drinks sit. "Do we have a clear understanding?"

He nods agreement.

"Please answer yes or no."

"Yes."

"Alright then, back to my original question. What do you have in mind?"

The question catches him as off guard the second time around as it did the first time. Having no rehearsed answer, he sees no option but admit the brutal truth. Besides, she's already seen him in action. Or inaction, as the case may be. He decides to throw himself at her mercy.

After downing another slug of scotch—again more to wet his mouth than for courage—he blurts out, "I want you to teach me how to act around women. Tell me what women want. Not just in bed—I mean, yeah, sure that's part of it, of course—but tell me what women want in a man day to day. You can probably see by just being with me how lost I am just sitting here with you and it's only been, what, maybe five minutes?"

A sense of relief floods over him for having confessed. Being a socially handicapped nerd is now a matter of record and there is no going back. Either this will or will not be successful, but if not, it isn't from not having tried.

Head cocked to the right, she studies him with a glimmer of interest.

God, those eyes...they're beautiful.

"You have a girlfriend?"

"No."

She nods thoughtfully.

"You gay and just haven't come out?" She quickly adds, "That's not something you should worry about. I've had that happen a couple times. If so, I'll simply help you find yourself."

He sighs. This conversation isn't progressing even close to the way he anticipated.

"No, I'm not gay."

She flashes a disarming, penetrating smile.

"No problem. I think I can handle this. Let's see what we can do."

"Thank you."

There is palpable relief in his voice.

"Again, no problem. And Toby—I hate to discuss business at a time like this—but instead of receiving a gift at the end of each day, I require the entire amount—for all five days—up front."

A buzzer screeches in his brain. He may not know the first thing about how to act around women, but money, well, that's an entirely different matter. Does he look that naïve? That much of a schlemiel?

Yeah, probably. Well, not probably, face it: yes.

Chance it and give her the money?

You gotta be kidding, right? What's to keep her from taking it and never showing up again? If so, what recourse do you have? Lodge a complaint with the better business bureau? Ha, fat chance!

To keep from making eye contact he picks up the crystal tumbler.

"No, I don't think I can do that."

"Oh? Why not?"

He sees no reason to back down and finds her question strangely annoying.

Simply cancel the deal now?

"I'll feel more comfortable if we settle things day today."

Sensing his suspicion, she brushes a finger across his cheek again.

"You're especially cute when you blush. Women like men who blush. It gives you an aura of innocence and vulnerability. Just be sure that innocence doesn't carry into the bedroom."

Pure bullshit. The cute part, that is.

He files away the other bit of information because it carries a ring of reasonableness. He looks up at her again.

"So, daily's okay?"

She smiles brightly.

"Whatever pleases you, Toby, because that's what I'm here for. Now, am I to assume you have a gift for me this evening?"

This, he realizes, is his first real discussion, negotiation, or whatever you want to call it, with a female and it wasn't all that difficult. He feels better already, having cleared this first hurdle.

"I can do that."

Moments later he returns from the bedroom with an envelope holding six one hundred-dollar bills. He hands it to her.

She doesn't move.

"No, Toby, please leave it there on the table."

He does as directed and sits back down for another sip of scotch. A moment later, without checking the envelope contents, she unsnaps her black purse and drops it inside.

"Money. Everybody wants it, nobody ever seems to have enough. Do you have enough, Toby?"

"I don't know. I don't think even Bill Gates knows if he does."

Her eyes roam the room again.

"Well, from the looks of it, you seem to be doing quite well for a man your age."

He interprets that as a statement in no need of rebuttal, so offers none.

She studies at his face again.

"Then here is your first lesson. You want to know what women want in a man? Answer number one is: money. Money and power. Each of those is a girl magnet. Put both of those in a guy and he'll trump any competition, no problem. Even the ugliest man on earth can score a good-looking girl if he has the money."

Again, he doesn't answer, and finds this point of view rather depressing.

What did you expect? That there is a Santa Claus?

Another touch on the cheek.

"Now that this discussion is over, why don't we turn to pleasure?"

Anxiety—with a capital A—comes crashing back, stealing his breath.

He wipes his palms on the thighs of his suntan Dockers.

"What's your pleasure, Toby?"

She stares directly into his eyes. Up until this very moment the evening has been only hypothetical, an intangible concept: sex with a woman. It's now segueing from an amorphous intangible concept to hard-core reality, making him suddenly see her anew and in startling detail: the small wrinkles sprouting from the corners of her eyes, the black mole just above her left collar bone, a skin crease traversing her neck, her ethnic hue of skin, particles of black mascara surrounding those beautiful almond-shaped eyes, the smooth edge between lipstick and skin. This is real. Right here, beside him is a living, breathing female willing to have sex with him. All it takes is to reach out and touch her and all the mysteries pondered during so many lonely nights of yearning will start unraveling. But here's a twist he never anticipated: this is just too easy. Sex for cash. Pay up and put out. Until this moment he'd always assumed one needed to exert some measure of mental effort, cunning, or whatever, to reach this point in a relationship. Like hunting an animal, you stalk them first or bait a trap. Maybe go out a series of dates, laugh at her jokes, be attentive to her needs. Learn things about the person with whom you'll share whatever level of mental and physical intimacy you elect. Here, none of that energy is required.

Strangely, it makes this reality frightening, for this is way too mechanical and it leaves an empty depressing void inside where there should be lust.

In spite of this, he realizes he must consummate this. It was, after all, the point of this trip. And, truth be told, he really does want to solve the mysteries.

What now?

He swallows, unable to speak.

She sizes him up again.

"Your first time? For sex with a woman?"

Too embarrassed to admit the truth, he opts for silence.

With a sly smile, she shrugs off the right spaghetti strap, allowing the dress to slip down and expose a breast. Reaching out, she gently takes his hand.

"Then I suppose you've never felt a nipple before. Here," lifting his fingers to darker flesh. "Feel how it grows hard when you squeeze it? Just like if I squeezed your cock."

Her use of that word startles and is instantly and stunningly embarrassing yet strangely exciting. He's never spoken of male anatomy to a female. This is so… different.

A part of his brain—a residual from who knows where—forces him to glance away in obvious embarrassment, which in turn, embarrasses him even more. He wants to die, yet wants to…

She forces his fingertips to play with the nipple.

"Touch it, Toby."

Sucking a deep breath, he allows his fingers to explore the tactile sensations that are being transmitted from nerve endings to brain and is amazed at the realization that as this moment he's having his first actual, honest-to-God, skin-to-skin contact. The Eagle has landed! Can't believe he's—

"Squeeze it gently. Make it swell," she murmurs.

He does, once more marveling at what he's doing. His world reverberates into a singular focus, concentrating on the tactile sensations turning on a deeply primitive region of his brain. His vision blurs as his ears become deafened with pulsations of blood.

From within this mental fog he hears, "I suppose this means you've never felt a clit, before either. Want to?"

He gasps.

She's shoulders him back against the loveseat as her hands mercifully release the tightness restricting his groin.

"Close your eyes," she whispers, her lips brushing his ear, "and just let go."

He's about to have a heart attack so pushes her away. Other than his mother and a family doctor, his genitals have never been exposed to a female, much less an erection. He needs courage to overcome the sense of shame at having something so private exposed.

"Wait, let me shower first."

Wrapped in a white Bellagio terrycloth bathrobe, hair still damp, he opens the bathroom door to the bedroom. Breeze has thrown open the drapes and turned off all the room lights, painting the spacious suite in kaleidoscopic neon and mercury vapor light. Flicking off the bathroom lights, enough light from the strip allows him to see her propped against the headboard, a sheet covering her flat abdomen, breasts fully exposed. His shower fantasy grapples with reality.

Flashing a seductive smile.

"Aren't you going to join me?"

Making sure the robe securely covers his body, he glances away from her breasts ashamed for staring.

"Will you to turn your head, please?"

"Guess what? I won't. One thing you need to get comfortable with is being naked in the presence of women, because most women want a take-charge-man in the bedroom. You can't do that by slinking around hiding your manhood all the time. Besides, what can you hide I haven't seen before? I've seen it all."

He walks to the foot of the bed and stops, takes hold of the terrycloth tie but can't seem to summon the nerve. She's right, he knows.

He needs to shed this paralyzing modesty, but by now the erection is back and throbbing.

"Guys are worse than girls in that regard," Breeze says looking directly at him. "Girls lose their inhibitions at a much younger age. Probably because what we endure in doctors' offices, laying back on an exam table legs spread with everything out there in the wind. It's hard the first couple times, but trust me, gets easier once you've done it."

He's at the foot of the bed still fully robed. She pats the sheet to her right.

"C'mon, Toby, show me that bad boy. I can see it's hard as rebar, so bring that boy toy over here so I can play with it."

Sucking a deep breath, he closes his eyes and drops the bathrobe.

"Lord have mercy, uh-uh-uh! You got nothing to worry about in the cock department. Bring it on."

He slips between the sheets and feels her hand firmly grasp his erection, amazed at how rapidly it returned. She squeezes and fondles it.

"You a virgin?"

"Yes," he admits, figuring there's not a damn thing left to hide, he's been stripped clean, so to speak.

After all, isn't this precisely the reason he came?

"Well, Toby, that sad situation is just about to end, so get ready."

8

ARCHING HIS BACK, Arnold stretches his arms high in the air, holds the pose for several seconds, working out the muscle kinks in his shoulders. Then settles back into the chair, eyes lightly closed. Morning sun angles through open curtains, warming his face in spite of the whisper-silent air-conditioner maintaining a comfortable 72 degrees. He relaxes and continues to sweep away mental cobwebs, a pleasant residual from the soundest sleeps enjoyed in...a...long time. He sighs, opens his eyes to look at Breeze again. She sits across the table from him, eating a room service breakfast of strong black coffee, a golden-puffy oven-fresh croissant, and a tall, chilled glass of freshly squeezed grapefruit juice. *CNN Headline News* plays softly on the television. Both are swaddled in soft, fluffy, monogrammed terrycloth robes. Arnold notices her red toenail polish for the first time.

"What would you like to do today?"

She pauses, a small chunk of golden-brown pastry halfway to her mouth.

"Need to run home for a couple hours before we go shopping."

Shopping?

"Oh," he says, unable to mask a hint of disappointment.

He'd hoped to spend the morning together. Doing what, he's not exactly sure.

This vague disappointment surprises him. Not solely because it's there, but also because he allowed it into his voice. How very uncool and unmanly. Most of all, he hates to develop an emotional attachment to her. Especially considering she is, after all, renting her affection to anyone willing to pony up the bucks. She is a professional caterer of men's sexual desires, a libido lightening rod. He means nothing to her. Yet this irrational affection burrowed into his heart last night after switching off the room lights. Soon as their sexual games finished and they readied themselves for sleep, he'd stretched out, hands knitted behind his head, waiting for fatigue to overcome him. Breeze had curled onto a ball a few inches from his right arm, her soft, scented body heat making him keenly aware of her presence. He liked that feel. Repeatedly he reminds himself she is an escort, a person paid to pamper him. Now he's forced to admit it's not like you're lovers. You've only known her a grand total of sixteen hours. His objective, logical mind knows all this. Subjectively however, he likes her a lot.

Don't be meshuganer.

He shakes his head, trying to fling off the emotional aspect of her response, and pretends to watch the news while reflecting on the events of the past night. Howie predicted correctly: getting laid has made a huge difference in his self-image and confidence. This morning he believes—no, he knows beyond doubt—he's no longer quite as little-boyish as he was twenty-four hours ago. His perspective on the world is now more that of a 23-year-old man. All because of accomplishing a rite of passage. Yeah, Howie nailed it. Maybe he should fly down every month, spend a few days with an escort, maybe even become one of Breeze's regulars. This thought had crossed his mind the night before as he lay next to her waiting for sleep, and it had evoked the first little prickles of jealousy. For some sick reason he pictured her in this very hotel room with a fat, bald, middle-aged businessman—maybe from the east coast—she kneels at his feet and lowers his pants as he pushes her mouth to…he shakes his head once again to rid the image from his mind. Why do this to himself?

Christ, it's so perverse.

As if required to justify her statement, she adds, "Need to swing by the house for a few minutes, pick up a change of clothes," before popping the pastry into her mouth and returning to the television.

Discussion closed.

He debates whether to ask. He knows better but can't resist.

"I could come with you." And quickly adds, "That is, if you want."

Jesus, what a lame thing to say. Sounds so pathetically desperate.

For a long, agonizing moment he waits for a reply.

She slowly turns, as if considering her words carefully.

"I have obligations."

Shit, she's married.

The bottom of his stomach drops. A flush ascends his face as he senses her studying him, but he can't bear to look her in the eye. He imagines the *60 Minutes* second hand sweeping around the dial: *tick tick tick...*

She sighs.

"Hey, look, I moved Mom here from LA a few years ago, okay? She's got a case of bad COPD, the smog was killing her. I'm it, an only child, so I take care of her now, give her medications. That, and I got this cat needs feeding." She pauses, as if testing his reaction.

Perhaps sensing a want to shore up her reasoning, she adds, "Mom doesn't like people dropping by. She doesn't want anyone—not even people she knows—seeing her so disabled. A pride thing, I guess. I'll be gone, oh, two hours max."

He scrambles for words with which to salvage a spec of dignity.

"No, no, sorry I even mentioned it. Take as much time as you need. Don't worry about me." Then, to change subjects, asks, "That where you're from? California? Initially, I mean."

"Yes."

She returns to the croissant and CNN.

He swears he detected a touch of east coast in her vowels last night. He's good at accents, makes a point of picking up on them. Boston maybe. For sure, somewhere up in the New England region. Just a word or two, then vanished.

Must be mistaken.

What's more, she has every right to keep her private life from customers. For any number of good reasons, now that he thinks about it. Still, she seems to be working hard on this present accent, a sort of

California West Coast generic sound. Makes him wonder…

She dabs the corners of her mouth with the linen napkin before tossing it back on the breakfast tray, checks her watch.

"Speaking of which, I should get going. We have some shopping to do when I get back."

This is the second mention of that particular activity. Shopping isn't anything he had considered doing. In fact, he hates to shop. If he needs new Dockers—which happens every couple of years—he runs down to Macy's, grabs a pair his size, pays, and is back outside the store in under ten minutes, nothing to it.

"Shopping?"

Out of the chair now, she glides into the bedroom.

"Yeah, I checked your wardrobe. Dockers the best you can do?"

"I guess."

What's wrong with Dockers?

"What, you don't like khaki?"

He sees half of her back as she sheds the robe, the sight of her naked body stirs his groin again. Wonder if she'd have time for…but figures best to not suggest it. Besides, how do these arrangements work? She on the clock? When does last night's "gift" expire? Or is there a closing time, like a bar, where business shuts down at 3A.M.? Was this the reason for wanting the entire five-day payment up front, to allow him free reign, so to speak? Too many questions to worry about them at the moment.

She's out of sight now, but he hears, "We need to get you a seriously cool suit for our nights out. Can you afford one?"

How much money she talking about?

He doesn't want to appear cheap.

"I don't know. What're we talking price-wise?"

Only suit he owns—a black single-breasted number purchased from The Men's Warehouse for his parents' funeral. The thought makes him flash on the bearded guy saying, I guarantee it.

He hears water running in the bathroom sink.

"A couple grand, thereabouts. Why? That a problem?"

Jesus! For a suit? She'd got to be kidding.

No piece of clothing could possibly be worth that much. A computer, sure, that he can understand, but clothing? Not a chance.

He opens his mouth to protest but muzzles himself. What will she think if he says no? That he's cheap? A jerk? He's already proven naïveté in bed, so why compound the lousy image by being what she obviously considers a bad dresser? Better pony up and buy it. Besides, now that he's a changed man, maybe he'll need it in the future. Who knows?

He raises his voice to be heard over the water.

"No, not a problem. Where we going that I need a suit?"

He saunters over to the bedroom door to watch her at one of the bathroom vanities brushing her hair. She's fully dressed now with her makeup refreshed. She looks at him in the mirror, never missing the rhythm of brush strokes.

"You're taking me out to dinner, aren't you?"

Hadn't thought that far ahead.

"Absolutely."

She nods, opens her purse and drops in the brush, primps once more in the mirror, smooths her dress and presses her lips together to smooth out her fresh lipstick.

"That's what I thought."

Satisfied, she turns to him.

"Okay, here's your next lesson: Women love men who are stylish dressers. Dockers and T shirts just don't cut it. So, we need to get you something nice. You'll arrange dinner reservations while I'm gone?"

She slides past, into the bedroom where she picks up her coat from the back of the couch.

He remembers Howie saying women like to be asked for advice.

"It's your town. What's your favorite?"

And for the first time this morning is proud of the way he sounded: masculine, in charge.

She moves to the front door, places one hand on the handle.

"What are you willing to spend?"

There it is again, an oblique probe into his finances. With the tip of his tongue, he works at dislodging a raspberry seed from the jam lodged between his teeth.

Hmm, how to answer...

"You name it."

Again, pleased with the way it sounds.

Smiling, "Get us a 6:30 seating at Il Mulino. We'll have an early dinner then come back for another lesson on satisfying women. How's that sound?"

Her words begin a stirring in his groin, but he's no longer ashamed of whether or not she notices. At the moment, he's more concerned with getting the name of the restaurant right.

"How's that spelled?"

9

THEY STROLL LIKE a couple, Breeze and Arnold hand in hand. Every so often, Arnold sneaks a discreet glance at other shoppers to see if they're checking him out. Do the men wonder how a skinny little weasel like him could attract such a stunning female? The women pay more attention to Breeze, he thinks, because they're stricken by fleeting jealousy for a figure that trumps theirs, or are trying to decide if she's more attractive, or younger, in spite of the high percentage of them who have obviously enlisted the skills of cosmetic surgeons on more than one occasion and are now held hostage by the puffy-lipped, amazed look. Having a beauty like Breeze cling to him this way really boosts his ego. Must be how Howie feels most of the time. Howie: the woman magnet, the guy who juggles three to four women at a stretch, sorting through the prime ones, never seeming satisfied with how lucky he is to have the affections of even one of them.

He's grateful to Breeze for the way she makes him feel in spite of the mental speed bump of acknowledging she's essentially his paid employee. But there's something else bothering him, a niggling doubt in the back of his mind that she really didn't visit her mother, that she was doing something entirely different. He shrugs off the suspicion and returns to enjoying having a knockout for a companion. After all, at the moment, she's earning good money to look like a million-dollar model. Which is exactly the reason she can demand, and get, top dollar. Or at least it seemed like top dollar when he was shopping for an escort. He's sure there are more expensive escorts available, but what more can they provide than what deadly odds he's enjoying now? Didn't even cross his mind at the time. Hmm…interesting thought, though. Perhaps he should investigate the possibility. He immediately experiences a twinge of shame for being mentally unfaithful toward her, especially with the affection he feels toward her.

They're casually window shopping on a meandering route to the men's store she's selected for him. He's never heard of the name until this morning but figures that's not surprising, considering he's never been interested in clothes nor been a slave to the elusive, ever fickle desire to be "in style." He doubts his time in Las Vegas with Breeze will change his attitude. If he possessed unlimited funds and was so inclined—which he isn't—he supposes he could hire a valet or butler to make sure his wardrobe remained fashionable. Then again, for what reason? Even if he turned into a clothes horse, his fundamental social personality would remain unchanged. He'd still be an introverted recluse who requires only a few good friends to make his life happy and satisfying. Simply put, he's not a social animal in need of constant external entertainment and stimulation. And unlike many of his peers, who are driven to "experiences," he isn't interested in travel and living for the here and now. And he sure isn't interested in accumulating "stuff," like his parents did. He realizes he's so wrapped up in thoughts that he's ignoring her.

"How was your mom?"

She stops to peer in a window, and without turning from it, replies, "Pretty much the same. Has bad days and good days. Last night she didn't sleep well because it was difficult to breathe and she's got this cough keeps her up."

"And the dog?"

He's not sure why he throws this out, but is interested in her response.

Without a moment's hesitation she answers.

"Fine. I let him out to do his business," and turns from the window to resume walking.

Arnold swats away the urge to ask why she must lie to him, to point out that during breakfast she claimed it was a cat in need of tending. Then again, maybe she has both a cat and a dog. Why assume she's lying? Maybe this is her way of protecting her private life. Maybe there have been men who, like him, grow attached to her to the point of being nuisances, or stalkers, or…besides, why should he give a damn?

Once he leaves town, he'll never see her again. What difference does it make? Still…

Giving his arm a gentle tug, she says, "In here."

The store is three walls of visually pleasing dark-stained mahogany shelving and hanging racks comfortably stocked with jackets, a window facing out into the shopping area with a display for foot traffic, four spacious islands stacked with shirts, ties, and sweaters. A decidedly masculine scent from the distinct fragrances of leather, cotton, wool, and shoe polish, the sum total produces a pleasant potpourri that, to his amazement, subtly encourages a willingness to shell out a ton of money to stock one's closet with more clothes than are reasonably necessary. A clever retailing ploy, he decides, similar to the way a hunter baits a trap.

"May I help you find something?" asks a skeletal male not more than a few years senior to Arnold.

With hands clasped together at chest level and deep-set wide eyes peering through black horn-rimmed glasses, he reminds Arnold of a praying mantis imitating Buddy Holly.

Breeze turns to Arnold and raises her eyebrows questioningly. Arnold clears his throat.

"I'm looking for a suit?"

Don't make a question of it, dammit.

With a wan smile, the humanoid insect nods.

"Very good, sir. Any particulars in mind? A designer? Color? Weight?"

Designer?

Arnold does his deer-in-the-headlight thing for a moment until he dredges up the only name he can think of, and only then because he remembers someone mention it in the distant past.

"Armani."

Is that even right?

67

Now he's not so sure.

Another nod, another smile, followed by a pirouette.

"Very good, sir. This way."

Breeze takes hold of the clerk's arm.

"Wait," stopping him in mid-stride.

She steps back a few feet, shoots Arnold a head to toe inspection.

"Naw. You're more of a Zegna type. Besides, you'd be paying a premium for Armani's name when you can get the same quality with Zegna. Maybe even save a few bucks in the process. What we save now can pay for dinner tonight."

Making them sound like an old married couple. He smiles.

He's never heard of the name—if it is a name—and decides to say nothing and just see what plays out. The clerk wags an index finger at her.

"You know, you're absolutely spot on with that." The finger sweeps left, to end up pointing toward a rack of suits on dark wood-and-brass hangers. "There we are." He appraises Arnold a beat. "Forty regular?"

Huh?

Then he gets it and wings it with, "Let's start with that and see what happens."

Hmm, that sounded okay.

The clerk leads them to a mahogany closet stocked with suits spanning shades of brown through black and on into more desert colors. He inserts his palm between two suits and the other a few feet away.

"The forties are in this section. But of course, if you don't see anything that seems to be what you're looking for, all our fabrics are there," pointing to one of the islands with identical wood shelves laden with bolts of luxurious muted material, "and our tailor would be more than happy to make one to your specifications."

Of course he would.

Breeze is already flipping through the suits, her hand moving with experience, inspecting a sleeve, discarding it, pulling out the next one until she's narrowed the choice down to one suit that she lifts off the hanging rod to carry into the mirrored alcove where the lighting is truer. Draping the coat over her left arm, she massages the fabric between her thumb and index finger, and then flips over the lapel to read a label. Apparently satisfied, she checks the liner, and holds the garment up for Arnold.

"What do you think? Want to try it on?"

What do I think? Looks like a suit coat, is what I think.

He nods.

"Sure."

He shrugs off his navy North Face windbreaker, and the clerk slips him into the coat. Soon as his arms fill the sleeves, the clerk palms both hands from the center of his back to his shoulders, smoothing the buttery material, then rotates Arnold by the shoulders ninety degrees to face the center of the three mirrors. Arnold stares at himself while the clerk flutters around, smoothing here and there, muttering sounds that aren't quite intelligible words yet strike him as pleasantly approving.

"Very nice fit," the clerk finally opines with a gentle tug to the left lapel, then smooths a palm over it to ensure a perfect lay. "Yes. A forty regular fits you like a glove."

Breeze strolls around him, eyes darting from shoes to collar, with brisk appreciative nods. Apparently satisfied, she steps back.

"What do you think?"

Arnold moves into the mirrors a bit more to take advantage of all three simultaneously, turning this way and that, assessing the back of the two-button coat, his right fingers absentmindedly luxuriating in the silky-soft weave of pure lightweight wool. The color is a deep, rich charcoal with tone-on-tone muted stripes. He glances at the left mirror, then the right, again rotating slightly one way then the other, seeing what looks like a man's suit. Nothing more, nothing less. What is there to say? A suit's a suit. But considering all this hoopla Breeze and the clerk are generating, he feels it necessary to appear to possess some semblance of a discerning eye.

Without thinking of what he is about to do, he reaches down to check the price tag dangling from the left sleeve. And is shocked. Twenty-five hundred dollars! Half off. On sale.

Jesus! What the hell could possibly make a suit this expensive?

Well, the shop, for starters. The overhead on this puppy must be ginormous.

Breeze and the clerk continue to await an answer.

Before he can say a word, the clerk hands him the pants still clamped to the hanger.

"If you'll follow me, I'll show you the dressing room where you can slip into these and evaluate the entire ensemble."

Now out of earshot of Breeze, Arnold lowers his voice.

"When I pay for this, I don't want her to see the credit card and I don't want you to say the name on it. Understand?"

The clerk gives him a knowing nod: the brotherhood at work.

"As you wish, sir."

Breeze inspects him again now that he's wearing the full suit.

"Have shoes to go with this?"

She stares at his sneakers.

Fifteen minutes later, as Arnold signs the credit card charge, Breeze instructs the clerk, "Please have them ready for a five o'clock pickup."

Flashing an ingratiating smile, "Yes, ma'am, very well."

10

A FEW DOORS from the men's clothing store—yet still within the Bellagio shopping arcade—Breeze pauses at a display window. Standing next to her, Arnold—still in shock from shelling out two and a half grand plus change for a wool suit and dress shoes—realizes the display contains nothing but purses, all of which appear to be exact replicas of each other except for size. He follows her eyes to one particular handbag prominently displayed atop a sleek pedestal. The smaller mates are scattered at haphazard angles, filling the wide interior windowsill. The purse of interest is black leather with an oversized square silver clasp in the shape of a stylized letter. He and Breeze stand side by side, engulfed in shopping mall white noise from myriad voices of various amplitudes echoing off of marble and plate glass, the clicking of heels, the squeals of children, and the flow of money.

The intensity in her eyes as she admires the pedestal display grabs him.

"You like it?" he asks impulsively.

She nods, mesmerized.

"It's gorgeous."

He cranes his neck for a better angle, searching for a price tag. No luck.

What the hell, can't be more than fifty bucks, right?

For some reason—perhaps an idea gleaned from casual conversation—he believes women love purses. He's never understood that particular fascination, but hey, whatever.

He says, "Let me buy it for you."

Breeze turns slowly toward him, the earlier pleasure gone from her face.

"No, you won't."

The words sting more than a slap on the cheek. His face burns in sympathetic response.

Momentarily stunned, he stares at her until the words, "Why not?" stumble out.

The feeling of being chastised like a naughty little boy hovers over him, inciting shame. He has no idea what he just did to deserve such a reprimand.

She studies his face closely, as if searching for something she doesn't find, because a second later her eyes melt into unmistakable sympathy.

Oy! So humiliating, her ability to so easily recognize his pain and awkwardness.

Why am I so fucking transparent? It's so...belittling.

She motions for him to follow her to a red velvet settee in the center of the promenade.

"Come here."

She sits. To him the settee seems so garish, so over the top, so Las Vegas. Yeah, the piece of furniture is so damn inappropriate it suddenly seems perfectly logical to belong here.

He follows like an obedient grade-school pupil about to be lectured by a playground monitor. In a moment of strange detachment, he studies the piece of furniture on which he's about to sit. Well, you asked for this, didn't you? How else are you going to learn these things?

She pats the seat next to her.

"Sit down, Toby. We need to talk."

A crate of butterflies is released into his stomach. This discussion—or whatever it'll be—can't be good. He settles in next to her, leans forward, elbows on knees, eyes straight ahead.

For almost a minute they sit in silence, leg to leg, as shoppers—all supremely gleeful to be gorging themselves on Las Vegas' air-conditioned palm-tree excesses—swarm past.

Breeze gently takes hold of his hand, the move compelling him to face her. There she is, studying him again, but this time with an expression too complex to gauge. Gone is the disappointment.

"Oh, Toby." She sighs. "You asked me to teach you things, so for what it's worth, here's your next lesson. Please listen carefully, because this one is really really important."

She licks her lips and inhales.

The weight of the moment forces him to look away again.

"I know you like me. I can see it in the way you look at me, talk to me, and try to please me."

He waits for the "but."

Silence.

He opens his mouth to say something, but she squeezes his hand again, silencing him.

"No, listen. Don't say a word."

The shopper cacophony seems to reverberate louder now, to the point of becoming noxious. Again, he wonders what he did wrong.

Doesn't matter.

Just listen to what she's going to tell you, because it's better to learn these things here while you're an invisible person rather than back home as bumbling Arnold Gold. This is, after all, the purpose of this trip. Pay attention to your tutor.

He's thankful for one thing, at least: Howie isn't here to witness this.

"Here's the deal. These feelings toward me are natural. For no other reason than I'm the first girl you've slept with. It's great that it means something to you, but—and here's the thing—you cannot let it cloud your emotions. Know why? Because we—you and I—aren't childhood sweethearts who finally got enough nerve to do it. Meaning, we don't have to kid ourselves into believing we're in love as a way to handle our guilt. You following any of this?"

He shrugs. She's right and he knows it.

"In truth, we didn't know each other existed until I knocked on your hotel room door yesterday and stripped you of your virginity. You experienced something you've wanted to experience for a long time, and you're grateful, but on the other hand, you're having problems with guilt. And now you feel new emotions that are hard for you to

73

categorize and, perhaps, deal with."

He starts to open his mouth, but she stops him again.

"No, don't try to deny it. I know it's true. I've seen it all morning in your eyes. Don't worry, you're like most normal men in this regard. Hey," another hand squeeze, "take it as a compliment, not a criticism."

She shoulder-bumps him as a way to dilute the humiliation her words cause. In spite of the wisdom of her words, they simply underscore the magnitude of his naïveté with male-female relationships.

Then again, he appreciates her sensitivity to care about this portion of his education. And now, viewing it in this light, he feels a stronger attachment to her more intimate than sex. In light of what she just said, it is stupid and counterproductive, he realizes.

"Thing you need to understand is that most men place more emotional attachment to sex than women. Seriously." She shoulder-bumps again. "And, like I just said, because I'm your first, and because I'm trying to please you as a customer, it's natural for you to feel attachment to me. I'm sorry if hearing this is hurtful. I really am, because I like you, too. But here's the take home message: never, and I mean never, let sex cloud your thinking. Got it?"

He nods. Not because he buys it, but because he knows she's probably right.

"Someday you'll find a woman to love and have sex with, but until then, enjoy sex with women for the simple reason that it's an important part of life, right up there with eating, sleeping, and breathing. I'll teach you how to please a woman. When I finish with you, girls will be shoving each other aside to be next to you. After all, sex is a primitive urge. We all need it or we start going a little crazy. Same goes for both men and women. Understand what I'm telling you?"

He nods.

"Yeah, okay, but I have to ask something. Okay?"

"Anything."

He hesitates, debating the wisdom of what he's about to ask. What he wants to ask is, "do you feel anything—anything at all—for me?" but decides that would be totally uncool, especially coming directly on the heels of her little lecture.

So, instead, he says, "That purse...do me a favor and let me buy it for you."

She cuts herself off from a kneejerk answer, seems to reconsider.

"You have any idea what that is?"

He feels another blush ascend his face and hates this kind of question. Makes him feel so totally stupid because the unstated implication is: no, of course you don't.

"Since you put it that way, obviously not. Least not in the same sense as you."

She shakes her head a bit woefully.

"It's a Fendi, Toby. They're expensive. They're nothing but trophy items. In reality they're no better or worse than any other well-made bag from some no-name designer working for some non-name leather factory in Bangladesh or wherever the labor costs are cheapest. See that little clasp, the little chrome rectangle holds the purse shut?"

A rhetorical question, he knows, so doesn't bother with even a sarcastic retort.

"That puppy is what you'd be spending two and a half thousand dollars for the honor of owning. Same price as your suit. Think about that a moment. And the woman who buys it? She wants it for show, knowing when she's out with other women, they'll immediately recognize it as a badge of feminine success. Believe me, the women who own the real deal are able to spot a knock-off at ten-thousand yards. And when you flash the real merchandise you send a message to the competition that you're successful at doing what most of those women are oriented to do: land The Big One. Get it? Besides, look at you, you're what, early twenties? How can you afford to throw around that kind of money on a woman you'll never see again once you blow this town?"

There it is again, another—although a bit more oblique—probe into his finances. Is he supposed to counter by saying he can afford it?

He ignores answering the question with, "Let's make this easy. I want to buy it."

She recoils slightly, releasing his hand.

"After all I just said?"

"Hey, look, consider it a gift, a special thanks for your gentleness last night. You could've made things harder."

Aw, Jesus, did I actually say that?

She laughs and shoulder-pokes him again.

"Seriously doubt that."

Now they're both laughing.

She shakes her head, giving a casual shrug.

"Hey, your money, you can do with it what you want."

"Good. That's settled."

She did raise a question he's never before had the chance to ask and suspects isn't something a guy—certainly not Howie—could answer.

"Long as we're on the subject of how women act, answer me this: do women dress for other women or do they dress for men?"

She laughs again.

"Think about what I just told you. Most women—unless they're out trolling for sex—want other women see who they are. Stop and look around on any downtown city street and you'll be able to know right away who are the executives, secretaries, students, or whatever. Same thing with guys. How we dress shows our personal identification, tells you a lot. Who has money, who has style, who has nerve? Artists, professionals, on and on."

"Let's go in and get your purse. What's the name again? Fender? Like on a car?"

11

BREEZE'S RIGHT HAND rests lightly on Arnold's left arm as they glide into the restaurant, a fashionable five minutes past their reservation time, Arnold decked out in his new suit, crisp white shirt, and black Ferragamo loafers, Breeze in a black, form-fitting, clingy, silky material with spaghetti straps, a single elegant strand of reasonably sized black pearls paired with black pearl earrings, a small sequined clutch in hand. Her gait is strikingly elegant, chin up, shoulders back, yet with a distinct air of casual confidence. In essence, classy. The black fabric sets off her flawless naturally tan skin and white teeth.

Arnold is amped on million buck exhilaration, a totally foreign feeling infused in him the moment he slipped into his butter soft Zegna, the fabric flowing over his body in ways he's never imagined possible. He finally gets what a custom-tailored suit is all about. But that doesn't necessarily mean he's going to run out and repeat the exercise anytime soon. One of these numbers will do for the foreseeable future. That's for damned sure. Still...

They approach the reception podium, where a slender African American hostess is conversing in hushed tones into a cordless phone, her left finger up in a just-a-minute signal. Classical music plays softly from recessed hidden speakers, competing with the irregular clink of silver against china, the pop of a cork, and the low white noise of dinner conversations. He catches a whiff of garlic, yeast, and grilling meat all mixed together and an appetizingly pleasant bouquet.

Breeze squeezes his arm: go ahead.

The hostess is off the phone now, he realizes, waiting for one of them to speak.

He stares back, at a loss for words. She smiles.

"Reservation?"

Jesus, Arnold....

"Yes."

He can't remember which name he gave and wonders if he was stupid enough to unwittingly use Gold? Panic time.

"For two," he says, stalling.

The hostess glances down at the reservation book next to the phone.

"Name?"

Breeze eyes him with a bemused smile, surmising he's caught in a trap of his own devising.

"Taylor?" he mutters, making a question out of what should be a straightforward answer.

The hostess smiles, extends a thin, aerobics toned arm toward the restaurant interior.

"This way, please."

They weave single file through tables, mostly groups of two to four diners, the restaurant almost to capacity with the early bird seating. The majority are couples, some strangely underdressed—it seems to Arnold, now that he's decked out in a new suit—for this restaurant. Open shirts and Levis. Is there no dress code here? All of which makes him feel slightly superior. Not just the new clothes generate this ebullience. It's also from having such a whiplash producing beauty clinging to his arm. Are people actually watching them out of the corners of their eyes? Is that a hint of envy from the middle-aged man leaning against the bar? For the first time in his life he feels not so ugly and undesirable. Perhaps even a tad cool. All topped off by a stunning woman, even if she is a rental.

Hey, might even do this again in a couple months. Perhaps a different escort? Hell, there're a couple web pages to pick from. This thought sparks another hint of guilt for being mentally unfaithful to her.

Then again, why feel guilty? No reason. Especially in view of her warning to not harbor emotional ties to her. Perhaps she's right, he's forced to admit. Still, he can't help but feel an ever-growing bond to her. She's been so good to him. Is it a crime to appreciate kindness? He thinks not.

"Here we are," the hostess says.

Arnold steps to the far side of the table and pulls out his chair to sit a second after he realizes he just cut a waiter off from doing that.

Fucked up already.

By now he's beyond blushing. After all, he reminds himself, since he won't see anyone here again after this trip, what difference does it make? And as far as the staff go, he seriously doubts they could care less. Probably they don't even notice. Nonetheless, he feels bad about hitting another social road bump at high speed.

But hey, this is supposed to be a learning experience, right?

So, he's learning.

He drops into the chair, pops his fine linen napkin, drops it on his lap, and is mortified to see the waiter—who just did the same for Breeze—stop in mid reach and retract his hand. Thankfully the waiter is tactful enough to cover the move.

Mom and Dad's fault, dammit.

They should've taught him these finer social skills.

That's not really fair. They tried. Sort of. Maybe they didn't know better?

Strange, not knowing the limits of one's parents' social skills.

He steals a glance at neighboring tables and wonders if other customers realize Breeze is a paid escort? If so, what do they think of him? That here's a guy too nerdy and inadequate to be with a looker any other way? That he's a married man bored with his wife? Or a horny Silicon Valley guru passing through Las Vegas? A player? Does it matter?

To his right, two tables over, a man in his mid-fifties entertains a woman close to, if not spot on, Breeze's age. She's clinging to his every word. Yeah, definitely hired. What other explanation could there be for a woman that age to be with such an old geezer? Well, she could be a gold digger or a daughter, but he doubts either. Then again, he reminds himself, he'll be that age one day, so don't be so judgmental.

"May I bring you folks a drink?" the hostess asks.

Arnold raises his eyebrows at Breeze. She nods for him to answer. *What?*

He has no idea what she prefers to drink, so he says to the hostess, "Yes."

The hostess smiles, like, you're kidding, right?

After a few beats Breeze bails him out with, "A margarita please, over crushed ice."

"And you, sir?"

Huh! Mostly a beer drinker. How weird would that seem in a fancy place like this?

Probably totally out of place.

"They do a great martini here," Breeze suggests encouragingly.

He's heard of the drink but doesn't know the ingredients other than some sort of alcohol. What the hell. He nods approval to the hostess.

"Twist instead of an olive," Breeze adds.

"I'll let your waiter know."

The hostess vanishes into plush surroundings.

Breeze waits until they're alone again.

"That's another thing: women like take-charge-type guys. Tomorrow night ask me what I'd like to drink and then order for me. Hey, look, relax. You look very sharp in your new suit."

This compliment buoys him. Slightly. Until he realizes he can't begin to initiate conversation. What do you talk about when sitting around a fancy restaurant? Everything that flashes through his mind seems trite and senseless or way too geeky. He wishes he had a menu as an excuse to do something. Anything to serve as a distraction from sitting here with such a moronic, vacuous smile. This, he tells himself, is exactly the reason you're here: to learn.

He decides to throw himself on the mercy of the court with, "You're seeing the problem firsthand. I don't know how to act when I'm with you. With any woman, for that matter. I can't come up anything to discuss that you might find interesting."

Smiling sympathetically, she reaches across to pat his hand, a move that seems more motherly than girlfriendly.

"No problem. Look at it this way: people love to talk about themselves. Ask questions, get them to make the conversation, listen to what they say and ask more questions. It's easy once you get the hang of it."

"Easy for you, maybe. You've had practice. This is my first time."

She adjusts the napkin in her lap by pulling two corners taut before replacing the linen at a perfect right angle to her thighs.

"So, tell me, Mr. Toby Taylor, what's your story?"

He starts playing with his fork, realizes it's probably not appropriate, and sets it back down.

"What do you mean?"

She leans forward, forearms against the table edge.

"You never talk about yourself. Tell me something about yourself and your life. What you do for enjoyment, what you read. Anything. Just give me a sketch of the real Toby Taylor."

What he'd love to tell her is his two passions: computers and artificial intelligence. Tell her about his uncanny ability to figure odds. But these are topics guaranteed to bore her straight out of her skull, and she'll probably leave and cancel the next few days, no matter how easy the money is. Discuss his gambling? Would she be interested? After all, this is Las Vegas, home of casinos. He's about to launch in when Howie's warning blazes across his consciousness.

Instead, he opts for, "No, let's talk about you. That's a much more interesting conversation. Where you from?"

He knows there's more in play now than simply grasping for a topic of conversation. He asked the question for a very specific reason: to find out how carefully she sticks to her story from this morning. Has she already forgotten the details? He realizes she might make up different stories for each guy to mask her real identity, so why even bother to worry about it? Well, for one thing, he's curious.

She laughs.

"Fresno, California."

Just as expected, different.

Then again, why am I being such a dick head about this?
He has no answer to that.
"What made you decide to come to Las Vegas?" he asks.
See, you're making conversation.
A waiter appears with one martini and one margarita on a round, silver serving tray.

With exaggerated flourish—probably in hope of increasing the tip—he serves Breeze then Arnold, and when the drinks are exactly the way he wants them, asks, "Would you like to see a menu now or would you prefer to enjoy your drinks for a few minutes?"
Breeze arches her eyebrows at Arnold.
He responds right on cue.
"In a minute. We'll enjoy our drinks first."
Breeze smiles.
See.
"Very good, sir. I'll keep an eye on you, check back in a few minutes."
He disappears.
Breeze lifts her glass.
"Cheers."
This time he knows enough to clink glasses before touching the chilled martini to his lips. He mimics the way she sips her margarita.

Clear chilled liquid flows over his tongue, laying down an almost breath-stealing numbing wake. He smothers the urge to gasp and forces a weak smile, thinks, so this is what a martini tastes like. Another lesson learned. A warm glow of pride warms his chest at tucking one more lesson under his belt. Howie had nailed it, of course: this was absolutely the right thing to do.

Dinner ordered, their first drink almost finished, Arnold is mellowing. In fact, he feels more relaxed than any time in recent memory. Certainly, he no longer worries about compounding one social faux pas on top of another. He credits this Zen-like tranquility as an equal split between Breeze's skills at putting him at ease and the martini. She effortlessly entertains him by making conversation so easy, so simple. Is he learning from this experience? Yes, he is. Maybe when he returns to Seattle, he'll be comfortable enough to sit down with Rachael and chat with her. He looks forward to that. Rachael…yeah, this will make the difference. Does she even know he exists?

He takes another tiny sip of elixir.

Order another before dinner? Yeah, why not! They're not driving.

He giggles at that. She asks him what he's laughing about, and he tells her.

Ask her if she wants another drink? Whoa, think about what she told you earlier: women like take-charge men.

So, what the hell, take charge. Soon as I see the waiter.

Breeze says, "Enough about me. I still haven't heard one word about you. What do you do for a living?"

A wrong answer buzzer alerts his brain. There it is again: another inquiry into how he supports himself. Then again, what's he being so sensitive about?

Well, because you don't want to slip up and tell her. And the way this martini is making me feel…

He surprises himself by asking, "Why do you want to know?"

Whoa, didn't mean it to sound like that, so harsh and aggressive.

He wants to apologize but stops short of doing so.

She hesitates, as if considering her answer, rubbing her lips back and forth over each other in what seems to be an unguarded moment.

"Hmmm, let me see. Several reasons. One, I find you interesting. Why? Well, for starters, the thing that's so very obvious is you appear to have a great deal of money for a man your age. And that makes me wonder, are you some kind of self-made Wunderkind or does your father pay you an outrageous salary for a nothing position in some big company he owns? Or are you a trust fund brat?"

"Trust fund brat?"

Interesting term.

"Why would you even think that's a possibility?"

Smiling, she settles back in the chair.

"I've run across my share. They all seem to have this air of practiced indifference to money. You definitely have a touch of that."

She reaches across the table to brush his hand. "I didn't mean to make that sound bad, or anything. An observation, is all."

He understands why she might come away with that impression.

Truth be told, he's gone out of his way to give her that impression as a way to enhance his Toby image. Buying the suit, her purse, expensive meals…in a perverse way, her observation shores up his self-confidence and pride. If she only knew his real story, she'd see the real man, the thing he's so proud of accomplishing. But he can't risk divulging any of that to her. Still, part of him yearns for her approval, doesn't want her to think of him as a piece of parasitic social driftwood afloat in his family sea of wealth.

"No. Far from it."

Her eyebrows arch.

"Very intriguing. You're becoming more and more a mystery man with each non-disclosure. Can't tell you how very sexy and interesting I find that. So, Mr. Toby Taylor, man of mystery, tell me: what's your big secret?"

Again, he's tempted to boast, to make her understand his extraordinary accomplishment, to be able to revel in the fruits of his work, but knows there isn't any upside to that other than giving his ego a boost, and Breeze is accomplishing that anyway. Besides, she probably wouldn't believe him if he told her. But he's deeply troubled by the possibility she suspects he's a trust fund brat.

Why should that bother you? What difference does it make?

Is this how a spy feels? Frustrated and isolated at not being able to discuss his day-to-day work with anyone, or to share accomplishment or problems.

This is not a new thought for him. It's surfaced again and again in recent months as he finally began to make good money. Ironically, so did the realization that if someone else had accomplished his high level of predictive analysis no one else would know about it either because that person would definitely be extremely circumspect about disclosing the details. So, he has every reason to keep the subject to himself. On the other hand, he can't help but wonder if the extensive security precautions he's incorporated into his home and computer network are

Deadly Odds

really that necessary? Where is the line between reasonable caution and paranoia? And what's to say he's not suffering from a bad case of self-aggrandizement? When you burrow into the depths of your own silo as much as he has, what's to keep your isolation from magnifying your accomplishments? Well, because Howie is genuinely impressed and he's a computer genius. Plus, there's the simple fact that he beats the odds more than is statistically reasonable. That fact just can't be ignored.

He realizes she's waiting for an answer.

He says, "I'm in finance."

"Finance? That's not very specific. What's that supposed to mean?"

Her persistence is becoming irritating.

"Make you a deal. You tell me why you became a," he catches himself from saying whore, "an escort, and I'll tell you how I earn a living."

There, that should shut her up.

$ $ $

Arnold kept finding it difficult to stay on subject instead of dwelling on Howard's final seconds of life, replaying his fantasy of how gut-wrenchingly terrifying they must've been. He kept replaying the mental movie of walking through the back door, pizza in hand, calling out to him, then Howard's warning, followed by the gunshot. Over and over, the horrible vignette shoved aside all other thoughts, derailing the story's flow detail by detail, causing Davidson to again and again prod him onward. Another wave of guilt swept over him, stealing his breath. Two simple facts kept coming back to him: if he hadn't gone to Vegas, Howard would still be alive. If Howard had gone to the pizzeria instead of him, Howard would still be alive. Howard was now dead, his body probably lying in the King County morgue. Tears welled up along his lower lids, his mind mired in self-loathing. His fault, all of it.

Davidson cleared his throat.

"You okay?"

Arnold shook his head and knuckled away the tears.

"I'll never be okay. Not after this."

85

Davidson tilted back in his desk chair and yawned, covering his mouth.

"That remains to be seen. So far, nothing you describe makes you responsible for Howard's death. How about a break? Stretch, get something to eat, coffee, stop by the toilet?"

Easy for Davidson to say. Once he'd heard the entire story, he'd change his mind and perhaps even drop him as a client. Now, he didn't want to finish the story because he wanted Davidson to think well of him, to not hold him responsible, but knew he had to continue, had to tell him every detail, regardless of how incriminating and embarrassing a light it would shine on him. Shit! Too many emotions vied for dominance, making it impossible to think clearly.

Davidson leaned forward, dropping his foot heavily from the partially opened desk drawer to the floor.

Clomp.

"Tell you what. Go into the men's room, rinse your face, take a few long deep breaths. Take a short break. Come back in here and finish the story. How's that sound?"

When Arnold didn't answer, Davidson pushed out of his chair.

"C'mon. I have to visit the little boy's room anyway."

Arnold leaned over the porcelain sink, cupping handfuls of cold water over his face, washing away tears and sniffing up the snot dripping from his nose. Fucking Firouz. He straightened up, stared at the face in the mirror and, for the first time since hearing the gunshot, felt a bud of resolve in his mind. Moving closer to the mirror, staring more intently into the bloodshot eyes staring out at him, he saw that resolve; hard, cold, intentional revenge. And knew in that instant something in him had changed forever.

Never in his life had he felt such raw rage building. If Firouz or Karim were to walk into the bathroom now, he'd have the strength to strangle to death both of those bastards with his bare hands. He held up both hands and studied his fingers, flexing and extending them, watching the intricate muscle and tendons stretch and relax under smooth skin. Not especially strong appearing, certainly not the hard muscles of a workman. So, okay, maybe he didn't have the actual strength to physically strangle either man single-handedly, but there had to be a way to kill those bastards. He thought about how that might feel. He realized that doing so wouldn't bring Howie back to life, but it would sure go a long way to settling the score.

He bent over, rinsed his face one more time before straightening up for one more intense look into those hard eyes. As of just seconds ago, his life now had a well-defined purpose. No matter what it took, no matter whether he had to sacrifice his own life in the process, he would exact revenge for Howard Weinstein. There had to be a way to destroy all the Jahandars and everything they stood for.

He nodded to the mirror image, quickly finger combed his hair, and after a deep, purposeful breath whispered, "I'm going to get you fuckers. Count on it."

$ $ $

"Can't you break into it?" Firouz asked.

"Eventually. It's password protected so I'm running a program to bypass that. It's using Windows. The Microsoft developers left trap doors for exactly this reason."

"If that's true, what good is a password?"

"Stop it, you're driving me crazy with all your questions. Patience, my friend. You must have patience. Is it not time for you to pray?"

Firouz nodded and motioned for Karim to follow him to the next room, where the prayer rugs were.

Allah would help, this he knew as truth.

$ $ $

Back in Davidson's office Arnold dropped onto the couch, leaned forward, and began popping knuckles.

"Where were we?" his mind now only half concentrating on their discussion while the other half grappled with how he might be able to nail those bastards.

Davidson ran the flat of his hand over the desk blotter, as if smoothing it.

"Looks like the break was exactly what you needed."

Arnold wasn't in the mood for chit chat now that he had purpose in his life again, preferring instead to bear down on business.

"Let's continue. Where did I leave off? I can't remember."

"You had just made a quid pro quo deal with Breeze. You'd tell her what you do for a living if she tells you why she became a prostitute."

12

ARNOLD TELLS BREEZE, "I gamble."

Her eyebrows rise as her mouth opens slightly.

She appears genuinely shocked. If not shocked, extremely surprised.

"No way! I don't believe it."

What's that supposed to mean? She trivializing him? Then again, maybe it'd be better to not have her believe him. Regardless, he resents her reaction because it implies...what, exactly? That a nerdy little geek is incapable of something so daring as gambling? That he doesn't have the balls? That he's trying to make himself something he isn't?

"Why not? Because I look like a geeky little nerd? Which therefore begs the question: how the hell is a gambler supposed look? Slicked back hair, shifty eyes, bad dental work, fidgety hands with nicotine stains?"

She's taken aback by his reaction, her face slowly morphing from serious to suspicious.

"Really? You gamble for a living?"

Just let it go, let her believe whatever she wants. Heed Howie's warning and don't say a goddamn word about your work or system.

But...

I'll make her respect me.

The martini isn't helping his self-control either, the alcohol greasing the skids between brain and mouth, encouraging him to tell her things he knows damn well he shouldn't. The wiser part of his cortex cautions him to go ahead, let her believe you're a trust fund brat who doesn't value his family's money.

You really don't give a rat's ass what she thinks.

He ignores his own sound advice and responds with, "Really!"

And likes the sound of his tone: assertive, direct, alpha doggish.

She seems to think about that.

"Yeah? Huh! Makes sense, I guess. Guy comes to Vegas and, yeah, who'd suspect? I mean you, right?"

There's a glint in her eye.

What?

Respect?

He would like to think so, yet he's not sure.

Breeze sips her drink and apparently considers this new revelation.

"Like, what are you into, cards, track, what?"

Howie's warning continues to reverberate through his mind like a mantra. But he finds the moment irresistible. Never in his life has a beautiful woman shown the slightest interest in his work, much less to ask a question about it. Then again, he reminds himself, how many times have you been with a woman? He reevaluates his position, thinks, would a few words really hurt? After all, he's hundreds of miles from home. Better still, she doesn't have a clue to his real identity, so....

Why the hell not? And if it makes him feel good about himself...

"Sports mostly," he says offhandedly, like, no big deal. "Football in particular."

And there it is: out.

Well, sort of.

That's just the gambling part.

"I do other things, too—" and cuts himself off before venturing into forbidden territory.

Howie's apparition continues to stand behind her, scowling at him over her shoulder, shaking his head in disgust, mouthing the words: Shut! The! Fuck! Up!

Again, she nestles back into her chair, appraising him with a strange smile.

Yeah, respect. That's it.

The smile widens.

"I don't believe it. You're jerking my chain."

See? Case in point. Why do people judge him just because he's not One Of The Beautiful People? Why assume that an acne scared skinny Jew Boy can't harness the power of artificial intelligence? Why do social retardation and a blasé taste in fashion automatically delegate you to the not-a-player trash heap?

Rhetorical questions, he knows. And this isn't the first time these thoughts have crossed his mind. Long ago, he decided that women like Breeze—attractive ones, not necessarily escorts—harbor stereotypical images of men who take risks—high-stakes gamblers, for instance—in a special category. They make the unfounded assumption that risk-taking men are more fun to be with and, as a consequence, cut them even more slack. The corollary, of course, is that geeky non-risk takers—such as himself—are, by some weird rule of life, conservative dullards. It's a circular argument that pisses him off because it ignores a person's intellect. Also, because he's a Jew, he hates the prejudice created by stereotypes.

He chooses to let her unintended slight pass unchallenged, preferring to shift the conversation back to her.

With a dismissive wave, "Whatever. Okay, we made a deal and now it's your turn. Why did you become an escort?" And immediately realizes how pejorative the words might sound. Apologize? Why? Tit for tat.

She laughs at him.

"Why should I tell you?" Then quickly raises a hand. "What I mean is, why should I give you a truthful answer when I figure you just lied to me?"

He just shakes his head and turns away, even more pissed than two seconds ago. Angry at her answer. Angry at being given the short shrift in the looks department. Angry at the way this conversation has ended up. Angry at his anger. He asks himself yet again, why can't I be happy with the gift of intellect, at being smarter than 90 percent of the population? But he knows the answer all too well: because in this world, physical looks trump intellect 99 percent of the time. For the gazillioneth time in his life he wishes he were handsome instead of smart.

"Toby?"

Just get up and leave? Walk out of this sick relationship and call it quits?

Or would that be juvenile, like a petulant adolescent?

Yeah, probably, but he'd sure feel a lot better exerting that kind of control.

Instead, he answers with, "What?" and hears the word come out sharper than intended.

She leans forward, arms to her side, like a child answering a classroom teacher.

"You asked me a question and I'm going to give you the answer. It's very simple: sex sells."

Her words take a second to register because he's been momentarily too self-absorbed to remember the question.

"Sex sells? That's why you've chosen to—" He can't believe it. "Yes, but—"

He stops. The simplicity of her answer strikes him as so cold-blooded, so calculated, that he's stunned.

Then again, why be shocked?

Well, because the subject of sex—at least for him—is an activity cloistered in taboos. He knows that everybody engages in it. But his problem is that he's always assumed the act should involve some degree of emotional attachment. Or at least that's what he's been taught to believe. By whom, he isn't sure, because his folks certainly didn't discuss sex with him like he thinks other parents normally do with their children. And now that he thinks about it this bias against discussing sex is rather silly, especially considering that losing his virginity was the sole purpose for coming to Vegas. Countless women and men, like Breeze, have traded in sex—as if it were any other commodity—since the first ape bartered firewood for vegetables. Is he just being too puritanical? Apparently so.

"But what?" Breeze asks, turning defensive. "Because I sell sex, I won't be able to find an aeronautical engineer to give me a cheesy half caret from an equally cheesy shopping mall jeweler so I can slave away my youth ferrying kids around in a SUV and cleaning toilet bowls?" She laughs. "Hey, screw that noise. I want money. My *own* money. And I want to do with it exactly as *I* please."

She penetrates his eyes with a defiant stare, daring him to challenge her.

When he doesn't comment, she continues.

"At my age, with my looks and skills, I can get top dollar for a night. You, case in point. You're willing to pay hard cash to be with me, take me out to high end places like this," with a sweep of her hand, "and show me off to other men. To top it off, you know that at the end of the night you'll be able to take me back to your hotel room and I'll put out. There's no mystery in that. I get paid to be treated like royalty. So, you tell me: why wouldn't I want this life?"

Her logic makes sense. In a way. If you totally ignore the fact that prostitution—okay, in general, maybe not her specifically—is strongly linked to other criminal activities, to say nothing of the risk of developing a serious case of non-treatable STD or HIV.

He sees no tactful way to mix this particular point into the discussion, so settles for, "Aren't you taking risks?"

She laughs.

"In this town? No more than any girl anywhere who goes out with a new guy. In this job I cherry pick and screen the men I go with by requiring they can afford me. Besides, the men I see usually don't want to leave any trail. They particularly don't want their wives or girlfriends to know what they're doing when they come to town. The way I do business isn't even close to standing out on a street corner waiting to blow some horny dirtball in the front seat of a Prius rental. I don't do drugs, so I don't have to work when I don't feel like it or take any John that comes along. And when I hit forty and my tits start heading south, I'll have enough in the bank to retire. Maybe I'll stick around this town or maybe I won't. Who knows? Haven't planned that far ahead yet."

A few strands of hair fall across her face which she promptly sweeps back with a finger.

"And in case you're wondering, no, I wasn't sexually abused as a child like a lot of do-gooder sociologists claim is the biggest reason," with mimed finger quotes, "a girl like me opts for the life. With me it was just the opposite. As a teenager I became curious as hell about sex, but all the clumsy dorks my age didn't want to do anything but find a hole to stick their dick into. So, becoming an escort gave me a way to explore my sexuality without any peer pressure or problems. And guess what? I get paid very well for satisfying my own curiosity and urges. And I'm not confined to the same guy every Saturday night whether I want it or not, but in case you're wondering, I get horny, too. So, what's not to like about the way I earn a living?"

He didn't have an answer for that one.

She wet her lips with the dregs of her margarita.

"So, Mr. Taylor, Mr. Big Time Gambler, you do races?"

Let it go, don't even bother answering.

But the glow from the gin, along with all the other factors, is putting a crowbar to his lips. Most of all, he wants to escape from his Seattle nerdy-geek persona, if only for the few days here in Vegas. All these forces conspire against him, compelling him to do exactly what he knows he shouldn't.

"Yeah, I do races," again throwing it out as casually as possible but figuring a nonchalant shrug might be overdoing things a tad.

Her face brightens.

"Cool." She considers this a moment. "But you can't do that one hundred percent of the time, so what's your day job?"

How irritating. She just didn't get it.

"That's it. That's all I do."

"So, guess that means you are a trust fund brat," she says smugly, as if playing a trump card.

He can't stand being trivialized this way.

"No. I keep telling you, but you refuse to believe me."

He figures what the hell, no one knows who he really is, so go ahead, get it off your chest, don't take this crap from her, make yourself feel better.

"I make predictions. That's what I do."

"Predictions? What's that supposed to mean?"

He immediately realizes his mistake. Can he cover it? Probably less than fifty-fifty at this point, so decides to just go with it.

The waiter appears with another round of drinks. Arnold's first impulse is to have him take them back because far as he recollects, he didn't order them, then wonders if Breeze signaled him, so maybe she wants one.

What the hell, relax and enjoy it. After all, you're Toby Taylor, player.

After a sip of the new martini he starts to explain: "Ever hear of Nate Silver?"

She sets her new margarita down.

"The statistician?"

Wow. Impressive. Most people had heard of him—if they could even remember his name—for the first time during the 2012 election when he nailed all the electoral votes, but few people know of his background in statistics. Other people learned of his work when his book, *The Signal and the Noise* became a New York Times best seller.

"I'm impressed you know about him."

She smirks.

"Why? Because a girl like me shouldn't read the news?"

Speaking of stereotypes...

Ignoring the jab, he says, "Well, I'm working on a system that's better than his." A wave of pride sweeps through him, prompting him to add, "I've done it, too."

"Really?" she says with what appears as genuine interest.

A debate of conscience starts in the back of his mind, the conservative side admonishing him for blabbing his secret while the new Vegas-emboldened side is countering with, why not?

You're Toby Taylor, what will it hurt to finally tell someone?

He nods.

"Really."

"Better in what way?"

Aw, Christ, better give her something, otherwise odds are she'll keep harping and chipping away at it all night. What are the chances she'll even remember the conversation by morning? Very slim at best, so what harm will it do?

He rotates the stem of the martini glass and synthesizes an easy explanation to a complex statistical phenomenon. The problem with not having explained this to anyone but Howie—who pretty much knows the theory anyway—is not having a practiced a bullet-point easy-to-understand explanation. He swallows and decides to give it his best shot.

"I analyze politics and economic situations. This allows me to model the outcome of pending or proposed legislation, for example."

She cocks her head as if her hearing is better in the right ear.

"Give me an example."

He's amazed she followed it. Or is she just good at asking questions that sound like she's tracking conversations?

"Remember the Newtown shooting? At Sandy Hook school?"

"Who could forget?"

"Right afterwards there was a big push to enact changes in the gun laws even if only to require background checks on prospective gun buyers. Right?"

"Yes, I remember."

"The common wisdom—at least in the media—was that coming right on the heels of such a senseless massacre, there wouldn't be a better time for passing legislation through the House and Senate. Well, I modeled all the data I could find, put it into my system, and predicted the bill wouldn't pass the House. I nailed every vote."

He sat back in the chair, his mind reliving the exciting validation that came from comparing the actual votes to his predictions, watching the incrementing score of right answers contrast to zero wrongs. He still amazes himself with that one, one of his first breakthrough predictions. He shakes his head in awe, now reveling in the glow of the memory.

"Fascinating. What else?" she asks, eyes sparkling.

He wonders if it's the tequila, or is she impressed?

Doesn't matter. He realizes he's disclosed way too much.

"Let's change the subject."

She reaches across the table to touch his hand.

"Really? But this is so interesting."

"I'd rather talk about you."

"Not fair, Toby. I'm not very interesting, and you are."

You didn't think so a few minutes ago.

He glances away, as if more interested in the little drama playing out at the tables around them. Some diners have left, others are arriving, others seem to be enjoying conversations over completed dinners while enjoying a glass of wine.

Breeze says, "Okay, we can talk about something else, but only if I get to ask you one more question. The example you just gave, that had to do with politics in the United States. What about politics in, say, Europe?"

So, she really *did* understand. Wow. How exciting. Her interest in his work becomes energizing and hard to ignore.

"Absolutely. It's a system with universal applicability rather than a singularly directed predictor. All you need to do to answer any question—and this is the really key thing—is figure out what variables to input in order to generate a meaningful output. Same thing Silver does. Initially, he started using his models to select baseball players for teams. He became wildly successful. Once he improved that system, he converted it to predict election results. Because his system is proprietary, no one else knows exactly how it's built, but the underlying concept is obvious. I've done the same thing. At the moment I keep two systems running: one deals with politics, the other sports. I support myself by betting sports and do the other because I love the challenge of improving it."

She beams at him now, making him feel for the first time that she's truly interested in his person instead of simply fulfilling the contract of being a full-service escort. And it makes him feel great. More than great. Wonderful isn't even close. He basks in the glow.

Until she says, "Why don't we bet a couple races tomorrow? It could be kicks."

And just as quickly, his high segues into free-floating anxiety. Weightlessness in the depths of his gut burrows straight up through his chest, making it impossible to satisfy an oxygen hunger. Howie is standing behind her again, looking really pissed this time, mouthing the words *Do Not Do It.* But the cat's out of the bag, and if he backs down...

He hates the feeling of being The Wimp. The Pussy. Especially coming directly on the heels of being The Elevated Guru.

Now what?

The Las Vegas persona urges him to go ahead, make a few bets, be a "Player."

Howie is countering, "Bullshit. You're not doing yourself any favors by playing the big shot gambler. Say no. Better yet, throw some sand over your tracks and say you lied and were only trying to impress her."

The mental voice of Las Vegas Gold counters with, "No! You need this for your self-respect. Finally, someone other than Howie can marvel at your accomplishment. Besides, what harm will it do to bet three or four races?

What would she think about you if you nailed them?

"Okay, why not," he says, downing another slug of martini.

13

ARNOLD FOLLOWS BREEZE up plush red carpet, through the tall glass doors into metallic-tasting, artificially cooled air, onto polished marble, then over more well-tended carpet crammed with row after row of slot machines, some populated with players stuffing in coins, others silent and waiting for the next sucker. The active slots fill the air with a cacophony of two bar mindless tunes and the occasional tinkle of coins.

For fleeting seconds, he may catch a snatch of individual melodies, some catchy ones burrowing into his brain like a worm. He hates those sounds. Hates the casino ambience. Hates the fact that willing people elect to devote hours knowing full well they will lose hard earned money yet continue to play. For some of these people, it's money they can ill afford to lose. In Arnold's mind, not even Bill Gates can afford to lose so idiotically.

How can some people be so stupid as to actually buy into chasing the dream of easy money?

There's no such thing as easy money. If they believe that, they're more foolish than an ostrich. Okay, sure, he bets and freely admits it. But the difference is he knows damn well he'll win a hell of a lot more than he'll lose. He knows this as fact, not hunch. He never actually wagered his first dime of real money until he'd objectively proven he could produce a win rate higher than 55 percent. Once he'd accomplished that he could throw the switch to the money machine, because if he bet the same amount each time, as long as he won more than 50 percent of the bets, he was guaranteed come out ahead.

By definition, it's not gambling if you know you're going to win. It's only gambling when the outcome is assuredly left to chance, which is always in favor of the house.

Occasionally he'll gamble in the true conventional sense. If the Powerball jackpot exceeds one hundred million dollars, he'll buy one six-dollar ticket. But he does so with the eyes-wide-open knowledge that the odds of winning are fantastically miniscule, and he is purchasing the ticket purely for its high-octane entertainment value. Way he figures, a week of fantasy is far more fun (and less expensive) than a ticket to a movie.

This morning, soon as he awoke, he used his laptop and the hotel room's complementary Wi-Fi to log onto the Internet. Then, to prevent leaving any digital trace between the laptop and his home network, he used the laptop's TOR browser to log onto his system. And in spite of such elaborate security measures, he still invoked a 256-bit encryption protocol. What people might consider overkill was, in his opinion, nothing more than a good dose of common sense. Why lead with your chin?

Took about an hour of work to select the win, place, and show horses for three Hollywood Park races. Three races should do it. And if not? Too bad. Now, having second thoughts as they entered the casino, he wonders if it would be smarter to just lose the bets. He toys with that idea a moment before discarding it. For some strange reason, he wants Breeze to admire him for something other than the money he spends on her. Although he'd never discussed it with Howard, he wonders if Rachael knows how smart he is. He's pretty sure he's been a topic of conversation between the brother and sister. How could the subject not come up, what with Howard being such close friend? Rachael...at the rate things are going he'll get the confidence to approach her when he returns to Seattle. For this, he is grateful.

She leads him over to an area of the casino with five betting windows and overhead boards displaying the odds for all the horses in each of today's races. His choices are listed on one flat screen. Betting at a casino—or anyplace public, for that matter—is a first for him. Until now, all his gambling has been online. Now, being exposed like this stirs an uneasy nervousness in the depths of his chest.

Time to get on with it.

With Breeze watching, he approaches a window, places his bets, slides the ticket into his Dockers pocket, and ambles back to her.

"All set?"

Arnold nods, pulls the ticket out for her to see.

"What would you like to do now?"

This area of the casino contains ten small tables and chairs with additional leather club chairs scattered around five large television sets displaying live feeds from several active racetracks and sports events. One set shows a soccer game in progress. Two tables have been shoved together to form one large table with five men around cheering the action, glasses of what looked like Bloody Marys within easy reach. From the sound of them, this isn't their first drink of the morning.

Breeze motions to an empty table.

"Why not sit and catch the races?" She checks her watch. "First one starts in thirty minutes.

Hmm…a Bloody Mary might taste good.

Why not?

Nothing better to do at the moment, and the outside air is growing hot. Even if it's "dry heat." To him, hot is hot. That's why it's called hot.

Within seconds of settling in a waitress materializes, asking if they wish to order food or drink. Arnold's a little hesitant to down alcohol this early in the day, but that's Arnold Gold's issue, the nerd. Toby Taylor, player, on the other hand, should have no hesitation. Without even glancing at Breeze, he orders two Bloody Marys, each with a splash of Tabasco and Worcestershire sauce and asks for the flat-screen closest to the table to be switched to the live feed for the Hollywood Park track. From the corner of his eye he notices a nod of approval from Breeze.

They sit side by side at the table, facing the screen.

With the waitress now gone, Breeze sets her purse on the floor between them, turns to him, asks, "You Jewish?"

Boom. Where's that coming from?

The question is startling, and immediately triggers several answers in his mind, but the overriding one is the urge to protect his real identity. He sees no upside to giving her one iota of accurate personal information, no matter how general it might be.

"Why do you ask?"

The corners of her mouth hint an apologetic smile.

"You just look Jewish, is all. I don't mean any ill will by that."

"What makes you think I look Jewish?" he asks a bit too sharply, although he's pretty damn sure he knows the answer: his nose.

So what if he's being offensive, she started it.

She adjusts her chair so as to not have to crane her neck as much to converse, and settles back in.

"You have an Eastern European look is all, one I commonly associate with Jewish people."

"In other words, a big nose?"

Again, too sharply, but he can't resist taking the shot.

"It's more than just your nose," she answers without the slightest embarrassment.

"My great grandfather and his family fled Germany just before World War II broke into full swing, when the handwriting was on the wall and Hitler's ovens were gearing up to full-tilt. Our family isn't religious, but because of someone's birth certificate they were all singled out for extermination."

One-hundred percent fabrication, but he welcomes the opportunity to provide any bit of disinformation he can. Plus, it makes for an interesting story. His ancestors immigrated from eastern Germany about the time the potato famine raged through Ireland.

"What's your heritage?" he asks.

"I'm Persian," she says with an obvious tinge of pride.

He has a vague idea of what Persia is, or was, but now, come to think of it, isn't quite sure.

"What does that mean?"

"My family came from what is now called Iran, but we consider ourselves Persian."

He decides to drop the subject and turns toward the television, wondering how Howie would handle this conversation.

She leans closer to him, catching his attention again.

"How do you see the Palestinian issue?" she asks.

Where the hell are these questions coming from?

"You serious?"

"Long as we're waiting for the race to start, we might as well discuss something. Or is there another topic you'd rather talk about? You said you want my help learning how to converse with women, well, here's a perfect opportunity. Talk to me."

"But politics? I don't usually discuss politics with people."

The waitress sets down their Bloody Marys and asks if there's anything else they'd like to order. Arnold says no.

Breeze takes his hand in hers and squeezes it a few moments.

"Women like to feel their intellect is valued. So, if not the Palestinian issue, what then? The latest fall fashions? Which movie star is cheating on his wife? Figure skating competition for the Olympics? I'm not sure you have strong opinions on any of those issues. I also have a sneaking suspicion you're not up on international soccer standings. Am I right?"

Valid point.

"What are you asking? Am I pro-Israel simply on the basis that you think I look Jewish?"

Grinning, she settles back in her chair and swirls the celery stick in her drink.

"No. The question isn't that simple. I'm not asking should Israel exist. It does and will, we can move on from that position. No, what I'm asking is how do you think Israel and Palestine might be able to co-exist in peace? As it is, both countries live in constant fear of each other while Israel continues to expand housing in forbidden territory."

Arnold runs his hand over his head, formulating his answer. He's never really given the topic much thought, mostly because the problem seems to have no viable solution, so why bother?

"Boy, I don't know...that's difficult. Otherwise it would've been solved years ago."

She cocks her head slightly. "And?"

Out of the corner of his eye, he catches the horses for the first race being jockeyed into the starting gates. Relieved to have a good excuse to dodge an answer, he points toward the TV.

"Race is about to start. Let's watch."

Breeze stares at the ticket in his hand, then back to his eyes, and back to the ticket.

"Win, Place, and Show. Nailed all of them. That's amazing. How'd you do that?"

Conflicting emotions struggle for dominance: pleasurable pride warms his chest while anxiety chills his gut. But the bottom line is she seems genuinely impressed, which stokes his ego. Never before has a woman looked at him with such glowing respect. Then again, he realizes the downside to all this is drawing too much attention to him, and this makes him extremely edgy.

"Tell you what, let's call it a day and go window shopping. I'll turn in these tickets," he says, holding up the ones for the next two races.

"You kidding? Now I'm really hooked. We're not going anywhere until the races are over. You get the next one right and I'll fuck your brains out. I'm telling you; this is a hundred percent turn-on."

They sit back down to await the next race as Arnold considers her offer.

Breeze pulls the celery stalk out of the Bloody Mary, starts nibbling it.

"This system of yours, tell me again what you plan to do with it."

He squirms in the chair and pretends to concentrate on the television off to his right, senses her waiting for an answer, decides on being as vague as possible, "Haven't given it much thought."

She coughs out a sarcastic laugh.

"Doubt that. Not you. You're thinking all the time."

"Seriously," he lies. "I wanted to see if I could do it. I reached the level you see now and I'm happy with it, but it's time to move on to other challenges, perhaps think about a graduate degree."

As if he had a bachelor's degree. He's never applied to the

University of Washington, much less attended a course.

She isn't buying it, he can tell, but too bad, he's not discussing this any further.

He misses the winner of the third race but considering the number of correct picks he's done extraordinarily well—too well, really—winning enough money to splurge on an expensive dinner. Breeze is clearly impressed, which is doing great things for his self-confidence.

That evening they sit in the Bellagio's Prime Steakhouse, into their second drink when Breeze broaches the subject again. The restaurant's interior decorating strikes Arnold as atrocious, what with the heavy velvet burgundy upholstery, thick carpet, dark paint on the walls, and thick blue curtains.

Someone with more money than taste must've received the decorating job, he thinks, but then again, what does he know? Obviously, someone high enough in the organization liked the plans enough to sign off on the project.

Their small table for two is positioned next to the back wall at a diagonal so they may sit at right angles to each other conversing while also being able to watch the action in the rest of the restaurant. The place has only a smattering of business at the moment.

She slides into the topic by saying, "I can't help but think about all the great things you could do with this ability you have to predict political events. That's pretty amazing stuff. What initially got you interested in that area of computing?"

He rearranges his silverware, lining up the salad fork tines directly over the dinner fork, then rearranges the tines into one straight line and decides it's a benign enough question to answer without disclosing anything truly personal. There's a point of being too cautious, especially if it raises more curiosity.

"Computers interest me."

"Yeah, but I get the impression you're really into it as more than just a passing interest."

Now he sets the salad fork on top of the dinner fork, aligning the tines as congruently as is possible. Breeze is slouched in her chair, one arm to her side, the other rocking her margarita back and forth, stirring up the crushed ice.

"I have this friend, Howard, got me interested."

And decides to not mention they are best friends.

She gives a nod to continue.

"And?"

He stops what he's doing to glance at her.

"Why all this interest?"

"Hey, look, cut me some slack, okay? I live in Vegas, gambling capitol of the world. Someone comes in, makes the bets you did today, hits one out of the park, I'd say that's pretty damn impressive. More than impressive. Phenomenal. You don't think I might be a little curious?"

She has a point.

"I just don't like to talk about it, is all."

She leans forward.

"Why is that?"

He's beginning to be irritated at the constant probing.

"Probably for the same reason you don't use your real name with clients."

That seems to sting. Or at least that's the impression he gets. She straightens in the chair, folds her arms across her chest, glares at him.

"I have my reasons for using a false name. Main one is for dealing with people like you."

Return zing.

The "like you" hurts more than he might have anticipated, because in spite of her warnings and his own trepidations, he's grown very attached to her and doesn't want her to be mad at him. Strange as that seems.

She continues with, "There are things about me that would surprise you, things you would never ever imagine or believe."

His turn for a personal question.

"Such as?"

She mutters a sarcastic, "Ha!" pauses a beat. "Why should I tell you my secrets when you don't tell me yours?"

This strikes him as a bit juvenile, a playground comeback. The martinis are making his head spin a little and he blinks, wondering when their steaks will arrive—they both ordered filets, medium rare—because he needs food in his stomach to slow down the effect of the alcohol.

He says, "Look, maybe this isn't working out and maybe I should just fly home in the morning, and we call it good. I'll give you your money for the day and you can line up another customer," emphasizing the last word.

Without missing a beat, she slides closer to him, slips her right hand under the table to his crotch, the gentle pressure of her finger evoking an erection.

"You sure about that?"

He gently tries to move her hand, but she holds it there, kneading the growing tension under the fabric.

"There are still so many things I haven't taught you about pleasing girls. Sure you don't want just one more night of instruction, cowboy?"

Her hand is achieving the intended effect, an effect his rational mind can't ignore or suppress. He suspects the decision to leave town was the correct one, but now...

"See?" she giggles. "At least part of you wants me to stay."

Still gazing out toward the restaurant, he picks up the cocktail glass. Only a few drops of martini remain, but at least he can focus on those while trying to decide. Another night in the sack with Breeze wouldn't be all that bad. Would it? Especially if he just kept his damn mouth shut about gambling. Yeah, that's the key thing, because the only real reason to leave is to extricate himself from her constant probing into his finances and system. He screwed up once. Unless he leaves there's a good chance she'll weasel more out of him. Right?

Right.

So really the decision comes down to whether he wants to get laid tonight. Then in the morning...

He briefly debates the finality of the decision, a niggling suspicion warning against staying, that to leave town is the best choice. But Breeze massages away caution as the rationalizations in favor of staying begin to pile up: she doesn't even know your real identity.

You'll be okay for one more night...

He sets down the cocktail glass and removes her hand from his groin before something embarrassing happens.

"Okay, but I'm still leaving in the morning."

She smiles, stretches toward him, plants a kiss on his cheek.

"I guarantee you won't be disappointed. I'll do anything you want, just name it." Then she slides out of the chair, purring, "Be right back. Need to visit the powder room. I'm getting too wet just thinking about it."

His erection is about to rip through his pants by the time they cross the threshold to his suite. The idea occurred to him to take her right there in the elevator on the trip up to his room, just hike her dress up, pull down her panties...but he's eager to learn the sexual secrets she so enticingly alluded to.

She plants one palm on his cheek and the other over his bulging crotch.

"Why don't you take a quick shower while I wait for you in bed?"

He undresses quickly, making sure to hang his prized suit carefully on the right hangers to keep the deliciously light wool from wrinkling, although he's convinced a fabric of this quality wouldn't show a crease if run over by a steam roller. Still, he wants it to be in nice shape when he packs in the morning.

Then he's in the shower, lathering down as quickly as possible while his mind fantasizes about what possible treats Breeze has in store. He flashes on her kneeling astride his hips, his head on a pillow, watching her slide up and down on him. Jesus, his groin is aching for release. But in addition to the raw sexual craving, there's an amorphous dark element lurking in the fringe: a tinge of fear. He pauses to wonder what it might be or what it means. What's the worry? Yet he knows it's there, but, like an irretrievable word on the tip of his tongue, can't quite grasp it. Has to do with Breeze. This much he knows. It started when he suggested terminating their arrangement. What is it?

With the stream of hot water full on against his face, eyes shut, he struggles to identify the meaning. There! He catches a glimmer of recognition. She started to radiate an aura.

Yeah, that's it. Okay, but of what?

Danger?

Yeah, danger.

But in a way, that made tonight's sex even more exciting, more real, more...and maybe that is one of the mysteries she intends to teach him, maybe this is a sexual trick.

Who cares, he'll be flying out of here tomorrow, heading back to Seattle.

He towels off, debates walking into the bedroom nude, his erection thrust out like a sword, and remembers his overwhelming embarrassment that first night. She's taught him things, that's for sure. Howie was right to suggest the visit. Totally worth it. He wraps himself in the white Bellagio robe, winks at himself in the mirror, opens the door to step into the bedroom.

Breeze sits against the elaborate headboard, sheet over her belly, breasts exposed. She pats the bed beside her.

"See? You've already learned a few things. Wow, looks like you're ready for some action."

Firouz recoiled from the news. Unbelievable.

Arnold Gold is a dead man! If it's the last thing he does, he'll kill that infidel.

Outside the stuffy, overheated apartment the lights of downtown Seattle glowed. It was now four hours since they had taken the Jew's computer. What had the killing of the Jew's friend accomplished other than make them a potential subject of a police investigation?

Nothing, absolutely nothing.

He'd kill the incompetent technician if it would solve the problem, but it wouldn't.

Leaving him what?

He needed to think.

Calm down, he told himself. Never, never trust your first reaction.

Allen Wyler

Only fools react. Truly superior warriors analyze and think.
Always turn adversity into advantage.
God willing.

14

THE NEXT MORNING is a repeat of the previous two: room service breakfast while Arnold scans the news on his computer and answers an email from Howie. Breeze does likewise on her smartphone. He's changed his mind about leaving early. The drapes are wide open, spewing squint producing desert sun into the room.

Arnold now understands why retired Seattleites who can afford to migrate to winter harbors in sun-belt cities such as Palm Desert. Although Seattle is beautiful in summer, the endless gray winter days of drizzle and fog really suck. The brilliant sun energizes him, makes him want to do something. Not sure exactly what, but just something, something different. Hanging around casinos is good for maybe an hour, two at the very most, but anything more than that, well...

"Toby"

Oops, that's him.

"Yes?"

She sets down her phone.

"Like you to meet someone today."

Huh? Right out of the blue.

"Who?"

"A friend. A close friend."

Strange request. He's not sure what to make of it, and on second thought, is not sure he wants to. Meeting friends implies an attachment that's definitely not on his list of things to foster with her. Seeing Breeze for sex is one thing, getting embroiled in her social life is quite another. Then again, they'll never see each other again after this trip, so why not?

"You up for that?" she asks.

"We can do that, but I have to ask you why."

She pours them both more coffee from the silver thermos pot.

"They're good people. You might find them interesting."

"Them? Thought you said you want me to meet someone, implying one person."

And is relieved of his initial, confusing, pang of jealousy. But on second thought, meeting two friends doesn't make any more sense than meeting one.

She smiles, replaces the coffee on the tray.

"Yes. Brothers. They're very close friends."

Without thinking, he checks his watch.

"When?"

"How about we finish breakfast then go for a walk? Such a beautiful day and we can be back before the sun gets too hot. We can meet them at Starbucks. I'll text them now."

"Okay."

He returns to his emails without another thought.

They are on the sidewalk heading for Starbucks, the heat of the sun already radiating from concrete sidewalks at only 10:30 in the morning. He hasn't checked the weather report but suspects today will be another scorcher. He wears a faded blue short-sleeve shirt and tan Dockers and high-top sneaks while Breeze is packaged into tight blue jeans and a white, form-fitting tank-top under a thin coat and floppy sunhat.

He's thankful for whoever invented Transitions lenses, because his are now in full tint, blocking the glares from all things shiny. The sun, glare, and heat serve as just one more reminder of Honolulu. One of these days, when the time is right, he'll live there. Wouldn't that be the life!

Especially if Rachael...*soon as I have the money*, he thinks.

As they enter Starbucks, Arnold's notices two Arabic-looking men at a café table near the window, signature white paper cups in front of them. They stand when Breeze and Arnold start through the door. Arnold estimates they're in their mid-twenties.

Breeze leads Arnold to their table, says, "This is Firouz," indicating the slimmer, shorter, of the two.

The guy smiles, offers his hand. Both wear expensive-looking designer shades propped up on oily black hair and flash smiles of what Arnold swears must be professionally whitened teeth. Both wear designer denims and expensive-looking sneaks undoubtedly endorsed by some NBA star Arnold has never heard of. Basketball is the one sport he hates and has no desire to bet on.

Arnold shakes Firouz's hand. What could this meeting possibly have to do with him?

Firouz sidesteps, nods to the other guy, a block of steroid and protein gym-bulked muscles in an orange tank top that showcases biceps, pecs, and oversized traps. His massive shoulders seem to connect directly to his ears.

"Toby, meet Karim."

Arnold chokes on a strong whiff of acrid body odor. Soon as they release hands, Arnold steps back. He decides fanning the air might appear offensive, so he suffers.

Smiling, Firouz asks Arnold, "Want anything? Latte? Tazo?"

"Naw, I'm good."

Firouz extends an arm, ushering them to the door.

"How about we step outside, take a walk."

Arnold catches Breeze's eye.

She says to him, "No worry."

And for some reason he believes her.

They stroll the manicured perimeter of Bellagio's triangular pool/ fountain to South Las Vegas Boulevard then turn north, following the sidewalk past Bonanno's New York Pizzeria to an unoccupied balcony above the pool where a sidewalk tree casts welcome shade in the blistering desert sun. Breeze pushes herself up to sit atop the broad concrete balustrade as both hands grip the edge next to her thighs.

Firouz and Karim face her, their backs to the sidewalk, the three forming a loose circle around Arnold like a wolf pack. He tries to read their eyes but sees only glare off their sunglasses, making him uneasy, especially given the mysterious nature of this meeting. At least they're out in the open if he has to run.

From what?

He feels stupid for even harboring the thought. Yet a primitive sixth sense sets his nerves on full alert.

Breeze says, "Relax, Toby, nothing to get upset about."

That apparent, huh?

"Going to tell me what this is about?"

Firouz says, "Sure, but you need to get your head straight first, dude. Okay?"

Arnold glances around and takes some degree of comfort in the nearby foot traffic, the slap slap slap of flip-flops, a rainbow of tank tops, shorts, and running shoes, and the fruity scents of sunscreen.

"Okay, but let's get this over with. Whatever this is."

Karim props his butt against the balustrade, arms crossed. Firouz remains standing, nervously pounding his fist into his palm.

Breeze starts in with, "We want to talk with you about something. Sensitive." And lets it hang a few seconds before adding, "You seem like someone who can keep a secret. Can you keep a secret, Toby?"

Making him even more nervous.

"Suppose so. Depends." He shrugs. "Dunno. Why?"

Breeze lowers her voice.

"What do you know about the United States intelligence services?"

Of all the things he might've expected, this isn't one. He's at a loss for words. They stand like this, the three of them facing him, waiting. Finally, another shrug.

"Not much. Nothing at all, I guess. Why?"

Firouz takes over.

"Heard of the Bureau of Intelligence and Research?"

Easy answer.

"Nope."

He shakes his head, now more befuddled than a moment ago.

"INR's mission is to provide all-source intelligence support to U.S.

diplomats. It's at the nexus of intelligence and foreign policy and plays a key role in ensuring that intelligence activities are consistent with U.S. foreign policy, and that other components of the intelligence community understand the information."

Firouz stops speaking, fingers his sunglasses up the bridge of his nose.

Arnold says nothing.

"That's us. Our job." Breeze says, "We work for the Bureau."

"Naw…uh-uh, no way."

"Why is that?" Firouz puts a sharp edge to his voice.

Karim turns away, to face the fountain, as if checking for potential eavesdroppers, stoking Arnold's nervousness and suspicions.

"Because…" Arnold scratches his cheek, scrambling for something less insulting than what first popped into his head. "I mean, a Las Vegas escort working as an intelligence operative? You gotta be kidding me."

Breeze lifts up her sunglasses to lock eyes with him.

"Seriously."

Back down go the glasses.

Arnold paces a tight circle, massaging the back of his neck, trying to believe her, but the idea seems too preposterous to swallow.

She adds, "You'd be surprised the types of people who visit Vegas for any number of reasons. Some good, some not so good. You'd be even more surprised to learn the sensitive information they tell an escort in confidence, especially after a few martinis and some pillow talk. Believe me, what happens in Vegas doesn't always stay in Vegas. Certainly not in our line of work."

Man, that's way over the line of credibility. But then, on second thought, it made a granule of sense. In a very perverse way, making him wonder, *really*? No way.

He says to Firouz, "And you?"

"And me what?"

"What do you do? Other than spy?"

"To call it spying is so old school, dude. We prefer to consider it intelligence gathering and analysis." He pushes up the nosepiece of his sunglasses again. "But if you really want to know, we tend bar. Both of us. You'd be surprised the things people tell a bartender. Even more surprising is what they'll talk about to each other while you're standing right in front of them wiping water spots off a glass. Easy."

"Now you're asking yourself, 'Why tell me this?'" Breeze adds. "Right?" the hint of East Coast accent creeping back into her voice.

Arnold emits a sarcastic grunt.

"Wouldn't you?"

She steps closer to him, lowers her voice.

"You're right, Toby, so here's the pitch. We want you to work for the Bureau as an independent contractor."

He's stunned, the day becoming one huge surprise right after another, boom-boom-boom, in such rapid succession, making it extremely difficult to process any of it.

He collects his thoughts enough to ask the obvious: "Doing what?"

"Intelligence analysis, Toby. What else would we want you for?" this said as if this were so obvious as to require no explanation.

He scans the three faces, wishing he could see their eyes through the cop-like wraparounds.

"C'mon, guys, this is really over the top. I can't believe you're serious."

Breeze drops her hands in a what-can-I-say gesture.

"Then I guess we have nothing more to discuss." She turns to her two partners. "Guys?"

Firouz shrugs. Karim continues to scan people passing by.

Arnold says, "I mean, what's the point? Intelligence agencies employ the best analysts and analysis software on the planet. Why even bother to ask me? Do it yourself."

His turn.

"Several reasons. Mostly manpower. We're drowning in data, more than we can possibly digest. Plus, we don't have enough good analysts to feed our computer the right questions. You, of all people, should know the rule garbage in, garbage out. And believe it or not, we're totally behind on work. Our mission, meaning the mission of the Bureau, is to ensure diplomats and other intelligence consumers have total access to focused intelligence products that help build the right decisions.

Politically, that is." A pause. "The Benghazi thing, a few years back? Now there's a perfect example of our government not being prepared. That's *our* fault—maybe not the three of us standing here," sweeping an index finger in an arc around the group, "but us in the general intelligence analysis groups."

"So," Breeze chimes in, "we think you're the perfect person to ask. You want to help your country, don't you?"

Arnold answers, "Jesus, that's a when-did-you-stop-beating-your-wife type question. It's not worth answering. The question specifically is what would I have to do?"

Firouz says, "We give you a target area of concern, say, the Palestinian peace talks. We give you three or four questions we need specific answers to, and you put your system to work figuring them out. Once you give us the answers you're on to the next problem. Pretty simple."

Not that simple.

There are still so many questions he doesn't know where to start.

"For you, maybe. Not me. I have to think about this before I can answer."

"Not a problem," says Breeze. "But I need to make one thing very clear. We asked you because you're a person we think can keep his mouth shut. I've been evaluating that for the past couple days. It should go without saying, you can't tell anyone about this discussion or our offer. And no one must ever know about the three of us. And that includes your friend Howard. We clear on this?"

No, not really.

"Don't worry. No one would believe me if I told them. Hey, I don't believe me now."

Firouz steps closer, right into Arnold's space, and Karim suddenly seems interested in what's being said.

"When we say to not say a thing, we mean it. You really don't want to fuck up on this. Understand?"

Even with those reflective designer sunglasses hiding his eyes, Arnold got the point.

15

"AND YOU BELIEVED them?" Davidson asked from behind the desk, leaning back in his chair with one foot back up on the half-open desk drawer again, the other in the well.

The question didn't carry any hint of incrimination or bias, just a flat-out inquisitiveness. Arnold appreciated this.

Arnold was pacing again.

"Not at first, but then I got to thinking…I mean, it sounded so preposterous that I began to wonder if there might be some element of truth to the story. You know, I started to do doublethink, like, something is so totally crazy it might possibly be true, along those lines."

With an encouraging nod: "Then what happened?"

Arnold did a quick knee bend, just to be doing something different, to relieve his nervousness. They were getting to the part he really hated to tell.

"The meeting broke up. Firouz and Karim headed off toward the city center and I went back to my room."

"And Breeze?"

"She came with me. I think she asked if I wanted her along and I don't think I answered, or at least I can't remember that part of it all that clearly, my mind was so…distracted. I guess she must've tagged along, not saying much. Maybe I thought she was coming to pick up her clothes. I don't know."

Davidson began tapping a Mount Blanc pen against his lower lip.

"Did she? Pick up her clothes, that is."

Arnold felt his face heating up.

"Not really. She got me into bed again."

A smile hinted at the corners of Davidson's face.

"Take much effort?"

The blush intensified.

"Guess not," with a nervous laugh.

The lawyer didn't probe that line of questioning further.

"Then what?"

"It's funny, she didn't really press the offer, either, like she wasn't trying to sell me anything. No hard sell at all. Later I went online, Googled the INR. Everything they said came right out of their web page, almost verbatim. I'd never heard of that agency before, so it was all news to me. The more I read, the more I began to buy into their story."

Arnold's voice trailed off as he drifted back through the memories.

After a few moments pause, Davidson asked, "Then what?"

"I started to become interested. Thought back to some of the conversations we'd had—Breeze and I—thinking maybe I could do something, ah, more productive with my work...after all, that'd be a good thing. Right?"

"Sure."

"I started asking her questions, like where would I work, and what would I do? She said I'd work from home, that that wasn't an issue, that they'd feed me situations to evaluate. I'd have to work secretly, but I could work on my own schedule and wouldn't be beholden to them in any way, like certain hours. It started to sound pretty good, so I agreed to one assignment, see how that went. If everything worked out okay, we could talk about something more long-term."

Davidson continued pen-tapping his lip.

"All this time you were using the Toby Taylor name?"

"Yes."

"And that wasn't going to be a problem?"

"Like what?"

"How would you communicate? How would you get paid? Those sorts of things."

"Told you earlier. I set up several false email accounts before contacting her the first time, so that wasn't going to be a problem. It was easy to set up a PayPal or even a bank account under any of those aliases. It was a done deal."

Davidson leveled an index finger at him.

"Right. Forgot." He leaned forward and jotted a note on a pad of legal paper. "Sorry to interrupt. Go on."

This was the part Arnold had been dreading. He reminded himself that this was his lawyer, the one person he should tell everything.

He gave a nervous laugh, "Now comes the hard part."

The room fell silent and Arnold briefly considered sitting down but decided to just shift his weight from one foot to the other and stay standing. This was making him antsy, embarrassed, humiliated, all rolled into one dysfunctional emotion.

"Okay, so they asked me to analyze three US embassies. One in Basrah, one in Riyadh, and one in Doha. Specifically, they wanted to know which one appeared most vulnerable to a successful terrorist attack." He saw the light in Davidson's eyes click on. "What are you thinking?"

Davidson waved off the question.

"Nothing yet. Go ahead, finish your story, then I'll ask."

"From the look on your face I think you already know what happened. Two weeks after I gave them my analysis the Doha embassy was bombed."

He waited for Davidson to comment.

Davidson chewed on that several seconds before offering: "Could be coincidence."

Arnold shook his head.

"Don't think so."

"Why?"

Unable to stand still any longer, Arnold went to the window to gaze down at the deserted streets and dark shadows obscuring the mouth of an alley while considering how best to explain it. The blunt, bitter truth would be the quickest. He needed to move on from this part and just get it the hell over with.

"When I first got wind of it, I was stunned. After all, this was exactly what my analysis was supposed to help prevent. At least that's what I was led to believe. But then I thought, hey, maybe it's all coincidence and some terrorist group hit it before our guys had a chance to evaluate my report. And if they read it, maybe they figured it was wrong. Maybe they were just testing out my accuracy. Funny what the mind does to rationalize stupid behavior. There I was, trying like hell to make myself believe I hadn't been duped. Christ!" He shook his head, the horrible feeling settling back over him. "Then I got to thinking oh, bullshit. How could I be so damn stupid? I mean, three Middle Eastern looking people con me into thinking they're intelligence operatives wanting me to work for them...I mean, come on. No vetting process, no evaluation other than an escort screwing my brains out? Jesus!"

How could he live with his stupidity?

"I can see how you could believe them. And it still might not be them. Still could be coincidence."

Arnold turned to face him.

"Oh, please! You're just trying to make me feel better. Once I saw the news reports we had an encrypted Skype call." Arnold paused to swallow and catch his breath. "They admitted the attack was theirs." He clamped his eyelids together, trying to lessen the impact of the memory. "They said they used my information to finalize plans, which, of course, made me an accomplice. Claimed that made me one of them now."

Arnold paused to catch his breath, the gut pain stealing his lungs. He held on to the back of the chair for support.

"You okay?" Davidson seemed genuinely concerned.

"Do I look like I'm okay? Hell no, I'm not okay. My stomach's killing me." Arnold swallowed hard and slid back into the chair then leaned over, hoping a change in position might ease it, but it didn't, so he fished the roll of Tums from his pocket and popped one into his mouth. "Never so much as had a cramp until all this happened. I should see a doctor, but..."

"Want to go to an emergency room? Swedish and Harborview are just up the hill. Say the word I'll drive you up."

Arnold shook his head.

"Not while those assholes are still searching for me."

Davidson yawned, both arms stretched high overhead, and held that pose for several seconds, his left shoulder giving an audible pop, but he didn't flinch.

"Offer's good you change your mind. Want to continue?"

Arnold nodded.

"Which brings me back to the obvious question: If all your interactions with Breeze were as Toby Taylor and you're sure about how well you laid down your false information, how did they know you're Arnold Gold? This the first time they showed up at your house?"

"Yeah, the only time." Arnold slowly dropped his head, humiliated by his own stupidity. He considered lying, say he had no idea, but Davidson should know the truth. "My bad. I screwed up."

Silence.

"I'm listening."

Arnold slumped against the soft, womb like leather couch and studied the ceiling, searching for an explanation that was truthful but wouldn't make him look like a complete putz.

"Don't know for sure, but here's the thing..." He started scraping out his thumb nail with the other one. "Jesus...so damn stupid, can't believe it."

"Go on."

With a grunt, Arnold pushed off the couch again to pace tight circles in front of the desk, too absorbed with berating himself to verbalize the answer.

A moment passed before he stopped and said to Davidson, "That second night, when Breeze went up to my room? She told me to take a shower? Okay, so I did. I mean, how was I to know? Right? My wallet was on the dresser. I'd purposely left it there as a test. Figured I'd check to see if she was trustworthy or if she'd steal my money. I had already put that night's fee in the envelope, but I left a hundred dollars for the tip in the wallet and locked the rest of my cash in the safe. Figured, okay, when I open the wallet I'll know right away. When I came out the bathroom, I noticed the wallet wasn't positioned exactly as I'd left it. It was at slight angle and I left it parallel to the edge of the table. But when

I checked later, all the money was still there. So, I thought, okay, she's not trying to rip me off and didn't give it another thought."

When Arnold didn't continue, Davidson asked, "You're saying you think she looked in your wallet?"

Arnold wiped his brow.

"Yeah, exactly."

His lawyer shook his head.

"Still don't get it. You say you went there with fake ID, that she only knew you as Toby. What I still don't understand is they obviously know who you are. How? How'd they know your name and address? You leaving out some key information or I'm going senile? Which is it?"

Time to come clean.

"Yeah, all that's true. The thing is, I had my real ID in there right along with the Toby stuff. Just in case..."

Davidson pondered this a moment.

"In case of what? How come that ID wasn't in the safe with the rest of your valuables?"

Arnold resumed pacing.

"Aw, Christ, I don't know...I was worried...I brought it because of the TSA and all. Started thinking, what if I get injured or sick, have to be taken to a hospital? What if I get arrested for *something*?" He held up a hand. "Yeah, I know, you're going to ask, arrested for what? I don't know. Anything. Jaywalking. Looking in store windows. Just something. I was also kind of worried about seeing a hooker. Made me twitchy. Yeah, I know the state of Nevada permits prostitution, but that's only in certain brothels outside of Vegas city limits." He shrugged off the statement with, "I was trying to be prepared, think of anything that could possibly go wrong. I know, I know, but it's just the way I'm wired, like when I write new code, I try to anticipate every possible eventuality and plan for it. Want to do it as bug free as possible the first time, have minimal troubleshooting. I admit that now, in retrospect, it was a stupid thing to do. And since I *did* bring my real ID, I should've put it and the wallet in the safe like you said. But I didn't, and here I am. Just another good example why retrospect's such twenty-twenty vision."

Davidson gave no reaction, just seemed to accept the argument and said, "Point made," in a tone vague enough to sound he was verbalizing thought instead of making a comment.

And this compelled Arnold to further justify his actions. "Thing is, ever since my parents..." Couldn't say the words "were murdered," so opted for, "died, I've been extremely security conscious." He raised both hands in mock surrender. "Yeah, yeah: to a fault. I get it."

Davidson dismissed the statement with a wave.

"Don't worry. I share your concerns, so you won't hear any criticism from me." Davidson cleared his throat. "Let's change the subject, move on to something else. You mentioned gambling for a living. That true?"

Arnold hesitated, still gun-shy about discussing the subject, but could see no reason to avoid it.

"Yes."

Davidson appeared to reevaluate him. Typical. Breeze's attitude changed soon as he proved he was a player.

Yeah, then look what happened.

"And the artificial intelligence bit, that true too? This isn't all just a story?"

"Yes, it's all true."

A vague smile crossed Davidson's mouth.

"Interesting. How does that work?" He quickly added, "The Cliffs Notes version. I wouldn't understand anything more complicated."

Arnold loved to talk about AI—lived for it, actually—but only with other geeks—Howard especially—because they didn't need complicated explanations. With like-minded people, he could sit for hours debating the pros and cons of topics outsiders didn't know existed, much less understand. He hated having someone ask him to explain a concept only to end up staring into a glassy-eyed receptacle of wasted breath. How do you explain something so complicated to someone so unprepared to understand? And cover it in thirty seconds or less? He knew Davidson hadn't asked the right question.

"What you're asking me to explain is what's on the computer Firouz and Karim killed Howie for. Right?"

Smiling, Davidson nodded.

"Since you put it that way."

Arnold dropped back into the chair, his steepled fingers tapping his chin.

"Ever hear of Nate Silver?"

Davidson frowned.

"Name's familiar but can't tell you why."

"Well, he's a god. Probably one of the coolest guys walking this planet at the moment. Mr. Prediction. The Man. He's called Super Bowls, presidential elections, any number of big-ticket items. Ring a bell now?"

"Maybe."

"Professionally he's a statistician. But he's parlayed statistical analysis into such a fine art he can accurately predict just about any phenomenon you might want to analyze. What're the odds the Eiffel Tower will collapse next year? He'll tell you. Who's going to win the Super Bowl this year? No problem. All the big Wall Street brokerages hire these guys— they call them Quants—to predict commodity prices. Each guy devises his own analysis paradigm in hopes of gaining a percent improvement over everyone else doing the same thing.

"No one knows Silver's exact paradigm, but they pretty much work the same. You use every bit of data you can find that might affect a phenomenon—commodity prices, presidential elections, just about anything—cram all of it in a supercomputer, crunch the numbers, and voila, you have a probability of something occurring. I do the same with sports, but I specialize in football. I'm constantly updating my database of players, both pro and collegiate. Guy sprains an ankle, boom, it's updated. Same thing for the coaches. Terabytes of data. I have Google searches running continuously. I practically update things before things happen. You wouldn't believe all the information I track." He paused for a breath. "Because even though we're all sort of doing the same thing, the biggest thing that separates one person from the other is the variables they track and the weight assigned each one. The more accurate the weighting, the better the results.

"For any given upcoming game, I update data right up until time to bet. I press a button and let the computer give me an objective point spread. No hunches, no emotional deviations, just purely cut and dried. Pretty simple, right? So simple, in fact, that everybody, including the dudes in Vegas who make the spreads, do the same thing. But you might ask, if everybody is doing the same thing, why doesn't everyone win? Simple answer is because they don't. And why not? Depends on your system. That's what makes it proprietary. And no one makes money just betting the point spread. The real money comes from being able to spot the games in which one team will beat the spread. That's what I do. I cherry pick the upsets."

Davidson said, "Not sure that really explains it, but I won't try to probe any deeper."

The room fell silent except for the muted sound of a jet out over the harbor on approach to SeaTac.

A few seconds later Arnold realized he'd slipped into a fantasy of being aboard that jet heading to some place far away, some place where he could begin a new, unencumbered life with no one chasing him, no one trying to steal his intellectual property, no reminders of his parents or Howard's murder. Seemed too good to be true.

But if that were to happen, where would he go?

Hawaii? Yeah, sure, where else? When he was twelve years old, his parents had taken him on a vacation to Oahu, to a hotel on Waikiki. He'd long since forgotten the name of the place, but he'd never forgotten the warm grainy sand between his toes or humid air embracing his embarrassingly white skin. To this day, the smell of coconut reminds him of suntan lotion and sepia tone memories of those few precious days, the experience long ago embedded in his memory. They were an intact family then. It was a wonderful time.

"Okay, moving on," Davidson said, breaking Arnold's train of thought. "Firouz now has your computer. Isn't this part of the dynamic now game over?"

And that was another facet he really hadn't had time to consider. So much had happened in such a compressed period of time.

"Not even close."

"Explain that."

"First of all, I doubt he can break my security."

Davidson leaned back in his desk chair and interlaced his fingers behind his head.

"Why not? I thought password busters were as plentiful as water."

Arnold laughed at that.

"Password? No offense, Mr. Davidson, but that's so old school. Nobody with any smarts and anything to protect relies on a password anymore. Why? Because you're absolutely right: they're too easily broken. I use biometric security, but even that can be broken by someone who knows their way around."

"What are you using?"

"Both right thumb print and left retinal identification. And," Arnold said with a glow of satisfaction, "if they get around that—say, by cutting off my finger—if you then don't use the right password in two tries, the hard drive self-destructs with a virus I call Revenge."

He warmed at the memory of the hours spent developing the routine. He'd written it simply as payback to anyone who did what Firouz had done tonight. The virus was never intended to be released for malicious use.

"And if those aren't enough reasons," Arnold said, "that laptop is only a workstation. The real software resides elsewhere." He decided not to mention where. In spite of Davidson being his attorney, he saw no upside to disclosing such information.

"Excuse me for asking," Davidson said, "but isn't that a bit excessive?"

Arnold couldn't help but smile.

"You mean paranoid?"

It was refreshing to see Davidson caught off guard. For once tonight someone else was feeling the sting of embarrassment.

"There is a fine line that separates paranoid from cautious," Arnold said. "You tell me where it is."

Davidson gave a concessionary grunt.

"Interesting point. Probably no different from distinguishing art from porn: all hinges on how appropriate it is." A pause. "Change of subject. Howard was your best friend?"

Was. Past tense.

He glanced down at his hands, the memory flashing back.

"Yes."

"And you saw who killed him."

The words came as more statement than question, but this time he felt obliged to answer. To claim differently would be to lie, and to not answer would carry the wrong implication.

"Yes."

"So, my obvious question is: why didn't you tell the police? Don't you want the killer arrested and locked up?"

"I do want them locked up, but..." Firouz's eyes flashed across his mind: intense lasers boring straight into him with the burn of dry ice. The moment he met the man in Starbucks, Arnold feared for his life. His words could never describe the intensity of his fear, so he simply said, "Trite as this sounds, he scared the crap out of me. If I finger him, he'll have me killed, no question about it. He's the kind of person who can get something like that done no matter if he's in or out of prison. In other words, I'm screwed regardless of what I do."

Davidson, still leaning back in his chair, listening intently, shook his head.

"I don't agree. It's always more difficult to manage people on the outside if you're locked up. Especially if he ends up in a prison for terrorists."

Well, shit, whether Davidson agreed with him didn't change facts.

"Look, here's the deal. He wants my system. I have to assume he's got someone who can break into my laptop. Fine. If they tried, it blew up in their face, so to speak. The moment that happens, it tells them what?" Being rhetorical, Arnold continued, "It tells them there really is something in there worth stealing because there's no other reason for such elaborate security. Meaning by now they're probably even more interested in getting their hands on my work. Meaning now I really am fucked. To make matters worse, Karim saw me. We looked right into each other's eyes. Meaning he knows damned well I can identify him as Howard's killer. All the more reason to want to find me." Arnold shook his head. "No, way I see it, I'm totally screwed."

Davidson was starting to say something when his phone rang.

16

DAVIDSON NUDGED THE phone a bit to see the caller ID and frowned.

"I better take this."

"No problem," Arnold said, as if his opinion meant anything.

He realized immediately it was a stupid thing to say but didn't dwell on it or try to change it. He was thankful for the break. So far this interview—if that's what it was called—was really stressing him out, coming right on the heels of the worst night of his life. He tried not to think of the sound of the gunshot, of Howie's last words, but quickly realized that trying to ignore those memories just made them all the more vivid.

Then Davidson was covering the mouthpiece, shooting him a strange look, and he realized he'd spaced out as to what was going on in the room.

"What?"

Davidson asked, "You willing to talk with an FBI agent?"

Arnold's initial reaction was to say, "Of course," thinking that if the FBI were involved it would help the police find Howard's murderers. Then, on second thought, it seemed odd for the feds to be involved in a local homicide.

Aw, shit!

An ice cube froze his gut. He nodded okay at Davidson.

Davidson leaned forward on the desk and stared at Arnold after hanging up.

"It's disconcerting that the FBI wants to interview you. Anything I need to know about? Other than your involvement with the terrorists?"

Was that sarcasm?

Arnold gave Davidson the benefit of the doubt.

"No. But that's the only thing makes any sense."

Davidson sighed and started drumming the Mount Blanc on the desk.

"I agree. But we don't know for certain yet. Still, we need to get your head straight so you can talk to them without disclosing too much."

"Why not?"

"We don't want to disclose anything important until we form a much clearer idea of what they're after and what they know for certain about you."

"Good point. Thing worrying me, is how did they zero in on me so quickly? That's making me nervous."

Davidson considered the question a moment, still drumming the desk, "As your attorney I advise you to listen to what Agent Fisher has to say but do not answer any questions until you and I have conferred in private. We'll decide jointly what you will or will not answer. Any question about this strategy? We clear on this?"

Not sure how he could make it any clearer.

"Yes."

"He called from down the street, so it should only take him a few minutes to get here. About enough time to go wring out a bladder." Then muttered, "Damned prostate."

Firouz disconnected from the call, slipped his cell back into his pants, saying, "His lawyer's name is Davidson."

He paused, mulling over what he'd just learned.

Karim asked, "What are you thinking?"

"Strange. Apparently, he told the police nothing about us."

"No?"

"I don't understand. He was questioned by a detective named

Elliott but refused to say who was in his house and why we were there. You sure he saw your face?"

"We looked straight at each other. There's no mistaking he saw me. Otherwise, why would he run like that?"

Still deep in thought, Firouz shook his head again.

"I wonder. I think I should talk with Breeze." He smiled at the false name, the hidden meaning. "Perhaps our little Jew is more fond of her than we think, or than she said."

"Are you sure of your friend's word?"

Firouz nodded.

"He's a true believer. He would never ever think of giving us false information."

Arnold wasn't exactly sure why—maybe the straight-back square-shoulder posture or the closely cropped well-groomed blond hair in addition to the way he carried the black leather attaché case—but Special Agent Gary Fisher struck him as ex-military. Efficient and serious. All business without coming across as brusque.

After Fisher showed his credentials, Davidson offered him the chair farthest from the desk and motioned Arnold to the closer one.

Even before they had completely settled in, Davidson started with, "May I ask what you wish to discuss with my client?"

Fisher shot the cuffs of his white shirt, taking his time to answer, defusing any momentum Davidson might have gained from such a direct approach.

"We're aware that Mr. Gold," with a nod toward Arnold, "has recently been in contact with people who have suspected links to a terrorist organization."

Knew it!

Arnold's gut knotted up again.

Fisher let that bit of news percolate a moment before going on to say, "Because of this, the homicide at the Gold residence earlier this evening—" with an exaggerated glance at his watch, "—correction, make that last night—piqued our interest."

Arnold shifted positions in the chair and realized his mouth was dry as dust. From the moment he laid eyes on Firouz and Karim he had suspected they might be terrorists but had discarded that thought for two reasons. Initially, because he hated to be stereotyped as a Jew, he hated to stereotype someone when meeting them for the first time. Later, as he started to buy into their story, well... in retrospect, his initial impression had been right. He was a fool to have believed them.

After a few beats Davidson asked, "And the point of this visit is?"

Fisher said, "Have a problem with allowing me to record this interview?"

Davidson pulled a yellow legal-size pad of paper closer and picked up the heavy ballpoint.

"Not a problem if I may remain in this room to freely advise my client."

"Fair enough."

Fisher balanced the attaché case on his knees, clicked open the top, pulled out a tablet computer, and activated a small recorder, which he set on the cushion next to his leg.

Fisher turned his attention to Arnold.

"Been out of town recently?"

Oh, shit.

Didn't want to lie but didn't want to answer either. He nodded for Davidson to answer.

Davidson said, "Yes, he has."

After setting the attaché case on the floor, Fisher handed Arnold the tablet.

"Recognize this man?"

The screen was filled with a cropped headshot of Firouz. The amount of background compression and blurring indicated the original picture had been shot through a high-powered telephoto lens, enlarged and cropped. Making it impossible to know if it had been taken indoors or outside. Arnold suspected the latter, not that it made a damn bit of difference. The chill in his gut quickly segued into the dull ache of earlier. He tried to swallow but his mouth was too dry to produce anything to swallow. His hands started trembling and the more he tried masking it, the worse the tremors became. Without saying a word, he handed the tablet back to Fisher and glanced at Davidson to answer for him.

Davidson asks, "Who is it you're asking about?"

Fisher flicked his finger across the tablet screen, changing the picture.

"The name on his passport is Firouz Jahandar. He works at a Las Vegas casino."

Fisher let the statement hang, as if there was more to it. Davidson tilted back his chair, began tapping his fingertips together.

"Interesting."

He too let the words hang, the interaction reminding Arnold of two professional tennis players lobbing volleys across the net, waiting for an opportunistic kill shot.

Fisher smiled at Davidson.

"I'm waiting for an answer."

"I fail to see how this relates to my client."

The pain in Arnold's gut grew more intense.

Here it comes.

"It has a lot to do with him." Fisher turned toward Arnold. "I believe Mr. Gold has more information about the homicide last night than his statement to the Seattle police indicates."

Arnold watched Davidson's expression. Damn, must be a killer poker player.

Davidson remained tilted back in the chair, still tapping his fingertips together, looking down his nose at the FBI agent.

"Huh! Interesting assumption. What makes you believe that?"

Fisher continued to address Davidson, as if Arnold was nothing more than a ventriloquist's dummy.

"Fine, then let's cut to the chase. Your client got himself into some very serious shit. Dangerous shit. He needs help, and we can give it to him providing he's cooperative."

Arnold's heart accelerated, his breath seemed to lack oxygen, certainly not enough to satisfy his air hunger. As a distraction, he stopped looking at Fisher and let his eyes wander the room at random, willing himself to remain still and act calm.

How would this meeting end? Better yet, would it?

Fisher turned to Arnold.

"Mind explaining why you registered at the Bellagio under a false name?"

Boom! Just like that.

Fisher's bluntness startled him. Or had he heard wrong?

Before he could open his mouth, Davidson interjected, "Is that an opinion, or do you have supporting proof of that allegation?"

Fisher shook his head woefully.

"Lawyers! Jesus. You guys."

Arnold swore Fisher had intended to say, "Fucking lawyers."

Fisher passed the tablet back to them, this time displaying a picture of Arnold and Breeze window shopping in the Bellagio Arcade, side by side, inspection a display of women's purses. The memory as vivid as the display.

"You were under surveillance the majority of time you were with her."

Oh my god—

"So what?" Davidson asked, still poker faced.

Having a lawyer looking out for him was worth every cent of whatever this little adventure was costing him, and he realized they had never discussed the fees. Arnold decided to let Davidson do one hundred percent of the talking. Why offer a word?

Fisher did not appear impressed by Davidson's aggressiveness.

"We have copies of your Bellagio registration under the name Toby Taylor, which we now know is not your legal name." He cocked an index finger and pointed it at Arnold like a gun. Gotcha. "Anytime a person of interest uses an alias, it perks up our interest. See where I'm headed with this?"

"So what?" Davidson was beginning to sound like an endless loop. "Guys go to Vegas all the time to get laid. No big mystery." He raised his eyebrows at Fisher. "Or perhaps that isn't the case for Federal employees anymore. So, it shouldn't surprise you that the tourist bureau banks on the slogan 'what happens in Vegas stays in Vegas.' That's the whole point."

Apparently, Fisher didn't find Davidson's sarcasm humorous.

"Yeah? Well this little working girl happens to be Firouz's wife."

Boom! Arnold almost recoiled from shock. Then again, he'd sensed some sort of connection between the two, just didn't figure...Jesus, how does it feel to know your wife is...he didn't want to think about it. The silence of the room closed in on him. He looked up to see both Davidson and Fisher staring at him.

"What?"

Fisher asked, referring to the picture of Firouz on the tablet, "You haven't answered my question. Do you recognize him?"

Davidson stood and walked between Fisher and Arnold.

"Mind if I have a few moments with my client? In private. Won't take but a few minutes."

17

"I DON'T BELIEVE you. The man must live somewhere." Firouz glared across the laminate table at Aasif, who was calmly sipping strong black tea. The diner is warm and humid, with the faint smell of Clorox and grease. Firouz also had a cup of tea in front of him but had yet to even sample it. He was too upset to enjoy it and really only ordered it as sufficient reason to be sitting there.

Aasif calmly set his cup on its saucer and patiently explained yet again, "There is no property record for this man in the city or anywhere in King County. Perhaps he rents or lives with another person. There is no phone record for a Palmer Davidson other than the one you already know of, his office. The one in the Smith Tower."

"And Gold?" Karim asked.

He was wedged into the booth with Firouz to his right and the wall flush against his left shoulder.

Both Aasif and Firouz turned to him.

"What about him?"

Karim, apparently annoyed with the question, snapped, "He could be seeing friends."

Firouz shook his head.

"So what? We are having no idea who they might be."

Aasif adds, "He was released under his lawyer's recognizance with the understanding he would be brought back immediately, so it's most likely he's with this lawyer, Davidson."

Firouz pushed out of the booth saying, "I want you to keep searching. There must be some way to find them."

He was irritated at Aasif for not finding the answers to his questions, at Karim for making idiotic suggestions, at not being free to visit a mosque so he could pray, at not having the Jew's secrets yet, at Karim's stupidity for killing the man in Gold's house.

"Where are we going?" Karim was sliding out of the booth after him. "To see what Ghayoor is finding on the copy of the Jew's computer."

Luckily Ghayoor had been smart enough to burn a copy of the hard disk before trying to break through the computer's firewall.

This time Davidson didn't sit calmly in his leather chair, tipped back, arms comfortably at his side. This time he was pacing back and forth on the Persian rug in front of his desk. He stopped to pinch the bridge of his nose before locking into Arnold's eyes.

"Why do I get the feeling you're not confiding everything to me?"

Arnold didn't know what to say. He had no idea what Davidson wanted to know. He wasn't intentionally withholding any information.

"Ask me anything you want. I'll tell you. I'm not deceiving you and I'm not withholding information. Least not that I know of. Go ahead, ask."

For a moment Davidson seemed more intent on his own thoughts than on Arnold's response.

"Just doesn't feel right, is all. We have an FBI agent out in reception looking like the cat that swallowed the canary. I know damn well he's only playing with us, seeing if we'll trip up or he can catch us in a lie, getting ready to unleash a load of government wrath on our heads. He's setting you up for something. I know he is and I hate that."

He started pacing again.

Arnold understood his point but still didn't know what to say that would alleviate the situation.

"What can I do to help?"

Davidson ignored the question, muttered, "If they knew about your involvement in the bombing, he wouldn't be here asking questions, he'd be here to take you down to their offices for questioning or to arrest you, depending on how much they know. So, it has to be something else. What?"

Davidson stepped over to the window to stare out. He absent-mindedly scratched the crown of his head and asked, "What about the gambling? Anything there I should know about? Like any involvement with organized crime? Anything?"

Arnold's stomach felt as if it were floating above his head instead of in his abdominal cavity.

"Jesus, not that I know of. I gamble, sure, you know that. That's it, end of story. What more can I tell you?"

Davidson shot him a don't-screw-with-me look.

"Anything we need to worry about far as that's concerned? Any huge debts? Owe someone who might be mobbed up? Any involvement like that you should tell me? Anyone involved in any sort of criminal activity? Anything at all you can think of?"

What the hell am I missing?

His mind drew a blank, which amped the anxiety back into flat out gut pain.

He said, "Look, here's the situation. If I say anything to him, anything at all, Firouz is going to kill me. Isn't that enough? Damned if I do, damned if I don't. Christ!"

Both eyes clamped tightly shut, he wished that somehow, he could magically be transported back to a time before Breeze entered his life. Either that or to make this situation miraculously vanish.

"I don't think you have much choice, Arnold." Davidson's voice grew closer, but Arnold kept his eyes shut. "Look at it this way: by now Firouz probably wants you dead regardless of what you tell anyone, FBI or not. You thought of that part of it?"

When Arnold didn't answer, he said, "Why not improve your chances and tell Fisher everything you know about the murder? And I mean everything."

And this is my lawyer talking?

"Because I'll probably have to end up admitting my involvement in the bombing. Then what happens? I end up in Gitmo or worse?"

Arnold kept his eyes clamped shut and a palm pressing hard against each temple. He tried to think but found that his gut pain and anxiety were keeping him from concentrating. Besides, Davidson was asking impossible questions.

Davidson scoffed.

"By continuing to stonewall, you simply incriminate yourself more. Face it, sooner or later he's going to find out. You need to tell him something, and that's best done now instead of later. Why not simply admit you hired Breeze for a few nights of sex and let it go at that? If they saw you meet Firouz and Karim, say she just wanted to introduce a friend. What's the big deal? Gambling and prostitution are fair game in that state."

Davidson was right: he saw very few options at this point.

"Okay, I'll tell him, but you screen the questions first. Deal?"

Davidson reached for the doorknob.

"Deal. I'll have him come back in now."

Arnold slumped in the chair, right hand splayed against his abdomen, the left arm at his side feeling strangely useless. He felt wasted, having given Fisher a detailed accounting of every event from the moment he left the pizzeria with the pizza until he ran back inside the place yelling "call 911." When he reached the part about Karim coming at him from the front room of the house, Fisher stopped him long enough to show him another picture on the tablet, this one of Karim.

Fisher asked, "This him?"

Arnold nodded.

"It is."

Fisher asked, "Just so we're straight, you saw both Firouz and Karim in the house?"

Had he said that? Now that he thought about it...

"No. Come to think of it, I never really saw Firouz. Just recognized his voice when I was in the alley, wedged down between bins, the fence behind me, holding my breath, praying Karim wouldn't see me."

Jesus, he couldn't remember having been more scared.

"But you're certain it was his voice?"

As he weighed his answer, another question popped into

consciousness, one that had come to mind earlier but had been quickly squashed by other, more pressing thoughts.

"How did you know?"

"Know what?" Fisher asked.

And now the stomach pain was trumped by a chill of paranoia. He leaned forward to hug his knees so he'd be doing something other than sitting there pressing his gut. He suspected he knew Fisher's answer but wanted to hear him voice it.

"You contacted me within, what, six hours of the shooting? How did you know it involved the Iranians?"

Fisher sucked a tooth for a moment as if weighing his answer.

"Wasn't hard once your name popped up on our computers. Since we had them under surveillance, we knew they came to Seattle. We also knew you live here. Our sources claim Firouz hasn't been to Seattle before. Not all that difficult to piece together, if you think about it." He paused a moment, changing tone. "Let me ask you something: you willing to come down to the Federal Building and give a sworn statement covering everything you just told me?"

Boom.

Arnold was back to holding his stomach again, wishing for a chug of Maalox or something to lessen the discomfort.

He knew Davidson and Fisher were waiting for him to answer, could feel their eyes lasing into him, but he kept staring at the maroon and blue Persian rug, unable to squelch the image of Karim targeting him for a kill, the segment playing over and over again, to the point he couldn't make a decision.

Way he saw it, if he signed a statement confirming their involvement in Howard's murder, he'd be required to testify in person in court sometime in the future. Meaning Firouz and his team would know exactly where he would be and what time he'd be there, making it impossible to hide when he arrived at and left the courthouse.

And if they didn't hit him in Federal court, they could follow him as he left. Unless, of course, the FBI placed him in the witness protection program. In which case he'd still need to physically appear in court. Sure, it might be suicide for the guy sent to hit him, but suicide seemed to be a popular weapon of choice these days for terrorists. And if he didn't identify them, they'd never know he hadn't, meaning they would still want him dead. Regardless of any of these issues, they still wanted his system. In essence, it boiled down to no matter what he chose, he was totally and irrevocably screwed.

"Well?" Fisher asked. "What's it going to be?"

Arnold shot a pleading glance at Davidson, handing the decision off to him, hoping his lawyer was smart enough to come up with a reasonable stalling tactic. Whatever that might be.

Davidson cleared his throat.

"My client is under a great deal of duress at the moment. He witnessed his best friend's savage, senseless murder only to narrowly escape a brutal execution at the hands of alleged terrorists. Since then he's been under ceaseless interrogation by police and now a Special Agent of the Federal Bureau of Investigation. I think the poor young man has been subjected to more than enough for one night, don't you? Why not allow him to recover and refresh himself so we may discuss this sometime in the future—perhaps tomorrow—once we're all a bit more rested. I suggest that unless you intend to charge him with a crime, this interview needs to be considered concluded. For the record, my client has willingly answered the majority of your questions, and I am absolutely certain he will be happy to answer more of them at a future, mutually agreed upon, time, but to summarize what he stated tonight, he visited Las Vegas for the sole purpose of obtaining sex and to gamble at the casinos. This concludes his statement."

Arnold turned to Fisher, but the man was staring at him, ignoring Davidson's words.

Fisher pointedly asked, "You're not going to answer my question?"

Arnold shook his head.

"You heard my lawyer. Perhaps another time."

"All right, then, we'll call it a night. But let me warn you that by refusing to provide a signed statement I consider you're aiding and abetting Firouz Jahandar and his terrorist organization, and this doesn't leave me much choice other than to make you subject to our ongoing investigation. Understand what I just told you?"

Not really. He just wanted the damned interview over.

Firouz pointed across Second Avenue to a white thirty-eight-story building, its highest section capped with a pyramidal roof.

"That should be it, the white one."

He knew nothing about the building other than its name. Odd and old looking, but, knowing nothing about architecture, either, he had no idea what style it would be called, if anything. The tallest segment with his peaked roof reminded him vaguely of a minaret.

Next to him, shielding his eyes from the streetlights, Karim studied the weird looking structure, but Firouz wasn't about to wait for him and started across the deserted street against a red light. Karim hurried to catch up.

Firouz inspected the heavy brass and glass front doors for a moment before slipping on leather gloves. Moving next to the glass he peered into the lobby of white marble walls and floors, polished brass elevator doors, large fica plants at the end of the hall to the elevator banks. More importantly, a small desk partially blocked the entrance to the hall.

At the moment it was not manned, but a cup of coffee sat on the left corner and he was sure he could see steam rising. He pulled a door handle but, as suspected, found it locked.

Without a word to Karim, he headed down Second to Yesler, east a half block, and was in the alley at the back of the building. Just as he turned into the alley, he heard a loud metal bang, stopped, held up a hand for his brother to do likewise, and peered ahead. An older man in gray overalls was lifting a black Hefty bag into a green dumpster, an open back door of the building casting light across litter strewn asphalt. Job finished, he slammed the lid, pulled a pack of cigarettes from his shirt pocket, and lit up.

Firouz put his lips to Karim's ear, whispered, "Wait here."

Then he was moving fast, back around the front of the building, north along Second to James, then east again, entering the alley from the north. Slowly now, he moved down the relatively darkened passage, staying as close to the wall as possible until he was directly behind the end of another dumpster. Peering over the top, he was now perhaps ten feet from the janitor. He glanced at the asphalt, saw a discarded Starbucks cup and picked it up and flattened it. Then looked for Karim at the end of the alley but couldn't see him.

A minute later, the workman glanced at his watch, flicked the cigarette against the opposite wall, wheeled his cart back through the door. Firouz was at the doorway just as the metal fire door swung shut. He slipped a flattened cup between jamb and latch only far enough to keep it from locking and prayed to Allah the janitor either didn't notice or wouldn't be security-conscious enough to make sure the latch seated.

He waited two minutes, whispered, "Karim!"

Then his brother was at his side.

Slowly he opened the door, only a crack at first to listen to the hollow sounds of an empty building. Then a bit more. No one around.

Quickly they slipped into the building and shut the door.

Allen Wyler

18

DAVIDSON STOOD AT the front door to his office suite watching
Fisher walk toward the elevator bank, making sure he didn't stop
outside, perhaps try to eavesdrop on any subsequent conversation.
Arnold heard the elevator ding and, moments later, the door rattle shut.
With a nod of approval, Davidson shut his door, turned to study Arnold
a few beats. He was pacing again.

"I don't understand why you didn't agree to simply give him the
statement. You sat here and admitted Karim shot Howard. Why not put
it on record?"

Davidson's tone was simultaneously questioning and accusatory.
Arnold watched him prop his butt on the corner of his desk with arms
across his chest, obviously unhappy with him.

If he knew the answer for sure, he'd certainly explain.

"It's a couple of things. Mostly, I'm afraid of them. Firouz more
than the FBI. You know that. We discussed it. If I agree to testify you
might as well paint a bull's eye on my chest. Besides, if you get right
down to it, which any good defense lawyer will, I didn't actually see who
pulled the trigger. I heard the gun go off. Period."

Davidson scoffed at that.

"That's one of the lamest excuses I've heard, Arnold. You just told
Fisher you walked in your house, heard Howard yell, heard the gunshot,
and then Karim came at you with a gun. Seems pretty damn obvious to
me."

Davidson pushed off the desk, dropped into one of the two leather couches in his office reception area. "Besides, if I were you, given your choices, I'd rather have the FBI be on my side than against me. You heard what Fisher said: they're going to investigate you. Which begs the question one more time: there anything, anything at all, you wouldn't want them digging up? Think carefully before you answer."

Arnold stopped at the corner of the desk Davidson had just vacated and leaned forward, hands flat on the top.

"You don't understand because you've never been face to face with Firouz. If you had you'd know why he scares hell out of me. There's something pure evil in that man. Shit!"

Another spasm of gut pain cut him off in mid breath.

"I understand all that. You've made that point repeatedly. But the thing is, if he's that much of a threat, why not at least attempt to put him behind bars?" Davidson's hand shot up before Arnold could answer. "Yes, I know what you've said, you're worried that even from prison he can reach out to you. I understand all that, but I also have to tell you, if I were in your shoes I wouldn't go down so easily, at least not without a fight. Granted, you're up to your neck in some serious issues, but at least fight to crawl out of it. Make sure the Jahandars feel the pain, too."

Arnold was leaning on his hands, his mind working on two issues simultaneously: a response to Davidson as well as a new idea, one that just popped up in consciousness.

"No, it's not enough to tell Fisher what he's after. That won't be the end of it. I have to find a way to finish this with the Jahandars completely, and I mean end it. I have to find a way he's never ever going to be a threat to me again."

Arnold's vehemence and tone seemed to catch his lawyer's attention.

Tense and concerned, he sat up and snapped, "What the hell is that supposed to mean?"

Arnold started pacing again, the gut pain less now that his mind was mulling over the idea.

He repeated, "What did it sound like? I got myself into this mess. I need to find my own way out."

Allen Wyler

"Oh, very illuminating." Davidson sighed, stifled a yawn, knuckled his eyes. "Look, let's take a step back and a deep breath. Obviously, we're at a standstill—at least it is for me—for the night." He decked his watch and amended that. "Correction. Change that to morning. We both need some rest. But one more thing before we pack it in: I need to ask you—and think carefully before you answer—is there any further connection between you and Firouz or his organization you haven't mentioned? Anything at all the FBI might uncover that they can use against you?"

With a dismissive wave, Arnold said. "You're kidding, right?"

"No, not at all. Just doing my job." Davidson pushed up off the couch. "I believe you. Now let's get out of here, go get some sleep."

This time Arnold gave a sarcastic snort. "No way I can sleep now. Not with this memory of Howie…"

He suspected that even when he could finally sleep, he would suffer nightmares, probably for a long time. This what PTSD's like?

Davidson reached behind the door separating the reception room from his office and came away with a raincoat.

"Need a coat? I have an extra one if you do."

A coat? What for?

He had no idea where he was going or if he was going anywhere. If Davidson was shutting down his office for the night, maybe he should just wander the streets and ponder a way out of this mess, to imagine what Howie felt in those seconds before dying. And if it was cold outside, maybe he should embrace the discomfort until he became hypothermic and numb. Maybe he'd stumble across a group of homeless huddled under an overpass, stay there long enough to drop off the face of the earth. He suddenly craved the idea of physical suffering as a way to assuage the guilt of responsibility for last night's senseless carnage. He ignored Davidson's question, now preferring to remain alone to think and suffer. And the more he considered it, what he really wanted was for God to suddenly strike him dead because that seemed the only way to rid himself of his terrible guilt.

Please God, strike me dead right now. No fuss, no muss, just zap, lights out.

146

Davidson patted his shoulder then held out his hand, offering him something.

"Come on. Believe me, things always seem better in the morning, no matter how dismal they may seem at the moment."

Davidson's palm offered a small, salmon-colored pill.

"What is it?"

"Xanax. Go ahead, take it."

Davidson dropped the pill in Arnold's hand before opening the hall door.

"This way," Davidson pointed the opposite direction from the elevators. "We'll take the stairs. Just in case."

Just in case? Of what?

Was this what his life was becoming? A hunted man in constant fear of discovery?

He examined the pill in hand. He'd never taken Xanax but believed it was used to treat anxiety. Might not be such a bad idea. Tossed it into his mouth and dry swallowed as he hurried to keep up with Davidson, who by now was almost to the end of the hall where the green EXIT sign glowed above the door.

No sooner had the exit door shut than the second west elevator dinged, and the light above lit up. Firouz stepped into the hall, looked right, then left, right, saw the frosted glass pane of the office door with *Palmer Davidson, JD* painted on it. No light shone through the glass. To be certain there wasn't another office in use in another portion of the office, Firouz put his ear to the glass and listened. Nothing. He stood in front of the elevators, working through their next move.

The streets, deserted this time of morning, would soon accommodate a trickle of commuters as the flow would rapidly grow into Seattle's notorious morning rush hour congestion. With the car radio off and Davidson not talking, Arnold heard only the soft thrum of road noise. The quiet in the car interior amplified his thoughts, a series of disjointed snippets, all fighting for dominance.

Things like: *if I was stupid enough to allow Breeze to learn my identity, what other stupid things have I done?*

What else did the Jahandars know about his personal life? Martini lubricated lips greased his willingness to satisfy her rapt interest in him, never once suspecting she might be obtaining intelligence for a terrorist cell.

Jesus, how nuts is that? Never in a million years...

He thought of Howie's parents and of Rachael, and was overcome with more guilt. Did they know yet? If so, how had they learned? He should've been the one to break the news, not a detached, unfamiliar face or an expeditious late-night phone call.

Pain gut-punched him again.

"Aw, Jesus, I need to call them."

He began searching his pocket for his cell and realized he was sitting in Davidson's car and it was still back on the kitchen table.

Davidson grabbed his shoulder.

"Hey, calm down. We're not calling anyone this morning."

He tried to shrug free, but his lawyer's grip was strong.

"No, you don't understand. It's my fault. I need to apologize, tell them how sorry I am."

He grabbed the door handle, but Davidson remained a step ahead of him by punching the kiddie lock.

Davidson curbed the car but left it idling.

"Settle down, Arnold. You don't need to do a goddamn thing right now but get your act together. Certainly, you're not going to telephone a soul until you're safe and this mess is completely finished. Think about it. Time to let the dust settle. Understand?"

Another wave of anxiety rolled over the effects of the Xanax. He wanted to throw open the door and run with no specific direction or destination, just run as far from all this insanity as humanly possible. "But what if Firouz targets them as a way to get to me? No, I need to warn them."

Davidson was almost shouting now.

"No, Arnold, listen to me...you listening?"

His mind was racing back through his conversations with Breeze, trying to remember every fact about his personal life he'd mentioned, wondering if he'd said Howard's last name? If Firouz were trying to find ways...

Davidson physically shook his shoulder hard.

"Listen to me, goddamnit!"

The physical movement jerked Arnold's attention back to the car and he realized they were illegally parked in the bus zone across the street from Macy's, the engine idling, Davidson sitting half turned in his seat, hand out, offering something.

"Come on, Arnold, here, take another one of these puppies. Think you need it."

For a moment Arnold stared at the open palm and oblong salmon pill, thinking, maybe it's not such a bad idea. Maybe he does need to get his act together before he stumbles through more stupid mistakes. As if he hadn't fucked up enough for one day.

He accepted the second Xanax.

Before he had it to his mouth, Davidson said, "Chew this one, it'll absorb faster that way."

He did as instructed, the pill tasting dry and slightly bitter, then rubbed the tip of his tongue across his gums and roof of his mouth, making sure to catch all the crumbs. He swallowed.

"Why do you have these with you? Have some sort of problem?"

Davidson laughed at that and didn't seem to be in any hurry to start driving again. But on the other hand, probably not too many busses were running this time of morning. Soon, though.

"For exactly this situation," Davidson answered. "You're not the only client who's had an emotional meltdown on me."

"Now listen to me," Davidson continued after a momentary pause. "You're not calling anyone tonight, especially not in the shape you're in."

It dawned on Arnold that they were heading someplace. Where? He had no idea.

"Where we going?"

Davidson checked the rearview mirror for oncoming traffic before pulling away from the curb.

"To my place. Make sure you get some sleep so we can map out a strategy to deal with the situation. The Xanax will help you calm down. Later today, once you're in better mental shape, we can start figuring out your best course of action. I think you mentioned you don't have family. That true?"

"Yes."

The admission made him feel sadly alone and isolated, especially now with Howard gone.

As if reading his thought, Davidson said, "Point is, if you don't have strong connections to staying in Seattle, we might be wise to consider exploring a possible deal with the FBI: your sworn testimony for a spot in the witness protection program. See, we have options available you haven't considered yet. Don't worry, we'll get you out of this. Trust me. It'll all work out. But for right now, you need to calm down and take a deep breath before doing anything."

Easy for him to say.

He'd never been face to face with Firouz. But Davidson's words did trigger a new idea.

The double dose of tranquilizer was really doing a number on his brain by the time Davidson took the Mercedes through a left turn off of Queen Anne Avenue onto a tree lined residential street on the south side of Queen Anne Hill. The street, narrow to begin with, was further constricted by cars parked to either side, leaving barely enough room for one vehicle to navigate safely.

Now slumped against the soft leather bucket seat, head lolling side to side, Arnold blankly watched vehicles slide past, wondering what it might be like to live in a neighborhood like this featuring such incredible panoramic downtown views. Expensive, for sure. Not that his neighborhood, Greenlake, was considered low-rent by any stretch of the imagination, but you paid more when views—especially like these—were involved. Money. That's what life is all about. Money: the root cause of this disaster.

To his surprise, his gut pain was gone now and his mind felt like it had been flattened by a steamroller, leaving him emotionally drained and unimaginably sad, resigned to a new life that would never again be as carefree and innocent as 24 hours ago. Nothing would ever be the same. Even if he was, by some miracle, able to survive and rid himself of Firouz and this Godawful mess, life as he knew it was over. This saddened him. The car turned left again, nosing into a short, downward sloping driveway to a large stucco cube with unlit windows and a garage door the same beige as the house, leaving an initial impression that the concrete driveway dead ended at the house. Davidson pressed a button at the base of the rearview mirror and the garage door began slowly rising, exposing a one car garage illuminated by harsh overhead lights. Soon as Davidson set the parking brake Arnold could hear the groan as the heavy door began lowering behind them. The garage walls were painted off white, the floor finished in a shiny epoxy made to resemble gray granite and clean enough to worry Arnold about dirtying them.

He'd never seen such an immaculate, shiny garage.

They opened their doors almost simultaneously, and as Arnold stepped out, he noticed the back-lit Mercedes Benz name along the bottom door sill.

Cool. Nice touch.

Shutting his door, Arnold asked, "What about your wife? Will my being here disturb her?"

What made me assume he's married?

Davidson came around the front fender.

"I'm divorced, so I live here alone. Long story not worth the time to tell." He approached Arnold. "Excuse me."

Arnold realized he was blocking access to what looked like a shoulder- height intercom grill with a keypad and blinking red LED. He stepped aside to give Davidson access.

Davidson pressed the single button just below the grill.

A synthesized voice responded with, "State your name, please."

Davidson leaned forward a bit. "Palmer Davidson."

A brief pause was followed by a metallic click from the door. Davidson pushed it open, the door movement automatically turning on interior lights. The lawyer stood aside for Arnold to enter.

"Access is controlled by, among other things, voice recognition," he said as Arnold passed, but Arnold had that already figured out.

Arnold stopped short, thought: what if Firouz knows I'm here and they're waiting?

Part of him realized this thought was over-the-top-paranoid.

Still...

Sensing his wariness, Davidson said, "It's safe. Believe me. As a criminal defense lawyer, I'm hyper concerned about some wacko gunning for me. As a result, I've become an expert on home security. No one but my closest friends know where I live. My property records are even under an assumed name, so see, we have a few things in common, Mr. *Taylor*."

The interior was as minimalist contemporary as the outside. The garage access entered a kitchen of stainless-steel appliances, slate gray granite counters with matching island, soft white walls, handle less European-style cabinets, and a slate gray polished concrete floor. The kitchen flowed into the living room area, providing an expansive feel. The far—south—wall consisted of floor-to-ceiling glass with two sets of sliders to a balcony with a million-dollar view of downtown Seattle, the harbor, and the Space Needle.

Arnold stood in the kitchen, gob smacked by the view, thinking, *Wow, wouldn't be hard to fall in love with a place like this. Someday...*

Davidson draped his suit coat over the back of a bar stool, unbuttoned his cuffs, loosened his tie, palm-wiped his face, and uttered a soft sigh while taking in the view.

"Much as I see this, I never tire of it. Makes the long hours worth it."

He pointed, said, "You'll take my office. It's this way."

Davidson disappeared into another room. Arnold followed. This one featured the same killer view of downtown. Arnold suspected the kitchen, and this small study formed the entire width of the house. Wood walls, same polished concrete floor flowing in from the kitchen, a small desk with a white Mac. Davidson hit a button and down came a Murphy bed craftily hidden behind wall panels, so well disguised you wouldn't realize its existence unless you were shown.

"There's a guest bathroom just off the hall you can use to wash up. I'll put out towels for you."

Arnold couldn't take his eyes off a vertically arching tube of about nine inches extending from an egg-shaped base.

"What is it?"

Davidson chuckled.

"A phone." He picked it up and handed it to him. "It's a Bang & Olufson Beocom 2. The design is now considered old, but I love their work."

After taking a moment to admire the craftsmanship, Arnold returned the phone, then stood in the hall admiring the interior. This was the kind of house he wanted to own someday, but he hadn't realized it until now.

Then Davidson was handing him some towels, saying, "Better try to get some sleep now. The Xanax should help. I suspect we'll have a lot of work to do later today. A lot of work."

Curled up on his right side, Arnold gazed out at multicolor city lights, the sky well into the first paling shades of dawn. He doubted sleep would come, but the double dose of Xanax had subdued his hyperactive brain, for which he was extremely grateful.

He knew Davidson had been right to insist they unwind before attempting to sort through the issues and map a strategy for dealing with this mess. Last night had been more horrible than any nightmare imaginable. He thought about how, at this very moment as he lay snug in bed, Howard's cold lifeless body undoubtedly lay stretched out on a steel gurney in the King County morgue.

And as Howard awaited autopsy, Arnold was actively hunted by terrorists.

How the hell do you deal with such perverse twists of fate?

He had no idea and at the moment was not able to even attempt to think clearly. There was, however, one thing he did know: the FBI and the witness protection program could never resolve his dilemma. There was only one person in this world who could accomplish that: Arnold Gold. Meaning it remained his responsibility to find a way to destroy Firouz.

Once that was finished, he could begin to construct a new life.

19

DAVIDSON AND ARNOLD sat at the kitchen counter with thick white ceramic mugs inscribed with the green Starbucks mermaid logo in front of them. Once again, his lawyer had him describe, minute by minute, the events of the previous night, clarifying even the minutest details, jotting notes, asking questions. He opened his mouth to ask another question when his cell rang.

After a quick glance at caller ID, Davidson muttered, "Better take this."

As Davidson talked, Arnold sat back to let his eyes wander over the city view, but instead of concentrating on the sights his mind began toying with possible ways of dealing with the Jahandars. Several options came to mind, but no one of them seemed any more likely to succeed than any other. What he needed was a plan that would destroy the terrorists while simultaneously shaking the FBI off his back, but he just couldn't figure out exactly how that might work with minimal risk of failure. Whatever he came up with had better be bullet proof. Then a thought hit: what if he were to die in the process? Wouldn't that resolve everything? Of all the options, this one held the most promise. But how could he do that?

For now, however, this would be the core of Plan A. Davidson interrupted his thoughts with, "Tell me about your finances."

Arnold realized his lawyer was off the phone now and talking to him. Once again, he had to think a moment to retrieve the question.

Where the hell had that subject came from?

"I've told you everything there is to tell. There anything in particular you want to know?"

Davidson started drumming his Mont Blanc on the note pad.

"How much you make in a year?"

Good question. Now, thinking it over, he realized he never kept track. Money came in and money went out for various bills and expenses. He could probably come up with a ballpark figure but couldn't cite a specific number with any accuracy.

"Tell you the truth, I'm not really sure. Enough to get by on, why?"

Frowning now, Davidson asked, "Mean to tell me you don't have a figure? Think back to last year's tax forms and the line titled 'adjusted gross income.'"

A queasy feeling bloomed in his gut.

"Never really looked all that closely at my tax form."

Well, sort of the truth.

No, don't kid yourself, not even close to the truth.

Davidson now appeared clearly puzzled.

"Why? An accountant does your taxes?"

"No, not really. Why do you ask?"

"That was Fisher on the phone. He wants us back in his office right now. He's charging you with income tax evasion." Silence, then, "Just so there're no surprises, you have been paying income tax, correct?"

Boom.

Aw, Christ.

"Uh... not exactly."

Davidson flipped the pen in the air, caught it on the way down.

"Oh, boy, not at all?"

"No."

"Just what we needed."

Fisher shut the door to the interrogation room and handed Arnold a two-page document and Bic ballpoint.

"It's a consent to record this interview. Sign it."

Davidson nodded for him to sign, so he did, and then slid the paper back across the table to the FBI agent. Fisher folded the paper, slipped it into the breast pocket of his suit coat. For several seconds the FBI agent studied Arnold with an expression that was making him even more nervous than when he walked in.

"Here's what we know about you, Gold. You're twenty-three years old, single, and living in what used to be your parents' home. You have no sibs and no other relatives that we could determine, so it appears you're all alone. Your parents managed their own small jewelry store. Five years ago, they were apparently robbed and, during the commission of that crime, were shot to death with a small caliber handgun. The store inventory was never recovered nor adequately covered by insurance. There was a still two years of lease in effect on the store at the time." Fisher paused to look from Davidson to Arnold, back to Davidson. "Either of you want to add anything?"

Davidson nodded to Arnold to answer.

"No."

Fisher looked like a gambler laying down four aces.

"Good, because I know this information is accurate. In addition to the store debt, the house was mortgaged to the hilt. Apparently, your parents leveraged the mortgage to start the business. Correct?"

Arnold shrugged.

"I guess."

"That mean a yes?"

"Yes."

"What I'm laying a foundation for," Fisher continued, "is that you inherited major debt at a time in your life when, as far as we can determine, and as far as Social Security records go, you weren't employed. Still aren't, for that matter. Have I overlooked anything?"

Arnold glanced at Davidson, who nodded at Fisher.

"Continue please."

"Point of this little exercise is, I find it extremely interesting that you not only paid off the house mortgage and settled the jewelry store debt, but in addition you also settled a few other outstanding debts your parents managed to accumulate."

Another round of glances between Fisher, Davidson, and Arnold.

"Your folks didn't have life insurance. Basically, every cent of their assets was tied up in the business."

Arnold was stunned.

How did they accumulate so much information so quickly?

Because they're the feds, stupid.

He didn't say a word.

"What's even more intriguing," Fisher continued, "is apparently you now have a half-million dollars invested in a discount brokerage account." He raised his eyebrows. "And guess what? You still don't have any obvious employment, and you're not a student. So, Mr. Gold, the big question is: where did you—and do you—get your money?"

Davidson cleared his throat.

"Just what, may I ask, are you suggesting?"

Fisher slowly turned to him.

"I'm not suggesting anything, not yet, but I do know one thing for certain: Your client has managed to come up with a substantial sum of money without any identifiable source of income. Don't you find this fact extremely interesting? I sure as hell do."

Davidson gave an almost imperceptible headshake at Arnold: don't say a word.

Fisher held up a finger.

"One possibility, of course—considering that the store inventory was never recovered and the security system had been defeated—is that the robbery could've been an inside job. To put it more bluntly, it's crossed my mind that Mr. Gold could've easily orchestrated the theft and fenced the inventory. But that's neither here nor there."

Arnold was struck speechless. How could Fisher suggest such a thing? Davidson was on his feet now, livid, pounding the desk.

"Are you accusing my client of murdering and robbing his parents? Because that, sir, is egregiously offensive and slanderous."

Pretty gutsy of his lawyer, Arnold thought, considering that they hadn't been able to discuss this issue yet.

Fisher sat back in his chair, smirking, digging something from his left eye, a granule of protein perhaps from fatigue, not showing the slightest intimidation from the lawyer's outburst. He flicked the something off the tip of his finger.

"Calm down, Davidson. I haven't accused anyone of anything. Every word so far is purely hypothetical. I'm simply stating the obvious scenario any investigator would consider. I haven't a clue who committed the robbery and murder, but the one thing I do know for certain is your client, Mr. Gold, hasn't paid one goddamn penny in income tax. Ever."

Davidson raised his eyebrows at Arnold as if to say this was the point of his earlier questions, that he knew Arnold wasn't divulging something important and here they were being blindsided with it. Davidson slowly turned to Fisher but said nothing.

Arnold was struggling to keep from lunging across the room to strangle Fisher for even thinking he might be instrumental in his parents' deaths. He remembered too clearly the events of that morning, of being called out of class and walked to the principal's office where a gray-haired school counselor with a compassionate face broke the news. He was a senior in high school, yet they were treating him as if he was a child. Shocked and numb, he sat in the small, overheated office smelling faintly of orange peels and damp wool, thinking this had to be some kind of sick joke. But the woman—he couldn't remember her name—seemed so serious and so compassionate that he kept telling himself it had to be true.

Later, when Howard's parents showed up to take him to their house, where he stayed until things settled down, he gradually let the reality seep into consciousness. For the next several weeks he tried to sleep in Howard's room in the spare bed while he processed the irrevocable non-negotiable change his life had just taken. Eventually he was able to convince Howard's parents to allow him to return home, and that he was sufficiently prepared to stay there alone. They finally consented to let him return home but only if an adult—usually one of them—checked on him every day for a few hours to make sure he was eating and wearing clean clothes and all the other things a teenager should have. Howard stayed over a lot in those first few weeks.

"Are you okay?" Rachael asks, deep concern reflecting from her eyes. They

sit in the Weinsteins' TV room, a football game on—he isn't tracking—with the entire family watching, trying their best to make Arnold feel at home. But it isn't working very well because he seriously wonders if life is even worth caring anymore. Even being here with Rachael doesn't mean anything now.

She takes his hand in hers and holds it. Not tightly, not loosely. Just perfectly. Soft, warm, caring, the human contact flowing into him, warming a very cold feeling he hasn't been able to describe or comprehend. It's just there, chilling him in spite of any number of blankets or hot showers. He's never missed anyone like he misses he parents. Not even when he got so damn homesick those first days at camp, when he cried himself to sleep on the top bunk, the other boys sniggering about it unabashedly.

It was in that moment he really understood the meaning of death.

Many a night since then he spent on his back, staring at the shadowy ceiling, wondering who'd committed the crime. He suspected—as did the police—the itinerant who'd been hired to wash the shop's windows, but the police were never successful in tracking him down. A point Fisher either purposely elected to exclude or, more likely, didn't know about.

Fisher seemed satisfied to have the income tax revelation and accusation weigh on their minds before pressing his attack. He finally broke the silence with, "In addition to the tax issue, we have evidence that your client associates with members of a suspected terrorist group. Can you finally appreciate where this discussion is headed?"

Davidson gave an overly dramatic sigh.

"What exactly is your objective in calling this meeting?"

Fisher continued to lean back in his chair, peering down his nose at them, a study of supreme confidence.

"For starters, how about your client giving me an accurate statement, one for the record. Once that's agreed to, we can talk about developing an understanding."

Red-faced, Davidson said, "I need to discuss this with my client first. In private."

Way the conversation was going—back and forth exclusively between Fisher and Davidson—he might as well be down at Starbucks enjoying a latte.

With Fisher out of the room and the door closed, Davidson leaned in close.

"Is he correct about the taxes?"

Arnold blew a long breath and nodded, feeling guilt upon guilt layering over him like thick coats of paint.

Davidson didn't flinch.

"Okay. What about the robbery?"

"Hell no!"

He resented the question. Anyone who knew him during the family's lifetime knew how much he loved them.

"What kind of person would do such a thing? To his own parents? My God."

Should've stopped at a drug store on the way here for a pack of Tums, because the pain was intensifying again, and he had nothing for it.

"You'd be surprised what people do when it comes to money. Hey, hey," Davidson shook Arnold's shoulder, "slow down your breathing. You're hyperventilating."

Arnold couldn't sit still, so he stood up. He decided pacing wouldn't help either, so, just to do something, he bent over and touched his toes and held that position while slowly counting to twenty, then straightened up, the move making his head spin.

Davidson waited for him to settle down before, "I prefer not to give clients ultimatums, but I'm giving you one now: tell Fisher everything you know about everything we talked about—gambling, the embassy bombing, all of it—or find yourself a new attorney. We absolutely clear on this?"

Arnold sucked an audible breath and nodded.

"Sounds like you're not giving me a choice in the matter."

Davidson went stone cold serious.

"You do have the choice. Full disclosure or a new lawyer, your choice."

Arnold looked up at the ceiling, dreading what he had to do. Embarrassing and self-incriminating as this would be, he feared losing Davidson more than any FBI repercussion. It left him little choice in the matter.

"Okay. Just don't leave me now."

Davidson stood there looking at the kid. What a mess. He felt palpable anger build inside. Hated being lied to by a client, especially over something as major as the tax evasion. Was Gold so stupid to believe that wouldn't be one of the first things the feds checked out? That was the question, wasn't it? Was the kid so far into his own world that the outside seemed irrelevant to him? Well, he intended to sort this out, and if the kid was a manipulator, he'd drop him as a client and do it in a heartbeat. His practice was prospering well enough that he didn't have to scrounge for work, especially some computer genius who might think themselves above those less digitally suave. So, for the moment, he said nothing to Gold.

In answer to Fisher's question, Davidson said, "Yes, he will make a positive identification of both Firouz and Karim, but in return we expect Mr. Gold to be placed in the witness protection program."

News to Arnold. Although they'd briefly discussed that possibility, it seemed like years ago and only as a hypothetical. Made sense. In a way. Yet a part of him knew he could never rest comfortably relying on some federal bureaucrat and a government computer file to maintain his new identity. Especially in view of the more recent self-anointed Keepers of Freedom who felt their moral duty was to disseminate classified or sensitive information regardless of employment agreements: Julian Assange and Edward Snowden served as prime examples. In addition, witnesses' true names and whereabouts were stored in a computer disk and no computer on earth was completely impervious to unintended penetration of information leakage. No, he would never rely on the WPP. If he were ever to safely extricate himself from this mess, it would have to be up to him and him alone.

Fisher answered Davidson with, "I—meaning the bureau—doesn't have the authority to negotiate the WPP. Justice handles all such offers. I'll talk to my contact but can't make any agreement until I have their thumbs up. Having just said that, I'll also say it's a very good chance they'll agree."

Davidson shrugged.

Fisher asked, "What about motive? Why's a person like Firouz Jahandar coming after a guy like Arnold Gold? Explain that one to me."

Davidson's turn to smile.

"My client will be able answer that. Once we're guaranteed protection."

Fisher yawned, covering his mouth with a hand.

"I'll take your word for it, but let's be honest here, we have a huge problem. For the sake of argument, say he fingers the Jahandars. As things presently stand, SPD doesn't have a shred of evidence that verifies either of the brothers was in his house. Ever. None of the neighbors saw or heard a thing—no car out in front, nobody or nothing suspicious— except the neighbor on the property to the south reports his dog might've heard something about the time the incident occurred and he let him out the back to investigate. But again, he heard and saw nothing unusual. On top of that, there was no sign of forced entry. Where I'm going to with this is, we need some supporting evidence to back your client's story, something to prove they were actually in the house at the time of the murder," now looking at Arnold. "Otherwise, any defense lawyer worth his salt is going to argue the brothers were in another part of town at the time this went down."

Arnold nodded for his lawyer to answer.

Davidson smiled again.

"We have solid and sufficient evidence to prove Mr. Gold's account of events."

This appeared to catch Fisher's attention.

"Yeah? What might that be?"

"My client's home is equipped with a state-of-the-art security system, complete with a motion-activated video feed from outside cameras covering both the front and back areas. Although we haven't had time to actually view those recordings, they should clearly document the brothers' arrival. The high-def video, by the way, is time stamped and good enough to read a license plate at 100 feet."

Fisher's face lit up in a broad smile.

"Then I'll—"

Davidson interrupted him.

162

"Just so you know, before you get any ideas of removing or accessing the evidence prior to any negotiations with Justice, the only equipment physically on the property are the recorder and cameras. That actual video is stored on a cloud and only Mr. Gold has the ability to access that. In other words, you'll need our cooperation to obtain it."

Fisher didn't seem too happy being handled this way.

Davidson added, "What does my client receive in return for full cooperation? In addition to the WPP, that is."

Fisher began picking at his left thumbnail, probably, Arnold thought, to avoid having to face Davidson.

"What does he want?"

Arnold wondered where his lawyer was going with this. Hadn't it been discussed?

Davison asked, "Who knows about the income tax allegations?"

"The other agents on my team. We haven't written up reports yet." "Good. We want that matter to go away."

Ahh. Good point.

Fisher scratched the angle of his jaw again.

"We can do that, but I'm sure you realize there's no way to hide his exposure if someone from the IRS were to audit him. In other words, we cannot and will not tamper with evidence or do anything to cover up the commission of a federal crime. However, we will see what an agreement might generate as far as withholding tax penalties."

Davidson glanced at Arnold, who nodded approval.

He said to Fisher, "Before he'll agree to testify, we want a written guarantee for the witness protection program and," he paused to emphasize this next point, "and immunity for any crimes that may have been committed, either by omission or commission, when dealing with any of the Jahandars, meaning both brothers and the wife."

He realized Davidson was trying to negotiate away his involvement in the bombing. Very smart, very crafty. His admiration for his lawyer increased another notch.

Fisher flattened his palms against the desk, as if preparing to stand.

"Can't guarantee anything until I talk to Justice, but I promise you I'll be as persuasive as possible."

Davidson nodded for Arnold to begin talking. Arnold gave Fisher a thumbnail sketch of his computing background, the system, and how he uses it to gamble online. Mostly sports, a lot of football both professional and collegiate. He admitted to Fisher the only reason he visited Vegas was for sex and that he'd decided on Breeze simply because her website appealed to him more than others. He went on to explain that in an attempt to impress her, he'd used his system to predict the outcomes of three races and had done well enough to catch her attention. Once he'd convinced her of being able to model a variety of political and sporting events well enough to fairly accurately predict their outcomes, she began grilling him on its potential applications. He stopped at this point in the story, figuring he wouldn't admit his involvement in the embassy bombing until after he and Davidson were convinced that he'd been granted immunity from prosecution.

When Arnold finished, Fisher ran a finger down the notes he'd accumulated on several pages of a yellow legal pad, got to the end of the list, and repeated the act.

Now, seemingly satisfied, he asked, "Your bets, where do you place them?"

Arnold didn't see any downside to answering, yet glanced at Davidson for approval, just in case he was missing an incriminating facet of the question. Davidson nodded.

Arnold answered, "Online."

"Right, but what I'm really asking is which site do you use?"

For some reason this struck him as funny. Naive funny.

"Wow, there're a ton of sites, depending on how much you want to gamble. For low-stake bets I use the commons ones you can find with a simple Google search. Type in "online betting" and see how many pop up."

Fisher made another note.

"What size bets you talking about when you say low-stakes?"

"Hundred dollars or less."

Fisher made another note.

"And for bets over a hundred?"

Arnold started to massage his left knuckles, worrying about where this was taking him.

"That's different. For those I don't use the internet. At least not as you might know it."

Oh, boy, here we go.

"Meaning?"

"I use various sites on Darknet."

Both Fisher and Davidson were looking at him questioningly now.

Arnold asked, "What?"

"Darknet?" Fisher asked.

"Yeah, Darknet, Deep Web, goes by a couple different names but they all refer to the same thing." Then, just to be sure they understood him, Arnold asked, "You know what I'm talking about, don't you?"

Are there really people left on this planet who don't know? Probably.

"No." Fisher glanced at Davidson, who just shrugged in reply. Fisher said to Arnold, "Okay, I'll bite. Explain it."

"Oh, boy…"

Arnold closed his eyes to collect his thoughts. Hated trying to explain these things, especially to someone he suspected wasn't computer sophisticated.

"Everyone knows what the Internet is and how it's used. But there's another part of it most people don't know about. That part you use for routine things like email or browsing with Internet Explorer or Firefox is only a segment of what's actually available. The other segment can't be accessed with a standard browser and is referred to by several names: Deepnet or Darknet or Deep Web, or even the Hidden Web. There are some areas that remain so hidden they can only be accessed by a handful of people, so remain very private areas. With me so far?"

"Huh!" Fisher nodded. "If that area is invisible, as you claim, how can anyone access it?"

It always amazed Arnold how many aspects of his day-to-day life—as it pertained to computers—were unknown to most people.

"That part of the Internet can only be accessed with a special browser. The most popular one is Tor, and they work on what's called an anonymity network."

Fisher held up his pen to stop Arnold.

"Anonymity network?"

"Yup. One of the biggest attractions of using Darknet is people can conduct business and remain completely anonymous. Pretty amazing, if you stop to think about it. And it works very well. Better yet, your average Internet user doesn't have a clue it's out there."

Fisher whistled softly.

"I didn't know. How long has it been," he seemed to search for words, "out there?"

He was thankful Fisher was following this without a having to ask a ton of questions and sidetrack the conversation, making this easier. Both the FBI agent and his lawyer were sitting up in their chairs, seemingly now glued to his mini-lecture. Having two well-educated men listen so raptly to a kid who had never attended a day of college felt great, buoying his self-confidence. He cautioned himself to not get carried away in self-aggrandizement.

"Since 2002," said Arnold. "That's when the US Naval Research Laboratory originally developed TOR. The original goal was to be able to operate on the Internet with complete anonymity."

"The Navy?"

"Yep. Think about it. The Internet allows rapid transmission of large chunks of data—such as aerial reconnaissance—some of which you might want untraceable and not prone to interception by your enemy. It provides serious military utility."

Fisher nodded pensively. "So how do users stay anonymous?"

"If you were to go on the regular Internet right now, say to use Google, you'd log on to your Internet service provider. Comcast or whatever. The moment you connect to that server, all the information about your computer—the city you're in, your name—goes right along with everything in the connection. It's one of the ways the NSA or Google can track your activities. Instead, when you use the Darknet you're handed off from one computer to another in a random pattern between you and your target site. And each time you log on, because it's a random path, it uses a different set of computers. It's this bouncing between random sites that preserves your identify. That and the Tor browser. But there's a huge downside to using it because any information transfer takes time, slowing things down. Imagine going on Amazon and having to wait a minute for them to acknowledge your search. So, the next question is where do all these random computers come from? Well, most Darknet users allow their computers to be nodes for linking other people using Tor."

Fisher whistled again.

"I can see where this could go."

"The Darknet is used more than you think. But not all of it is evil like the name implies. It is used for legitimate purposes but, as you've probably already figured out, the anonymity makes it perfect for conducting criminal activities. In fact, there's a virtual eBay for criminal services; sites for professional money laundering, another where you can buy hacked PayPal accounts with balances ready to transfer to an offshore bank, you can order illicit drugs, obtain false IDs, including US and Canada driver licenses and passports. Want to hire a professional hacker? Easy. Want a contract killer? No problem. You name it, it's out there. But unlike the normal web, the Deepnet doesn't use self-evident addresses like Hitman-dot-com. Instead, addresses are strings of random looking characters followed by dot-onion instead of dot-com. So, you need to know a complicated address to access a site. There's a Darknet Wiki site that provides a directory of some legitimate and criminal sites, but even that is not widely known."

Arnold paused to catch a breath.

"But to get back to your original question about where I bet. I use the regular Internet for small bets but I move around between them to keep a low profile and not attract attention by winning too much on the same site. For bigger bets, I use DeepNet sites."

Fisher jotted another note.

"When you say bigger bet, how much we talking about?"

Arnold swiped his palm over his hair.

"Depends on how much of a sure thing I think the outcome is. When I'm really convinced it'll pay, I lay down up to fifty bets across as many as ten sites. And the reason is, most of them have a two-thousand-dollar limit." Arnold laughed at what he was about to say. "Every now and then, especially if I think a bet's weak, I bet a loser simply to keep my profile more kosher. Don't know for a fact, but I'm pretty sure the online bookies keep tabs on who wins and who doesn't."

Davidson was listening raptly, eyes darting from Fisher to Arnold and back like a tennis match.

He interrupted with, "Okay, okay, enough explanation. He's cooperated. We're done here," and started to push up out of the chair.

"Sit down," Fisher said sharply, leaning forward and pointing at Davidson's chair. "We're not done yet."

Davidson paused in mid stance.

"Wait a minute, we—"

"Had a deal?" Fisher finished for him.

Davidson glared at the FBI agent before sitting down.

"That was my understanding."

"Only thing we talked about was your client's income tax issues." Fisher paused long enough for Arnold to begin pacing again, "There's another issue we haven't discussed." Then, turning to Arnold: "What's your relationship with Naseem Farhad?"

"Who?"

Fisher studied him a beat.

"Naseem's an Iranian name. Means breeze. Farhad was her maiden name, before becoming a Jahandar."

Arnold felt his face pale. He dropped back into his chair and turned to Davidson for help.

Davidson said, "He already answered that. He hired her for sex. What's your point?"

"Simple question. Deserves a simple answer. Why is your clientsuddenly twitchy?"

Davidson leaned forward and stabbed a finger at Fisher.

"Because your tone is unquestionably accusatory. We don't appreciate your attitude and we certainly don't have to put up with it any longer. This discussion is over." He motioned to Arnold. "Let's go."

Before either could rise from their chairs, Fisher waved them down.

"Don't push it, Mr. Davidson." Fisher's face stone-cold serious now. "Your client could live to regret it."

Davidson snapped back, "Are you threatening us?"

"No. Purely a statement of fact. We know his involvement with them is more than simple sex for hire."

Arnold slumped back in the chair, prepared to be charged with a felony.

Fisher said, "Relax, Gold, I have an offer for you, one that should be attractive, given the alternatives."

He doubted that.

"What?"

Fisher began twirling his ballpoint between fingers like a little baton, a trick Arnold assumed he'd practiced for a long time before becoming any good at it. Probably developed the skill in high school to impress classmates.

Fisher said, "Just out of curiosity, how many years you been hacking?"

Arnold caught Davidson's slight tight-lipped headshake.

"Don't know what you're talking about. I do online gambling, nothing more."

"Oh, bullshit. There's enough computing technology in your basement to run NASA. You're a hacker and a gambler and maybe a few other things I'm not quite sure about. Yet. But I intend to find out. Hey, don't be giving me that innocent look. It doesn't become you, Gold."

Arnold swallowed.

"You said you have an offer for me. What?"

Fisher stood and headed for the door saying, "Before we discuss this any further, the two of you need to sign confidentiality agreements."

Agreements signed and secured in the manila file folder, Fisher propped his butt on the desk corner.

"Our intelligence sources indicate the cell the Jahandars work for is planning a major bomb attack somewhere in the United States. We also believe it's scheduled to occur within the next thirty days, perhaps even a week earlier. We have nothing to indicate where the attack is supposed to occur or what magnitude it will be. Might be as small as the

Boston Marathon or a big as the Oklahoma Federal Building, but the chatter from overseas indicates it will be huge. We strongly suspect a mortality on a scale of the Twin Towers."

Fisher wiped the corner of his mouth.

"So far," he continued, "our attempts at intel gathering have been totally frustrated because we haven't been able to determine how the cells communicate. Believe me, we've tried to find out but have been unsuccessful. There's nothing to indicate they use email or text messaging, and there's no evidence of a courier. But we know they must be communicating somehow. This, by the way, is the reason the Jahandars were under surveillance when you became involved."

A nauseous feeling developed in Arnold's gut as he waited for what he figured might be coming.

Fisher slid off the desk and stood behind his chair with his hands holding a corner. Made him look more like an actor giving a speech than an FBI agent ready to screw him.

"You," with a nod at Arnold, "for obvious reasons, are in a perfect position to help us on this."

Davidson silently raised his eyebrows at Arnold as if to say this might be an important bargaining chip.

"Any questions so far?" Fisher asked, glancing from one to the other.

Neither Arnold or Davidson answered.

"Good, then we can go straight to the punch line. We want you to get involved with them, Mr. Gold. And when you do, we want you to get us access into their communications flow."

Although Arnold had suspected this was where all the foreplay was headed, nothing had prepared him for the impact of actually hearing the words. He held onto his own chair to keep from falling over and sucked a deep breath to stop the room from spinning. His gut was aching again, a deep gnawing pain boring through him.

Davidson broke the heavy silence with, "Just so I'm absolutely clear on this, you're asking my client to spy for the federal government? Do I have this right?"

Fisher shook his head.

"Wrong. On several counts." He went back to sitting on the desk corner. "The difference is this isn't a *request*. This is an ultimatum. Mr. Gold is being given the opportunity to either play ball or be prosecuted as a terrorist involved in actions against the interests of the United States." Fisher drilled both Davidson and Arnold with knowing eyes. "And I think Mr. Gold is aware of what I'm referring to."

Arnold wanted to scream, kick, or thrash his arms but knew it would solve nothing. He felt like the skipper of a small boat caught in a hurricane, unable to get away from the weather but knowing the boat would be swamped and sink. And there was no one to call for help. "This isn't fair."

"Fair?" Fisher gave a sarcastic snort. "Everything's fair in counterterrorism. There wasn't anything fair about flying jets full of passengers into heavily occupied skyscrapers, either. This is war. We deal with a very simple principle: get these assholes before they get us. You're a person who might be able to help us do just that."

Davidson was on his feet now, getting into Fisher's face.

"No, this is not as cut and dried as you're making it. What you're doing is forcing my client to spy for the United States government. If he gets caught, we all know the outcome: he is dead. But should he refuse and take his chances fighting your trumped-up charges in court, he'll at least stand a chance of winning. And say he does lose in court. In that case he goes to prison but he still stays alive."

Fisher's face was turning crimson with anger.

"You both know that's not how it'll work. He's a dead duck in prison. He knows it and I know it. Everyone in this room knows anything short of the disappearing into the witness protection program means he's a dead man. There's no prison on this earth that offers complete safety to any prisoner.

"Okay, yes, I'll concede we're appealing to his patriotic sense of duty by asking him to help his country, and that is precisely why we create law enforcement agency and military branches, but we also ask individual citizens to share the burden in numerous ways. Think freedom comes without risks and sometimes loss of life?"

Davidson said, "Last time I checked our military was all volunteer.

The draft went away with Vietnam."

Arnold wedged between them like a referee in a boxing ring.

"Whoa. Simmer down, let's discuss this."

He knew Fisher was right, that he was a target in or out of prison. He had some questions in need of answers.

Fisher and Davidson exchanged glares before backing off.

Arnold said to Fisher, "You mean to tell me you guys—meaning all the governmental intelligence agencies—haven't been able to infiltrate that group?"

Fisher nodded vigorously.

"Exactly. And this shouldn't be any big surprise. Not after your mini-lecture a minute ago."

"I don't get it. Is not infiltrating communications networks what the NSA and other intelligence agencies do for a living?"

"Absolutely. But they've tried and so far, haven't been able to get to first base. But these guys are sophisticated, they know everything you just described, probably even better than you do. We're not talking about a bunch of primitive village hicks anymore. These guys are extremely technologically sophisticated, they know all about communication tracking. That's exactly the reason bin Laden used a courier instead of digital communication."

Arnold opened his mouth to ask if they had the Jahandars' cell phone numbers when he realized how stupid that would sound, considering there was a huge market for disposable cells that could be easily purchased at any of a number of retailers like Walmart, Rite Aid, that would never be traceable. Use one to link a cheap notebook computer to the Darknet and no one would be able to trace you.

Fisher had a point. Besides, there was his own neck to consider here. Unless the Jahandars were permanently gotten rid of, he'd be looking over his shoulder for the rest of his life. Might be best, after all, to have the feds on his side. At least for the moment.

"What exactly are you proposing I do?"

Fisher didn't hesitate.

"We want you to work for them."

Boom!

A thousand thoughts converged at once: Karim in the archway, gun in hand, the detonation of the discharge, an unnecessary, cold blooded murder. A wave of revulsion came over him, forcing a swallow of bile.

"How could you ask me to work with the people who killed my best friend? The same ones who want to kill me?"

A slight smile played at Fisher's lips.

"You'd love some revenge, wouldn't you?"

"Absolutely. But they'll kill me the moment they lay eyes on me."

"Maybe. Maybe not. I really don't think so. Depends how things play out. Think about it this way," Fisher said. "At the moment you're basically screwed, a dead man walking. Why? Because they know you can eyewitness them for your friend's murder. Until yesterday, they've been able to live in this country without being charged for any crime in spite of our suspicions. Okay, we're one hundred percent certain they're members of a terrorist cell, but just like the Boston Marathon killers— the Tsarnaevs, the kids who couldn't be arrested before detonating those bombs—there is nothing we can do about them simply because we suspect they're on the cusp of doing something huge. But there is something we can do if you testify. Don't testify, and they remain free. Simple as that. And believe me, they know that. Based on that alone you're extremely important to them. But you need to also consider that you have something they'd love to have. I'm not sure exactly that I understand what that is, but it's obvious it involves your computer. Am I on target about that?"

Fisher looked at him closely.

Arnold couldn't help steal another glance at Davidson, who wisely ignored him. Arnold didn't answer, which was probably answer enough.

"As if that weren't enough, you now have us breathing down your neck. Either way, you're up against it. You like to gamble? Fine. Say you decide to take your chances and have us prosecute you: you lose. Why? Because if you end up in prison, you can bet your ass Firouz can and will eliminate you there, because at that point you have nothing to keep you alive. Realistically, you're safer out of prison than in, meaning it all boils down to one chance at redemption, at making it all go away. That one chance is if you work with us on this."

Davidson stepped between Fisher and Arnold, his hand on Arnold's shoulder.

"My client and I need to talk privately outside of this room. Preferably outside of this building."

He made a show of glancing around at places where a microphone might be concealed.

Fisher stood.

"You've got four hours. Then I want a decision, a definitive decision. In the meantime, that'll allow me sufficient time to touch base with Justice and explore their thoughts on offering the witness protection program. I broached the subject with them earlier, so it's not like it'll be a complete shock. But at the time I wasn't sure what you could or couldn't deliver, so they were hesitant to deal. We good?"

Arnold nodded.

"Yeah, we're good."

As they headed toward Davidson's car, the lawyer weighed his trepidation about continuing on as Gold's attorney. On one hand he despised hackers. But Gold didn't seem like the type to maliciously destroy others' computers for kicks.

Was he simply influenced by bias?

If so, what did that make him?

And wasn't there more on the line here?

Food for thought, that was for sure. There was also the terrorist angle. If those bastards were planning an attack possibly on the scale of the Twin Towers...well, that was something to consider...

20

DAVIDSON SUGGESTED THEY'D do best to completely leave the building and get into some fresh air, someplace completely away from the Federal Building's influence, so they could talk openly without risk of being monitored.

They walked back to Davidson's Benz and he drove them to Alki Beach, a hugely popular area along the southwest coast of Seattle with panoramic views of the harbor and city skyline. Historically, this location was notable as the spot where Seattle's first settlers homesteaded when founding the city.

They now plodded through sandy beach cluttered with kelp-scented driftwood, eye level with a concrete bulkhead and street to their left, the downtown business district at their backs and the harbor to their right. Overhead, seagulls—fattened on handouts of scraps—circled, screeching shamelessly for food. Crisp 68-degree salt air carried a potpourri of seaweed, creosote, and rotting wood. A white Washington State ferry slid past on its way to the downtown terminal.

They hadn't spoken during the ten-minute drive here.

"What are you thinking?" Davidson asked.

Arnold responded with a sarcastic laugh.

"I feel pretty much like what Fisher said: unquestionably and totally fucked."

Davidson nodded pensively.

"At the moment things might seem dismal, but there is a way out of this mess. Might not seem all that clear to us right at the moment, but we will figure out something. There are limited options, so that simplifies it a bit. But I guarantee we'll get you out of this. Let's start by throwing out some ideas, no matter how ridiculous they sound. Never know, we might brainstorm a solution we haven't considered."

Arnold waited for Davidson to continue.

Davidson started walking again.

"Option one: we make you disappear. The downside, of course, is you'll have both the FBI *and* Firouz searching for you. Which brings up a point I've intended to ask: how portable is your…"

Arnold finished the thought for him.

"My system?"

"If that's what you call it."

They continued moving, slowly kicking through sand, their arms and faces soothed by a refreshing breeze off the water.

"My software is stored in chunks across several 'clouds'," Arnold said, using finger quotes. "I do this for obvious reasons. It's a great way to protect it from someone like Firouz. Turns out it's a good strategy. If I were to disappear, all I'd have to do is buy new hardware, network it together, and rebuild it. It'd be a ton of work, but it's certainly doable."

"Very good. That's one issue solved. But then you'd still have Firouz and the feds hunting you. What are the chances you could stay hidden the rest of your life?"

Arnold hadn't had the time to consider that in detail, but the thought had crossed his mind.

"Oh, man, I see some huge problems, especially considering how I screwed up so badly with Breeze."

Davidson kicked at a piece of driftwood.

"True, but you're pretty sure you know what went wrong there. If you were to vanish, it'd mean destroying any trace of Arnold Gold. I doubt you'd make the same mistake again."

"True. But here's the deal, I don't speak another language, so moving to a foreign, non-English-speaking country won't work. Canada's a very good possibility. And I've already thought about that, but I'd need to get a fake passport. Might take some time."

"Sure, but it's something to consider."

Arnold paused to glance out across the harbor, amazed that Davidson, a person tasked with upholding the law, was suggesting he break it.

How did that square?

It didn't.

Davidson cleared his throat and raised his eyebrows at Arnold.

"Moving on, there's always the option of making a deal with Firouz to either work for him or have him buy your system."

Arnold shook his head.

"Thought of that, too, but once he has it, he'd kill me. Besides, I can't stomach the idea of selling it to anyone."

Davidson picked up some sand and slowly let the grains slip through his fingers.

"Afraid you might be right. Okay, then, this leaves only one option: spy for the FBI. The downside to it is, of course, it puts you in imminent risk from the Jahandars. On the other hand, the upside is you'll have the Bureau watching your back. Then, once that cell is neutralized, they can squirrel you away in the witness protection program. Sounds like your best option, unless you can think thought of another one we haven't covered."

"There's a downside to the last one you missed: if I work for them, they might just end up with my system and use it against us. That's a huge risk. You willing to chance it?"

"How do you figure?"

"Okay, say I'm analyzing a situation for Firouz. I guarantee that if his people are smart enough to keep hidden from our intelligence people, they're slick enough to penetrate my security and steal my software. Once they have it, they'll pick it apart and put it back together to make it functional. Soon as that happens, I'm dead. Don't think for one minute they'd keep me alive. I'm never going to be one of them, and they damn well know that."

Davidson stooped to pick up a small, smooth piece of driftwood.

"All that means is you have to be smarter and quicker than them. All the more reason to help Fisher take them down and do it before they can get you. To me, that seems like another strong argument in favor of siding with the Bureau. Bet you ten to one Justice will agree to relocate you with a new identity. Once that happens, you're right back in business." He inspected the driftwood more closely, rubbing his thumb back and forth over the surface smoothed by years of being buffed by sand and wind, brushing away grains of sand and salt.

"Naw, that's not going to work. I don't trust the feds all that much. There's always the risk of a leak or, worse yet, someone hacking their files. That happens, I'm toast."

Arnold watched Davidson inspect the wood.

Almost seemed as if his lawyer was grappling with a decision.

He dismissed the thought.

"No, if I do this, I need to do it on my own." He let the word hang as he gazed across Puget Sound to the distant islands, thinking back to his plan, working out the finer details, finding it difficult to stay on any subject for more than a minute. "There's one thing you're forgetting."

Davidson tossed the driftwood toward the water.

"What?"

"I have limited skills. In fact, I only have one: computers. Right now, I'm making good money. I'm not about to throw that away and start over by having to go to school, and I'm not planning on doing unskilled labor for a living. If I somehow work my way out of this mess, I'm still going to have to gamble. Firouz and company know that, so unless they're taken totally out of play, it's possible they could track me down by discovering where I bet. Any plan I finally come up with has to completely eliminate any link back to the Jahandars or the FBI. I have to cease to exist."

"Not sure I buy your suggestion they could track back through your bets, but I won't argue that." Davidson appeared to mull things over. "With a totally fresh identity, you should be able to work around that. But until we come up with a better plan, your best shot is to ally with Fisher."

21

DAVIDSON, ARNOLD, FISHER, and an attorney from Justice sat around an eight-chair walnut conference table with Arnold and Davidson on one side facing the feds on the other side. The room had no artwork other than a picture of the President and another of the head of the FBI. A wall of windows showcased a view across First Avenue and out over the tar roofs of smaller buildings. The room smelled faintly of stale coffee and the Justice lawyer's deodorant.

The Justice Department lawyer, a sour-faced woman in her late thirties with short hair and horn-rimmed glasses, said, "It's crucial for Mr. Gold to testify in court that both Jahandars were involved in the homicide assault. And his testimony must be unequivocal."

Davidson said, "We understand that part. What I want clarified is what happens if it becomes impossible for Arnold to provide you with access to the Jahandars' computers?"

The Justice Department lawyer closed the manila folder on the table in front of her.

"That's Mr. Gold's problem. Our offer becomes effective only if he provides us with access to their communication system in addition to testifying in court. In person, I might add. A videotaped disposition isn't going to cut it. Offer's non-negotiable. And before you object, try to see it from our side. Say he can't come through with the access. If so, how do we know he made a good faith effort? What's to say he decides it's too risky and simply claims he can't do it but tried? We can only judge results, not performance. So if he delivers, great, problem solved. And don't forget, we're under the threat of attack within the next couple weeks. Meaning, we don't have time to play games here. We can't do this any other way. Mr. Gold?"

All eyes turned to Arnold.

Arnold, looking down at his interlaced fingers, shook his head slowly from side to side.

Fucking bastards.

Miss Legal Brilliance had no clue of the risks involved. Or, if she and Fisher did, they really didn't give a damn what happened to him. To them this was just a job, and he was the quickest way to perhaps finish it. He wanted to scream at them, tell them they were…what, exactly?

What would he do differently if he were in their place?

Probably exactly this. Still, he resented the hell out of them strong-arming him.

Davidson filled the verbal void by telling Fisher, "I believe my client is willing to work with you. Isn't that right, Arnold?"

Arnold shot him a look of disgust and squelched saying, "whatever," because that would sound too much like a petulant, sullen. Whiny teenager.

"Right."

Fisher said, "In that case, I'll introduce you to our head of forensic information technology, John Chang."

Chang's office was on the fourth floor in a different building two blocks from the Federal Building on Second Avenue. The halls to his office, as well as the room itself, were painted in greenish beige, a look that struck Arnold as stereotypical government. No artwork on the taxpayers' dime, two windows with northern views up Second Avenue toward the city's main retail district, and three banged up metal desks. The thing that caught Arnold's eye and evoked pangs of envy was that each desk was outfitted with two ultra-cool high-def 40 inch monitors side by side in V formation.

Slick!

Chang was an Asian scarecrow with jet black glossy hair, thick puffy lips, and bushy eyebrows so close together that they resembled a caterpillar crawling across the bridge of his nose. Instead of standing when they entered the room, Chang simply leaned back in his rolling chair, fingers interlaced behind his head, to squint at Arnold.

"You the computer guy?" he said, as if surprised by something.

Fisher said, "John, like you to meet Arnold Gold. Arnold, John."

Arnold extended his hand, but Chang didn't make the slightest effort to stand or to shake it.

"You tell him what we need?"

Fisher said, "I did, but you need to go over it again in computer speak."

Chang leaned forward, eyes on the screens, and began playing with a wireless mouse.

"My team's been tasked with infiltrating the Jahandar network for the past three months but hasn't found any evidence that one exists, much less tried to penetrate it. We believe the Jahandars, the three people you met in Vegas, are members of a much larger organization with cells throughout the United States and Europe, possibly Asia. Because we don't have access to their communications system, we have no idea of their size other than some miscellaneous intel. But it's clear that a group this large must communicate and do so rapidly. We have reason to believe they're not using a courier or one of the parcel shipping agencies. Which leaves us the Internet. But we have no evidence to support that idea, either. Personally, I'm convinced that's exactly how they communicate. We also haven't been able to insert anyone into any of their cells, so in this regard, you're unique. We believe you might be our best hope. In fact, we're counting on it. Once you have access to them, we want you to provide us with a portal. Do that, and we'll take it from there. That's your job," he said, pointing a finger at Arnold's chest.

The mouse didn't seem to be doing anything and, far as Arnold could tell, Chang was fiddling with it only as an excuse for not making eye contact. Arnold could relate to this tactic, having been guilty of the ploy numerous times himself. Arnold figured the guy was probably embarrassed at being one upped by a group of terrorists. Made Arnold wonder if the terrorists handled their own communication system or outsourced it.

Arnold threw up a question for either Chang or Fisher: "You guys sure they're communicating electronically? I mean, we already mentioned bin Laden using a courier because they knew the NSA and other intelligence agencies were all over electronic communications.

Chang answered.

"We investigated that angle and think it's highly unlikely."

"What makes you so sure?" Fisher said

"Good question and, obviously, one we've already considered. Simple answer is that intense physical surveillance doesn't support it. If they are couriering information, they've figured out a way to do it that we haven't been able to spot. Especially since they're undoubtedly aware that's the way bin Laden was finally located. Bottom line, I seriously doubt they're using that method. Besides, we estimate an eighty percent likelihood they're passing files too big to fold into small envelopes. Copies of blueprints, information like that. Much more likely is that files large as that are being transmitted electronically."

Suddenly the intellectual challenge of solving a difficult puzzle intrigued Arnold, shifting his resentment at being forced into this job into the mindset of game playing. This was a challenge he could relate to. He dropped into one of the three metal chairs.

"No offense, John, and I have no way of diplomatically asking without simply sounding insensitive, but out of curiosity, what's your background?"

Chang, clearly annoyed by the question, drilled Fisher with an I-told- you-so look.

Fisher shrugged, so Chang answered with, "Undergrad at Carnegie Mellon, two years post-grad at the Stanford AI labs. Now the bureau." Then, with a slight smirk, "What are your credentials?"

"Hey, guys," Fisher said before Arnold could answer. "Stay focused. We have a job to do."

Realizing he'd bruised Chang's ego, Arnold scrambled to make amends.

"Didn't mean it the way it sounded. Sorry, bad choice of words."

Which was a bit of a lie. He resented the way Chang had snubbed his offer of a handshake. "What I meant was, you obviously know what you're doing, so the thing I'm confused about is what makes you think I can do something you can't?"

Aw, shit. That sounded even worse.

Frowning, Chang asked Fisher, "Seriously?"

Fisher said, "Get on with it, John."

Chang turned back to Arnold.

"Thought I already covered that: you have a personal tie to these guys," pausing for effect. "From what I understand, you've had an intimate relationship with at least one member of the group." He smirked. "Making you uniquely positioned to infiltrate them."

Chang smugly sat back again in the chair.

Arnold sucked in a long, deep breath, held up both hands in surrender.

"Okay, my bad. Let's start fresh. What's been your approach so far?"

Chang uttered an intolerant sigh.

"John?" Fisher said, taking the other metal chair, prepared to sit and listen.

Chang picked up the mouse and again began absentmindedly sweeping it back and forth across a mouse pad while explaining.

After ten minutes of questions and answers, Chang asked Arnold, "Fisher says you use the Darknet. That right?"

Arnold glanced at Davidson.

Okay to answer?

He nodded.

"For some things, sure. Mostly for gambling."

Chang gave a confirmatory nod. "All our leads—which aren't a lot more than basically a hunch—indicate this could be their preferred route for information transfer. And because you're already familiar with using it, you'll appreciate just how impossible it is to track anyone on it, much less try to find one of their portals."

Arnold was beginning to feel a connection with Chang now.

"Yes, I get it. Makes you realize just how dependent we are on search engines."

Chang was no longer playing with the mouse.

"Exactly." Then addressing Fisher and Davidson, "There's no Google for that. Sites are passed on mostly by word of mouth. Some sites are only known to a few people." Back to Arnold, "We suspect that access to their cell is known only by their lieutenants. If we can uncover the address to their main communication site, you better believe we'll penetrate it. Once we do that, we can be fairly sure of discovering where they're headquartered."

"Sounds easy," Arnold muttered. "And if I get caught?"

Chang glanced at Fisher to answer.

Fisher moved to a large whiteboard on one wall, uncapped a black Sharpie, and pointed the end at Arnold. "Time to discuss strategy." He printed the number 1 in the upper left-hand corner.

"Not surprisingly, their organization places a huge premium on security," said Fisher. "If you start working with them, you'll be under constant surveillance by their security people as well as ours. This means you must be extraordinarily cautious with any communication to us. It goes without saying that all communication must be minimized to only what's absolutely—and I emphasize absolutely—essential. John?"

Chang cleared his throat.

"I know you know this, but I'll emphasize it just so we're perfectly clear: no text messaging, no emails. Nothing that has even the remotest chance of leaving a digital trace. We'll give you a special cell phone with a special number on speed dial in the unlikely event you need to get in touch. We monitor the number continuously until this operation is finished. But—and I can't emphasize this enough—use it only in an extreme emergency. All other routine communication to us will use the draft message technique."

Davidson raised his hand.

"Whoa, hold on. I don't know what you're talking about."

Chang explained, "It's an ingenious way for terrorists to pass messages surreptitiously. We don't know for certain, but believe it originated with al Qaeda. Problem is, it's so damned effective it's now the terrorists' preferred means of communication. Works like this: Agent 1 wants to send Agent 2 a message, but they both assume their emails and phone lines are monitored and they're being tailed, so they can't use an internet café or other public portal. So, they set up a new email account with G Mail, Hotmail, or whatever. The particular choice doesn't matter long as the account is web-based. Or, in the cloud, if you prefer to use that term. Both agents have the account name and password and can access it from anywhere in the world with an internet connection: an internet café in Moscow, Istanbul, Peoria, or wherever. Agent 1 logs onto the account and starts a message but instead of sending it he saves it as a draft. Once that's done the message sits in the email account until it's erased. Agent 2 can now log into the same account and access the same draft. Soon as he's read it, he deletes it. Bingo, the information is passed between them without actually sending an email that could be intercepted. Meaning that anyone monitoring either agent's email activity externally doesn't see a thing. Get it?"

Davidson nodded, a faint smile across his lips.

"Tricky."

Chang returned the smile.

"Damn right it is. What it means is that unless we have the account name and password and are logged on and monitoring it 24/7, we'll miss it."

Fisher asked, "We finished with this part? Can we move on to the next topic?"

Chang nodded.

Fisher said, "There will be times when we need to pass Arnold information. But because he's very likely going to be either under Jahandar surveillance or have a guard physically next to him, it won't be safe to approach him directly. This is where you come in," speaking to Davidson. "All communication other than a dire emergency must come through you."

"Won't that be suspicious?" Arnold asked.

"No. You have every reason to have conferences with your lawyer. After all, there's an ongoing investigation into Howard Stein's murder, and you're a person of interest until the case is officially closed, which I guarantee won't happen until this issue is settled. I'd also be very surprised if any meeting between the two of you isn't monitored by one of Jahandar's group, so you need to exercise extreme caution on what you say and how you say it. They could be surveilling you with highly directional mikes and video and could use lip readers. So, you'll have to assume any discussion is not secure. So be proactive soon as this meeting's over and set up some codes."

Arnold's palms were sweating, and his mouth was dry again. He realized he was pressing his gut, scared to death. He forced himself to think of Howie, of how sweet revenge would feel. Revenge would make any risk worthwhile.

Davidson tapped Arnold's arm.

"Hey, you okay?"

Arnold, now dizzy, grabbed the edge of the table to keep from falling over.

"Hell, no. The thing you guys seem to be ignoring is while I'm trying to steal their information, those assholes are going to be trying to do the same with me. It's going to be a race. If they penetrate my system first, I'm toast."

Chang smirked.

"Means you need to be the first, is all."

Fisher handed Arnold a cell phone.

"Here's the phone. Remember, only for a dire emergency. Familiarize yourself with the speed dial."

Arnold inspected it: simple clamshell, small and compact, easy to use, probably disposable.

"Show us you can use the speed dial."

Arnold flipped it open, powered it on, demonstrated how easy it was to operate.

Fisher said, "At the risk of being irritating, I repeat: use that only for a dire emergency. Everything else goes through Davidson."

"What about something urgent but not quite emergent? Say, I need to set up a meeting?"

Chen fielded that one with, "In that case, Tweet Happy Birthday Gary, Palmer, or John, depending on which of us you need to meet.

We'll try to get there soon as we can. Which is the next point to discuss: the meeting place. What's works for you?"

Arnold considered that a moment. Someplace near the house would the most likely spot. Also, it should be somewhere that was part of his normal routine.

"How does Greenlake sound? I jog or walk the outer path several times a week, so it makes perfect sense for me to go there. How about the field house with the swimming pool? Evans pool. How about just outside the front door in the parking lot."

Fisher nodded.

"Yeah, that works."

Silence.

Fisher said, "That about covers it unless somebody has something more to add. Questions? John? Arnold?"

"Yeah, I have one," Arnold answered. "What am I supposed to do now? How do I get things going?"

He could think of no way to contact the Jahandars other than through Breeze's website and wasn't overly thrilled about going there.

Fisher nodded.

"Right now, nothing. Go home, act normal, wait."

"Really?"

Minutes ago, this was urgent. Waiting didn't make much sense.

"Yes. Way I see it, Firouz and Karim now know a couple things. One: they know your laptop is worthless. Two: they know you witnessed the murder. If it's true they also want your system, then it makes sense that they would prefer you alive and too intimidated to testify. They also want your help. In all likelihood, they believe that because of your previous involvement in the embassy bombing you'll keep your mouth shut. So, it's very likely they'll try to contact you soon. Howard's funeral is tomorrow. We estimate that's the first place they might try. In fact, it's a very likely place. It's out in the open where they can observe you to make sure you're not under surveillance. They'll contact you once they believe it's clear. If so, let them. Listen to what they offer and get back to us straightaway through Palmer."

Arnold wasn't so convinced Fisher had it right. His gut pain increased.

"What if he tries to kill me?"

Fisher shook his head.

"Doubt they want to do that. Besides, we'll have your back. You'll not be able to see us and they'll not be able to see us, but we'll be able to see you. Have faith, play your part, and we'll get you through this."

Arnold wanted to vomit.

"Oy!"

22

DAVIDSON CURBED THE Mercedes in front of Arnold's home, a small, two-story Tudor-style house with a high peaked roof and mature shrubs filling the surrounding beds.

He cut the engine, asked, "Want me to sweep the place for bugs?"

Arnold stopped reaching for the door handle, startled for not having thought of the possibility, which was strange, considering his usual security consciousness. Made sense. In a way. What he found even more interesting was that Davidson would have equipment readily available for the task. More and more, Davidson impressed him as someone you should never try to outwit without a lot of thought and preparation. And perhaps not even then. Did Davidson go out of his way to appear so harmless and unsuspecting? Did that strategy serve him well in the courtroom? Probably.

"You can do that? I mean, you just drive around with equipment in the trunk of your car so you can sweep for bugs any place, any time."

He hadn't bothered to look in the backseat of the car and certainly hadn't inspected the contents of the trunk. But now he craned his neck for a glimpse and noticed a black case about the size of a briefcase on the back seat. No telling what it might be. Jesus, no telling the things Davidson might be hiding in the trunk.

The lawyer chuckled.

"Matter of fact, I do. Never know who might want to eavesdrop on me. Especially when preparing for trial. You'd be amazed what your opposition will stoop to. In addition, there are people who just flat-out hate criminal defense attorneys."

Which brought up a point that had always bothered Arnold.

"The people you defend, you know for sure they're criminals?"

"Some of the time."

Arnold let go of the door handle and turned to face him.

"Then how can you, in good conscience, defend them? How do you justify that? Is it the money?"

Yeah, of course it was the money. How else could someone stoop so low?

Davidson chuckled, a tired sounding laugh.

"It's complicated and probably a lot of things all rolled into one. I've never tried to analyze all the reasons, but the standard one you'll get from any criminal defense lawyer is that everyone deserves to be defended in a court of law. It's written into our constitutional rights, and they'll correctly point out that any person charged with a crime is innocent until proven guilty, etcetera, et cetera. For me, it's pretty simple: I thrive on the challenge. Makes me want to get up in the morning and work on the next case, see how well I can stand up against incredible odds and some very smart prosecutors. And, I'll admit, it doesn't hurt when it pays well. What can I say?"

Still didn't make it acceptable, and the favorable impression Arnold had had of Davidson a moment before waned significantly. He reminded himself that he, himself, was technically a criminal for not paying taxes, but that really didn't seem like such a crime because it wasn't directed against anyone. At least not directly. And it wasn't violent. But the real point was that not paying taxes was an unintentional act, an act of omission. At the moment, he was employing a criminal defense lawyer in the hopes of being able to beat any charges, especially the ones for abetting the Jahandars.

So, what did that make him?

Still, it didn't seem quite the same.

"But what about a guy like Dzhokhar Tsarmaev, the Boston bomber?" Arnold asked. "There's no doubt he's guilty. In fact, he admitted as much when he and his brother hijacked the SUV. How can anyone with a conscience defend a bastard like that?"

Davidson shook his head.

"His crime still deserves a fair trial. Doesn't mean he won't be convicted. It certainly doesn't negate his right to have a lawyer—who knows the legal ropes—to defend him."

"But what about those times a defense lawyer gets a guilty person off purely on some weird legal technicality? How do you justify that?"

Davidson seemed to relax back into the bucket seat and dropped his hands into his lap, obviously resigned to defending his chosen profession. He appeared bored, perhaps from having faced this subject ad nauseam throughout his career. For several seconds he seemed to be collecting his thoughts or marshalling a counterpoint.

"Isn't it true that in your computing career you've broken into other people's computers and networks?"

Arnold grudgingly allowed a half shrug capitulation, now aware where Davidson was taking this. But he reminded himself, he started it. "I guess..." Davidson ran his palm back and forth over the top of the steering wheel, polishing the glossy wood.

"Without getting into an argument over semantics or philosophy, that's considered hacking. Am I right?"

Arnold turned to look at his house instead of Davidson. He pretty much knew how this would end and was peeved by Davidson's point. He knew that none of his motivation or activities had ever been malicious. Perhaps Davidson was like the majority of people who didn't realize that the true meaning of the term "hacker" referred to a person with an in-depth understanding of computers and their operating systems instead of the Hollywood inspired stereotypic image of the destructive, pimply-faced intruder intent on destroying or exploiting.

"I guess."

"You guess? I believe that exactly what it's called. What justification do hackers give for illegally breaking and entering other people's computer systems, be they personal or institutional?"

Arnold didn't bother to answer because he knew his silence was, in itself, an answer.

"I know the argument you guys make," Davidson continued.

"Hackers self-righteously claim they're simply exposing security flaws in whatever system they unlawfully enter, and by doing so, they cause better software to be developed."

Arnold couldn't stand not saying something in rebuttal. "So, you're saying it's okay to get a killer off because it'll result in better laws? I don't buy that."

Lame, true, but at least it was something...

"Then that's your problem, not mine."

Davidson opened his door to step out.

"Yeah, okay, let's do it."

Arnold was more curious to see what kind of equipment Davidson would come up with than argue the point any longer. Besides he grudgingly had to admit, Davidson had skillfully made his point.

Arnold led Davidson into the house through the front door, into a small living room with a dining room to the right. An archway directly across from the front door led to a stairway to upstairs and a hall connecting a small TV room to the left of the stairs and the kitchen to the right. Hardwood floors except for the tiled kitchen floor, painted plaster walls from the days when builders had used real plaster, muted wall colors.

The compact Tudor was a typical design of this neighborhood and was probably mirrored numerous times within a few blocks. Arnold took only one step into the living room before he froze with the realization of what he was seeing. The place was a mess: two end table lamps overturned, several latex gloves strewn haphazardly over the rug and furniture along with ripped paper bandage wrappers. One corner of the rug remained folded back. Black fingerprint dust smudged on tables and walls. Flies buzzed around a pool of crusted dried blood on the floor. He realized this was probably the exact spot where Howard had died. The thought almost caused him to vomit.

Davidson stood to his left, hand on his shoulder.

"Soon as I sweep the place, I'll help you clean up."

Arnold gulped a breath, held up a finger. "Give me a few minutes. I feel...dizzy."

He stepped back outside to the porch, sat down on the steps, and buried his head in his hands, eyes clamped tightly shut. What he'd seen inside kept reverberating through his mind's eye. He couldn't get the image out of his head until, in a flash of clarity, he knew he would revenge Howie's senseless murder no matter if it cost him his own life. He didn't notice the sounds of Davidson working inside.

A couple minutes later he became aware of Davidson clomping down the stairs from the second floor, saying, "Nothing up there, either. Feel a little better now?"

Arnold raised his head from his hands, stood on shaky legs, went back inside.

"Not much. Doubt I'll ever feel better about what happened. Never. My life will never be the same." He squeezed the bridge of his nose and blinked, trying to clear his head. "And I'm not saying that just to be dramatic. I really mean it. After my folks died—especially the way they did—life changed. All the security I felt as a kid suddenly vanished in one brutal, senseless act. Part of me died along with them, corny as that sounds. It's like the entire experience repeated when Howie...guess this is one of the reasons I'll be happy to disappear into the relocation program, get an entirely fresh start in my life with nothing around me to remind me of Seattle."

Arnold stared at his interlaced fingers, feeling sorry for himself while at the same time angry at God, if there was one.

"Life never is the same, after something like this." Davidson waved toward the kitchen. "Come on, show me this basement room I've heard so much about, then let's get this place straightened up."

They entered the basement stairs from the kitchen, the flight directly underneath and paralleling the stairs to the second floor. The basement had lived its long life as a large unfinished room with exposed overhead joists, large old lumber supports, and a cracked unpainted concrete foundation with a lint clogged drain near the old wall mounted laundry sinks. Along the south wall stood a washer and dryer, with a natural gas forced air furnace in the corner. A separate room had been built directly under the living room.

Arnold opened the door and reached, threw a wall switch, illuminating a panel of bright overhead LED lighting.

"Watch your step."

He stepped up onto a floor elevated three inches off the basement cement to ensure the room would stay dry if the floor accumulated any moisture during the wet Seattle fall months. Arnold had built the floor by fitting sheets of three-quarter plywood over a simple frame of three-by-fours. He'd covered the plywood with squares of linoleum, all of which had been purchased from Home Depot and fashioned with Howie's father's power tools. The only window was a narrow horizontal rectangle five feet off the floor but only a few inches above the ground outside, the confined view obscured by the flowerbed shrubs. Although the window was too small for anyone but a child to squeeze through, further security was enhanced by stainless steel bars securely bolted into the surrounding cement. Because the computer equipment generated heat, Arnold had also installed thermostatic air conditioning to maintain a cool 65 degrees year-round.

"They're LEDs," he muttered, referring to the overhead lights. "I try to minimize wasted energy. Also, they run cooler."

Along the left wall stood two floor-to-ceiling gray steel racks with shelves spaced three feet apart. The shelves held two servers with numerous external disk drives all ganged together with a rat's nest of cables. Snug against the adjoining wall ran a plywood workbench on which sat three additional tower computers in various states of repair.

"Wow, now I appreciate what all the fuss was about." Davidson stood in the center of the room, taking it all in. "What's that?" he asked, pointing to what looked like a portable generator under the left end of the workbench.

"It's a dedicated cooling and air circulation unit. Runs constantly to regulate the heat computers generate. Keeping the room at this temperature ensures they run well without overheating. They don't like being too hot."

He realized he sounded like a parent bragging about his kids and felt his face blush.

An hour later, Davidson exited through strike in the front door, paused and turned, right hand on the door jamb, left hand holding the screen door open, a concerned look on his face.

"You okay?"

You kidding? Hell no.

Arnold glanced down, lips pressed tightly together, inhaled audibly through his nose. "Yeah, I'll be fine. Eventually...just need to get my head straight, is all. Wow, just hit me that this will be the first time I've been alone since all this started. Boy, seems like it's been going on weeks now," and shook his head.

Davidson glanced at his watch and made a decision.

"Want me to stick around few more minutes? I got time if you want."

"Naw, I'll be okay. I've taken enough of your time."

Davidson punched him lightly on the shoulder.

"Okay. You're a smart guy. You're going to come out on top of this. You sure you're straight on everything, have Fisher's and my number?"

"I do."

"All right, then, be strong and call the moment something breaks."

The lawyer turned, walked wearily down the cement steps to his car.

Arnold watched Davidson's Benz move slowly down the narrow curving road and disappear around the corner, leaving him feeling isolated and afraid of an uncertain future. Instead of going inside and shutting the door, he remained standing on the small porch, concentrating on each of the familiar sights, sounds, and smells of the beloved neighborhood of his childhood, embedding each in his memory for retrieval sometime in the future, when he knew loneliness would envelope him. In a few days—whenever that might be—he'd be forced to leave the only home he'd known. It was, he realized, a place he'd taken for granted. Soon he would never be able to return. This realization made it all the more imperative to burn these images into his brain forever.

He was realistic about the odds he faced in going up against the Jahandars, and they were heavily stacked against him. But if he were going to die, he'd be damn sure to take as many of those fuckers as he could along with him.

Finally, he gently shut the door and wandered into the kitchen to make a hot chocolate, an indulgence he allowed himself when feeling out of sorts. If Fisher were correct, his enemies would make contact tomorrow at the funeral. He needed to plan his next moves carefully.

From this point on, he could afford no mistakes.

His life depended on it.

23

THE DENSE PEWTER overcast—so characteristically Seattle—
produced misty drizzle befitting Arnold's mood. The deceased's young
age coupled with the violent and senseless cause of death amplified the
solemnity of the gathering.

Arnold stood among the graveside mourners; the smell of freshly
overturned sodden earth unmistakably pungent in the chilly breeze.
Drops of water glistened like diamonds on the freshly mowed emerald
lawn as the rabbi's monotone droned through the service. Arnold had
dressed too lightly for the miserable weather and was now shivering in
the marrow penetrating chill, fists shoved deeply in his pockets,
shoulders hunched so tightly his neck muscles ached. Only fitting, he
decided, that he should suffer physically now, a menial penance for his
guilt. He owed Howie a debt that wouldn't be repaid until the Jahandars
were killed. To make matters worse, he repeatedly caught himself
stealing glances at Rachael.

*What kind of friend are you to be coveting his sister during his
funeral?*

Jesus!

Another wave of guilt swept over him.

I'm such a jerk.

As they began to lower Howie's simple pine box into the ground,
Arnold wished it were his body inside instead. If he'd been at home
when Firouz and Karim arrived, he would've simply handed over the

computer without any argument. Let them have the damned thing. For all the good it would do them. But he wasn't home, and when he did return, Howie tried to warn him and, in the process, gave his own life to save Arnold's.

I'll never forget you, brother. Never!

Howard's family and friends began approaching the grave, bending down to pick up handfuls of damp dirt to toss on the coffin, each impact causing a gut-wrenching thump as the rabbi slowly recited Psalm 91 and El Maleh Rachamim. Arnold had purposely arrived at the last minute so he wouldn't have to stand next to the grave and come face to face with Howard's parents, but now he watched as each family member tossed a handful of clay into the grave. And now, to his shock, he realized the similarity between Breeze and Rachael.

Jesus, did I pick Breeze because I want to fuck Rachael?

He felt his self-esteem drop even lower.

Service now over, the people began drifting into a line to Howie's mother, father, and Rachael. Arnold shuffled into the queue and glanced toward the outer edges of the cemetery, searching for Firouz or Karim, but didn't see them. Just as well. The sight of either man would only have upset him more. He considered what to say to Sarah, Howard's mother. This would be his first words with her since…Christ, it was difficult to even think the word "murder."

Then he was next.

He wrapped his arms around Sarah, hugged her tightly, mumbling, "I'm so sorry. I…" but words failed him.

He squeezed a little more before releasing her. Seemed as though she was also reluctant to let go, as if holding on to the last living remnant of her son.

She gently held him at arm's length, looking deeply into his eyes.

"Howard loved you, Arnold, like a brother."

He saw her red-rimmed tired eyes and mascara slightly smeared from tears.

"I loved him, too," he said, wanting to say so more. Instead, he moved on to Herbert. They shook hands without a word.

Next came Rachael and their first encounter since Vegas. For a fleeting moment he flashed on Breeze and the things other than sex she'd taught him. He realized he was no longer intimidated by her presence and could actually speak with her. Without thinking he wrapped his arms around her and hugged.

"I'm so sorry, Rachael, so sorry."

To his shock and pleasure, she nestled her head against his chest and hugged him tightly.

"I know you are," her warmth a delight against his shivering body.

Without thinking, he kissed her on the forehead and, as he did, she hugged him closer. Then, he held her head in his hands to directly into her eyes.

"This is awful for me to say under these circumstances, but when the time's appropriate, I would love to see you, maybe take you out to dinner if you want."

And now you're hitting on her? Jesus, what kind of friend are you?

He bent down and kissed her forehead again, a move he never in a million years would've ever considered.

She smiled, her eyes twinkling with an emotion he'd never seen before, but then again, had he ever really had the nerve to make eye contact? And at that moment he knew a nonverbal message had just passed between them. She liked him, too. He smiled.

"I'd like that, Arnold, I'd like that a lot."

She squeezed his hand before turning her attention to the next mourner in line.

For a moment he stayed frozen in place, marveling at what had just transpired between them. And, truth be told, he knew this was Howie's final gift to him. A tear welled up, and he turned away. Then, eyes down, began trudging the winding path to the parking lot, making no attempt to acknowledge the smattering of friends and family doing likewise. No one talked anyway, they just moved wordlessly to their vehicles, the mood too solemn for conversation. That would change, he figured, soon as they were inside their warm vehicles driving away, trying to forget the message funerals impress upon us: death is certainty, leaving only the question of when and how it will occur.

Having been one of the last to arrive, he'd parked at the far end of the rectangular asphalt lot. Now pausing to allow a car to back up and exit, he heard the overhead whine of a jet on landing approach to the nearby Seattle-Tacoma airport. Up until now, his plan had been to simply disappear under a new identity, go to Hawaii maybe, start a new life. But now, with the possibility of seeing Rachael…

He paused and glanced around, reorienting himself, having wandered here so deeply in thought that he momentarily forgot which direction to go. About fifty feet ahead, parked at the end of the lot, was his green Jetta. Looked empty, but he couldn't tell for sure at this angle because the front seat headrests obscured his view. Interestingly, the area immediately surrounding the car appeared deserted. And this was not what he'd expected. Fisher's suggestion had caused him to anticipate running into a Jahandar sometime during the event, and it made the most sense that it'd be here and now. And now, looking, he didn't see anyone at the other end of the lot coming his way, either. Then, as he moved closer to the Jetta's front door, he saw the silhouette of someone in the passenger seat. Who? How had they gained access to the car? He distinctly remembered locking the door. His heart began pounding, engulfing him in the prickly flush of fear. Firouz. Has to be that bastard. His fear morphed into rage.

Hold on, hold on. Take a few breaths.

Isn't this what is supposed to happen? Didn't Fisher hope you'd make contact this way?

He bent down for a closer look.

Aw, shit, Breeze.

And now he hated her, especially with the sight of her coming on the heels of his encounter with Rachael. He straightened up, scanned the area again. No, no one else nearby. Was the FBI watching? Sucking in another deep breath, he reached for the door and, to his surprise, found it unlocked.

Slowly he slid into the driver's seat.

"What do you want?"

She faced him.

"Come on, Arnold, I think you know. Or do you prefer I call you Toby?"

He slammed the door and fired up the ignition. His encounter with Rachael had temporarily distracted him from the chill now in his marrow, giving him shivers. The sooner the heater began pumping out warm air, the better. He turned the seat heater to high. His clothes, he realized, were soaked with drizzle.

Stupid to come without an umbrella or raincoat.

She seemed to be waiting for an answer, so he sniped, "What's the matter, couldn't get the computer to work?"

He goosed the gas and checked the rearview mirror.

Anger was churning his gut now that his initial shock was subsiding. He felt a warm glow of satisfaction at the mental image of them struggling to discover a way through the multiple layers of the laptop's security only to watch helplessly as the hard disk destroyed itself.

Yeah, that's probably exactly what happened.

He couldn't suppress a self-satisfied smile.

Assholes.

Breeze glanced around as if looking for something. Like? Maybe she was looking to see if he had surveillance. Or perhaps it was a sign to her own people. Any number of possibilities. But the game had now officially started.

"Why don't you take me downtown and we can talk during the drive?"

He muzzled a sarcastic reply and concentrated on driving his initial course to Aurora Avenue, also known as old US Highway 99. Once out of the cemetery and headed north toward the city, Breeze began running her hands over his chest and legs. He swatted her hand away.

"The hell you think you're doing?"

"Just checking."

She pulled his cell phone from his pocket and slipped it under her flank, effectively muffling the microphone.

"For what?"

Then realized how stupid his question must sound.

Apparently satisfied, she said, "Politics aside—because I know you don't have strong feelings one way or the other—there is money to be made. Firouz can make you very rich, you know."

He can also make me seriously dead.

"Since you're calling me Arnold, why don't you tell me your real name?"

"Naseem."

Well, at least that's truthful.

He thought he'd mentally prepared for this moment, trying to script a tactic that would make him seem hard to get while at the same time convincing them he could be recruited. Now, his mind was awash in questions, most of which were inappropriate, and some just flat-out hateful.

Shame on you for even thinking them.

Yet several still surfaced, questions like: "What kind of man lets his wife fuck other men for money?" He realized his best strategy would be to just shut the hell up and let her do all the talking. He flipped the turn signal, pulled into the passing lane and overtook a tractor trailer freight truck.

Finally, he said, "Go on, deliver your message."

She settled back into the seat, hands in her lap, eyes straight ahead.

"I'm not the one to negotiate with. Firouz is. I'm simply here to set up a meeting. But what I can say is he's prepared to make you a very generous offer; that is, if you're willing to listen."

Arnold realized he'd been white knuckling the steering wheel so tightly his fists were aching. He let go with his left hand and began to flex and extend his fingers, loosening up the muscles. He then repeated this with his right hand. It was all he could do to keep from verbally lashing out at her but knew that would be counterproductive. Everything had changed and he was now an actor, playing the part of the stand-offish-yet-willing-to-listen geek for hire.

"Why would I even consider working with you?"

"Like I said, there's a lot of money for you. Isn't that enough? And then there's the other thing. If you don't wish to cooperate, we can make certain the FBI discovers your prior involvement. Is that what you want, Arnold?"

For a moment he almost laughed. Knowing the FBI was actually behind him, talking to them gave him a sense of power.

"You find this funny?"

He realized his mistake: smiling. He shook his head, serious once again.

"I think it's funny you seem to forget something very important. Firouz and Karim murdered my best friend. Not only that, it was so cold blooded. Now you want me to work with you? How can any of you expect me to accept that?"

Stupid question.

Hey, don't overact. Tone it down.

"Arnold," she said, placing her hand on his thigh, "be practical. What's done is done. He's sorry. He didn't plan that to happen. It's what your military refers to as collateral damage. Exactly the same thing that happens when a drone murders innocent children and defenseless women. Besides, Karim pulled the trigger, not Firouz."

"So that's an important distinction?"

He gave a sarcastic laugh and started to remove her hand from his leg but reconsidered.

Go on, let her believe she's getting to you through your dick. Stay focused on the final goal. Your best revenge is to take them down. Never lose sight of that.

He'd make a lousy spy, he realized.

A car in the rearview mirror caught his attention, causing him to do a double take.

Have I seen it before? Yeah. Twice now.

He reached up to adjust the mirror slightly for a better view, maybe distinguish whether the driver is Middle Eastern.

"That supposed to make everything wonderful?"

Stop it! You're supposed to be malleable.

"For someone who's supposed to be very smart, you don't sound so smart to me. We're willing to pay you extremely well for your work. But I guess if you don't want to be involved, we can always have Karim kill you, too. After all, we have little to lose other than your help, which isn't all that essential. Your choice. Think about it."

She cupped his crotch.

"And, to sweeten the offer, you can have sex with me anytime you wish."

The car stayed behind him, always one or two cars back, hanging in there. Who was it? Fisher? Firouz? His gut started killing him again, and he fought to keep from pressing against his abdomen and reveal how much stress this was causing. He wondered if they'd bugged the car and put a GPS device on it, like you see in spy movies. Or was his mind playing tricks on him?

"I must warn you," she continued. "Mention any of this to the authorities and we'll know. Just like we know you said nothing to the police. We have many sympathizers, so we know more than you might think. Try to double cross us, we'll kill you. Straightforward. I know you think you're a smart man, but don't kid yourself into believing you can outsmart us. Do you doubt we have sympathizers? Would it convince you to know, for example, that you didn't give the police our names?"

Boom!

Jesus! She isn't kidding.

A chill slithered down his spine. The gut pain throbbed.

What about the FBI and Davidson? Do they know about them also? I need to let Davidson know ASAP.

"This surprise you? It shouldn't. If it does, you underestimated us." She fondled his crotch again. "Relax, Arnold. Be smart and realistic and you can become rich. Besides, you really don't have other options. Not anymore, you don't. You will work with us."

"Or?"

"I don't think I need to answer that."

Enough for one day.

He moved his hand.

"Where should I drop you?"

She resisted long enough for one last gentle squeeze.

"Macy's is good."

He turned onto First Avenue, heading toward the business district and, in the process, checked the rearview mirror again, but the car was now gone. Replaced by someone else? Was he being overly paranoid? Or were they—whoever *they* were—using two cars?

He couldn't leave things on a negative note, so asked encouragingly, "What exactly do you have in mind for me?"

"Firouz will give you the specifics, but essentially you would do pretty much the same as before. We supply a target, and you provide an analysis of what is necessary to complete a mission."

Arnold realized his hands were clamping the steering wheel too tightly again and worked his fingers some more to relax them.

I'd rather die than help you assholes.

But knew he must do differently.

A small black handgun suddenly appeared from her purse.

"Really? Careful what you wish for because I could kill you right now if this is what you want."

She read his mind, or had he actually uttered the words?

He cut across two lanes of traffic, ignoring a honking horn, curbed the Jetta at a bus zone, threw the transmission into park, and turned to her.

"Go ahead. Do it."

And for a moment wished she would. At least then he'd be at peace.

He tensed for the blast, but several seconds ticked past before she slipped the gun back into her purse.

"You haven't answered my question. Will you meet with Firouz?"

Realizing he'd been holding his breath, he inhaled deeply.

"Let me think about it."

"Do that. You have twenty-four hours. I'll arrange for you to meet Firouz tomorrow. I'll call, let you know where."

She opened the door to step out.

"This isn't Macy's."

She shrugged and continued out of the car.

"Talk to anyone about this, we'll know. Believe me, we will."

She tossed his cell phone on the passenger seat, slammed the door, and was gone.

24

UNBELIEVABLE! ARNOLD BLINKED and did a double take. A parking spot. Only two blocks away from where he needed to be. Arnold crept the Jetta slowly past the space, sizing it up. Yeah, might be too good to be true, decidedly tight, but ultimately doable. He loved parallel parking—which he knew seemed totally weird to other people—and considered challengingly small spaces especially fun to conquer.

He shifted into reverse and jockeyed back and forth until the car was wedged in an acceptable distance from the curb. Took three minutes with his credit card before the parking meter coughed up a two-hour sticker that he dutifully pasted to the inside of the passenger window for the benefit of the meter patrols that notoriously prowled this area. More than enough time, but you never knew. And considering the excessive charge for overtime parking, purchasing a tad more time than estimated seemed to be a very cheap form of insurance, considering the Draconian overtime penalties.

He cut down Marion Street, walked past the old Maritime Building, caught a break in traffic, so jogged across Alaskan Way to the sidewalk bordering the harbor. The tangy smells of saltwater, car exhaust, and maritime diesel spiced the air. Then, across the street to Ivar's Acres of Clams—an iconic waterfront fish and chips tourist trap just north of the ferry terminal, offering both inside and outside dinning. Arnold found Karim at a small plastic table at the far end of the pier.

On the table next to him was a grease stained discarded cardboard boat of partially eaten fish and chips and several balled napkins to either side of a red plastic catsup dispenser. A fat seagull perched on the nearby railing begged for fries or any other food scraps anyone might wish to donate to The Seagull Welfare League.

Approaching Firouz, Arnold realized it'd be difficult for the FBI, or anyone else intent on surveillance, to monitor a conversation out here even with a good directional microphone. Not impossible, just difficult.

Was he being followed?

Smiling, Firouz waved him over to a molded plastic chair at the table. Arnold dumped himself into the one directly across from the terrorist, his back to the street, facing the harbor with a view of the islands and Olympics in the distance.

Firouz said, "Good. You came. Want some lunch? Their tartar sauce is excellent. Haven't had chips this good since London."

He broke the end off a fry and tossed it to the waiting gull. The gull caught it without so much as fluttering a feather.

"I'm not hungry."

"What a shame. These are excellent, you know. Karim and I both think they're better than any in Vegas, and Karim considers himself a fish and chips connoisseur."

He smiled, as if this were an inside joke he was now sharing with one of the family.

He screwing with me?

"I'm not here to eat. Naseem gave me your message," deciding it would be best to use her real name if he intended to collaborate with them. "She said you wanted to talk. What about?"

Firouz dabbed the corner of his lips with a paper towel, an almost effeminate motion, Arnold thought, way too precise for eating damn French fries.

Trying to impress someone?

"I'm offering you the opportunity of a lifetime. And the chance to become a very rich man in the process."

Arnold made a point to glance around, looking for anyone who might be listening, or perhaps spot whoever was supposed to be his tail.

"Why don't you be a bit more specific about what that would entail?"

Firouz pushed the half full boat of chips a few inches away and wiped his fingers on the one remaining unsoiled napkin.

"This is quite simple, really. Your computer was of no help to us, but I think you already knew that." His face reflected mild irritation, which, Arnold hoped, was only the tip of an emotional iceberg. Hard as he was trying, the terrorist seemed to be incapable of suppressing all of it. "Since we still don't have what we want, we're offering to buy your system from you."

"My system?" He shook his head. "Not for sale."

"You misunderstand. We don't want your computer or your system—we probably wouldn't know how to use it if you donated it to us. No, we're more interested in what you can do with it for us, your analysis capabilities. And we're willing to pay quite handsomely for your work. Your assignments would be very similar to the work you so graciously did with us previously."

Now, if anyone were monitoring the conversation, Arnold's complicity would be a matter of record. Again, Arnold felt comfort in knowing this was already in the FBI file.

Arnold began scratching away a glob of old dried catsup stuck to the white enamel tabletop with his thumbnail.

"What sort of price you offering?"

Firouz didn't hesitate.

"One hundred thousand dollars."

"For?"

"Six months' work."

"Naw, not worth it."

Firouz rubbed his chin a moment.

"Three hundred, then."

Laughing, Arnold shook his head.

"You kidding? With the risks I'm taking?"

"That's a shitload of money, Arnold. If not three hundred, then what price is fair?"

This was the tricky part: making them buy into really being

contractible, yet not exceeding a figure they would think ridiculous. Everyone had a limit, and regardless of who was funding their activity, there was a point at which to decline.

"Let's not make it time dependent, because as Einstein pointed out, time is relevant only when comparing to other things. Let's say a half-million for each problem I analyze. Furthermore, I want the money transferred to my offshore account within twenty-four hours from the time you assign me the problem. Here," he handed Firouz a folded yellow Post-It with the name of a Grand Cayman account under the name Toby Taylor.

Firouz unfolded it, held it up to view from a better angle, smiled.

"No problem."

No hesitation at all, which told Arnold he was being played, sure as hell. The moment they had pirated his system he would be killed.

"But," Firouz said, refolding the paper and slipping it into his breast pocket. "The duration of your employment is performance driven. You understand what this means?"

Yeah, soon as you screw me, you'll kill me.

"I get it."

The gull on the railing watching the negotiation leaned forward and screamed at Firouz. This time he threw an entire fry over the rail, away from the gull so he'd have to at least fly to catch it.

After carefully cleaning his greasy fingers on a fresh paper napkin, he returned to Arnold.

"Then we are agreed?"

Arnold nodded yes and realized he was applying counterpressure to his stomach again. Did he notice? He fished a roll of Tums from his jeans pocket in a stupid attempt to disguise the pain as simple indigestion instead of anxiety.

"There are differences from the way we operated last time," he said, "because I assume you prefer to remain in Seattle at your home. However, our activities will be elsewhere. Vegas, for example, where we presently work."

Arnold asked, "How will I communicate with you?"

And here it comes, he thought: the door to his system they would surely try to exploit. He caught another hint of a smile and thought the guy had to be a doormat at poker.

Firouz opened his wallet, removed a small piece of paper to hand him.

"This is how you contact my computer specialist. His name is Nawzer Singh. The two of you can work out the particulars of how to pass information, but from what I understand—and I don't know much about computers—he'll give you remote access to one of ours. You transfer our information there. For obvious security reasons, it's isolated from the general internet. Nawzer emphasized to me you must keep your activities restricted to that drop box only. Nothing else. He says it will be impossible for you to explore anything but what is contained in that one folder. And if you do try to access any other areas in the system you will face extreme consequences. I can't emphasize this strongly enough, Arnold. Is this clear?"

Arnold nodded agreement, thinking they'd provide him access to a directory for only one reason: to provide themselves with an access link into his system. And once they had that, they'd start robbing him blind. He now faced a simple, straightforward strategy, pitting his skills against some geek named Nawzer. How good was he, and how good was their geek?

Well, I'll find out. Let the games begin.

"Okay, then. We done here?" Arnold asked.

Firouz leaned across the table to him and lowered his voice.

"Not yet. One more thing. Try to fuck me on this and there are no words to describe the hell you will endure before you die."

They got ready to stand, the meeting now over with, until Arnold remembered...

He held up a finger.

"One more thing. Almost forgot. I need to talk now and then to my lawyer in person."

Firouz's eyebrows arched.

"Oh? Why?"

Good thing he'd rehearsed this line.

Not missing a beat, he said, "Surprised you have to ask, especially with a spy in the police department. Howard's murder is still under active investigation and I remain a prime suspect. Until it's closed..." holding both palms up in a gesture of innocence.

Firouz made no attempt to mask a smile.

"Oh, and I almost forgot," mimicking Arnold's innocent tone and gesture. "You have a roommate."

Arnold waited.

"Karim will live with you for the foreseeable future."

Yeah, until he tries to kill me.

"Shoot. Was hoping for Naseem."

With a smirk, he said, "Wouldn't want to waste her talents. She makes too much money."

25

ARNOLD TILTED BACK his chair and massaged the rock-hard cords of muscle on the right side of his neck. They were especially knotted tonight, sore from sitting with his head cocked to the right, a bad postural habit acquired during childhood, before his astigmatism had been diagnosed and corrected with glasses. He listened to the familiar 2 AM house sounds: the soft hum of the air exchange fan, the cooling unit down in the computer room, Karim's guttural ragged snoring from the upstairs guest room, a distant siren. He could smell the now cold slice of pepperoni pizza to the right of his mouse, a can of warm Diet Coke just beyond that. Dinner from hours ago. He used to be able to devour an entire medium size pizza, but not lately, not since Howie's....

The gut pain had first appeared the night the police interrogated him about the murder and had waxed and waned ever since, depending on his level of stress, causing him to chew Tums like candy. Now, as he worked on a strategy to access the Jahandars' computer, the pain seemed more intense. It would stay with him forever, he believed, and become one of those chronic ailments older people complain of, just another dysfunction accumulated as a result of coping with life's ravages.

The problem needing a solution went like this: the FBI wanted access to the terrorists' method of communication but had been thus far unable to determine what that mode might be. Could be digital, courier, or even FedEx shipments, for all anyone knew. That had been their biggest stated concern. Now, at least, he knew that some of their communication was digital. But, in spite of Fisher's reassurances, he knew the FBI wouldn't be satisfied with one link into one isolated computer because that would not yield a method to locate them. What they really wanted was access to—and the location of—the mother organization.

In contrast to terrorist groups such as al Qaeda, these jokers hated publicity, believing they could operate more effectively by remaining anonymous. Although some members might occasionally use a disposable cellphone for limited communication, the ears of the NSA and other intelligence agencies have proven so effective over the years that terrorists had to assume all cellular conversations were monitored. Routine email was equally vulnerable. Bin Laden had solved the issue by using a trusted courier to hand deliver messages, in spite of the method being slow and cumbersome, and, in the end, knowing how easily it could be broken if the courier was fingered.

This is why so many terrorists had recently migrated to the Deep Net. Although anyone could download the Tor browser, finding desired websites was problematic because, unlike normal websites such as eBay, Facebook, or Amazon, Deep Net web sites did not have user friendly "dot-com" URLs or addresses. Instead, addresses were made up of a seemingly random string of characters followed by ".onion." Sophisticated users knew where to find online directories—such as The Hidden Wiki—that provide addresses to some Deep Net sites.

The really scary part was that these directories only scratched the surface of the illegal activity and content available within the Deep Net. The deepest dot-onion addresses were known only to a select group of people, and it was these sites that contained the darkest contents.

Recently, there had been speculation as to just how good Tor actually was at keeping online activities anonymous. Some claimed it provided absolute anonymity whereas others disputed this. One Tor hidden online narcotics store, Silk Road, was brought down by authorities in March 2013, but the authorities had difficulties prosecuting the online narcotics sellers because they had been operating in disparate jurisdictions, so most still remained free. In contrast, an FBI investigation into child abuse and porn was completely frustrated by

Tor.

The time and effort needed for law enforcement agents to track Tor users—even when possible—was not feasible. Tor "end nodes"— the computers supporting Tor traffic—could reside in any country having Internet available, which nowadays was pretty much everywhere. In addition, it wasn't uncommon for unsuspecting computer owners to be completely unaware of the criminal traffic passing through their machines.

Politicians and governments might like to believe they could police the internet, but the difficulty of actually enforcing online legislation was close to impossible, partly because well-defined sovereign borders simply don't exist. The good news was that some people are not willing to wait and watch cyberbased crime go unchallenged. A few years ago, the infamous hacker group Anonymous took matters into its own hands by shutting down several child pornography websites, including Lolita City, as part of Operation Darknet.

The FBI strongly suspected the Jahandars were communicating via the Deep Net and now Arnold possessed the proof of that. He had discovered this from their first contact this evening. But things weren't that simple. Never were, Arnold thought, staring at the monitor.

He picked up the one remaining slice of cold pizza, nibbled off the limp apex, dropped it back into the box, and slumped back into the chair.

Think! This is important.

Okay, as of a few minutes ago, he knew how they communicated. That part of the puzzle was solved. But Fisher wanted more. He wanted the ability to intercept all their messages and not just the ones to Arnold. Meaning he had to discover a route into the mother computer.

That would be a total bitch!

If he had a single Tor address to connect to, the solution would be mind-numbingly straightforward: pass that information on to Fisher and let the FBI geeks work through the massive headache of trying to track the originating computer back to the country, city, and physical address—if there was one—of residence. Then again, who's to say the computer wasn't a laptop in the front seat of a car roaming the streets of

Mogadishu and connecting to the Internet via a satellite phone uplink? Apparently, whoever was in charge of the terrorists' computers had anticipated this risk and had taken the precaution of constantly varying their Darknet address. Meaning when they wanted information from Arnold, they gave him a dot-onion site that remained active for maybe only ten minutes. If he didn't log onto the site within that period of time, it went dead and the terrorists moved onto the next, completely new, address. Had to hand it to Nawzer: he—or she, he had no idea which—was very canny when it came to being elusive.

He decided his only hope would be to write a Trojan horse, a tiny bit of software to upload to their computer next time they linked up. It, in turn, would send back a simple intermittent message—a digital beacon, of sorts—that would allow him, or the Homeland Security geeks, to track back to its origin. Simple in concept, difficult to pull off. For if Nawzer was as clever as Arnold suspected, he would have anticipated this tactic and would be screening any incoming bits for an attached code each time they linked up. Meaning Arnold had to be better at disguising his Trojan horse than Nawzer would be at detecting it. This was the problem he now faced, and time was running out.

He glanced at his watch, realized how late it had become. Plus, he was dog tired, having slept only a handful of hours these past few days. Worse yet, he found himself slipping into fantasies about Rachael, about how intimately she had hugged him at the funeral. He shook his head, trying to focus on the task at hand. But he also needed sleep. Otherwise fatigue would cause him to start making stupid errors.

What are my most important chores tonight?

Well, one was to transmit this new information—that the terrorists were using the internet—to Davidson to pass on to the FBI. Easy enough. He sent an email to Davidson to meet mid-morning.

Last thing before hitting the sack was to start his security scans running. Those bastards knew the only way to obtain his system would be to steal it. Meaning, they would try to upload a similarly stealthy Trojan horse to his network. This was no longer a hypothetical mental exercise; it was a given. So, on top of his usual antivirus/spyware routines, he initiated another scan to scour his system in minute detail for any bits of code that were new to his system since his contact with Nawzer. The scan would take hours to complete and would run while he slept. The last precaution he took before heading off to bed was to disconnect from the Internet.

For a moment Arnold sat listening for Karim's snoring. Yes, still there. The tough thing was knowing the smelly bastard would remain in the house until Firouz gave him permission him to kill him, a task he suspected would please Karim no end. But he assured himself, that would not happen unless they had his pirated system working for them. Moving over to the kitchen cabinet, he opened the blue plastic Maalox bottle and chugged a slug, waited for the first swallow to work its way down to the ache before taking a second hit, then wiped chalky residue from his lips with the back of his hand and capped the bottle.

For a moment he stood, bottle in hand, butt propped against the edge of the kitchen counter, reflecting on the battle taking place between himself and Nawzer, the terrorist computer jockey: the race had begun.

Who'd win?

The pain smoldering in the pit of his stomach wasn't helped by the chalky liquid, so he grabbed a handful of Tums from the bathroom to stash on the bedside stand. That's when he noticed the still untouched amber prescription bottle on the cabinet shelf, exactly as it had remained for the past year. Ambien. He shook it, feeling the weight and listening to the rattle.

Almost full. Enough to kill myself? Hmmm.... Interesting...

Death would certainly solve the immediate issues and relieve the stress tearing him in half, as if the FBI and Jahandars each were tugging an arm and leg like a medieval torture device.

In retrospect, life had been going along perfectly until he decided to visit Vegas. Well, except for his overwhelming desire to overcome his awkwardness around women. And if he hadn't flown there he'd still be grappling with that issue, so it *had* resulted in a few positives. But now, with the aid of hindsight, he knew the trip hadn't been worth it. Had he known...well, that wasn't exactly true either. He really had wanted to experience sex. Hell, had even dreamed about it frequently. Yet had he selected another escort, who knew what his life would now be like? Less complicated, for sure. Then again, who's to say that would be the case? He'd never know.

With a resigned sigh, he shook the bottle again, listening to the rattle of pills. Yeah, upend the bottle and wash them all down with a glass of water or, better yet, a slug of vodka, slip into bed, feel the pleasure of sleep settle over him and never wake up.

Easy enough.

He tried to imagine what it would feel like to actually go through with it, to experience the sensation of the pills slipping down his throat to his stomach, where they would slowly begin dissolving, first crumbling into paste and then on into fluid, at which point the drug would begin to be absorbed. Soon as that happened, his fate would be cast. Unless he chickened out and got himself to an ER to get his stomach pumped. But was death the only way of extricating himself from this bind?

No. Not yet.

At least he hadn't reached that point of despair. Yet. Besides, he had a morbid curiosity to learn how this chapter would end, to see if he was really good enough to beat Nawzer and Chang. By now, helping the FBI wasn't the overriding motivator to see this little game to the finish. At this point, the game itself, the challenge of putting his life on the line, was the ultimate gamble. It had become an adrenaline rush of sorts, like bungee jumping or sky diving. For the first time the reality of gambling for the ultimate stakes really sank in. He could win only if he could devise a foolproof way to stop the Jahandars and then disappear forever, leaving everyone, including the FBI, to believe he was dead. Interesting problem. Replacing the Ambien on the shelf, again pondering his situation, he wandered back to the kitchen.

A new kernel of an idea popped to mind. A possibility. He stood at the stove inspecting the six burners, absent mindedly massaging his front teeth with the tip of his tongue.

Could it possibly work?

He mentally began searching for flaws in the plan.

Yes, it might.

No longer exhausted—and in fact feeling strangely excited—he microwaved a mug of water for hot chocolate. Back at the table he began critically analyzing the idea, forging it into a solid plan, a simultaneous solution to several problems at once, a way to reconstruct his life and free himself. Howie would never come back to life. He felt terrible about that. But vengeance for his senseless murder would go a hell of a long way to alleviate his guilt.

Patience would be the key, and patience wasn't one of his strong points.

But for the first time he glimpsed a possible way out.

26

ARNOLD SET THE parking brake and climbed out of the Jetta, Karim doing likewise from the passenger side, sticking to him like a booger on the tip of his finger. Once again, he'd been lucky to be a half-block down from another car as it started to pull out, free spaces at a premium along this stretch of Alki Beach. The sun warmed the salt air, heightening the pungent shore smells of beached seaweed and decomposing barnacles.

He recognized Davidson sitting on a large piece of driftwood about three hundred yards west on the beach, tossing rocks he picked up at his feet. Arnold waved, and Davidson returned the acknowledgment but made no effort to stand, seemingly content to sit on the large, weathered log and watch them approach.

As they neared the lawyer, Arnold said to Karim, "That place across the street, Spuds?" nodding to a cubic, single- level building of glass, white painted wood, and a blue, weathered canopy.

"Uh."

Which Arnold interpreted as an affirmative.

"Great fish and chips. I strongly recommend them."

Karim glanced from the stand to the beach and back again, his pace slowing as he considered whether to feed his face or stand around ogling the women on the beach.

"That bench?"

Karim had started taking to asking questions similar to the way

Arnold did. He was referring to a park bench bolted to the concrete sidewalk, facing the harbor.

"You sit there."

Too much!

"Oh, for Chrissake, you think I'm going to run out on you? Here, take the fucking car keys if that'll make you happy."

He was getting fed up with his evil twin constantly at his side.

It was a stupid question to ask because the answer was obviously yes. Everywhere they went it was always the same, as if Karim were accompanying the transfer of a notorious prisoner from one prison to the other instead of simply making sure Arnold didn't take a powder. Shaking his head in a show of obvious disgust, Arnold dropped down onto the bench, wrist to his side so Karim could handcuff him to the round iron leg. Davidson was standing next to them by now, watching with obvious bemusement.

Soon as the cuff was secure and Karim satisfied, Davidson plunked down next to him but continued looking straight across the blue harbor to the Magnolia neighborhood. A white and green Washington State ferry was slicing across the panorama toward the downtown terminal. Neither man spoke until Karim began dodging traffic on his way across the street.

Davidson gave a sarcastic snort.

"Doesn't cut you any slack, does he?"

Arnold turned from watching his guard to his lawyer.

"Figured the idea of food—especially fish and chips—would give us a chance to talk in private a few minutes. They're busy this time of day, so that should allow a few extra minutes."

"How you doing?" Davidson asked sympathetically.

Arnold sat back, trying to enjoy the sun on his face and view as much as possible with his hand shackled to the bench.

"You asking about me personally or are you asking about the information I'm supposed to get for our federal friends?"

Davidson crossed his legs, right ankle on left knee and shot the cuff of his suit pants.

"Don't be so cynical. Both. Start with you."

He wanted to open up and tell him how tired and frightened he felt every second of the day, how he wished to hell he'd never selected Breeze, how he'd picked up his mother's amber bottle of Ambien and actually toyed with the idea of swallowing the whole lot of them with a vodka chaser. But that would be whining, and he hated that. Instead, he stole another reassuring glance over his shoulder at Karim, saw him queuing up at the order window. Quickly, he pulled a slip of folded yellow notepaper from his jeans and handed it to Davidson.

"Here."

Soon as Davidson had it, Arnold put his hand back to his side. All he needed was for Karim to catch him passing notes. For a second, he felt as if he were back in grade school, dodging the teacher's all-knowing eyes.

"What is it?" Davidson asked.

Arnold checked on Karim again. Still in line.

"Two things. The most important is the number of two of Firouz's offshore accounts. A good way for the feds to finger him is to work back through those. I got them off the initial payment he sent me. Have them follow the money, although I suspect the accounts might've been changed by now. But at least it gives them something to play with."

Davidson nodded.

"Good work. I'll pass it along. You said two things. What else?"

Arnold blew out a breath and wiped his palms on his jeans, his heart pounding faster and harder than normal.

Yeah, I'd be a shitty spy.

"Fisher said he suspected they were using the Darknet. Last night was my first contact with Firouz's controller. They gave me an assignment. But I suspect it's total bullshit, a nothing job, just something to test what I'll do and how I'll react. The important point to tell Fisher is he's right, that's one way they communicate." He thought about that a moment and added, "At least with me it is. I have no idea how they pass information between each other."

Davidson gave a quick nod of acknowledgment.

"Got it."

Arnold saw something in his lawyer's face, and it wasn't good.

"What?"

"Bad news." Davidson was staring into the distance now, making it apparent this wasn't going to be easy for him. "They want you to do more than only provide a link to their cell."

Davidson stopped, as if undecided how to deliver an unpleasant message.

Arnold shook his head in disgust.

Why am I not surprised?

"Go on. What?"

Davidson cleared his throat.

"They want you to tell Firouz to let his handler know the FBI asked you to spy for them. Then—"

"You fucking out of your mind? They'll kill me, they find out."

Davidson raised a hand.

"Hold on and listen to me. I didn't say I agree with them; I'm just telling you what they instructed me to pass on. Do with it what you please. You listening?"

"Yes."

His head felt ready to explode and he realized he was grinding his molars, making the angle of his jaw ache on up to his temples.

"They figure that not only can you obtain more information this way, but you can also feed them disinformation. See the logic?"

The pressure in Arnold's temples spiked, throbbing, producing a migraine like headache. He started to make a bitingly sarcastic remark but caught himself.

Fuck it, I just need to get out of this.

When he didn't answer, Davidson added, "Perhaps it's time we consider plan B. If you can figure out a way to slip away from Karim, I can hide you for a few days until we decide on a way to make you vanish for good. What do you think? We can do it right now, today, if you want."

He'd considered this option already. It had, in fact, been a recurrent rumination since the beginning. But he couldn't do that. Not yet. Not as long as he still owed Howie revenge, some payback for being murdered. He was also torn by the specter of a possible connection with

Rachael. As long as that remained a possibility, he wasn't going anywhere.

He shook his head.

"Can't do that. Not right now. Soon maybe."

"Your call. I'm just saying, consider it. We can do it anytime, just give the nod."

Arnold turned to glimpse the fish and chips place again. Karim was now standing to the left of the order counter, sprinkling vinegar over a double order of golden fish and chips. Arnold turned back to the beach view.

"If I don't settle this for good, I'll be on the run the rest of my life. If the FBI isn't hunting me, Firouz will be. And if he doesn't find me, you can pretty much count on him coming after you. You prepared to deal with that?"

"Well, since you put it in those terms, no. But I still think we should consider getting you out of the action before something bad happens. I have a real uneasy feeling that nothing good is going to come of this."

Arnold kept facing the water with his voice lowered.

"I'm working on a plan."

Davidson repositioned himself on the bench at an angle, left arm draped over the back, legs crossed, partially facing Arnold.

"What?"

Arnold leaned forward, elbows on knees, and spoke toward the water.

"You're better off not knowing."

Davidson mimicked Arnold's position, so both were speaking away from Karim's approach. "No, tell me."

Arnold shook his head.

"You're not hearing me. No. How can I make that any clearer?"

Davidson didn't answer.

Arnold felt guilty for the cutting tone of his last remark, so he added, "I think I'm making some progress in finding them, but you're better off not knowing any details."

Davidson scratched his chin and frowned.

"Fisher's getting antsy. Says upper management is demanding some traction on this case. It's been two weeks with nothing to show for it. He doesn't want to sit around with his thumb up his ass while these guys put the finishing touches on an attack next week. Their chatter says that's when it's happening."

Arnold shifted positions, bent his right knee enough to prop his right heel on the edge of the bench so he could awkwardly retie his Nikes, the task painfully difficult with his right hand tethered by the handcuff. Big orange and silver shoes with air cushioned heels.

"You tell him I'm paying quarterly taxes now? Least that should put a smile on his face." Davidson shifted positions too and raised his hand to shield his eyes from the glare. "I know you're frustrated with this. I am, too, but there's no need to shoot the messenger."

"Do me a favor."

"Sure, what?"

"Howard has a sister, Rachael. Can you contact her and have her use Howard's computer? Tell her to use Tor to access this email account. She'll know what I'm talking about." Arnold passed another slip of paper. "Will you do that, please?"

"Yeah, sure, no problem."

Arnold paused to blow a long, slow breath, slowly shaking his head.

"Jesus, I hate this. Getting squeezed from all sides. You would, too. Besides, I just gave Fisher something so that should make him happy for a while."

"Only if it helps prevent another bombing or killing."

"Shit," Arnold mumbled with another glance over his shoulder. Karim was holding a white paper sack in one hand and a soft drink container with a straw poking out the top in the other, waiting for a break in traffic. "Long as we're talking taxes, what's the statute of limitations on income tax evasion?"

Davidson raised his face to the sun and closed his eyes.

"Three to six years from the commission of the crime, meaning from the date the return should've been filed. If no return was filed, which is the case with you, the statue begins to run from April 15 of each year taxes weren't paid. Meaning that you're still fully exposed on multiple counts."

"We're done, Karim's coming." He leaned closer to Davidson. "I need more time. Fucking Jahandars know exactly what I'm trying to do. That makes it much more difficult. If getting inside were so damn easy, Fisher's geeks would've been there months ago. Pass that on to Fisher."

Standing up from the bench, Davidson nodded.

"I'll tell him, but remember one thing. They're under pressure, too. They know an attack is imminent. They need to know where and when it's going to happen. And then they need to know how to find these bastards. Who knows how many lives depend on that? And I'm not being a drama queen when I say this."

"I know."

The gut ache was back.

27

WITH THE SUN warming his back, he watched in envy as Davidson walked away from him with the easygoing stride of a man with few pressures, certainly not even remotely close to the pressure he was feeling bear down on him now. Arnold realized he was holding his stomach again and popped another Tums from a half-eaten roll in his pocket.

Karim was standing ten feet away, facing the shore, toes of his shoes over the edge of the concrete sidewalk above the sand, his left hand holding the grease stained cardboard boat while his right hand shoveled catsup coated fries into his constantly chomping mouth. Karim turned to him.

"You are right. Very good."

He tossed the empty grease-soaked boat into a trash can, licked his fingers clean, wiped the glistening saliva on a paper napkin before bending down to unlock the handcuffs.

"We go now."

Arnold stood, massaging the redness the steel cuffs caused from his wrist. If he were bigger and stronger, he would try to take those cuffs from Karim and stuff them down the bastard's throat. But he wasn't, and couldn't, so just shook his head and followed.

Arnold backtracked the Jetta along Harbor Avenue South West to the onramp of the West Seattle Bridge, crossed over the tip of Harbor

Island to where he caught the Alaskan Way viaduct heading north.

As they approached the Battery Street Tunnel, Karim said, "Take the exit."

"What?"

That exit would not take them north on Aurora to Eightieth, where he planned to cut east toward Greenlake.

"Take the exit!" Karim waved repeatedly at the off ramp.

Arnold slid over to the right lane, turned on his blinker and headed down the off ramp, the uneasy feeling churning his gut. "Why? What's up?" Trying for an unconcerned tone that was exactly opposite his present state of mind.

"Go straight." Karim pointed, as if there were other options here along Western Avenue.

A half-mile later Western Avenue forked into Elliott Avenue, a row of eight-story office buildings buffering them from the harbor to the west, a string of various trashy businesses between the road and Queen Anne Hill to the east, some of the small buildings in the process of being destroyed to make way for concrete foundations destined to become taller, view-obstructing buildings. Urban progress at its finest.

Having received no explanation the first time, Arnold asked again. "Where we going?"

Ignoring the question, Karim used his little fingernail to pick at something between his front teeth. Finally satisfied, he closed his mouth, swept his tongue over the teeth, but remained mute.

He pissed Arnold off. Then again, most things Karim did pissed Arnold off.

Unable to stand it any longer, he asked, "Karim, where the hell we going?"

"You will learn. Up ahead. The ramp, take it." Referring to the Garfield Street Bridge on ramp.

Once on the ramp only two options remained: continue up to the Magnolia neighborhood or take the exit down to the Smith Cove docks that service cruise ships and ocean-going fishing boats. Soon as they blew past the down ramp without a word from Karim, Arnold realized Magnolia had to be their destination.

But why?

Magnolia was a residential area with one small village like shopping area of two or three blocks.

Wait a minute…what about Discovery Park? The 534-acre parcel of land occupied most of what had once been Fort Lawton, an army installation originally built in the late 1800s to protect the Seattle harbor from naval attack. The government gifted a substantial chunk of the fort to the city for a park that now contained large, desolate fields and woods along the high bluffs overlooking Puget Sound. But with the park so immense, there were vast areas where no one ventured…

Karim pointed for him to turn onto Magnolia Boulevard, a curvy street running the cusp of the bluffs on the way up to the south entrance of the park, making their destination a certainty. What's there? A drop of sweat seeped from his armpit to slither down the side of his chest.

Shit!

At the moment, he couldn't think of a better place for Karim to kill him. If that were the reason for the visit. Dump a body over the cliffs and no one would find it for weeks, possibly never. Coyotes would dispose of the bones within days. Or as the body rotted, the smell would be totally obscured in the obnoxious odors wafting up from the tide flats.

Up ahead, the south entrance of the park came into view.

"Where to?" Arnold asked, hoping Karim would tell him to take a right or stop, or turn around and go back.

"Straight. Into the park."

Aw, Christ! Could he talk him out of it? Or was he getting cranked up over nothing?

He nosed the car past the entrance in the cyclone fence, followed the asphalt road through a right-hand curve into a spacious parking area containing only three other empty cars and an increasingly desolate vibe. This being a workday for most people, the area would likely remain relatively empty except for an occasional dog walker probably from the nearby neighborhood.

"Park," Karim said, waving at no particular space.

As they stepped from the car, Karim pointed to the road they'd just traveled.

"We go that way."

From the few sketchy details Arnold remembered, the trail would take them west to a crest of the property where a series of two-story peaked-roof officers' homes looked out over overgrown grasses and blackberry vines rolling down past the now empty parade fields and on out to the high, Dover like bluffs above the saltwater of Puget Sound. Arnold started walking, Karim on his left, matching his pace, neither one speaking. What was there to say? Arnold casually glanced around to see if any other person was nearby, perhaps even a park maintenance worker, but saw no one, not even a dog. The park was so huge the occupants from the empty cars could be anywhere. And if he saw someone, what could he say? Hey, this guy is going to kill me?

Another wave of gut pain rolled through him, causing him to press his stomach as they walked. They were cresting the hill now, exposing the expansive view to the west, out over the fields where he imagined troops once marched in formations, drilling, preparing to fight the war du jour. He thought he could even hear the ghostly clanking of tank treads grinding up the clayish dirt but knew it was only his racing mind playing tricks, maybe the result of wind blowing through the massive blackberry tangles bordering the expansive field.

They started down one of three dusty paths heading west with diverging angles toward the cliffs. Several hundred yards to his left the southern border of the property was defined by a ten-foot cyclone fence hidden by a row of tall pines. The path Karim chose curved northward, through one particularly high tangle of blackberries, toward a clump of dense forest. Arnold stole a glance at the smelly bastard, checking to see if the gun was in his hand. No, both hands remained empty, swinging in concert with his long lumbering gait, but this meant nothing. The gun could easily be hidden in the small of his back by the shirt he never bothered to tuck in. Precisely for that reason, probably.

They continued in silence, Arnold's legs growing more wooden and less willing to move the closer the tree line grew.

Unable to tolerate the suspense any longer, Arnold asked, "Where we going?"

Better question, he realized, would be *why are we even out here?* Might as well hear what the steroid bulked Iranian had to say.

"You will see."

He considered a quick cut to the right and then simply running flat out, fast as he could to lay down as much distance between them as possible before Karim could draw the gun, aim, and squeeze off a shot. The greater the separation the more room for error, meaning the less chance of being nailed by a bullet. He'd done it once, so he could do it again. How quick was Karim with that gun? What kind of accuracy did he maintain? But as sensible as that option seemed, Arnold couldn't build up the nerve to act on the urge, to actually learn the answers to those questions. Chickening out like this made him think of all the Jews passively allowing the Nazis to herd them into humiliating showers and mass graves. Was he now demonstrating his heritage?

The path entered the woods and continued for another twenty feet before t-boning another path paralleling the edge of the cliffs. Ahead was a small clearing with a protective railing that allowed visitors a 120-degree westerly view of Puget Sound. Karim led him to the railing and stopped. The terrorist stood, three hundred feet above the crashing waves, shielding his eyes from the sun with both hands.

This it?

Arnold stood behind the large man, thinking, now is the time. Run! But once more, he couldn't will his body to act on the urge. Something, perhaps a curiosity about why the terrorist had brought him to this secluded spot, caused his hesitation.

Karim turned to him.

"The money, what do you plan with it?"

Huh? Of all the possible topics...the hell's he talking about?

Karim's eyebrows scrunched together.

"You are making good money with us. What are you planning for it?"

I was making even better money before I started working for you bastards. So what?

"You mean, how will I spend it?"

Karim nodded before returning his attention to the view.

"Huh. Hadn't really thought about it." True, he's had other things to think about, like how the hell to extricate himself from this mess. "Why do you ask?"

Karim turned his back to the panoramic view and sat on one of the rail supports and crossed his massive arms.

"This life I am living. Is not my whole life. Soon, maybe, five years, I will retire."

A distant look settled into the man's eyes, a thousand-yard stare.

This conversation was making Arnold edgy.

Why all the questions?

What could his possible motive be? He licked his lips, glanced around again for other people. And saw no one.

This some sort of diversion so someone, Firouz perhaps, can sneak up behind me when I least expect it to send a bullet through the back of my head?

He licked his lips and wiped his palms on his jeans and ignored another butt-puckering urge to run.

"There is a place," Karim turned back to the view. He leaned forward, holding onto the rail, and faced the southwest sun shimmering off the water, the Olympic Mountains in bold relief in the horizon. "Is on the Black Sea. You know this Black Sea?"

"No."

Arnold turned his back to the view to keep an eye on the path behind them just in case...this sudden buddy-buddy brotherhood shtick of Karim's was making him twitchy.

Karim hawked up a ball of phlegm, sent it sailing over the railing in an arching trajectory.

"By then, I will have money for dacha, a house. You know this term, dacha?"

"No."

"I live there, fish, maybe find a young woman who needs husband." He shrugged. A who-knows, anything-is-possible shrug. "This," pointing at the water, "makes me think of it."

Only the rustle of the breeze through the trees and an occasional distant screech of a seagull could be heard.

For a split-second Karim's confession—so seemingly heartfelt and human—evoked a momentary warmth toward him. But just as quickly Arnold reminded himself, this is the man who shot Howie to death in cold blood.

He stifled the urge to shout, "Where the fuck do you get off? We supposed to be buds now? This supposed to be a male bonding experience now that we're playing on the same team? Well, fuck that." Instead, he said nothing.

Karim remained standing, both hands stuffed deeply in his pockets, facing the view with a look of reverence in his eyes.

"Where will you go with your money? You will stay here?"

As if he simply assumed Arnold wanted to be someplace other than his life-long home.

A warning bell rang in the back of his mind. Had Nawzer uncovered his secret bank account? Probably. He might just have burrowed far enough into his system to realize Arnold was moving the majority of his funds to hidden offshore accounts. Perhaps they assumed Arnold planned on disappearing before they could kill him. After all, he and Nawzer were playing the deadly game of winner takes all. If the terrorist could steal Arnold's system before Arnold could steal his, they'd kill him. So, this trip to the view spot could be nothing more than a tricky way of interrogating him for information, to give them a head start in tracking him down if he fled.

Interesting question, the one about staying or leaving. A question Arnold had repeatedly considered these past sleepless nights while tossing under the blanket. Leaving would mean abandoning all hope of ever finding out what might happen between Rachael and him. Also, Seattle was home. Always had been, and he loved it here. But the house and the neighborhood had been his home as long as his parents and a best friend lived. Now that Mom and Dad and Howie were gone... but what about Rachael?

"Would you leave?" Karim asked.

"Yeah. I'll go to Tampa Bay in a blink. Anything to get away from the weather here."

"Tampa Bay? Why?" Karim asked with what appeared to be

genuine interest.

"Our family spent a vacation there a few years back. Loved it. All the boats, the nice weather, the sun." All bullshit, of course. "Fell in love with the area. Wanted to live there ever since. Maybe get a fishing boat for the Gulf."

"You want a boat? To fish?"

In for a pound...

"Yeah, deep sea fishing. Marlin, fish like that."

In fact, he hated fishing, felt sorry for them. Catch and release seemed especially cruel.

Anyone ever ask the fish what they thought about it?

"I like to fish, too." Karim mimed casting then stood very still, gazing at the water, sun sparkling off ripples, the breeze fresh and salty. After several moments, he stepped away from the railing and turned to head back up the path.

"We go now. Just wanted to show you this."

There was a tinge of resignation in his voice that gave Arnold pause. By now Karim was ahead of him, not seeming to care whether Arnold remained there or was following, the distance between them increasing. Arnold expelled a deep breath and hurried to catch up.

What did all this tell him, he wondered. And mulled that over as they walked. Well, for one thing, it meant Nawzer must be further ahead than he thought.

Time was running out faster than he had predicted.

He would have to finish his plan in the next day or two.

28

THEY DROVE BACK over the Garfield Street Bridge in the opposite direction.

At the bottom of the ramp, Arnold turned north onto Fifteenth, then immediately pulled into a parking lot in front of a single-story industrial-looking building with a sign across the top that read "Albert Lee Appliances."

Soon the hand brake was set and the ignition off, Karim clamped onto his right wrist.

"Why this stop?"

Arnold tried to pull free from the vise-like grip.

"Jesus, Karim! Let me go."

"Answer me."

Arnold glanced around for help. No one. He jerked his arm again.

"Let go and I'll show you."

Karim studied him a moment before releasing his wrist.

Arnold snaked a finger into the front pocket of his jeans, fished out a folded paper that he handed to Karim.

"Here."

The Iranian unfolded it, stared blankly at the series of letters and numbers before returning it.

"What is this?"

Arnold turned the paper so they both could read it and pointed to the letters he'd printed in ballpoint.

"This is my stove model," and thought about how that might sound. He added, "My cook top, you know, the burners I cook on? The starter for one of the burners doesn't work, so I have to replace it."

Karim seemed skeptical and suspicious. Arnold didn't know what else to say, so simply reached for the door handle. This time Karim didn't object and climbed out the passenger side.

"I go with you."

Fifteen minutes later, Arnold walked out of the appliance store with a new igniter.

29

ARNOLD DROVE THE Jetta slowly along the narrow alley, bouncing over potholes. Ten feet from the garage door he braked, clicked the garage opener, and waited for the door to slowly rise in a screeching protest of metal against metal.

Jesus, I really need to oil that puppy.

Which only brought to mind the myriad other chores he never seemed to get around to completing. The door was going to have to wait and now might never get oiled.

Seriously, what do I do all day?

Easy answer: write software, play video games, watch porn and old movies.

I should read more.

For some reason he couldn't quite identify, he'd lost interest in reading, both fiction and non-fiction. Now he read only emails and text messages, a routine that had started on the heels of his parent's murder. Used to love crime fiction in particular, authors like Michael Connelly, John Sandford...but then, considering...nope, he doesn't read anything anymore.

Emails and text messages, that's about it.

What was the world like before smart phones, when people wrote long letters and waited weeks for correspondence to cross the continent or oceans in prop planes and ships? A world without the Internet seemed unfathomable, so excruciatingly slow.

Garage door now open, he nosed the car into the narrow interior—allowing more space on Karim's side to wedge his bulked-up body out the passenger side door. Being considerate toward the slob would be another step in playing his role of sympathizer to the Jahandars and their cause. If he had to play the double agent game, he'd better appear to be the real deal. There wasn't much time left. But more important, he didn't want the asshole damaging the door by slamming the edge against the greasy power mower.

Now out on the cracked and oil-stained cement floor, he punched the garage door control. A moment later the agonizing grinding noise began afresh as the heavy door reversed directions and started back down. Arnold unlocked the side door to the backyard without bothering to check on Karim's extraction progress. If that retarded gorilla couldn't squeeze out of the car, well, that was his problem. Since Discovery Park, Arnold had been stewing in an unsettling brew of hatred of the Jahandars and everything they stood for, making it extremely difficult to act civilized toward Karim.

But what really helped stabilize his mood was that during the drive back here he'd been going back over his plan, refining the final act, savoring the idea of how sweet revenge would taste. Arnold bounded up the stairs from the backyard up to the back porch and French doors into the kitchen, opened the right-hand door and entered, and stopped short, dumbfounded. Firouz was sitting at the square Formica table enjoying what appeared to be a mug of tea, sections of the Wall Street Journal spread haphazardly over the tabletop.

The bastard had even had the nerve to use his favorite mug.

Firouz glanced up as if annoyed at being interrupted from reading an interesting article.

"Well, well, you're back." He smugly folded the section of paper and sat back in the chair with the trace of a smirk, the deliberate sequence of moves clearly intended to emphasize who was in charge. "Have a nice chat with your lawyer?"

Arnold, so furious at the sight, found himself speechless. He thought: *what gives you the right to break into my house?* In shocked muteness, he realized his home security system was under computer control. Did this mean Nawzer had already burrowed into his network and disabled the security system for Firouz? A move designed to show technical superiority?

"How did you get in?"

Firouz paused for dramatic effect.

"I walked."

Don't give him the slightest hint of how angry you are. Not now. Here is the perfect time to be friendly.

Arnold forced a smile, wondering, is it as transparent as it feels?

"You left the back door unlocked."

Bullshit.

He was a stickler for security. And even if that were the case, the back gates required a numeric code to access.

Unless he climbed the fence.

He glanced at the door to the basement stairs and saw the deadlock still engaged. Then again, it could just as easily have been relocked. Does he know about the equipment room? Did he have the knowledge to actually install a virus or Trojan horse? A trick that would certainly facilitate Nawazer.

"Been waiting long?" Arnold asked, his gut killing him, but he'd be damned if he'd pop a Tums in front of this asshole.

"Long enough to brew tea. Sit," he said, motioning to the chair opposite his.

Karim wandered in through the kitchen and continued on, saying, "I'll be in the other room watching TV, you need me."

For lack of anything better to say, Arnold asked, "Water still warm?" "Should be. Give it a feel."

Arnold checked. Enough hot water remained in the pot for a cup, so he dropped a bag of green tea into the water.

"What's on your mind?" he said as casually as possible, setting the cup on the table and then sliding into the corresponding chair, trying his damnedest for an air of indifference.

Firouz smiled.

"We're quite pleased with your work."

"Doubt you came all this way just to tell me that."

"Hardly." Firouz folded the newspaper, carefully aligning the pages. He muttered, "Newspapers!" while pausing to fold the volume along its original crease. "Dinosaurs. I'm surprised there's anyone on the planet who still reads them. But I must admit I still love them. There is something about the feel of the newsprint, so coarse, and, of course, the newsprint smell is all very pleasing, don't you agree?"

Why the game playing? Why not just get on with whatever was on the agenda?

"Haven't ever thought of it, I guess because I don't read them."

Firouz picked up his mug and inspected the contents.

"You're not interested in what is happening in the world?"

He replaced the ceramic on the table without taking a drink.

"I am. It's just that I read online. It's a green thing, I guess. Don't like the thought of using trees to make a product with such a senseless life. Besides, it's just one more thing to have to recycle. Might say it's a pain to do that."

Firouz's eyes narrowed.

"Tell me, Arnold, what is it, exactly, you discussed with your lawyer today?" his voice taking on a much different edge, cold and cutting.

Arnold laughed.

Perfect. Couldn't have asked for a better opportunity. Maybe there was a God after all.

The terrorist's eyes turned questioning. "What's so funny?"

Arnold held up an index finger and swallowed to buy a few seconds, knowing he needed to play this part flawlessly or else he'd give himself away. He sat back and looked Firouz in the eye.

"You won't believe me."

"Try me."

Arnold snorted another laugh, figured he'd assembled a sufficient story to pass muster.

"Several things. Three things, actually. First, the investigation. He seems to think the police are going to clear me as a person of interest, but they're no closer to discovering who did it."

Firouz leaned forward a bit, studying him more closely now.

"And you still did not tell them about us?"

"No."

He frowned.

"This makes no sense. I don't believe you."

"Naseem," Arnold continued, using Breeze's real name as a display of respect, "said you have a source with the police. I assume they're keeping you in the loop on this?"

"That's beside the point. The police can keep things secret if it serves their purpose." Firouz made a get-on-with-it motion. "You and your lawyer. Continue."

Arnold saw the moment as a pivotal point in the discussion, one he needed to play very cautiously. He thought of the lesson his father had taught him for selling a desirable piece of jewelry that was more expensive than a customer planned to spend: make the price non-negotiable and the customer will want it even more.

Arnold forced a laugh, dragging out his response.

"I give him tips."

"Tips?"

"Yes. Point spreads on football games, so he can bet them. Can't afford his fees, so this is how I pay him. It works out well."

Firouz appeared doubtful about this.

"You said three issues. What else?"

Arnold lowered his voice slightly and glanced from side to side.

"That's something I wanted to talk with you about, so it's good you came by." He cast another glance toward the hallway, as if checking for Karim, but as expected, didn't see him. He heard the TV come on in the other room. "An FBI agent contacted Davidson."

His posture straightened, eyes flaring.

"FBI?"

Arnold nodded.

"Yeah."

And let it hang, making Firouz work for the answer.

Firouz must've realized his body language revealed too much, so tried to relax, but Arnold interpreted the move as forced and disingenuous. He gave another get-on-with-it motion.

"He said the agents want to talk to me, find out what I know about you and your, ah, colleagues."

Firouz chewed on the words a moment.

"They know about me? How?"

Now came the tricky part: weaving a web that would make Arnold the focus of attention, a position in which no liar would willingly place themselves. Arnold dropped his eyes, sighed, shoulders slumped. The best lie, he knew, was one close enough to the truth to lessen the risk of screwing up the story later on.

He shook his head.

"I fucked up. With the IRS. I haven't paid taxes and for some reason, they found out about it as well as my gambling."

Firouz sat back in the chair and rubbed the side of his nose, studying him several seconds, perhaps weighing whether or not to believe him.

"Interesting. But this raises other questions. This doesn't explain why they would talk with to your lawyer about me. Why would they assume you and I know each other?"

Thank God I anticipated this.

"I'm not sure. I think maybe it's because of Naseem."

"Naseem? They were in Vegas? These FBI?"

And this was where the story really became treacherous.

"No, no. My lawyer believes they had Howard's funeral under surveillance, looking to see who I associated with. He doesn't know this for sure, because I asked this specifically. But she was in the car when I was left, so..." letting him fill in the blank.

Firouz paused to sip tea with affected casualness. After a few seconds he nodded to himself as if accepting the fabrication.

"Why don't you pay taxes? Isn't this risky, especially given you gamble?"

Was he buying the story or simply probing for lies? No way to tell for sure, and this time his body language revealed nothing.

"Couple reasons. For one, why give the government money if you can keep it?"

The terrorist's eyebrows shot up.

"And?"

Time to bait the hook.

"The other reason is personal."

"Tell me."

After a resigned sigh and a calculated pause, Arnold explained, "Pretty simple, really. Tax dollars pay for drones and other weapons of mass destruction this government uses for reasons I don't morally or philosophically agree with. Killing innocent civilians, for one. The same money that otherwise could be spent rebuilding our bridges and roads or supporting our schools, and God knows, our infrastructure needs work. Our politicians have their priorities backward. It sucks."

This said with convincing contempt.

"I didn't know you felt this way." Firouz appeared to regard him with a different glow in his eyes and tone of voice. "And this is why you said nothing to the authorities?"

"Already discussed that. They're not exactly the same reasons, but I guess in a way they are related."

"I see." Firouz pushed out from the table to stand in front of the window over the sink to look at the limited view to the neighbor's house. After several seconds, "And your reason for telling me this is?"

"You asked me a question," putting a shrug into his voice. "I answered it. That's it."

He nodded.

"So I did."

Arnold suspected he'd convincingly sold the story, so decided to move to a different topic.

"You still haven't explained why you're here."

Firouz turned from the sink after what appeared to be a decision-making moment.

"We have a special job for you, an important one. Not like the ones you've been given so far."

Uh-oh. Here it comes.

Just as he suspected, the previous jobs had been nothing more than tests to evaluate his allegiance and how compliant he was, to explore whether or not he would be a problem. Arnold simply listened.

Karim appeared in the doorway between the kitchen and the hall, suddenly interested in the conversation.

"In about an hour we will contact you and give you the assignment. We expect the results by Saturday."

"Saturday? Seriously?"

"Seriously."

"That's ridiculous. There's no way I can guarantee a deadline without knowing what the hell the task is."

Firouz shook his head.

"Not an option. You will complete the assignment and that's that."

"Hey, I'll try."

"I probably need not to remind you of this, but I will: you try to cross us, I'll fucking kill you. If it comes to that, I won't think twice. Your system isn't worth the grief. Are we absolutely clear on this?"

Interesting. This was the first reference to trying to steal his system. A slip of the tongue or intentional?

Did it make any difference? No, not really.

He could feel his blood pressure jacking up to dangerous levels, intensifying the gnawing pain in his gut. He wanted to slap the smug look off the bastard's face but had to be satisfied with knowing that if his plan worked, he'd bring down not only both Jahandars but the entire group's infrastructure as well.

Without waiting for an answer, Firouz turned toward the front door. "Back to work. Both of you."

Karim stepped out of Firouz's way, apparently content to carry on his day as if nothing had happened.

Still seething, Arnold walked into the first-floor bathroom and closed the door. He stood at the sink, rinsing his face, taking in deep, controlled breaths in an effort to soothe his temper and lower his blood pressure.

For another moment he enjoyed the isolation from the Jahandars. He sat on the closed toilet, mentally reviewing his plan. If they needed an analysis by Saturday, it could only mean that their attack was imminent and that Nawzer was closer to penetrating his security. It occurred to him that Firouz had done an excellent job of distracting him

243

while Karim had been elsewhere in the house.

Doing what, exactly?

No way he'd gotten into the basement, so that part was safe. Then again, Karim had done a good job delaying their return with the trip up to the park. How long had he been in the house before they returned? Could he be more computer savvy than he let on?

And what about Karim and his damned smartphone? Had he texted Firouz?

Was the trip to the park nothing more than a way of giving him more time in the house? That had to be it. He had planted something in his computer.

Arnold went straight from the bathroom to the kitchen table without bothering to check Karim's whereabouts. Didn't really give a shit. Besides, Karim could be standing right behind him looking over his shoulder and wouldn't have a clue what he was doing. Not so with Firouz. That was one sneaky sonofabitch.

The laptop was closed. Which was unusual. He always kept it open. But so what? Firouz had been sitting at the table reading the paper and perhaps he needed more space. Maybe that was sufficient explanation.

But he doubted it. There had to be something fishy.

He angled the screen back to its usual position and now saw that the logon screen was glowing. The machine was set to power-down after an hour of inactivity, meaning it should now require a partial reboot instead of idling.

Rather than log on to the computer, he left it as it was and disconnected the power cord, flipped the box over, slipped out the battery, and waited a full minute by his watch before reinserting it.

30

WITH THE MACHINE now plugged back in, he punched the power button. But before the computer could boot, he pushed F1, aborting the routine into safe mode. One by one, he loaded only those routines absolutely essential for running Windows. Once the laptop was safely up and running with only the bare essential software, he initiated a scan for any segment of code that had been loaded into the computer since midnight. While the scan ran, he brought up the system configuration and studied the programs scheduled to load during a routine boot, searching for anything different.

He found the alien program.

Nothing fancy.

Nothing remotely sophisticated. Just an off-the-shelf chunk of software anyone could purchase online or in a computer store for under $100, a small bit of software to record keystrokes and mouse activity. Just the thing a prying parent or suspicious spouse might use to spy on a loved one. Okay, he now knew the real purpose of Firouz's visit. Only required a flash drive and a few simple instructions to install this bit of spyware, so even if he was a complete computer idiot, he could be easily coached by Nawzer through the installation.

He surprised himself at not even getting mad.

On reflection, he realized he might've been really steamed if they'd gotten away with it, but its presence on his machine told him a great deal. Most importantly, the little gem's presence undoubtedly meant the terrorist had also embedded a second piece of software that, when activated, would be capable of linking his machine back to the terrorists' computer. This second piece of software would allow Nawzer to sink his digital hooks into Arnold's computer. Once that happened, it would only be a short matter of time until they possessed his complete system. The moment that happened, Firouz would order Karim to kill him. So time was now rapidly expiring.

Unless Arnold killed Karim first.

Arnold leaned back in the chair, interlaced his fingers behind his head.

What to do?

Disabling the bug would immediately tip off Nawzer of the device's discovery. Leaving it might lull the terrorist into complacency. Better yet, by leaving it untouched he could use it as a perfect conduit for disinformation. Hmmm....

Time to think carefully and to not react hastily out of anger. The really good news was having anticipated the possibility of becoming infected with this type of virus long before any involvement with the Jahandars, he'd developed and installed a series of well-disguised defenses in his system. Malicious hackers scoured the net for computers of unsuspecting, security-lax users whose machines could be hijacked for any number of reasons, including pirating them for use as Deep Net transfer points.

How much exposure an individual's computer risked was directly proportional to the number of hours a day it remained connected to the Internet and powered. Because Arnold spent time on the Deep Net, he guarded against malicious intrusion by partitioning the laptop into two virtual machines. The first—the one a hacker would encounter through illegal access—would appear as a generic Best Buy laptop in the typical entry level user's home.

The other, hidden hard drive, which could be accessed only via a hidden password, was the real gateway into his artificial intelligence system. Nawzer would realize the dupe but only after looking carefully at the hardware installed on the machine. Once he tumbled to that, he'd search for the hidden partition. So, again Arnold considered whether or not to destroy the implanted spyware or ignore it. The downside to removing it would be destruction of any trust the Jahandars had in Arnold. Once that happened there would be no more reason to keep him alive. Then they could simply kill him and walk away with all the hardware in the basement. But his hardware alone was worthless. They had to know how his system worked, and it was quirky enough that it would almost be impossible for Nawzer to figure it out. Long as Arnold was alive, they would watch him work only until they could reverse engineer his system's use. Then, game over. Ignore the spyware? But the longer he allowed the alien code to remain installed the more deeply he could burrow into his system.

Tough decision.

He paused to massage the kinks in his neck. Of the two options, he decided it'd be best to simply ignore the virus and let them believe they'd outfoxed him. This, however, meant he had to end this in two days. At most.

Having a clear course of action now energized him. First thing he needed to do was check to see if Rachael was online and if so, spend a few moments chatting. After that, he needed to dig into work. He smiled at the thought of her. He pinged her and she immediately responded with:

Rachael: Hi. What u up to?

Arnold: Work. Got a job.

Rachael: NK? What?

Arnold: Can't tell U. Classified.

Rachael: LOL

Arnold: No, really.

Rachael: When can I C U?

Arnold's heart skipped a beat. He couldn't believe what he had just read. He scanned the line again and thought about it and realized his mistake. Did the Jahandars now know about her?

Arnold: CU.

He cut the connection.

Aw, shit!

He erased all evidence of the chat and then double checked that the few lines had been exchanged over the Tor browser, meaning her address would be difficult to track down. But now they knew her name. Making it all the more urgent to destroy everything. The last thing he wanted was to place her in danger, too.

Dumb shit!

He stood, took several deep breaths to calm himself, then went into the bathroom to rinse his face with cold water.

Back at his computer, he tried to concentrate, to see if he was missing anything other than the plan he'd selected. The obvious downside to vanishing into the witness protection program would be the need to abandon any possibility of a relationship with her. His heart ached at the thought.

Press on, don't get mired in self-pity.

A quick check of his offshore account confirmed a new deposit for the $20,000, payoffs from bets last weekend and another $5,000 from the terrorists. A few mouse clicks moved the money from that account to another one he felt certain remained unknown to the Jahandars and FBI. Certainly, if the FBI were monitoring his offshore account in an attempt to backtrack into Nawzer's system, they'd realize the balance had suddenly zeroed out, but what could they do about it? Arnold, after all, was their asset.

Arnold pushed out of the chair again to stretch and relieve the kinks in his spine. Move! Do it. He grabbed his toolbox and the replacement stove igniter purchased earlier today at Lee's Appliances. As usual, Karim was spread over the TV room couch next to the French doors, taking advantage of the bright sunlight angling in, a paperback in hand and a glass of tea on the end table.

Karim didn't even glance up to acknowledge him, just grunted something unintelligible while flipping the page. Arnold set the toolbox on the counter next to the stove, opened it, and rummaged around noisily. He watched the Iranian's reflection on the stainless-steel microwave above the stove, but the smelly bastard didn't seem to pay any attention. Arnold pulled the black iron pot support from the burner and set it on the counter, where Karim could see it if he glanced this way.

He unpacked the gas igniter, selected a small crescent wrench from the toolbox, and stood at the stove pretending to work. Two minutes later, satisfied of a convincing performance, Arnold repacked his tools, replaced the burner cover, and slipped the new, recently purchased burner igniter into his pocket. He turned the burner on and off a couple times, testing it, watching the electrical igniter spark and ignite a flame. "Okay. Burner's working," he called, as if Karim could give a shit.

He walked to the basement stairs, opened the door, yelled, "Be downstairs for a while."

Now in his special electronics room, Arnold knelt next to the rack that housed his computers, routers, and networking equipment. Over the past few days he'd accumulated all the needed parts here: a standard 110V extension cord, a voltage transformer, and some standard dual-wire cord with the insulation off one end and a USB plug wired to the appropriate computer jack. He quickly soldered the bare ends of the 110V line to the transformer and wrapped them in electrical tape, then did the same to the transformer and stove burner igniter, creating a mechanism to trigger a spark. He used electrical tape to affix the igniter to a strut on the computer rack, plugged in the AC line. This circuit complete, he typed a preprogrammed command on his smartphone. The igniter fired each time he hit enter. Now he had a way of triggering the igniter remotely via the house Wi-Fi system. He tried it three times to make certain it faithfully triggered a beautiful arching spark.

He smiled.

So far, so good.

Phase I of his plan was now finished. Next the tricky part. He turned off the room's special air conditioning but allowed the ventilation system to continue running. The HVAC was powered by natural gas brought into the room via a thick, high-pressure hose from the house furnace supply. He severed this line and inserted a T valve between the severed ends. The T portion of the valve was turned off, allowing the gas to flow normally to the HVAC. Next, he attached a three-foot length of new tube from the T portion of the valve. He duct taped the hose's free end to the equipment rack so the open end was only a half-inch from the igniter. Then, for additional stability and support, he duct taped the hose vertically to the struts. The T-valve could be used to divert the natural gas from the HVAC into room air with the highest concentration next to the igniter. He had, in effect, created a bomb that could be detonated from his cell phone similar to the way Middle Eastern insurgents triggered improvised explosive devices, or IEDs.

He smiled at the ironic parallel.

He started the HVAC again and brushed off his hands while inspecting his handiwork. Not bad. Not bad at all for a nerdy computer geek. Back upstairs, he turned his attention back to one of his most daunting tasks in the entire plan: he still needed to write the most important chunk of computer code of his young life. With Nawzer's spyware recording his every keystroke, time seemed to be evaporating at warp speed, making it imperative to infiltrate the terrorists' system within the next 24 hours. Even 48 hours would be too long. The pressure bearing down on him was both exciting and dreadful, exhilarating yet painful, rolling waves of pain through his stomach. From this point on there was no room for any mistake.

He kicked himself for not having factored in the possibility of a Jahandar implanting the keystroke monitor in his laptop, for now the odds of success had been shifted from Arnold to Nawzer. The question was, could he turn that advantage into a liability?

Yeah, maybe. Well, no maybes, you damn well have to. How?
Jesus!

He blew a breath, wiped his palms on his thighs, stood.

Stop farting around. Press on!

Okay, think. The problem with a keystroke recorder is it's only good if you can use it. Which means you eventually have to read it to retrieve any information. Either that or it has to be programmed to automatically send you information when reaching a predetermined buffer size. So, sooner or later a connection had to be made directly between him and Nawzer's computer. Unless Karim or Firouz intended to copy the information and send it to him, which he believed was highly unlikely. Besides, that would take time, and Arnold suspected Nawzer needed the information as soon as possible.

Meaning it'd be very likely that he would try to upload the

information later today, when he gave Arnold his assignment.

Yeah, that's perfect!

Meaning if Arnold were to have any prayer of establishing a route back into Nawzer's computer to tag him instead, his code would have to be flawless.

Shit, do I have enough time to write it?

He had one advantage: he'd written similar software a year earlier so that would be a good start. Problem was, it wasn't particularly sophisticated, making it difficult to slip past a professional as good as Nawzer.

He blew a long slow breath and continued coding the software.

31

WHEN THE CALL came an hour and a half later, Arnold had barely finished coding. The instant his cell rang his heart began hammering in his chest. Palms damp, he pushed speakerphone, grabbed a pen, sucked a deep breath.

"Yes?"

"Is it clear?"

He immediately recognized the voice from prior calls.

"Yes."

They running a stress analysis of my voice?

Not knowing, he kept his answer as short as possible.

"Repeat please: alpha, mike, dash, thirty-four, fifteen."

Soon as the words were out of Arnold's mouth, the phone connection cut off, giving him only ten minutes to connect with the terrorists' computer before the site would cease to exist in the seamy Darknet world. On one screen, using the Tor browser, he typed AM-3415.onion in the address field while he kicked in another program on his second window. A few months ago, his cable connection had died for two hours. He prayed similar problems wouldn't happen now, when every second was crucial. He double-checked the typing, confirmed it was typed correctly, hit enter.

And started drumming his fingers, watching the first computer hand off the connection to the next, then on to the next, until the multiple links wormed across the globe to finally link up the desired destination. Soon as the connection secured, he typed the command to transmit his Trojan horse to the recipient computer while muttering a brief prayer that Nawzer wouldn't notice it coming. Without making any attempt to confirm receipt—for any hesitation might, in itself, draw attention—he moused a big red button on the center of the screen. One second later, the icon vanished and the screen filled with several lines of typewritten instruction: his assignment.

Having anticipated this would be their method for passing the information, he quickly snapped a screenshot which he immediately saved to a protected directory. He snapped a second insurance shot in case the first one had somehow been corrupted. Before he even had time to log off the site, the screen blanked, terminating his connection with the terrorist's computer. The entire process of information transfer had taken less than sixty seconds. No one—not even the highly skilled NSA computer scientists—would have been able to trace the connection on the regular Internet, much less via the Darknet. Which underscored the importance of cyber warfare in fighting terrorism.

Arnold stood and inhaled a deep breath, felt like moving but had no idea where, took three steps, decided that wasn't helping, so returned to the chair. Shit! Restless body syndrome. Standing once more, massaging both temples, he tried to relax and stop grinding his molars.

Jesus! Is Karim watching?

For Christ sake, don't look.

He believed the bastard was too computer illiterate to realize what he'd just done even if he had been watching. On the other hand, the bastard possessed a coyote's nose when sniffing out stress. He continued to stand, eyes closed, massaging both temples, counting one, one thousand, two, one thousand...

Get. A. Grip.

The question was would Nawzer discover his Trojan horse? If not, would it work? The most efficient and stealthy spyware, Arnold believed, must be an artwork of engineering parsimony. Effective, short, free of any bug. Most of all, it had to be sufficiently functional to flawlessly execute the intended task.

I'll find out soon enough.

Within the next ten minutes, most likely. He knew this would mean each second would pass with sub-glacial speed. He tried to distract himself by reading his new assignment. After five futile minutes, he simply gave up.

He left the laptop to pour a glass of cold water from the plastic container in the fridge. At the sink now, he sipped and stared out the window over the weathered cedar fence to the neighbor's Tudor.

What do I do if Karim's phone rings?

For that would only mean one thing.

Forget getting information for the FBI and move on to phase II.

Attractive as that seemed, another part of him knew he had to follow through and play out this game to the end, even if it meant his life. He owed Howie.

Yeah, very noble, but if his phone rings, you know what's coming next.

Grab a knife for self-defense? Yeah, that'd be a stretch. Had no idea how to fight with one, never having dreamed of ever getting into a hand-to-hand combat situation. Then again, you probably picked things up quickly when your life depended on it. Then again, Karim would probably use a gun like he had on Howard, so…would he really? Especially knowing his fingerprints were all over the place? Sure, if he figured his prints weren't on file. If he even thought about that angle. Or maybe he'd make some excuse to return to Discovery Park and do it there. Maybe that's what that trip was all about, sizing the site up, getting Arnold used to the idea.

Jesus! Too many things to worry about.

Finger combing his hair, he tried to slow his mind from rabid bat mode, different thoughts zinging through it with millisecond half-lives, making one coherent thought impossible.

The laptop dinged.

An email.

Cardiac arrest time.

Back in the chair now, mouse in hand, he double clicked the email icon. And froze. Did a double take, looked again, just to be certain.

Holy shit!

His little Trojan horse was successfully embedded in Nawzer's computer, laying down a series of breadcrumbs for Arnold to trace. But it'd take time, because Nawzer kept the machine online only a few minutes at a pop with no regular schedule. But hey, he was grateful for anything. In the meantime, he had an assignment to finish.

Rachael. Jesus, If I could only see her and explain what's going on.

Has to be some sort of karmic injustice. After all I've gone through to get close to her...

He shook his head.

Fate is making damn sure that's impossible.

Allen Wyler

32

ARNOLD COLLECTED HIS grande mocha from the barista's oval serving counter to carry over to the table, where Davidson waited with an open bottle of Perrier. Karim sat camped out with his Tazo at a separate table next to the front window, probably where the reading light was brighter and he could rest easy that Arnold couldn't sneak out.

They'd decided to meet at the Starbucks on the 2300 block of First Avenue and were fortunate enough to catch a lull in patrons, allowing the luxury of separate tables with sufficient distance in between to not worry about being overheard. Not that he thought the big terrorist really gave a rat's ass, but you could never predict the machinations of that primitive mind. Karim's blasé attitude could just as easily be a clever ruse to lull Arnold into slipping up. But perhaps that was giving him too much credit. On the other hand, the accurate predictions Arnold had provided them the past couple weeks made it entirely possible the Jahandars now considered him fully on board.

Arnold chose a chair perpendicular to Davidson's instead of directly opposite, allowing his voice to project away from Karim. He paused to reflect on how strange it was to have his life degenerate into worrying about such otherwise insignificant details.

Leaning closer, Davidson lowered his voice.

"Are my eyes deceiving me, or is that a romance novel your friend's reading?"

Without bothering to look, Arnold nodded.

"Reads nothing but. Devours them, in fact. Never seen anything like it. Can you believe it?"

Davidson continued to stare past Arnold's shoulder for another moment before slowly shaking his head.

"Who'da thunk it, right?"

He was absentmindedly rotating his coffee cup.

Arnold peeled the white plastic lid off his own cup, leaned down to blow steam away from the black surface, trying to give Karim the impression of casualness. He loved the smells of roasted coffee and rich pastries so characteristic of these stores. He supposed Starbucks was all too aware of that also.

"What's up?"

Unable to suppress a slight smile, Arnold answered in normal volume, "Nailed them all. Well, except for one." And felt obliged to defend the one incorrect point spread. "You probably saw the game, but the Seahawks field goal kicker sprained his ankle in the first quarter so ended up on the bench. Second string guy missed a thirty-five yarder with one minute to go. Pathetic." And gave a couldn't-be-helped shrug. "Those are the weird twists you can't account for. So, missed that one by two points."

He stole an over the shoulder glance at Karim. Good, still engrossed in his Harlequin, not seeming to pay any attention.

Davidson put his hand next to his mouth.

"Have anything for our friends?"

Meaning the FBI. How to answer?

He'd figured Davidson would ask. Telling him everything at this point would put the lawyer at risk and, having grown fond of him, he didn't want that. But, he repeatedly reminded himself, the man was at risk no matter what the hell he did.

He nodded and lowered his voice.

"Couple things. Tell Fisher the attack's planned for the Consumer Electronics Show in Vegas. That's probably why Breeze and company have been living there, establishing a cover. It's going to happen this weekend, but I'm not sure exactly which building yet. That convention center is pretty damn big. What they want me to is decide the best spot to plant the explosive for maximum damage. I'll pass along that information soon as I make the determination."

Davidson whistled softly.

"Yikes. They're going to want to know ASAP. No one short of the Secretary of Defense is going to be able to shut that convention down, so they'll have to deploy more security."

"I'll find out what I can, but it's hard to get an accurate read on this. It's possible this assignment is fake, nothing more than a test of who I'm really working for. So until I can verify the accuracy, simply warn Fisher to be extremely careful how they decide to handle this. Understand my point?"

Davidson's face remained blank, showing Karim nothing, if perchance he really was monitoring their conversation.

"I do. And?"

Arnold licked his lips.

"I may have a chance of finding out their location. Nothing nailed down for certain, but I'm working it hard. A few more days I might just have it."

This time Davidson couldn't mask concern.

"Aw, Christ, Arnold, if they're planning an attack this weekend—"

Arnold cut him off with, "I know, I know. But I'm really getting jammed here."

"You mentioned a plan. What's the story with that?"

Again, better to say nothing. Especially not with the wheels in motion and all the preparatory work completed. No one, not even Davidson should know.

"It's off the table at the moment."

Davidson studied him a moment.

"Why am I having a hard time believing you?"

Because I'm a shitty liar.

"Seriously. I'm not going to do anything until I can locate the main cell."

"If you say so."

But clearly Davidson suspected Arnold of lying.

Rather than apologize—for that was getting really and seriously old—Arnold asked, "We done here?"

Just get this over with and press on with the plan.

He hated how he had to act, hated what he'd become these past few weeks; all the paranoia, the lying, mentally and physically looking over his shoulder, the constant dread gnawing away his mind and stomach.

But fate had trapped him in a vise of opposing forces, slowly squeezing him to death. His only hope—at least as far as he could see— was to stay on point and play the game. Win or lose, by the first of next week he'd be free of this intolerable situation.

He was taking the biggest gamble of his young life by placing that life on the line.

Allen Wyler

33

THE COMPUTER DINGED, interrupting a daydream about life
before having been sucked into this clusterfuck, about how much he
wished to turn back the clock, miraculously teleporting to a time before
meeting Breeze, a time when Howard lived and life was good. Had he
known...

The ding had signaled an email. From Nawzer. He moused it open.

A request for a dialog on the secure instant messaging.

It was at that moment he heard movement behind him. He spun
around, his nerves raw from the physical and mental fatigue brought on
from unremitting tension. Karim filled the doorway, a paperback in one
hand, the door jamb in the other. Jesus, he'd forgotten all about him.

"Why don't you answer?"

Arnold opened his mouth, thought, *why bother saying anything?
He knows something's up.*

*Well, for one thing, this isn't the time for petulance. Time to
appear cooperative and pliable and gain their confidence.*

He yawned.

"Guess I fell asleep."

He clicked the instant message icon.

The screen segued to a video of Firouz instead of Nawzer, the
fisheye webcam lens distorting his image into a cartoon like bulbous
nose on a receding forehead and jaw. Firouz leaned forward toward the
camera, disfiguring his face further. Arnold could barely keep from

laughing.

"Arnold, my friend! How are you this evening?"

His upbeat mood made Arnold nervous.

He trying to sucker me into a false sense of security?

The numerous computers for the Darknet annoyingly desynchronized the audio and video.

Arnold could see the shoulder of another man behind Firouz. Probably Nawzer running the instant messaging app for him.

Forcing a smile Arnold said, "Fine. And you?"

"Good, good. Couldn't be better. And the computer, it is running well?"

Firouz changed the angle of his face as if trying for a better view, perhaps searching for Karim.

Strange question. Why ask?

Did it mean Nawzer had just penetrated his security and was now copying the system? Did they find his Trojan horse? He shifted uneasily in his chair, looked for Karim's reflection in the screen but the light was wrong.

"Why?"

Firouz raised his hands in an empty gesture.

"No, no, nothing to worry about. Just asking. Wouldn't want anything to happen to our chief analyst."

Bullshit, especially considering you're going to try to kill me.

Arnold stared back at webcam, mouth shut.

Sonofabitch is up to something, that's for sure.

Firouz leaned forward again.

"So, this weekend is big, yes?"

Arnold rechecked Karim's reflection and got the light right. Yep, still there, arms folded across his massive chest, legs spread, almost filling up the doorway between kitchen and dining room.

Why is he listening in this time? Never has before.

Probably because he knew the topic of conversation and was anxious to finish his job and get out of the States.

Arnold rubbed his fatigued eyes.

"Yes, it's big."

So what?

Firouz's entire face became one large toothy smile.

"Your system, it is doing very well, very well indeed."

And your point is?

Arnold stifled another yawn by protruding his lower jaw and popping his ears.

"Yeah, so?"

Firouz checked his wristwatch.

"So, you should have no problem completing the analysis by six o'clock P.M. Yes?"

"Tonight?"

Still had things to do, arrangements.

Rachael, I need to talk to her.

"No way," said Arnold. "That's not the agreement." A glance at his Movado: 4:30. Giving him ninety minutes to finish Phase II. "Why the rush?"

Arnold suddenly realized the problem: Nawzer had made more progress than anticipated.

Meaning they planned to kill him *tonight.*

They never intended to use his analysis because the assignment was nothing more than a diversion to keep his guard down. Fuckers!

He sensed Karim's body mass shift and checked his reflection off the screen. No longer holding the book, he was dry washing his hands, permeating the room with his sour body odor. Arnold sucked a deep breath and nodded at the webcam.

"Yeah, no problem. Six it is."

34

ARNOLD CUT THE connection and settled into in the chair, his mind frantically scrambling for traction, a sense of primitive self-preservation making him keenly aware of Karim's nearby mass.

Probably wringing his hands like the smelly village idiot he is.

What exactly were the fat bastard's instructions?

Would Firouz call again to order the kill, or it already been planned? But then, why wait? Why not try to kill him now? And why the urgency to transfer his analysis to Nawzer by six P.M.? Did that mean they'd keep him alive then? No way to know for sure. Meaning he had to finish the job now. Ignoring Karim, Arnold carefully inspected his system's security measures, checking tripwires to determine exactly how far Nawzer had penetrated.

Not that it made a hell of a lot of difference at this point.

Well, that's not entirely true.

He'd be damned if he'd allow that bastard to steal his intellectual property. Then he realized, *No, of course Nawzer doesn't have it. Not yet. Because, if he did, I'd be dead.*

But every indication suggested that he was closer than Arnold had thought. After ten minutes of intense concentration Arnold slumped back in the chair, massaging his neck muscles, relieving the ache from his unconscious habit of hunching both shoulders when working. Apparently, he had made progress.

Significant progress.

Grudgingly he had to hand it to the bastard for expertly avoiding the two most apparent tripwires. He pictured him rolling around in front of his desk, laughing and fist-bumping or high-fiving his second in command, ridiculing Arnold Gold, security rookie, for being so naive as to actually rely on such an obvious trap.

Yeah. Right.

Arnold's turn to laugh. What Nawzer didn't realize was that by skirting those tripwires he'd unwittingly turned loose a virus that, two seconds earlier, had unzipped itself into ten bots that were presently scouring the terrorist's silicon, gathering information. The infection had deployed beautifully and was now dutifully sending back crucial data. Armed with this information Arnold could launch the final phase of his plan.

That was the good news.

The bad news was that sooner or later Nawzer would find one of the bots and decode it. The moment that happened there would be no question that Karim would be given the green light.

Arnold increased his pace of work yet again, racing against the inevitable phone call, one ear constantly cocked for the ring of Karim's cell in the other room. He routinely kept his entire system backed up on cloud drives scattered across the globe.

Now it was time to destroy every bit of software on every computer in the house. Broke his heart to issue the command, but he saw no other option. He called up the program that would begin his digital scorched earth policy.

His finger was poised over the enter key when the email beep sounded. Not just the regular email, but one indicating the return of a bot from the Iranians' computer. He hesitated.

Read it, or go ahead and destroy everything?

It'll only take a few seconds, go ahead, read it.

A quick glance over his shoulder.

Nope, Karim wasn't there.

He double clicked the message, opening it. Three lines of information scrolled down the screen.

Stunned, he sat staring at the blinking words.

Jesus, this for real?

Working quickly now, he transferred the GPS coordinates to Google Earth, and voila, he was looking at the location of the terrorists' communications center, pinpointed to within a hundred yards, the limits of his non-military technology. Immediately, he copied the coordinates onto two thumb drives and forwarded a third copy to one of his cloud storage addresses. With the information now secure and in his pocket, he issued the command to destroy his system.

For one gut-wrenching, regret-filled moment, he listened to the soft hum of hard drives destroying billions of bytes of software and databanks, the culmination of and refinement from years of hard, diligent labor. This was not the pseudo deletion that occurs if an email or file is dumped into the Windows recycle bin. Instead, it was the total reformatting and blanking of each disk sector.

He attempted to assuage his regrets by assuring himself the system could, with time, be reconstructed to exactly the same state it was in the day before. Sure, the artificial intelligence system would have to relearn the refinements of the past few months, but he could still get it up and running. If he lived past the next few hours.

His watch now showed 4:45 P.M.. How long before Nawzer discovered a bot? Unfortunately, he hadn't had time to devise a self-destruct program for them. In a perfect world, that's what he would do to wipe out all evidence of their existence.

Get moving!

He found Karim on the living room couch reading and picking his nose. The bastard had the disgusting habit—an unconscious one, Arnold hoped—of wiping the snot on the underside of the coffee table. Even after Arnold had complained about it several times, the bastard wouldn't stop. Arnold turned to go the basement door when Karim looked up.

"What you doing?"

Arnold stopped. Success of this phase relied on Karim not bothering to follow him downstairs.

For a moment he was at a loss for words but quickly recovered with, "Just need to check the computer," and mimed lifting the hood of a car, which was probably something Karim could relate to.

Karim studied his face.

Looking for? What? A lie? Shit.

After what seemed like a millennium, Karim made a grunting sound, which Arnold took as permission. Without waiting a second longer, he was on his way downstairs, heart beating wildly, mouth dry, hands running along the wood railing. Hit the concrete floor and in three long quick steps was in the computer room, door closed.

He faced the two side-by-side five-foot-high racks of shelves stocked with computers and support electronics, saw the glowing LEDs on the scrubber used to remove surges from the 110 volt supply, the battery backup to maintain functionality during a power outage, the special cooling system designed to prevent the room from overheating. He listened to the muted hum of the power supply fans; the sound more soothing to him than a lullaby. He loved this room almost as much as the memories of building it.

Wasting time, dude. Get on with it.

He tested the stove igniter, confirmed it worked exactly as planned. Now squatting on his haunches, he switched off the HVAC, turned the T valve on the gas line to shunt the natural gas into the room instead of to the HVAC unit. He stood and listened to the hiss of escaping gas, his nose already detecting the unmistakable odor of the chemical used to tag it.

Similar to dill pickle juice, he thought.

Very soon the entire room would be filled with the foul-smelling explosive gas. The computer hard disks were now silent, having completely destroyed all content, allowing him to finally throw the main power switch to power down all the equipment. The room went strangely silent except for the faint hiss of escaping gas.

He double checked the high narrow window—ground level outside, shoulder level down here—making certain it remained tightly sealed with the duct tape. Then he was out the door. He closed and double checked the latch, engaged the dead bolt.

Back upstairs he went directly to his one remaining functioning machine, the laptop, signed onto his Twitter account, tweeted: Happy

Birthday Palmer, the code to convene an emergency meeting ASAP.

His heart refused to stop galloping, stoking the anxiety freezing his gut almost to the point of becoming mercifully numb. He blew a long, deep breath through pursed lips, rubbed both palms against his thighs.

CALM THE FUCK DOWN!

Fingers tingling—probably from hyperventilation, he realized—he headed for the front door, yelled, "Going for a walk."

Jesus, what if Karim insists on coming?

Well, figure something out.

Shit, don't want to have to deal with that right now. Not now.

As if he were dreaming a nightmare, Karim yelled, "Wait."

The pit of Arnold's stomach fell through the floor.

He stopped, one hand already on the doorknob. Karim's hulk appeared in the living room. For a moment the two men were silently facing each other, Arnold willing him to stay.

"Where you going?" Karim asked with a distinct edge of suspicion.

Sunlight angling in from behind the Iranian made his face appear shadowed and impossible to read, not that the ape ever showed a speck of emotion....

"Greenlake. Need a walk, just too tense right now, need to loosen up, clear my head."

Don't overdo it, dude.

Karim stepped close, his eyes boring straight through Arnold's on into his brain, a primitive feral sense reading his thoughts. They remained this way for what seemed to be an eternity.

Karim asked, "Finished your work?"

Jesus!

Arnold suppressed the urge to wave away the nauseating halitosis.

"What are you, my mom?" Karim obviously didn't find his sarcasm amusing and Arnold immediately regretted having said it, so quickly added, "Sorry. Yes, almost done. I just need a break, is all."

Besides, Nawzer's about to figure out I sabotaged him.

Arnold made a show of checking his wristwatch.

"I'll be back in, what, thirty minutes?"

Or so. Depending on how long it takes Davidson to show up.

267

He decided to gamble on a touch of reverse psychology by adding, "Hey, feel free to join me, you want," with a glance at Karim's belly.

Looks like you need the exercise, asshole.

Karim grunted and shot him one last heavy-lidded dose of feral eye before lumbering back into the television room.

35

ARNOLD HAD ALMOST reached the Evan's Pool building when he saw Davidson's Mercedes nose into what had to be the one remaining empty parking space in the lot.

He headed straight toward the coupe, wanting this encounter to be brief as possible so he could start back before Karim became suspicious and decided to see what he'd been up to in the basement. And just in case the bastard was following, he turned to check but saw no sign of him.

What are you worried about? He knows you meet Davidson. Yeah, but if he catches me in a lie...can't afford to risk it.

Davidson climbed out, stood by the car door, looking toward the front of the big rectangular Evan's Pool building when Arnold yelled, "Davidson," because for some reason addressing him as Palmer just didn't feel right.

Davidson turned, nodded, shut the door, glanced from side to side, obviously being cautious, too.

Of what, Arnold wasn't sure.

FBI?

Their paths intersected at the curb, so they moved onto the lawn and away from vehicular traffic, the air traced with scents of lake water, pollen, and athlete sweat. Davidson offered his hand and Arnold shook it, expertly palming him a flash drive. His lawyer's eye flashed a half-second of surprise.

Then, not missing a beat, discreetly slipped the device into his pocket.

"What's up? You look fried. Everything okay?"

Arnold absentmindedly began massaging the base of his neck, working out the kinks.

"That goes to Fisher ASAP. It's the GPS coordinates of the main group's communications center. Where that is in relation to the group's leader, I have no idea, but at least that fulfills my side of the bargain." He glanced nervously around, relieved to no longer have the evidence on his person. "And there's one other thing. Do me a favor, okay?"

Davidson flashed a questioning look.

"Anything. What?"

"Howard has a sister, Rachael. Call her. Say I'll try to contact her sometime in the future, but have no idea when that might be. And that if things don't work out, tell her...ah, tell her...ah, man, I don't know...I have to go."

"What the hell are you up to, Arnold?"

With the information transfer now complete, he needed to return home to complete the final phase. He was already turning when Davidson took hold of his arm.

"Wait! The hell's going on, Arnold?"

Stomach aching like hell, Arnold paused to look at the clouds in an azure sky. He inhaled a long, savoring breath of lake air in an attempt to dampen the ten thousand watts arcing through his nerves. His brain seemed on the verge of exploding.

Would telling Davidson lessen the anxiety?

Part of him knew his best action was to say nothing, not even to Davidson. But didn't he owe this man—who had perhaps literally saved his life—an explanation? After all, he'd sheltered and protected him through his most vulnerable hours.

With another nervous glance at his surroundings, he said, "I set a bomb in their computer."

Davidson chewed on that a moment.

"What? Who? Who the hell we talking about?"

Shifting from foot to foot, wiping both palms on his sweatshirt,

Arnold explained, "Not a physical bomb. A small bit of software that's programmed to wipe out their computers."

Now that the words were out, relief engulfed him, making him secure in the knowledge that if Karim killed him before he could destroy them, he still had successfully obtained an ounce of payback for Howie. And if he escaped? That payback would taste even sweeter.

Davidson whistled softly, shaking his head side to side.

"Jesus!"

Now Arnold felt compelled to explain more.

"See, Nawzer, their IT guy? He's been trying to steal my system." Although he'd told this to Davidson numerous times in recent days he felt compelled to repeat it. "Now he can't."

"Aw, Jesus!" Davidson shook his head again. "Can you stop that?"

Puzzled, Arnold thought about that moment.

"No, why?"

"Here's the problem. That'll wipe out evidence the FBI needs."

"That's irrelevant. They're outside this country. The feds have no jurisdiction. And by the time they can possibly negotiate a collaborative arrangement, it'll be too late."

"Shouldn't the FBI the ones to make that call?"

"Screw the FBI. They knew about the Jahandars before Howie was killed, and that didn't stop the murder. This is now way too personal. But, if it's any consolation, tell them the virus won't trigger until midnight our time, so if they get on it right now, maybe they can salvage what they need. But I seriously doubt they'll be able to."

"I'll take your word for it." He paused. "Aw, Jesus, Arnold, Firouz is going to kill you."

He realized he'd gotten ahead of himself.

"So what? He's already given Karim permission for that. Makes no difference what I do, everything's already in motion. I just have to hit them first."

"Why do you say that?"

The park started closing in on him, his gut pain ratcheting up to unbelievable levels. He needed this conversation to end.

"Trust me, I know."

Davidson didn't seem anxious to release him.

"Wait. You have another option."

Shit. 5:20 already.

The entire afternoon seemed to be a live variation of a recurrent nightmare that went like this: as he packs for a trip, he can't seem to move fast enough to make the airport in time because every move seems mired in molasses.

Don't panic!

Yet the harder he tried to stay calm, the worse it got. He tried to slow his mind but couldn't concentrate even on that.

Davidson was saying, "Just drop everything and get in my car right now. I'll call Fisher as we drive. He can relocate you somewhere safe. Come on, let's go."

Davidson pulled him toward the Mercedes.

Arnold wrenched free.

"No! I have to finish this and do it my way."

His lawyer seemed genuinely puzzled.

"Finish what?" At this point, he realized, his best strategy would be to simply shut up and walk away, but he owed Davidson an explanation. Sort of. "I've started something I have to finish. For Howie. Trust me."

For a long moment Davidson stayed still, intently studying his face, trying to read an explanation from his eyes. After several seconds his lawyer melted into resigned agreement.

He nodded.

"All right. But I'll keep my cell on and keep any calls brief, just in case you change your mind. If so, call. I'll come get you, no matter what time of day."

Arnold shook his head.

"No, see, this is where we part company. I won't be seeing you again. Ever."

Davidson recoiled.

"What's that supposed to mean?"

"Exactly what I said. I won't see you again. As of this moment I'm gone from the face of the earth. Arnold Gold ceases to exist."

"Horseshit. You can't say that and expect me to just walk away."

Arnold gently put his hand Davidson's shoulder and without saying a word, he knew this simple gesture conveyed everything his words couldn't: heartfelt fondness and gratitude.

"Thanks for everything. I mean that from the bottom of my heart. But my life here is over. And I now have a very big debt to settle. I've thought this through more than you can imagine. Nothing has weighed more heavily on my mind these past few days. But I *have* to do this."

Davidson nodded slowly.

"All right then, I accept that." He shook Arnold's hand. "Great knowing you, Arnold Gold. You're a good man."

36

KARIM WAS STANDING on the front porch waiting, muscular arms crossed over his hairy chest, a nasty scowl on his face as Arnold rounded the corner to start up the curving narrow street to his house.

Arnold slowed, wondering, uh oh, what now? Then figured, screw him, the asshole wasn't about to try to kill him out here in the street.

Would he?

Probably not.

Unless Nawzer had found and decoded his virus. If so, all bets were off. His confidence drained.

Turn around and run for it?

He knew this neighborhood well enough to beat the odds of getting caught, besides, he'd done it before. But if he did, then what? Call Davidson and hide? No, he had to taste the satisfaction of inflicting some serious hurt on the bastards.

So, he approached the porch with his most innocent face.

"What up? You look so serious."

Karim glared.

"What took you so long?"

And started the handwashing thing again, clearly ready to get on with it.

So, just for spite—as juvenile as that might be—Arnold paused at the bottom of the concrete steps up to the small bricked-in front porch. He turned his back to the bastard and let his eyes wander the neighborhood one final time, burning the images of where he'd spent his entire life into memory. He'd miss this place, the familiar sights and smells, with the womb-like security it bestowed. But life was always about starting over. Always.

"Get in here!" Karim yelled. "Firouz wants results. He called several times while you were out wasting time."

Arnold started slowly up the stairs, thinking carefully about his next moves, going over each one once more, because he'd only get one shot.

Timing would be everything.

Now passing through the door jamb, he glanced at the carpet, to the spot now a shade lighter than the surrounding fabric as a result of having removed Howie's blood. He hesitated for one final glance at the furniture so seemingly ingrained into his DNA, every piece an intimate part of his life. My past life, he thought.

"Go, go!" Karim made a shooing motion toward the laptop on the kitchen table.

Arnold noticed Karim sweating.

"What's wrong?"

As if I really give a shit. Or don't know.

Karim grabbed his shoulders and shoved him toward the kitchen table.

"Is not good that you're behind schedule like this. I told Firouz when he called to talk to you that your stomach is problem, you were in bathroom. I make excuses for you. Now you are making it difficult for me. Go!"

Arnold slipped into his chair and checked his watch. 6:15. No wonder Karim was irritated. Apparently, the Law of Fecal Gravity applied to terrorist cells. Where was Davidson now?

Had he handed off the flash drive to Fisher?

Were the FBI geeks ready to relay the intel to whomever would take it from here? Arnold moved the mouse, clearing the screen saver, exposing the desktop. He paused to wipe his palms on his jeans, took a deep breath, and popped a Tums from the roll next to the mouse pad.

Then he was on the instant messenger ringing Nawzer, a fresh bout of second thoughts exploding through his mind.

The screen flicked over to the distorted webcam image of Nawzer's face and it wasn't happy.

"Where you been? I've been calling."

"Good evening to you, too."

Could he see or sense his nervousness? He willed himself to act as if everything was normal but now wasn't sure what that might be.

Think about it too hard, you'll screw up.

Nawzer disregarded the comment.

"Hold on. I'll get the boss."

The boss.

As if they were all one happy family working in concert for a common goal. He used the opportunity to check Nawzer's hacking progress. Amazingly, it appeared he hadn't made significant progress since the last check. But he was still way too close to discovering Arnold's hidden hard drive. Then again, in addition to stealing Arnold's work, Nawzer and crew had their regular job to contend with, which now that he thought about it, he needn't worry because all his hard drives had been totally destroyed.

Regardless, once they figured out Arnold had scuttled his own ship, Karim's order to kill him would be cast.

Firouz was now peering into the webcam.

Just give me a few more minutes.

"Hey, my friend, how you doing?"

"Sorry I'm behind. Am having some stomach problems."

Supporting Karim's little white lie might give him pause, maybe ease the rush.

Ten more minutes I'll be done here.

"No problem, no problem. Are you finished?"

"Will be. Soon as I'm off this call I'll upload the analysis to your computer."

Asshole.

"Good, good. See any problems?"

Arnold's confidence grew.

"No."

Apparently, he was a better liar than he gave himself credit for.

"Go ahead, send it then."

The instant messenger disconnected, leaving Arnold stone still with an aching gut and hunger for air. But with Karim watching from the doorway, he knew he should breathe normally.

Do it!

His hand seemed paralyzed.

For Christ's sake, do it!

When is Karim supposed to kill me?

Soon. He could sense Karim's anticipation, and his heightened sensory system could hear the friction in Karim's nervous handwashing.

It was then he caught the first faint whiff of natural gas. Jesus, the computer room must be saturated with the stuff by now.

For Christ's sake, do it.

Why had he wasted so much time? Time was running out.

A fresh wave of resolve hit.

He grabbed his smartphone, scraped back the chair, and was up, heading into for the back door, calling, "I'm done. Going out now to pick up some pizza. What kind you want?"

But Karim came at him, moving fast. Karim's iron grip clamped Arnold's biceps so he couldn't move.

"No, no. You stay."

Whoa! That look on Karim's face...this is it! Get out. Fast.

"Aw, c'mon, Karim. Pizza. Aren't you hungry?"

Playing to the slob's endless appetite. He reached for the door with his free hand, thinking, break free and run! Karim released his arm.

Arnold grabbed of the doorknob.

Beat him last time he chased me out the door, I can do it again and this time, ankle's fine.

The knob turned but the door didn't move. Shit! The deadbolt was engaged, and the key wasn't in the lock like it always was.

Oh, shit, this is it; bastard's going to kill me before I can get him.

"You're not hungry?" he asked Karim. Karim shook his head.

"No. We wait."

"Wait for what?"

As if he didn't know.

Karim's phone rang, the sound so startling that Arnold jumped. He hadn't noticed the terrorist's cell on the counter next to the opened paperback.

And in that moment Arnold knew it was Firouz telling Karim to go ahead, kill him.

37

STUNNED AT WHAT he was seeing, Arnold watched Karim reach to the small of his back and withdraw a flat black 9mm Glock. Just fucking watched him do it without even trying to struggle, his mind again flashing on Jews obediently marching into Nazi gas chambers knowing they were about to be executed, some still clinging stubbornly to the unrealistic hope of actually having a shower.

Think!

For a moment, Karim inspected the gun with a detached, clinical air about him.

Like, "Let me make sure I got this straight, one in the chamber..."

For Christ's sake, do something!

Yeah? What? Run? Fucking door's locked and there's no way around that big sonofabitch.

Fight. Least that's better than just standing here with your thumb up your...

Try talking him out of it?

And say what, exactly: I wouldn't do that if I were you?

Yeah, that sounds about right.

Karim smiled with satisfaction that the gun appeared to be in perfect working order, just like he always kept it. His gaze came up to meet Arnold, and for a moment Arnold thought he detected a spark of regret, as if somehow they'd bonded in a reverse Stockholm Syndrome of sorts.

Arnold held up a hand.

"Stop. Wouldn't do that if I were you."

Karim's brow furrowed, perhaps wondering if he'd heard right.

"Smell that?" Arnold said, sniffing in an exaggerated audible manner. "Gas! Pull that trigger, this whole place goes up. Kaboom! You with it."

Karim stood motionless, as if replaying and evaluating Arnold's statement over and over, word by fucking word. Arnold could almost see the syllables sequentially processing through his lizard brain: flash, gas, ignite, kaboom! Karim sniffed, turned his head slightly with his chin raised, sniffed again, as if having difficulty discerning the gas. His eyes flashed back to Arnold.

"Is in the basement, this gas line?"

Arnold nodded vigorously.

"Yes. Want me to go check? Must be a leak."

Any chance to break out a window and crawl out before Karim had time to scramble down to stop me?

An old chair was next to the washer and dryer, and a monkey wrench on the workbench, perfect for smashing the glass...

Karim flicked the barrel of the gun toward the den.

"In there."

"Hey, look, let me go down and see what's wrong. I know the—"

"In there. Go."

The good news about the den was that it wasn't directly above the computer room. Close, but not directly over it. If he could bust out that window and slip out and ignite the gas, he might still have a chance. He pictured Karim bending down with a puzzled expression, looking at the open T valve with the gas escaping. But was he dumb enough to actually go down there? And would he be smart enough to look in the computer room instead of only at the line to the furnace?

Soon as they entered the den, Karim pulled a pair of handcuffs from his back pocket.

"Stand there," and pointed to a spot next to the desk.

Arnold looked at the location, thought, so what? And didn't understand.

Until Karim rough slapped one end of the cuffs around his right wrist, squeezed it until the sides pinched skin, then yanked his arm down, buckling Arnold at the knees. With Arnold now kneeling, Karim secured the other cuff to the desk leg immediately below the bottom drawer.

Shit!

Wasn't working out even close to the way he'd planned.

The gas odor was growing stronger by the second and he was damned sure it wasn't his imagination.

"Hey Karim, it's me, Arnold. You can trust me. Don't just leave me here."

Karim, halfway through the door jamb, now his bulk filling the space. He turned and shot a dead-eyed stare at Arnold and said nothing.

If he could just talk him into undoing them...

"C'mon, Karim, don't leave me cuffed to the damn desk."

Without a word the big terrorist turned and vanished around the corner.

Arnold heard the door to the basement open followed by the clunk-clunk-clunk of heavy steps down the wooden flight.

No! This isn't how I planned it. I was supposed to go out to empty the garbage or get pizza or take a walk—just anything to get out the house—and then trigger the igniter with the cell phone.

He jerked against the cuffs on the off chance they hadn't been secured. But all that did was send a bolt of pain through his wrist. He tried to curl his hand and wrist into a small round mass to slip through the cuff like he'd seen a prisoner do on the TV show *Lockup*.

That didn't work either.

Time was flying past. By now Karim was probably inspecting the furnace, finding the gas line.

Jesus, he'll be back up in seconds.

Frantically, he glanced around the room for something to help him free his hand. Tried to push up the corner of the heavy oak desk with his back, but the damn thing weighed a ton and didn't budge, and the corner cut into his skin. He tried again, ignoring the pain. This time he was able to lift the desk high enough to slip the cuff underneath. *If* his arm were long enough to reach.

Which it wasn't.

Glanced around the room again. Nothing!

Seconds continued to fly, tick tick tick tick...*shit!*

He didn't see any other option. More than anything in the world, he wanted revenge for Howie's senseless murder. He wanted Karim to die at his hands, even if it meant sacrificing his own life.

He used his free left hand to reach across his body to fish the cell from his jeans. Working quickly now, so Karim would hopefully still be in the computer room to receive the full force of the blast, he opened the app to wirelessly trigger the stove igniter, figuring the rack and the computer fragments might even act as shrapnel.

With the app now open, all was needed was to press enter and 110 volts would spark across the contacts, igniting the natural gas. But would the explosion kill him, too?

Then again, what did he really have to lose, considering Karim planned to kill him anyway the moment he came back up the stairs? Would he rather die at his own hands or at the hands of that big stupid asshole?

Do it now, don't waste another second! Press the damned button, you pussy!

Arnold swallowed hard, closed his eyes and thumbed enter.

38

ARNOLD BECAME VAGUELY aware of intense heat and violent hacking coughs, the pungency of smoke, and more coughing. Nothing like the smell of fall, when people illegally burn maple leaves raked from yards or enjoy fires in fireplaces. No, this was the smell of burning rubber and drywall, plastic, and wool.

The stench of a burning house.

His head pounded on the threshold of exploding.

A split-second later he realized he was flat on his back, right arm still tethered to the desk, left knee bent at a painfully awkward angle. Slitting open his eyes, he could see only thick anthracite, nose-clogging haze, backlit with flickering glowing reds and yellows. He became aware of a familiar crackling roar.

Of?

Fire!

Instinctively, he rolled to his right, freeing his pinned left leg from under him, sending a bolt of pain up his thigh and body, his right arm still tightly tethered to the heavy oak desk. He tried to jerk his hand free, but the metal cut further into skin.

Fucking handcuffs.

Suddenly he realized what had happened: the computer room had exploded as planned. He'd survived. But now he was trapped in an inferno, handcuffed to an immovable oak desk. Again, he tried to push up the corner of the desk with his back. No go.

Allen Wyler

Think!

Well, dude, if you can't slip the cuffs, unlock them...

Yeah, great. How?

The heat from the crackling, raging fire was growing more intense with each passing second. Already he could feel flames singeing his skin. He remembered leaving a fork on the desk yesterday when he was eating pizza. Had it moved? If so, where was it now? The smoke was too thick to see a damned thing, leaving him so disoriented he didn't know how far the desk had moved—or even if it had moved at all—in the explosion. He started groping at his surroundings like a blind man, hoping for some sense of orientation. He found the corner of the desk and gingerly explored the hot top with his fingertips. Nothing remotely familiar remained there, probably having been thrown somewhere by the blast.

Soaked with sweat, clothes and soot clinging to him, he was verging on panic.

Panic and you die.

True, but I might die anyway.

Think!

He let loose with a hoarse, chest-heaving cough, and, without thinking, inhaled another lung full of smoke. Which triggered another time-consuming bout of coughing, doubling him over in a wheezing mass tethered to an anchor.

Coughing fit subsiding, he struggled up into a kneeling position, and in doing so, his fingers brushed something. Blindly, reflexively, he groped for it, found it and immediately identified it.

The fork.

Aw, man, there must be a God!

He remembered reading that all handcuffs share a common locking mechanism that requires only one simple common key. Thereby making it seamless for various law enforcement agencies to hand off and transport prisoners without having to worry about keeping track of the keys. This, in turn, meant the locks were easily picked with a rudimentary instrument such as a bent tine. Exactly one of the reason prisoners were not allowed metal forks.

Working totally by feel now, ignoring the burning heat, he bent one of the three tines to a right angle from the others. Then, with the help of the desk leg against the edge of his cellphone, he bent a quarter inch of the tip as close to a right angle as possible without hurting his finger. Still using only touch—the smoke too thick to see at all now—he wiggled the bent tip into the key slot and rotated the fork until he felt resistance. Applying steadily increasing pressure and a prayer, he rotated the fork counterclockwise until he felt the lock release. The handcuff fell apart, freeing his wrist.

Okay, now how the hell do I get out?

With the smoke so thick, he couldn't see the doorway to the hall, and the desk wasn't a very accurate landmark because it had been moved in the explosion. He simply started crawling away from the flame, feeling his way, remembering something from the distant past about staying low as possible in a burning building because that's where the smoke is less dense and oxygen more plentiful. With the hot floor burning his hands, he continued crawling until he felt the door jamb. At the same time, he heard what sounded like a blood curdling scream over the roar of the fire.

Karim?

Can't be. Bastard has to be dead!

He paused long enough to listen again. Now he heard metallic banging, like someone pounding against a furnace air duct.

Ignoring the sound, he resumed crawling, left hand feeling his way, using the hot peeling molding between floor and wall as his only guide. His stinging eyes were now completely dry, making it painful to blink.

The bathroom.

Get to the bathroom.

With the backdoor locked and the key gone, his present route was impossible.

A bout of wracking coughs doubled him up again, his throat and sinuses so clogged with gritty irritating soot each breath seem more and more impossible.

Move!

A crash thundered above the roaring crackling fire. Arnold glanced right, just as the floor and wall between the hall and the living room caved in, opening a gaping hole into the basement, providing a direct path for fire to roar ferociously upward. The heat intensified, but the flames provided slight flickering light.

Shit, sure this isn't Hell?

Then he reached the bathroom door, shoved it open, crawled inside, kicked it shut. At least in this room the smoke wasn't so thick, allowing him to see dim light through the window.

Break the glass.

How?

To his left was a linen closet. Struggling to his feet, he opened the door, grabbed a bath towel, wrapped it around his hand for insulation, and then locked the door.

If Karim tries to get in here, the door should stop him.

At least for a second or two. *If* he had survived the blast. Couldn't possibly still be out there. Could he?

He grabbed two more bath towels, wrapped them around the first one, making his right hand a large bundle, moved to the window and rammed his fist straight through the center of the pane, shattering it, leaving jagged shards protruding from the frame like shark's teeth. Quickly as possible, he knocked out as many jagged shards as he could from the bottom and sides of the frame, deciding there wasn't enough time to even bother with the top ones, that cutting his back was the least of his worries. Then he was back at the linen closet grabbing the two remaining towels just as a horrendous thump cracked the center of the bathroom door.

Shit! Can that be? Bastard should be dead.

Back at the window, he layered the towels over the bottom edge of the sill as fast as he could without dropping them. Then climbed onto the toilet, grabbed the sides of the frame, and was thrusting his left leg through the opening as another horrendous crash splintered out the center of the door. Arnold glanced over his shoulder long enough to see Karim's face, most of the skin burnt completely off, exposing bone, his hair singed to crisp scalp. The monster was pushing through the opening with inhuman strength, gasping and coughing for air. The big man threw his shoulder into the remaining door panel, smashing it to splinters, letting him in.

Holding both sides of the window frame, Arnold climbed on the sill and jumped. He slammed into earth with a jaw popping impact. Then was up, running along the garage to the high cedar fence. He reached the door and opened it, spun around for one last look. Karim stood inside the broken window screaming, the fire silhouetting his huge body just behind the window frame, the bastard too big to squeeze through the narrow opening.

Arnold stopped to stare—overwhelmed with a strange mix of horror and sympathy for the way the terrorist was about die. He wanted to yell back, to apologize for the way his life was about to end, to explain that all he really wanted was to free himself and seek revenge for Howie, that he never intended his death to be so horrid.

Instead, he raised a fist and yelled, "For all of us, you sonofabitch!"

A second explosion shook the evening air, shooting a fireball through the open bathroom window, swallowing the terrorist. Next came the crash of an internal wall collapsing, burying Karim in the conflagration. Arnold stepped through the gate into the alley and began jogging toward Greenlake as the wail of approaching sirens competed with the roar of the fully engulfed house fire, the alley now thick with the cloying and acrid stench of burning plastics and household goods.

Allen Wyler

39

ONE WEEK LATER, Davidson's private line rang in his office. The lawyer glanced at the caller ID and saw it was Fisher calling, so carefully placed his Mont Blanc on the desk and punched the call into speaker phone.

"Davidson."

"Palmer, Gary Fisher. How you doing?"

Davidson knew the FBI agent wasn't calling simply for a health update and hoped he would provide an update on the investigation.

"Up to my ass in alligators at the moment. What's up? Any word?"

"Matter of fact, good news. Word just came down the chain of command that a SEAL team took out the Jahandars' mother ship, lock, stock, and barrel. Gold's GPS coordinates were perfect. Never would've gotten those bastards without it. We also nailed the two operatives who were setting up the bomb for the Vegas convention. So all in all, it was a clean sweep."

Davidson felt a rush of elation. But that was immediately supplanted by sadness that Arnold Gold would never know the good he had accomplished, would never receive the thanks he deserved.

"And Firouz?"

"The New York police nailed him in downtown Manhattan when he was walked out of Grand Central and tried to hail a cab to Kennedy airport. He had a one-way ticket to Karachi via London. Would've made it, too, if it hadn't been for a sharp transit cop who recognized him.

Lucky."

Davidson nodded appreciatively and peered out the window at the business district.

"That leaves Breeze. Any news?"

"That's the bad news. She's in the wind."

"Shame."

"Yes, it is. But all things considered, it worked out well, wouldn't you agree?"

"Not really. A really fine young man died in the process. Guy was a genius with artificial intelligence. A real genius. Your interactions with him were quite different than mine, so you may not appreciate his qualities the same way I do."

"Point made. Still, he did an incredible job. I applaud him. By the way, you happen to know if the fire department ever found the bodies? I haven't had time to check."

"Not really. Talked to Detective Elliott yesterday. She just received the official report from SFD. Seems the house was completely destroyed. By the time the fire department arrived on scene it was all they could do to keep the neighbors' places from going up, too. But they did find DNA evidence that Karim was incinerated."

"All right, then. Anything else I can tell you?"

Davidson hung up the phone and sat back in the chair, letting his gaze travel up Second Avenue, thinking how unjust life can be. The sun was beginning to set behind the Olympics, yet he still had a pile of work to complete. But now his attention was elsewhere.

Go get a latte and bring it back up to the office?

Might as well, it would be a long night. With a weary sigh, Davidson pushed out of his chair and headed for the elevator.

As Davidson enters Starbucks, a man and a woman walk through the front door of a single-story house perched on an ancient lava flow.

"I brought the papers."

The slender, long-haired woman leads Arnold across the granite foyer, the scrape of her sandals echoing off bare walls, down three shallow steps to an expansive room of floor-to-ceiling sliding glass walls.

Her right hand holds a thin leather portfolio. With her free hand she effortlessly slides open one of the glass panels onto a wide deck. Warm humid air wafts in with the scent of salt water and bougainvillea. Sunlight sparkles off distant water, a warm glowing ball high overhead.

He follows her down the granite steps and across the great room onto the balcony with a solid railing of tempered glass that Davidson would approve of. For a moment he stands gazing out at Diamond Head far off to the left, the city skyline directly ahead, Pearl Harbor in the distance. He inhales warm balmy air deeply, his lungs still purging smoke particles. He imagines, like a cigarette smoker, his lungs will harbor permanent stains. But each day brings healing, and soon he might not cough so much.

"Lovely, isn't it?" she says.

She's tall and thin.

Maybe Japanese or a mixture of Polynesian, Caucasian, and Japanese. Can't tell for sure.

Long black hair flows over the shoulders of her brightly colored floral dress.

"Yes, it is."

She turns to face him.

"We can sign the papers in the kitchen, if you wish."

He nods, thinking of the furniture he needs to buy and the work that reconstructing his artificial intelligence system will require over the next months. He'll need to purchase a shitload of computer gear. And that's when he realizes his gut no longer aches.

When was the last time I felt it? When was my last Maalox?

Funny how we notice the appearance of things more acutely than their disappearance.

It saddens him to know he'll never see Rachael. He'll never know if things might've worked out between them, but no one from his past—not even Davidson or Fisher—must ever know he didn't die in the fire as had been reported in the Seattle Times.

"I can't tell you how lucky you are to be able to get this piece of property. Primo, really prime."

He follows her back inside, into the kitchen area, and watches her set the portfolio on the granite counter, open it, remove a stack of papers and a pen. A black and white Mont Blanc, like Davidson's.

"We could do this at the office, if you'd prefer."

"No, this will be fine."

From the attaché case he's brought, he removes a small, silver frame with a picture of a woman and sets it beside the papers.

"Your wife?" the agent asks, sounding a bit surprised.

"No, just a friend from the past." He looks at the picture of Rachael and smiles. "We can get on with it now."

She hesitates, the papers held with both hands, inspecting him again.

"Sorry if this is too personal—and if so, no need to answer—but I can't help ask, what with you being so young to afford a house in this price range, I mean…oh, and may I call you Trevor instead of Mr. Taylor?"

He smiles and nods.

"And your question?"

"May I ask what you do for a living? You're not a trust fund brat, are you?"

The question triggers an eerie memory of a night in Vegas, of sitting at the table in a restaurant, of the start of everything bad.

He smiles.

"How did you guess?"

About the Author

ALLEN WYLER IS a renowned neurosurgeon who earned an international reputation for pioneering surgical techniques to record brain activity. He has served on the faculties of both the University of Washington and the University of Tennessee, and in 1992 was recruited by the prestigious Swedish Medical Center to develop a neuroscience institute.

In 2002, he left active practice to become Medical Director for a startup medical device company (that went public in 2006) and he now chairs the Institutional Review Board of a major medical center in the Pacific Northwest.

Leveraging a love for thrillers since the early seventies, Wyler devoted himself to fiction writing in earnest, eventually serving as a Vice President of the International Thriller Writers organization for several years. After publishing his first two medical thrillers, *Deadly Errors* (2005) and *Dead Head* (2007), he officially retired from medicine to devote himself to writing full time.

He and his wife live in downtown Seattle.

Visit Allen Wyler at www.allenwyler.com

CPSIA information can be obtained
at www.ICGtesting.com
Printed in the USA
BVHW071535211220
596069BV00002B/107